I0690600

Hand and Glove: Hell

First Edition

Published by The Nazca Plains Corporation
Las Vegas, Nevada
2007

ISBN: 978-1-887895-59-0

Published by

The Nazca Plains Corporation ®
4640 Paradise Rd, Suite 141
Las Vegas NV 89109-8000

PUBLISHER'S NOTE
Hand and Glove: Hell is a work of fiction created wholly by *Bob E. Genz's* imagination. All characters are fictional and any resemblance to any persons living or deceased is purely by accident. No portion of this book reflects any real person or events.

Cover Photo, Sandra vom Stein
Art Director, Blake Stephens

Dedication

Hand and Glove is an analogy. The Hand represents the dominate, the Glove the submissive each as individuals knows their roles in the realm but when the two combine as equals they becomes something greater than the two individuals. They become the ultimate Ying and Yang, harmony at its best. Being passive does not mean you are weak. Being passive means you have a strength of character that allows you to submit to freely explore variations of sensuality.

Have no friends not equal to yourself.   Confucius

I speak for myself when I say that we each personify the Hand and Glove analogy by how we structure our lives; associate with others and by how intensely we love. I am dedicating this book to my friends. These friends come from every walk of life and social structure. They are creative, brilliant, fun and in their own way extremely Spiritual. We believe in self-empowerment, walking in balance with our inner natures and struggling against the mediocrity of our world today.

To my friends, thank you...Chuck Higgins, Lady Dee, Hal, Lee, Julian and Scott, Kevin Hiza a.k.a. the Pup, Jenna V, Lin F., Lady V., Lawrence F., Timmy Brough, Goddess Lakshimi and Sweet Limey, Peter and Craig, Daddy Brian and boy jeff, dog blu, Papi David, Gene and Master Will, Eric L., Bearman, Richard S., Papabear and Gary, boy jim F., danny T, Grande Mistress Carla, Amy O @ Marvelous Mayhem, the Sabers M.C.C. of Ft. Lauderdale, the Wildcats M.C.C. of Norfolk, SLLAP of Ft. Lauderdale, SPICE of Ft. Lauderdale, and most of all to my Number One...for your friendship, support and love as we walked this road together.

There is only one good, knowledge, and one evil, ignorance.
Socrates

Hand and Glove: Hell

First Edition

Bob E. Genz

Contents

Previously

No man ever really showed me just how much they loved me until I met my Lord and Master retired Major Bruce Hunter. Too often we hear the catch phrase, 'tuff love or hard love' usually applied to someone else who needs a very hard lesson about reality. Well I was just such a person. I came to Buena Vista like a wolf dressed in sheep's skin thinking I was fooling everyone when in fact I was only fooling myself. I blamed society for making me into an animal. An animal bent on survival at all costs. I didn't care how many I had to climb over, how many backs I had to stab as long as I was climbing that ladder towards success. Like before, I knew that if I could become Hunter's slave I could top from below problem is; he, Cappy and all the handlers knew what I was and were waiting for the chance to trap this animal, break and rebuild him into a functional servant within our society.

Everything would have been wonderful or so I thought until I did the unthinkable. I struck my master with intent to harm and maim so I could flee like so many times before. Yes, I struck him, that is to say the animal within me struck him with nothing less than an appliance cord when his back was turned; so that, when he turned the cord cut a fiery path over his shoulder, up his neck, over his right cheek, the bridge of his nose and impacted just above his left eye. A smiggin' either way would have cost him an eye and me my life instead I gave him way too many stitches and reason enough to destroy the animal that I had become.

His punishment was just. I never really knew just how many boys when I was a top that I damaged until it was time for me to take my punishment; they all seemed to be present for the show. I must have been the most hated, arrogant snotty nosed brat of a slave on that compound by the way people lined up to have at me. Even Doc, one of our more twisted rubber wearing doctors, joined the festivities and supplied Hunter with a very special custom made single tail that would according to Doc, "skin the hide off a bull elephant". Like so many other animals that had bled out while hanging they swung me from the blooding tree. A place normally used for wild game to drain from blood before they were skinned and butchered for our freezers nevertheless it was fitting end for this one.

One third of this animal died when Hunter, Cappy, mike and j.d. wrapped a white hot band of steel around my neck denoting by scars and collar I was no longer a wild beast. The second third died the day I was shown the newspaper article detailing my death while racing my corvette around the Blue Ridge Parkway. The final third the self-hating animal died in his pit. My ego-beast died within his cage of cold hard steel which easily matched my coldly detached calculating self. Locked away from all like any beast after attacking the one man that really ever loved this animal. In that cage I learned the tangibility of real honest fear. Alone, confined to darkness, silence so profound that it hurt in a bad way. In that pit I found there was only one real truth in my life of lies, Hunter loved me. In the soul-dark delirium of my mind one source of light, Hunter. When all the other prayers died mid-throat I prayed to my personal God and he came. His touch no matter how harsh made me crave him. He spent months retraining me to serve and I became is greatest creation, his glove, a slave like no other.

Chapter 1

Pain and Pleasure, like light and darkness, succeed each other;
and he only who knows how to accommodate himself to their returns,
and can wisely extract the good from the evil, knows how to live.
Sterne

"Lets go to Vietnam. My patrol and I ran into some heavy fire while in a rice patty we radioed in for a chopper. They did not arrive in time for most of my men, 2/3's died in the patty and the last of us got captured as we were dragging out our wounded. I got separated from my men by the damn gooks. They shot three right before my eyes and took the balance in a covered truck. They stomped the crap out of me. Then bound my hands backwards with bamboo at my elbows placed a noose around my neck. When I lost my footing as we marched they beat me senseless with bamboo canes until I crawled to my feet. The fast paced march seemed to go on for days. When we finally arrived I thought I would be given chance to rest, not so. They tortured me for days seeking information on patrols, men, ammo, and supplies. When I didn't give them the information they wanted I was beaten, bound and tossed in a pig sty. Kids nailed me with rocks; old ladies tossed buckets of piss and shit on me. It was absolute hell!"

"Days turned into weeks then time stopped all together. All I knew is that they wanted information and none of what I knew was any value to them. It did not matter, they continued to beat me daily, fed me crap, had me crawling around on a stone floor naked on grains of rice until my kneecaps bleed. I told them everything I knew still it was not enough. Hell continued, over and over, day by day until I was about to give up, but I knew Hunter would find me. He was my only hope and even that was beaten out of me. I gave up told them everything I could imagine, had to sign papers, just so I could eat. Then they gave me a bowl of rice. One single bowl of rice was more food than I had in weeks. What I had eaten I caught if it hopped into my cell, yes, I ate bugs. It was food, damn fine food but the way my stomach felt."

"I must have been delirious cause I could have sworn that I heard a whippoorwill, a bird that lives in the north east United States. My eyes began playing tricks on me, as I could have sworn the low growing underbrush was moving inwards towards my cage. Under brush was moving, crawling in towards the cage. The gooks has suspended my cage from a tree near the village so that everyone would know what an ugly American looked like. I watched in silent amazement as the underbrush, shrubs and clumps of grass crawled ever closer then all hell broke loose. Then I heard that damn bird again and could have sworn Hunter was standing at the edge of the village. All hell broke loose as mortars began dropping bombs all over the village. Bamboo and grass huts blew up all over the damn place, people were running, children screaming and in walks Hunter. Painted like a fucking redskin Indian, wearing his war paint and blasting anything that ran into his path as he walked directly to my cage. A few clips from wire cutters and he had me draped over one shoulder. Just as easily as he walked in he walked out with me again."

"While he was carrying me back through the jungle, he paused to cut me free of the wire they had used to bind my wrists and ankles. I begged him there to leave me bound and fuck me hard. He did and I passed out right after he came. He had to have carried me all the way back to home base from what I was told by some of the men on the recon mission. He let no one carry me. Once I was released from the hospital he nursed me back to health. Taught me to trust again, trust in him. When my strength returned I begged him to use me like one of the boy whores he would rent on the streets, eventually he did. During basic training, I was his master after my rescue we became lovers. Hunter was the only man I trusted we reversed roles as he turned into my master and I his slave for the balance of our tour."

"The night before we both were to ship out for home. We had a private dinner party at our home. Very romantic just the two of us, jonathan had put his hand out and touched our Lord. "He offered me his collar and the chance to be his number one boy when we got back to the States. That night I ran away. I wanted the collar, I really did, it just scared the shit out of me. I wanted his collar really bad, but I kept saying to myself that I wasn't queer. Hunter was forcing me to do the acts that I did, made me, when in fact I loved submitting to him, but then my head wasn't screwed on real tight."

"You twins have to understand. I love Master Hunter more than life itself. You, 9-745 and you 9-777 may just understand how I feel, he is the air that I breathe, without it I am nothing, empty, a hollow man. You twins helped me find myself, helped me come to terms with who and what I was and for that I will be ever grateful, but when Hunter called and invited me to Buena Vista. I came dragging you both."

"I have been living a double life on the estate. My days off were spent usually within our private dungeon in bondage or being corrected for my arrogant ways when topside. Remember those days when I wore shackles for a week? We joked about it saying that I had lost a bet. Yes, I stomped and bitched and was a royal pain in everyone's asses, but hidden within my pants was a hard on that would not quit! Both of you accepted my welted back as another lost bet. I bet you two must think I am the unluckiest man alive. Then you laughed it off, I want the two of you to do that now, laugh and go on."

"God knows how much I want his brand now. You would too take it if it were offered. It means security that goes beyond words, actions and locks us together like no other relationship on this planet. The collar that we each wear brands me as well as the shackle on my right ankle as a slave. His brand elevates me from the norm. His brand makes me His personal property to use as He sees fit."

"Yes, I ran when he offered his collar to me again. I got to the end of the highway before I realized I was repeating Vietnam. I turned around and drove back to the cave entrance and begged Hunter to come to me there. I had almost given up when he appeared like that day in 'Nam. He made me sweat and wait for him this time. He wanted to be certain I was not going to run away again. Now, I am certain, this is what I want and need."

"Normally, Master rules those he owns with a light touch however some of us in this room have forced him to use excessive force. When we were together in 'Nam, I was in every way his slave. When I ran from his offer to the States, I thought I was free. When he called me while I was pimping pipeline in the oil fields. I dropped everything and ran home. I needed him just like you two needed me. When I arrived here with you two. We made a contract that I would live a double life until you two came to an age where schooling was necessary. Boys, I want you to accept my good fortune. I really want Master Hunter's brand he has been riding my back for years and I adore him beyond any words. Hell I worship him as my God!"

"Any questions mike or JD?" jonathan asked them while studying their faces.

JD cleared his voice, and looked up to Hunter, "Sir, what will happen to the two of us. Now that you have these new slaves to serve you?"

"Glad you asked that question," said Hunter. "Well, mike will be going to culinary school in Williamsburg this fall and you JD will be attending medical school. Both of you when you have finished your education will report back to the Deus of Castle Enterprises for your new assignments."

"Sending you both away for schooling was my choice," said jonathan. "I had been planning it for years just waiting for the two of you to come of age. I wanted you both to have the best I could offer. Hunter pulled strings and got you into the best schools we could offer. Each of you have worked your self nuts on Buena Vista. Its about time that what you paid in is paid out. Buena Vista will be paying for your schooling, clothes, books, apartment and whatever else you need, that's a gift from Master Hunter."

Hunter began talking, "I will be branding three slaves while we are out here." His boot collided with my butt, "9-745 will be branded as my number one and jonathan will be branded as Buena Vista's number one. That bound lump of meat over there is going to be branded as my number two, 9-777."

"I must ask a favor of you JD. Can you train your replacement by fall? He graduated from college with a degree in animal husbandry as well as horticulture. He was raised on a big farm, one of the largest in Illinois. Who, oh, I didn't tell you did I? Well," Hunter laughed and flashed one of his big toothy grins, "Having a slave under foot helped a member of the Black Watch Security team reconsider a proposal. Eric Wilson has agreed to join our Buena Vista team. If I could toss in a slave like the last one he had to sweeten the deal?"

"What did you do to that man jonathan, or should I say what didn't he do to you? Should I tell him anything for you jonathan? By rights, as my number one Buena Vista slave he would need something like you under foot to help him until he catches hold of the reins properly. We will talk later."

jonathan began speaking, "Twins, I know a part of you has to be hurt by these changes, but I really want us to get back to normal as soon as we possibly can."

Hunter stated, "Mike you seem perplexed, talk?"

Mike was never one for a lot of words, "ssshhurr, how do I relate to my master now?"

"Mike its real easy," blurted JD, "he has a collar that means slave, equals. This way its much better, we can share him with the man we love."

Hunter interjected, "basically mike, JD and you," he looked at jonathan. "JD, mike and jonathan you all owe allegiance to me and Buena Vista. Handle yourself accordingly. 9-745 and 9-777 are to be my personal slaves they own nothing except what I give them, they will be trained how I see fit when I see fit."

"Ok, is everyone square with what's going down? Good; JD, you and mike have double duty, tell those of the handlers to ask about Cappy's transformation and

9-777 that if they have questions they need to approach me. Or you can be cruel and tell the whole truth just as we have said it here. Most of them are fucking romantics anyway! Yeah, tell them the truth, its time everyone knows everything about their new Deus, no more skeletons in the closet."

"Let's hit the deck and watch who brings in the first pot of gold. Let's be seen as the happy family we are. OK, boys and jonathan dismissed. Slaves, I need to be properly dressed for the day, attend me!"

Having dressed our Lord in what he termed more appropriate clothing; translation, leather and boots, we joined the boys and jonathan on the deck. Pillows had been pulled together to form a nice little nest. An umbrella had been placed over the pillows giving those of us who needed shade the extra protection; a platter of fruit and a pitcher of chilled wine with tropical juices were at hand. It had to have been something like a "love in" by the way we had to have looked.

Our master Hunter was in the center of the pillows. His back supported none other than me as I rubbed his back, shoulders and neck easing away any tension that might have been left from the family chat. JD was hunkered over a goblet of flavored juice trying to skewer chunks of fruit to feed mike and jonathan. While 9-777 laid between Hunter's open legs. Sirs boot was resting on the slave's ass as the sun was massaging 9-777's back. We were alone on the deck save for a few deck hands. The few that were present were diving going after conch and other rare delicacies that were destined for our dinner.

We were lost in our own happiness and did not hear the screams from the shore until the Captain of the Watch sounded a god awful air horn signifying to all that someone had found the treasure of 200 pieces of bullion. The handler that made the find was coming up to our boat to show off his good fortune and to show it off to master Hunter. We did not know until mid-week that our Buena Vista flag was flying from the tallest mast indicating to all that our Lord was on this ship.

Like an excited child, the handler jumped up the ladder, danced around until he spotted Hunter and came a running. He dropped to his knees and skidded the short distance to our pillowed domain, "Sir, oh Sir. Look!"

He opened a leather pouch and spilled out small bars of pure gold. "Sir, I never won anything before, not never! I used the maps and the star charts and found it just where I thought the clues said it would be." He grabbed Hunter wrapping his arms around him in the moment and kissed him firmly on the lips to the shock of all of us. Then the handler realized whom he had just kissed. The color drained out of his face and he was begun to stammer then began to apologize when Hunter stopped him.

"Handler...."

I whispered, "Kevin. Sir."

"Handler Kevin, congratulations are in order, I think; no a toast to you Handler Kevin. Congradufuckinglations Handler! You are a hell of a lot richer than you think. That gold goes for $285.00 per ounce and you have about 300 or 400 ounces but then I could be wrong. Do the math boy. You could have over $1200 dollars in that leather bag. Not bad for one days pickings huh? Son if you will listen to me a few minutes. Pull out one or two pieces to show off and ask the Captain of your vessel to put the rest of it in the safe. There you will not tempt people to help themselves. Gold tends to make people crazy."

The boy was nodding his head in agreement, thanked Sir. Climbed to his feet and went seeking the Captain to have his gold locked away before all the other handlers returned.

As the handlers returned our little band dispersed to the wind. JD and mike found younger people they wanted to pursue and were dismissed by Sir. The diving team wanted volunteers to gather more fish from the bottom of the ocean so jonathan joined them and Sir was left with two horny slaves. For a time nothing happened, he laid back pulling each one of us into his arms. We took pleasure being at his side luxuriating in the sun, wind of the ocean, and just being there with him. The galley disturbed us asking for slaves to help with kitchen prep and 9-777 was turned over to the chef with strict orders not to wander off.

Sir took me downstairs into our cabin and ordered a hank of rope. Once I produced it he set to binding me until I was hogtied with extra rope cinching my arms to my sides. Once bound he used me as his boot rest while he conducted some pressing business and spoke on the phone to Eric at Buena Vista.

He may have hated working on his vacation, but I sure as hell loved it. His boots were walking all over me while I was under the table. All was fine until the door of the cabin burst open and a slave none other that 9-777 bounced to the floor at Sir's feet. Sir stood and demanded to know what was the meaning of this intrusion. A handler followed 9-777 through the door.

"Beg your pardon Lord! You had asked that I keep a watch on it and if it wandered off to toss it in shackles and bring it down Sir. I have done as you requested Sir. But it put up a fight," he pointed to fresh whip marks on the slaves butt, "and we had to gag him when he became disrespectful. Used my preference knotted rope, Sir."

Hunter had crossed the room to inspect the handiwork done to his property, "Thanks for bringing the slut home, Mark." This one does not seem to follow orders well unless I am near it to enforce its obedience. "Had it wandered off from the galley, it was suppose to be working in the kitchen."

Mark, a chubby bear cubbish type fellow, "the chef had finished with it and dismissed it. "Sir if you will forgive an observation. It would seem this slave does not have any homing skills. It seems to think that when it is done with one job that it is free to do as it wishes. Was it free to do at it wished? Did I overstep my rights in dragging its hide down to you, Sir?"

"You did right, Mark. It may not have been told to report to me after it was finished with that assignment; still, it should have known."

Master got to his feet, walked over to look down at 9-777, "Mark, help me if you have time. Help me get this piece of meat up and on its feet."

Hunter used the toe of his boot between 9-777's butt cheeks to get the animal to crawl across the room. When it faltered his boot dropped crushing its nuts to the floor until the animal found more speed. This way Hunter directed his slave towards a corner area of the room. Together he and Mark got it to its feet, released the shackles replacing them with Hyatt leg irons and cuffs before relocating its hands at its back.

Rope was attached to the center of the cuffs and Sir pulled forcibly down on the rope, lifting the slave's wrists upwards forcing its head downwards at crotch height. Master directed Mark to bind the animal's legs at its knees and added extra rope around its elbows. Completed they stood back admiring their handiwork. By the look on 9-777's face the position was painful and would grow worse as time wore on.

"Join me for a drink, Mark, I could use a man's company. That is if you are not busy or have pressing business?"

"Sir, I would be honored to join you for a drink." Mark replied.

Hunter pointed at a chair, "care for some of that wicked fruit punch the chef makes here. Tasty stuff but after a few cups it nails your hide to the deck! Care for a nice iced glass, Mark?"

They were sipping and chatting about nothing in particular until Hunter brought up the bombshell. "Mark, tell me what the handler's are saying about 9-777 and its reduction in rank. Anyone upset or out of sorts?"

"Well, Sir," Mark began, "some of the boys think its only fitting that the whore that got them in so much trouble should be stripped of all rank and enslaved. A couple, want its nuts, seeing as they think you are not hard enough on it. Slavery is only as brutal as the master or mistress can be."

"They think it's having an easy life then?" Hunter was thinking, "perhaps they are right. I could be allowing my love for the beast to cloud my judgment? Would that be your assessment, Mark?"

"Sir, you know better than I. But it does seem that is the case," replied Mark.

"You are probably right, Mark, thanks for pointing it out to me. Care to hang around and help me adjust my attitude and its headspace?"

"Sir, I can think of nothing else that is pressing. What would you like to do to it?" Mark was getting excited or should I say his crotch was getting tented and not from bugs either.

Master turned to look at the struggling slave at his back, "its back is still kinda ripped up from the braided cat I used on it the other night. I could use a couple of leather paddles on its butt and thighs. That alone should help it understand that I want it under my feet when its not assigned elsewhere. But is that enough, I wonder?"

My Lord came to where I was lying knelt down to one knee and checked my vitals. Liked what he saw climbed back onto this feet and left me to groove on my bondage. I had the pleasure of watching them prepare 9-777 for the paddling of his life. They relocated it on the edge of the bed with its legs still bound. The position Mark selected was one of a kneeling slave with its head pressed to the floor. The animal was bound so once in that position it could not wiggled out of it. No matter how hard of a beating it would not move easily. Hunter's final act was to remove its gag, telling it to scream its lungs out and just maybe if it begged forgiveness they might stop. All of us in the room thought they knew the answer. He would stop only when he wanted to stop.

Two heavy leather paddles with wooden handles were pulled from the toy trunk; it was as if Hunter had foreseen their need on this trip. Hunter allowed Mark to give the beast a warm up using lighter paddles until its ass glowed a pretty pinkish red then they each took turns laying hard solid blows to that slaves ass and thighs. With the first blow from those huge paddles they had to be all of 4 feet long and 6 inches wide, it voiced its displeasure. Hunter's sadistic chuckle told me that this is just what Sir needed.

They took turns working the slaves buttocks and thighs with the huge paddles. Each blow would make a huge whacking sound as it struck the flesh. The skin went from pinkish red to white then began assuming other colors and by the time they finished its butt and legs were a deep rich purplish black! The color alone would inform all that Hunter was not a softhearted bastard but was anything but.

"Thanks Mark for your assistance with 9-777. Want ta fuck its hot hole?"

"God, yes Sir! That would be GREAT!" Mark all but danced over to where 9-777 lay sobbing.

Hunter had this shit eating grin plastered across his face, "care to make your fuck a more memorable for the slave, Mark? I got an old toy I loved to use when I gave a slave a punishment fuck. You will not feel anything but that slave under you will feel every thrust of your hips intimately?"

Master had walked to the toy chest, pulled a spiked cock and ball shield out of it, and was holding it out to Mark. It looked like a flat of heavy leather with a hole in it. Master explained, "Slip your cock and balls through the hole. Yeah, that's right. Pull the straps around and buckle them tight around your waist. Here, let me help."

My Lord, helped buckle Mark into the cock shield. Straps wrapped around Marks hips and were buckled in the back, another strap ran up between his ass crack then he turned so Hunter could inspect. Sheet! The whole front of Marks groin was covered by heavy bulldog spikes 9-777's ass was about to be transformed into ground hamburger. Each thrust of his hips would force those sharp spikes into the slave's beaten ass and if Mark liked to twist his hip when he withdrew or pushed in he would rip 9-777 a new hole.

Mark had an average sized cock with handsome veining and a lovely mushroomed head. He slipped his cock into that slave's ass and began riding it like there was no tomorrow. It did not take long for him to strike gold, blood began trickling down 9-777's legs which only seemed to spur Mark into more action.

9-777 began singing his solo from the first impact of Marks hips with his. Its song never varied much at first but broke when Hunter pointed out to Mark that blood was running down the slave's legs. The rich baritone solo changed from low moaning screams to begging accented with pleas. Its voice cracked and transformed into low growling as the slave's endorphins finally dropped a load of body created morphine into its system. The animal rode the waves of pain muttering and begging Sir to forgive it all the while Mark plowed that bloody red furrow. When Mark came he made the whole ship aware of it by screaming a most distinctive cry likened to a rooster on acid.

Hunter had sat watching Mark work on 9-777's backside his hand jerking on his own cock in rhythm to Mark slamming his cock into that slaves upturned ass. Mercifully I worked myself to where my Lord sat by lip crawling the short distance and was present when his load took flight. It landed with a warm splat on my chest as the other droplets rose up to my chin. God what a feeling of accomplishment that was for me and to have Hunter look down our eyes lock and him smile made the struggle worth every drop of his cum. Waste not want naught.

Mark was given the option to shower there or go to his cabin. He chose to wear the blood and the cock shield. He left the room like a cock on its walk, strutting! He was mighty pleased with himself and his abilities to serve his Lord.

I was released from his bondage and given the job of cleaning up 9-777 by taking it into the shower and bathing its cuts. Amazingly the animals backside was not as badly damaged as the blood would have indicated, true, it would be sore for the greatest part of the week but it deserved its treatment.

Returning with it, it dropped to the floor and crawled to where master was seated. It placed its head between Sir's boots, pulled its arms around his booted feet, placed its lips to them and cried. Sir basically ignored it until it was finished its sobbing then he ordered it to lift its ass and he stretched out one boot dropped it to the sore butt. The animal gasped, Hunter chuckled and said, "you are not forgiven. You must do better than all the others or you are not worthy enough to wear my brand. Now shut the fuck up or I will give you something to really cry about!" Sir crossed his other boot over the first, leaned back into his chair called me to his side. He read his reports, answered a few on his laptop while he absentmindedly rolled my nipples erect and played his hand over my body as if to comfort me

The vacation on our South Seas cruisers was grander than anyone had expected. It literally shaved exhaustion and time from our lives and forced us to look towards each horizon as a new adventure. Our team went native and became the pirates we envisioned ourselves to be. Well, somewhat civilized pirates when we landed at the islands and had to act the part of tourists. Hell of a way to treat a world. I was thinking when I was ordered to dress my Lord in of all things Bermuda shorts and a Hawaiian print shirt, that he added of all things, flip flops to complete his ensemble. Never in my wildest dreams would I have even seen him in this get up. Still he was on vacation and that shirt did open to reveal his handsome graying chest hairs and budding dun-lap, dun-lap meaning his stomach done lapped over his belt. Age has a way of messing even with the most perfected body. His workload and the time he had dedicated to the gym or working in the fields was showing in minor ways. Still he was older and wiser model as we both were.

We dropped anchor early in the afternoon around 3 bells. Sir having completed his reports pulled 9-777 and I to our feet. He was in a painfully playful mood. He had me pull out a pair of long bondage shorts these he installed on 9-777 covering his badly blistered backside. Master took extra care in sizing these shorts as they had lace panels on both legs and down the back over the ass crack. He first placed the animal into a heavy posture collar, added steel collar and its own hands by way of a pair of arm shackles thus keeping its hands out of master's way. Hunter and I pulled the pants up the animal's legs, literally lifting him off the floor in attempt to get them well seated. Then Hunter began tightening the leather panels around its legs until they were skin tight leaving no room for it to gain any freedom of movement. Each leg was buckled in place just above its knees and he added an extra strap and buckle just near the bend of the thigh. Sir wanted the leather to increase the pain the boy would feel with each movement. Its ass panel was left to last, Hunter forced a rather bulbous plug into the slaves ass before cinching the panel closed giving it no place to escape if it dared attempt an exit. A thick latigo belt was woven between belt loops. Before he closed the belt he added a pinprick athletic cup over the animals well-proportioned cock and balls, zipped up the double zipper closure, locked the panel to the belt and secured the belt with a padlock.

He had me walk it around the room as he watched smiling. 9-777 moved as if every fiber of its being was on fire and in a way that was just what the paddling must have felt like with the glove soft leather over it. Then he sent me to the closet to retrieve one of his old cowboy boots. One of those with the needle toes. 9-777 was dropped to its knees, its ankles were placed in restraints and put into a spreader bar and just before master laid it to the floor its mouth was wedged open and he inserted the toe of his cowboy boot. The boot was forcibly wedged between 9-777's lips and buckled in place so there was no way it could dislodge his boot. Once complete master lowered the animal to the floor and told it to rest. Then he turned his attentions in my direction. I just knew by the way he smiled he wanted some of my flesh and amazingly enough I gave it to him without hesitation.

He placed me on his highboy fuckbench that had me bent at my waist, arms down before me and locked to my ankles. He spread my ankles and locked them in place before departing my side. When he returned he carried a few good canes and one of Cappy's old crops. He began tapping my butt with the canes, layering the blows so that my ass warmed rapidly. These warming blows were laid into my flesh, from my butt down to the tops of my knee's before he worked the tapping inwards going to work on the inner thighs. The well-laid light taps became heavier single blows. First one thickness of cane then moved onwards to a heavier cane, this way again he covered my backside with ever-growing layers of welts. He applied three layers of welts to my backside before he took the thickest of the canes, the one that was almost a thumbs width and began carving up his pig. I had gone from a low moaning to a deep growl to a loud blistery scream when he applied the thickest of the canes to my butt with huge swings from his arm. They ripped into my mind flaring and spraying white-hot lava down my cherry red shoals. He would slam that damn cane into my ass forcing me up on my tippy toes then withdrawal the cane and lightly rub his hand over the well-placed welt. God I hated how I loved it when he did this to me. Each blow rocked my world making me crazy with pain and yet opening a door on pleasure as the endorphins kicked into high gear taking my head into spaces few can imagine without the aid of drugs. I was on my drug of choice Hunter, and endorphins, and he was making me beg for them. The bastard knew me too well as he could hold his hand until I would fucking beg him to slam his cane yielding hand into my hide, than I would scream. Scream and choke it back down inside me, as his hand magically wiped away the pain turning the welt into more pleasure than I would beg again.

It was like being mind fucked; yet I knew it was not that at all. He was seriously twisting me into his pain pig just like he was training 9-777 to take it his way. That is what he wanted from both of us. To serve him totally in all functions without question or doubt. "Oh, god please, my Lord," I begged in a whiney voice, "Please Sir, hit me again!"

"Aaarrggghhh!" I would scream then that would turn into a sobbing moan and I would be right back up and at his door knocking until he answered and gave me what I so richly needed from him, his pain.

Master kept at me until he had his desired creation a crazy Scottish tartan etched by canes deeply into my slave hide and when he released me I crawled to where he stood looking down at me and begged for more, "One more please Sir, pleasseee, Sir!"

He laughed and spit at me instead and like the trained pig I was, I caught his spit showed it to him and swallowed on command. I should have known he was not finished with me when he dangled before my eyes another pair of bondage pants. He said my eyes actually lighted up when I saw them that day, sadly I do not remember. I wanted those bondage shorts on me in the worse way. I was a slut in heat and I needed either him in me or those shorts on me cause I knew one way or another I would have my way tonight and he was going to be dinner.

He installed onyx eggs into my ass about six I think, bound my nuts nice and tight in a circle eight pattern making them go in opposite directions and connected my cock piercing to my guiche with a lock. Yummmm, my head was reeling with slave lust as I could work those eggs within my hole as he stood there lacing me into those wonderfully damned shorts. My shorts were different that 9-777 as they had a zipper down the back giving him access to my ruby rose and like 9-777's they got laced super tight from the inside of my legs down then belts around my upper knee, another belt around my waist and I was set on automatic pilot. Sir added his favorite toy to my arms, binders, set the cinch belts and lay me on the floor. Then he turned to his dressing, leather jock and his thigh high engineer boots, and we were ready for the evening.

Once he was dressed to his liking he released 9-777 from its boot plug and spreader bar and helped it realize that it was to care for our needs tonight. Added to 9-777 its tit bar that ran from one nipple piercing to the other giving it a nice handle for master's hands should he need to grab a hold of something during dinner. I was lifted and together the three of us ascended the steps to the upper deck and were greeted by the Buena Vista herd in mass already in knee deep into their dining pleasure. He directed us towards an out of the way zone and sent 9-777 to fetch us platters of food. While the animal was away, my Lord drew me close to him, protectively put me between his boots and allowed me to rest my head on his thigh. The beast of burden 9-777 returned and began its duties of feeding us the tastiest morsels of the plates. Interestingly Hunter refused it food until we had completely eaten all we wanted then the animal was made to eat on all fours. The redness in its face was more pronounced than its ass had been earlier.

The ships did not combine into one flotilla this evening as we were all making way for the next destination and the next treasure hunt. The winner would be completing for the chance to get a key, the key would open a trunk and in the trunk was the prize. This treasure hunt was designed to get the handlers to work as teams. Teams of three persons where created that evening after dinner, all duly noted in the charts and on the morning the three would work as one to find the buried treasure. The team that won the key would win times three.

As the night wore on small collectives of people would form to watch some scene develop on the deck and that's where we found jonathan knee deep in a fire scene. The top that was using it was using flash paper to ignite an anointing of alcohol illuminating slave jonathan's back and face with a huge smile. The fire scene transformed as the lights grew dimmer and a top began shooting sparks from his fingertips at jonathan. Both seemed to be in pig heaven, loving the scene as the flares of fire arched out of the tops pointing finger to grab a hold the slave who was screaming and dancing in delight of the connection.

Sparks showered down from above us as another top entered the picture. He had his female slave bound to an old fashion wooden boat wheel and he was standing back using an electric grinder on steel gauntlets attached to his arm. He was using the sparks of the metal grinder to burn lightly his slaves back and by her wiggling she was in heaven.

Flogging scenes evolved from the darkness and cascaded over the deck as if choreographed. Others were writhing in bondage, still others in the ecstasy of wild wonderful sex it was as if everyone had gotten drunk on the lust of this voyage. Everyone was having fun expressing themselves, as they should with people that support their choices. That night seemed to be the turning point for all of us. It was as if the reality of our world, our choices came to the surface and were accepted by everyone on board for what they were an extension of themselves. They found others that enjoyed various scenes and those paired off; still others found common unity within their community and those paired off.

It was amazing transformation to watch from my advantage point, secure with my Lords arms or legs. People that were normally so GD prim and proper when at Buena Vista had let down their hair and were enjoying golden showers, others were enjoying the pleasure of being flogged, all seemed hell bent to explore new possibilities on this neutral ground. In a location that brought out the beauty and ugliness of the world and they found acceptance. And yet there was one that made the mistake of going against our prime directive as a people. There was a pedophile among us who had kept his secret so well hidden even his closest friends were not aware of his perversion. When we had stopped on the last island he had struck taking a small boy off into the jungle. It was not until we set sail that we had communications from the island police. We were in as much shock as the child that one of our own would have done anything like that to any child. As a people, our shield mates and Manor houses condemned one form of sexual predator a pedophile. Children were scared to us, we may not be breeders but that does not make us less in a child's eye. If nothing else we are staunch protectors for our children of the future. They are a valuable asset by reaching them, protecting them we can destroy hate and disharmony more rapidly than by trying to reach the parents who were already programmed.

Our ship had turned back once Hunter and a group of his peers had gleamed the truth from the handler. Luckily the fellow admitted his wrong and was willing to return to the island to stand trial. Hunter had spoken to the constable in charge of the case and found out what the handler would face if he were found guilty, castration. When Hunter shared the knowledge with the handler he was oddly overjoyed. It seems he had sought castration in the States but it had been denied to him. He was hopeful that with his nuts removed that he would no longer have the desire or harm any other children. Like our ships they had set their course so had this handler and the currents would take him a different path than we now journeyed.

My Lord found a sling hanging from the ropes attached to one of the masts. Tossed my ass into it placing my feet in the stirrups, draped my arms over the upper edge and lowered my head. He ordered 9-777 down on its knees and ordered it not to move then he disappeared, returning with a handsome man by the name of Brian. Tall stately fellow, lean swimmers and gym body with big well-veined muscular arms and torso. Brian and Hunter stood talking over my body. Brian being at the rear had opened the zipper while Hunter ordered me to play the Easter bunny role. Meaning I should give Brian an egg or two. His easy laughter made him a winner for me that and the fact that he pocketed the eggs slipped his cock into my ass and walked closer all the while talking to Hunter about his fishing trip today.

Hunter dropped my head and placed his cockhead on my lips. Opening my mouth he entered my mouth and the two quickened their movements. They must have practiced their dance steps before tonight cause they would withdrawal and heave too as one body in two holes. Someone cranked up my reception by adjusting my knobs, working them hard as if to get great reception from Russia while another opened my pouch and grabbed first one nut than the other squeezing them heighten their experience. They sawed my body into pieces as if they were both master magicians doing a stage show left me tittering on the edge begging for cock and air then shot their loads. My guts seemed to swell just from the volume of their deposits. They withdrew their cocks as one leaving me empty and withdrew. I thought I was alone until another pair of cocks entered me. These two did not have the same affect on me as the two who fucked as one. These just sawed away at any random rate that they could muster. One dropped his load almost as fast as he slipped in the other worked my hole for days gaining no ease for his pressure and finally withdrew perhaps out of boredom. A third pair of cocks used my holes for entertainment before my Lord returned to rescue me from the horny handlers aboard our ship.

Returning to our cabin earlier than anticipated my Lord slipped me into a sleep sack, laced me in securely and with the aid of 9-777 they got me locked within suspension. It was my Lord's choice where I would sleep that night as any night. I slept cocooned within a wonderful leather bag, laid out flat facing the ceiling, encapsulated in leather, laced with heavy belts. Secure almost as much as if I was with my lord in his bed. Having digested six loads, five from strangers, and locked in his bondage for the night I all but purred myself to sleep.

My bladder was aching for release when he finally lowered me from my position and released me so that I could crawl into the bathroom to clean up and out. Making my way to the bathroom I noticed that 9-777 was still within the bed as Sir had bound it tightly in place, ass upright and ready for action. No doubt, my Lord had used it too as he was in a chipper come fuck me mood. Returning I found remnants of breakfast laid out on the table and master nowhere to be seen.

He returned carrying a rubber hood of sorts. Opened the toy chest pulled out a bishop's hood and tossed them both in direction of 9-777's prone body. Hunter crawled across the bed to 9-777's head. Like a calf roper he grabbed the animals head forced the mouthpiece between its lips pulled the rubber hood over its head allowing it to snap tight around its neck. Quickly Hunter bound the bishops hood over the rubber mask setting straps in record time as the slave struggled turning its head this way and that as if to knock his head free, and with a flourish of a well practiced calf roper Hunter lifted his hands into the air. Revealing a slave's head encapsulated in rubber and leather buckles its mouth impaled on a rubber tube that connected to a funnel on top of its head. 9-777 had failed to drink master's piss for the last time it would seem. After this lesson, it would drink his piss and relish it.

A knock came to the door. I was signaled with his head to open the door. The handler from last night, Brian entered. With his help 9-777 was catherized and taken up to the deck to begin its time of service to all handlers in need of the head before they went ashore to begin the second search for the lost treasure of Buena Vista. The teams were all present and ready. Our ships were not docking; part of this hunt would require them to swim ashore carrying one on a float. Tools were taken earlier according to Hunter as the teams needed to do more than just dig to find this treasure, they would be needing rope, a pick axe and then a shovel once they got to the site. Hunter addressed his people telling them that once everyone had jumped ship that the ships would lift anchor and would await the first team to arrive on the other side of the island with the key. That dinner would be held on the island. Everyone have fun, be safe and good luck. With that he hit the button to the air horn and the world took to the water laughing and screaming as they swam, waded and ran up shore to grab the necessary but limited tools.

No sooner than they had departed did the four ships weight anchor turn on their engines and putter around to the other side of the island. The balance of the day was used to build fire pits, set out huge mats of woven palm leaves to ferry pillows and items of comfort to the island. Torches were planted down the shoreline, the crew of the ship with the aid of 20 slaves worked like fevered beavers setting up the banquet area for the evening's winners. Among the slaves working hardest was one black-headed slave that had to kneel for anyone wishing to use it as a urinal. It was damn lucky that it was working hard and its sweat was super charged with the piss it was drinking cause without a handler or master present there was no way it could release the catheter that was inserted into its own penis.

When we were permitted to return to our ship it did seek out its master post haste and it was drained but not removed as it may have hoped from its imposed punishment for failing its master.

It was late afternoon before a team found the treasure and made there way down to the shore where they signaled the Captain of the Watch, who in turn blew the horribly loud air horn signaling to all the treasure had been found and all should return. The entertainment committee reclaimed 9-777 early in the evening. It was later found bound kneeling to a palm tree within easy access of all handlers having need of a very personalized urinal instead of a green jungle. The golden waters flowed richly and that slave had all it could ever imagine handling as they found out who it was everyone had to help it understand its duties to our Lord.

We arrived as the last stragglers hit the sand. They were carried bodily by their brethren to the banquet table given large chilled goblets of fruit drinks an allowed to relax before the festivities were started. We were directed to sit where two huge woven palm mats came together forming one huge banquet table. Fresh fruit covered the greatest distance of the table, pitchers of water and spiked fruit juice were littered down the table. A dais was erected just up from where we sat it was littered with pillows and just to the left of the dais was another smaller platform holding one of Hunter's steamer trunks holding a huge padlock.

Torches were lighted by runners coming from the far end of the shoreline drawing closer up and to the picnic area were we all sat in stunned silence here too torches were ignited. We heard a loud drumbeat being played on what sounded like a hollow log and with that as the fanfare a figure covered in grasses and an elongated facemask jumped out of the jungle. It waked towards us banishing a wooden club went to the trunk and tired beating the padlock off, tossed the club away and called for the winners to step forward. They too jumped from out of the jungle naked save for grass skirts. Our world went wild with cheers and boos from those that did not find the treasure, it was all in good fun.

The three were lead by the witchdoctor to the trunk they proceeded to open the trunk and everyone at the banquet held their breath. The trunk opened and the three literally dived into it. One jumped up screaming holding an envelope that was passed to the second who started screaming then to the third who joined the unholy riot. They were permitted to dance around in excitement until the witch doctor came and took the letter. He too joined in their dance but led them towards the dais and pointed that they needed to sit while he read what they had won. They were given by the Buena Vista Leather guild a $2800 voucher for custom leathers and $200 voucher for boots. Which easily translated into pants, vest, boots or something more fun. Anyway the crowd went nuts when they realized the prize was worth $3000 worth of leather goodies for the winners.

Three more prizes to go and we were only on the fourth day of the cruise. Each would climb in price and hardness to find as Hunter announced. One prize was beyond compare as it was a custom built Harley Davidson built by none other than Rob Roy of Richmond and the winner of that prize will receive their hog at the October Manor run. Then the party raised a notch as our dinner arrived carried by slaves dressed in grass skirts. Everyone including the slaves had a great evening and retired to the ships easily as all but a few were damned exhausted from the miles they had to cover to get from one side of the island to the other. Our ship was quiet that evening only a few of us were about on the deck.

Hunter, 9-777 minus its headgear and I were present to watch the moon rise from the ocean. 9-777 had its face buried into its master crotch most of the time and missed the greatest show when the moon seemed to rise giving the water its own illumination as two moons filled the space. Still 9-777 had learned a valuable lesson it will no longer refuse its Sir anything. It was worshipping its Lord properly caring for his needs no longer concerned at who watched as he mouthed and sucked on his Sirs cock. It was after all about making master feel good. If Sir was happy we too would be happy.

The ships weighted anchor once the last remnants of the crew were aboard and set sail for the next island in our merry jaunt around the South Sea Islands. What lay ahead of us only Hunter and perhaps jonathan knew. It was not my calling to know only be there to give my Lord pleasure however he wished. Right there at that moment he wanted my lips attached to his nipples, I complied even as 9-777 nursed his cock with his throat muscles. Three pigs in heaven under the moon and stars, two slaves one the Master.

We slept that night bound, as we slaves should be kept. I at his side, the other bound on the floor beside the bed. When we awoke we would be seeing a different world more beautiful than anything I could have ever imagined. I traveled in perfection as if in a dream with my Lord at my side and my brother too. How could it get any better this slave could not know, to me at that time this was perfection.

Chapter 2

No life is so hard that you can't make it easier by the way you take it.
Ellen Glasgow

Awaking the following morning we found a shivering fevered 9-777 at the side of the bed. A sick slave is a burden to its owner. That is not always the case if you have a caring and understanding owner as we did with master Hunter.

Once we realized 9-777 was really sick. Hunter dropped to the floor besides his slave and I was sent for the doctor and Hunter's medical bag. He checked his vitals while I ran for a sheet and a blanket to place around the sick slave. Afterwards, I ran to find the doctor who was at the time on the fourth ship and returned informing Sir that the doctor would be quiet awhile. They had rigged up a chair that was pulled from one ship to the other by way of a taunt line strung between the two ships.

Returning I found that 9-777 had crawled into master's lap and was resting more freely as it was unbound. Every movement caused him some pain. As he wore a coat of many colors and looked as if he was beaten from his neck down to its knees.

Hunter was hushing 9-777 with quieting noises as he loaded a hypodermic syringe with a vial from his doctor's bag. Hunter was so gentle, I knew that side of him intimately and loved him all the more. Master cleaned the boy's thigh with a cotton swab then stuck the boy. The shot was quick and over with before it even knew. Together while we could still get him moving we lifted him from the floor and placed him on master's bed. More covers were added as the manimal 9-777 lay there watching, studying Sir's face as if he was fearful Sir would hurt him again. His slave had a temperature of 103 degrees.

Master leaned over and placed his lips to the boy's forehead by the slave's reaction you would have thought Hunter's lips burned. Hunter refused to give up and placed his hand on one side of the boys face, the slave flinched as if he had been struck. 9-777's eyes went wild and he tried to push himself away from our master who was having none of that action from the slave. It was as if the unexpected kindness that Hunter was showing to the slave was just too brutal to bear. When he couldn't break free his struggles subsided and tears began to stream down his face. The kiss, gentleness had caught 9-777 totally off guard that alone cracked 9-777's facade more completely than all the pain Sir could have given the slave. 9-777's defenses were not primed for this type of assault; but then again, who defenses were? Too often I had seen Hunter work; now, I knew 9-777 was his!

Hunter lay on his side next to 9-777 lightly weaving his hand over the fevered boys flesh as the shot worked its charms making the layers of pain and exhaustion disappear. It tried to fight the affects of the shot by slowly rolling its head to and fro as it looked up at Hunter, "daddy, I am sorry that I misbehaved. I will be a good boy daddy, I…"

9-777 fell asleep mid sentence and Hunter climbed off the bed, added blankets and called the Captain asked him to cancel our need for the doctor. Rang off and cursed not knowing the whereabouts' of jonathan. I was ordered to the kitchen for breakfast materials and ran into jonathan there fetching coffee for the top who had used him hard by the looks of his welts the night before.

Our morning passed like sands running between open fingers. We waited to see if 9-777 would come around when it did we fed it a super tasting broth the cook in the galley had made for him with chunks of shrimp and kelp flakes. We frolicked most of the morning on deck Sir and I until a hand drawn chair floated overhead. The doctor had arrived from one of the other ships and was taken to 9-777 by Hunter as I followed. My Lord explained. The doctor eyed the slaves back and groin without many comments gave us a big tub of numbing salve, an antibiotic shot and cautioned us to not allow him into the ocean until his cuts healed then make him swim. As it will be the best thing for him the water would limber up his sore muscles and help cure out its battered hide.

The balance of our day found us hiking through the rich forest seeking out a waterfall called the Tears of Love. It was suppose to be a waterfall created when one of the native ancestors watched her one true love die at sea. Her tears created the water falling from fresh water into a basin of salt water. Interestingly enough the seawater was warmed by volcanic activity. We found the enchanted fountain and joined the many that worshipped her grief by diving into the sea basin and luxuriating in the toasty natural salt spa and climbing out by way of the river. Our afternoon was delicious and made more so when we found that we have been followed by a native couple that having taken the waters crept aside into the heavy fern embankment and made sweet music. We joined their suggestion finding our own bed of soft ferns. Their Hunter made love to me giving me tender caresses combined with heavy lovemaking.

We were disturbed by the ships air horn sounding departure. Calling all the tourists that had gone ashore back to the launches before the ships set sail. This way our tour had to have boosted the local economy hugely as it seemed we stopped at about every small island as we journeyed from shore to shore.

Two lovers ran across the burning sands to the launches hopped onto our ship and descended into our cabin finding Nurse Hellga (jonathan) at work caring for 9-777. Our evil nurse had moved the slave onto a folding cot, secured its hands to one end of the cot and locked its legs in leather fetters and a spreader bar per the doctors orders. Supposedly to stop its hands from gouging or scratching it's healing scabs. jonathan had gone ahead and cleaned the slave's backside applying literal appointments of the salve, which assisted the slave with a deeper sleep. We joined the slave in slumberville as the three of us piled into Sir's bed and napped until dinner.

When we awoke jonathan was informed that it would be on guard duty for the evening and that it should report to the galley for its dinner. It brought its bowl of slave goop richly laden with fruits and meat back to the cabin there it dined under master's watchful eye.

Once completed it was permitted to clean itself out and prepare for its time of service as one of the guards for the evening. Problem is while on the ship we did not need any guards or so I thought, but Hunter had other ideas. When we exited the bathroom where we had been sent we found a heavy sleep sack laid out on the floor and Master standing nearby with his shit-eating grin plastered all over his body. He was up to no good and jonathan would be soon in his uniform for the evening, his own private sleep sack.

Carefully jonathan slipped his arms and egs into the sleep sack and lay back as Hunter cinched him tightly into the confines of the luxurious soft glove leather. Laces were cinched firmly over the top of the body; an inflatable hood was added with one breathing hole and a thick posture collar. Then belts were wrapped around the bound and helpless man within the suit those were buckled securely in place. While I held its head Hunter pulled the ropes working the pulley system hoisting the slave up off the floor floating mid air. There it was left while I dressed my Lord for dinner.

We had dinner amidst a horde of men and women hurriedly checking their maps, going over there star charts and checking the heavens with sextants to see if what they had pulled from the computers were correct. Everyone was a buzz filled with excitement of the next challenge that was before them on the morrow. We enjoyed a quiet private dinner, Sir laid back in the comforts of his slaves lap while the slave fed him finger foods.

When dinner was complete we descended into our cabin to check on our wards.

9-777 was awake and thirsty; I attended to its needs while master attended to jonathan's needs. He had removed its hood when he got my attention by snapping his fingers and pointing at a bag of MandM chocolate covered peanuts on the table. I brought him the bag of chocolate the same candies that melt in your mouth not in your hand. Hunter was laughing while he worked one of his nastier tastier raunchy jocks he had been wearing since he was here over jonathan's head making certain the pouch would lay across the slaves nose and mouth.

Hunter tapped the slave's head lightly to get its attention, "you are on guard duty slave for the balance of the evening. Do not let anyone steal my diamonds!" Hunter spoke to jonathan with his eyes twinkling and over flowing with mischief.

I thought these two had way too much sun while I attended to 9-777's needs and listened to them carrying on.

"slave, you have to guard my valuables. I can trust only you. You are willing aren't you, meat?"

"Sir, yes, Sir," mumbled the slave!

Hunter had torn open the bag of candy-coated chocolates as I watched him from the far side of 9-777 in disbelief at their game. Hunter held up a yellow MandM, "this is one of my finest yellow diamonds," Hunter giggled and shoved it into jonathan's mouth. Hunter followed the yellow diamond with greens, blues and reds filling the slave's mouth with candy all the while laughing. Then he pulled his cock raunchy jock over the slave's mouth and added his codpiece to the super structure the chinstrap was closed and the slave was locked into heaven. Having worn that same head harness, I knew this was just next to being in heaven the smell of master was sucked in with each breath, scrumptious!

Hunter leaned over getting right into jonathan's face, "when I return all those diamonds had better be in perfect condition or...."

The twinkle in jonathan's eyes told me all I needed to know about the game these two were playing. We exited the cabin and returned to the party upstairs knowing when we returned the diamonds in jonathan's mouth would be long gone and the slave would be tortured for his failure. Reward and punishment was never really a game played with Master and his slaves except when it was just that a game. He chose to use a slave as he saw fit be that with kindness or brutality both were suitable gifts for a slave. Should a slave fuck up then it was punished with something far worse than any slave had ever expected. Each slave has his or her own fears. Punishment usually involved its fear being used in a corrective assessment thus the lesson was burned into the slave's psyche and it would remember the lesson more completely. Some slaves fear public exposure, still others fear piss its one of the master's jobs to find and isolate a slaves most personal fears. Once known they can be used to affect change within the beast and help it over come one of its own self inhibitors thus making it a more focused beast. The key is focus, only one exists within a slaves mind, that of its Owner. Even its own self image is set aside for the preferred image of its owner, this way a slave is willing to give totally of itself wherever and whenever it is called to serve.

We departed the room seeking the private dungeon that had been set up below deck found it and realized it was packed with heaving bodies in various forms of entertainment. We returned to the deck; found a handsome handler bound in a sling, and master nailed his tail while I kneeled below caught the juices. Completed, we dropped down the steps to check on jonathan and 9-777. In passing we ran into mike that was literally helping a handler down the hallway while holding on to his huge bloated cock. Mike gave Sir a bow and Hunter laughed knowing that boy just might have found the size that he needed to scratch his itch. Mike was a size queen, the bigger the better for that boy. Hunter had sent him on a mission to find the largest cock within our fleet and if I knew mike he would do them all to find that one.

We entered the stateroom each of us crossed to our wards, I to check on 9-777 who was wiggling his ass seductively and Hunter to check on his diamonds. I heard Hunter saying, "spit out my diamonds guard. What are these? I gave you jewel toned diamonds and you give me back nuts? You will pay for this..."

Hunter released a panel and pulled jonathans cock and balls out of the confines of the leather. He crossed the room and returned with his sounds and a tens unit. One of the largest sounds I had ever seen was installed into jonathans cock before an electrode was taped in place locking the sound deep within the slaves cock. Hunter then bound the slave's nuts in heavy gauge copper wire added another electrode and began turning the knobs watching his slave react. A smile covered master's face, he placed the unit on the slave, added a lace to hold it in place and moved up to another pair of panels on the slaves black bound body. Sir's fingers worked its tits then grease was added to each and suction tubes were applied pumped hard and left. With all that done, Sir bent over kissed the slaves lips. Raping his mouth signaled that we should leave and we returned to the party for the balance of the evening.

Hunter and I had just finished his cigar and I was reeling from its affect. Nothing finer than having a hunk of a man force me to take his smoke by him placing his hand over my mouth, his lips over my nose and filling my lungs with his cigar smoke. This way I enjoyed the pleasure of his cigar and the other ways were to lie at his side as he scorched my flesh or fed me its ashes. He had me writhing in no time as he slowly burned off any real or imagined hairs left on my body. I could not help myself when he had a cigar in his hands or to his lips. It was as if the cigar became my fixation and I loved watching him place it to his lips or bite and chew it when he was aggravated and angry. Just the act of him placing his lips around that cigar almost always gave me a hardening cock. Thank God, I was locked in chastity it would never have done for him to see my cock hard when he was smoking.

Initially Sir had kept me locked into a solidly made set of rings that forced my cock down in a deep curve. It was a device created by one of our more twisted blacksmiths. Later he added piercing's that kept my cock neatly tucked between my legs and with the addition of his padlock it was not going anywhere. Of course there are other piercing's that will do the same thing and rings that line the cock all have the same intended purpose to train a slave or submissive that that piece of meat is no longer theirs to use. Interestingly enough it keeps my head focused on my job and has refreshing side effects. Since I have been in chastity my Lord no longer needs to use lube on my ass its now a self lubing butt one that he calls Juicy butt affectionately and well, I am much happier no longer having rule over my cock. He uses it or milks it as he sees is fit for my health or allows me the chance to cum when he inflicts great pain on it. But other than that, my cock is his cock and he has control over it as he does me.

Having finished the cigar he allowed its hot embers to fade before he placed it into his private ashtray and watched as chewed and swallowed. After all it was nothing but nicotine and fiber it would come out in the morning. He climbed to his feet ordered me to follow and we went to check on his diamond mine.

Returning to the cabin he made final adjustments to the slave jonathan by only lowering his feet, reconnected the suction cylinder on its tits, removed the tens unit and sound, added a little lube and began jerking on jonathan's cock until it got nice and rigid. He placed a large cylinder over both jonathan's cock and balls added the pump and applied pressure. It was amazing to watch the cock swell as the vacuum pulled more air into the flesh. Once done to his level of satisfaction he raped the slaves face repeatedly with his tongue and finger then bade it good night.

Before bed he placed me in a leather straight jacket, leg binders and a heavy hood with penis gag, tossed me into his bed and used me as his pillow teasing my cock throughout the night. Taking it just to the point of no return before he withdrew his hand. No matter how I tried to move I could not get off and he knew it. He drifted off to sleep and I drifted off into agony as my blue balls rose a notch.

I was allowed to stay in bed when he rose and he went about his business. I drifted in a dark world filled with bright images of Sir and I at play. Images of him using me before his peers, using me as a boot rest, having sex with me in the pool and tender moments where I knelt before him filled with admiration of his control over my every waking moment. He returned to increase my bondage. Straps were added to tighten his control over my legs, and a cylinder was pumped over my cock making my tongue and tits sensitive like antennas feeling radio waves. Then the bed rose as he departed leaving me to writhe and hump flexing my body against the straps that encircled my body and mind. He kept me this way for the greatest part of the day. Sexually focused and alive; aware of nothing and everything. It was as if my body was his focus for sexual energy, and I was frying in his skillet.

When he removed the hood, I could not tell what time it was as the portholes were draped, it could have been the next day for all I knew. He fed me while I lay in his bondage still bound to the bed, encased in his straps and leather jacket. He fed me food and kisses all the while stroking my cock forcing me to focus on him. When he had had my fill of food, he pulled me onto his chest at nipple height, "make me feel good slave," he said. Knowing full well all I could access due to his bondage was his nipple and armpit. So I got him back and went to work sucking and chewing with my teeth until he was wheezing and moaning like an old teapot. He pushed my face from his chest. Began releasing my straps and leg binder. Lifted me to my feet escorted me to the bathroom should I need to piss or shit, I pissed. Then took me into the office area and placed me on my knees. Neither 9-777 nor jonathan were present just my Lord in all his glory.

He pulled from his closet his tallest pair of Dehner's all freshly spit shined by my own face and body. Pulled from the closet his leather breeches and a muscle shirt, added gloves, his cigar case then turned to me.

"I am going to hurt you today slave. I am taking you to the dungeon where we can play the day away," he said this as he dressed himself.

There was nothing I could do to stop what he wanted he was telling me this for what reason? Perhaps so I could steel myself for what was to come perhaps to psyche me out. It did neither only make my cock hard and dripping in anticipation of a whole day with him in the dungeon. I was ready for him today! He had gotten my motor started last night and I was all but humming with sexual energy.

He stood there handsome as hell itself. Ranger breeches of black leather, Dehner boots and a blue rubber tee shirt that conformed to his body like liquid. His nipples were erect and very visible through the rubber. He grabbed a hood and tossed it in a bag along with other items then came towards me, placed his boot between my legs and pulled my head to his leg. There he stood, I kneeling on the floor my cock dripping pre cum on his spit shined boots trapped in a straightjacket and not seeking release any time soon. Just happy as a pig in shit kneeling there feeling his sexual energy arching out like a bolt of lightening to me and driving me fucking nuts with desire for him to be in or on me.

He pulled me to my feet, grabbed his bag, opened the door and pushed me towards it and snarled, "get your ass into the dungeon you fucking slave! I need to correct your errant ways."

Who was he kidding? I all but ran the way in my excitement. Would have made it but a handler who thought I was running away from Sir caught and detained me until my stalking Hunter approached. "Thank you John for catching my runaway pig. I will take it from here."

Sir latched onto my neck and drug me the short distance to the dungeon. We entered closed and locked the door. In the corner of the room was another slave by the looks it was 9-777 but hooded and bound in such a way that it could not get up or get down. Sir had it in a deep squat, knees spread wide, ankles bound in a spreader bar and its ass slipped over the largest damn dildo I could ever imagine working its way into a butt. The slaves arms were elevated bent over a steel bar hanging from the ceiling and bound down in upon itself wrists attached to its steel neck collar. Its tits were drawn away from its body by thread bound tightly around nubs on its chest and weighted. Any struggle seemed to be met with resistant and made the beast slip down on the plug in its ass.

He caught me watching the struggling slave "see you like my handiwork slave, its what 9-777 needed to realize its got no more choices left open to it but serve."

"My dark side is ravenous. Its craving man flesh and suffering slaves."

He pulled me into his chest, grabbed my chin lifting it and forced his tongue down my throat as we battled mid mouth for supremacy. He knelt placed tight steel shackles around my ankles, moved me into position and locked my feet to the floor. He stood, released the straps containing my arms in front then stepped behind me releasing the leather jacket and pulling it off. He wiped me down with a dry towel and fed me water in preparation of what was about to happen. He made me watch him as he pissed inside the leather hood allowing the leather to drink up the moisture before pulling it over my head and cinching it tight. Metal went around my wrists and my arms were lifted until high overhead. He took my nipples added something that hurt like hell then went to work on my cock-n-balls. Those he laced tightly drawing them deep into their sack before wrapping my cock tightly. Then he backed away lighted a cigar and left me to hang and wait for his attention.

A gentle tapping began on my calves, nothing painful, like a switch gently tapping a beat. The switch rose up my legs over my thighs across my buttocks up my back and up my arms to my hands then back down the front before it was repeated and repeated each time getting harder. Each repeat got harder, stronger, as his tapping made my body sing with electric sexual tension. My panting breath became harder with each cycle over my body. My tits hurt, my balls ached, if I tried to turn to miss a blow he would pull on them and yet, something odd stuck out in my mind. He was avoiding two areas on my body the skin cn my right buttock and the area above my right tit. Why was he not hitting these areas's I wondered. Nothing came to mind as the strokes got harder and harder whisking my mind into another Zen like trance. Screams were not necessary still I sucked on the leather hood until it seemed to catch in my throat cutting off air. I panicked when I could not get air he must have realized what had happened as the tapping stopped. He removed the blockage before tightening the hood another notch. Then he resumed his pattern using another tool, a belt perhaps?

The pattern was beaten into my hide over and over using the belt. He took his own sweet time as he worked me into a burning ember. Never varying the speed neither fast nor slow just keeping the belt moving up, over, around, and down. The belt was dropped and another tool was added to my burning hide it felt like a swarm of bees striking my flesh, stinging me and biting into my flesh. I imagined I was a drum on which he was beating out a dirge; mine if he continued the way he was going. Another tool changed and the beat became faster double sticks were being used to increase and cover my whole body with angry red welts or so I imagined. I was delirious with pain and could not stop humping the air with my cock, jumping this way and that as his sticks set me on fire.

I knew I could not take any more of this and screamed a horrible blood filled scream. His pace quickened the intensity ncreased a notch and my screams were ignored as he kept beating and beating me. I started struggling as if I could get away from his blows, I knew better but knew I could not take this much longer. I was on the cusp about to fall into the pit again when it stopped.

My body burned like a flash fire, hot and brutally clean!

I did not know if he was present but I clung to a lifeline, a hope, that he was standing just in front of me jerking off watching me wiggle and turn in the agony of ecstasy. He was there, his cock in his hand, a cigar in his lips and he was fisting his cock down the length to his balls then rising up to the purple cock head, hard hands gruffly fisting his hard cock. Pre cum by the gallons seemed to be dripping to the floor at his boots. I wanted to scream please master let me taste it! He did but only in my imagination.

I jumped half out of my wits when he hit me next and screamed in anger as he was using electricity. Jolt after jolt ran across my skin his hand was a fire with the damn stuff and he kept me twisting around like an old lady in a hoola hoop. God I hated that shit! Thankfully it did not give him the desired results and he halted after a few attempts to get me to jump up and do the boogie-woogie.

He released my feet, cock n balls and tits then my hands and pulled me into his chest. There his arms closed around me holding me upright and making my body tingle. I felt like a battery locked to a charger. His hands caressed my hooded head and it felt so damn good just to wrap my arms around him that I could have climbed into his skin just to be closer to him.

Instead he turned me and with one hand on his arm he guided me towards my next station of the cross and more suffering for his pleasure. I did not care at that point as I was riding a body high that would not quit any time soon. He was the conductor on the ride and I knew he wanted to take me into and beyond the outer limits.

Using his hands on my shoulder he pushed me downwards until I was seated. One at a time my feet were fed into heavy boots, they got laced tightly and I thought I knew what he was going to do, reverse suspension. But he pulled me to my feet onwards to the unknown until I bumped into a barrier. He kicked my legs open and bound them, pushed me forward over a rounded surface and secured my neck by a chain to the hood collar fusing my body over the barrel. My arms were lifted behind and up until they were secured overhead. This position I knew would be a bitch if left here long.

Once positioned his hands began to weave their spell working out knots in my neck and shoulders forcing me to relax into his bondage his forced position, making me accept what he wanted. My body awakened to his touches as if a spark was blown into flame. The hairs on my body began to ache with the energy that was being transferred from him to me and back and forth. I tingled with his excitement, and he felt my pain and my needs. Looking through his eyes I could see my body bound wiggling under his hands. I could feel his frustration his needs for me to endure more pain for him. He needed my pain like I needed his cock buried deep within me. Then it dawned on him and me that our minds had fused into one mind. We were feeling each other's emotions, needs and sharing each other's pain-pleasures.

I watched him as if I was outside my body. Watched him walk across the room and fetch a heavy wooden paddle. He walked back swinging it, getting the feel of the device and swung his arm back, then forward and my ass exploded with a loud thwack! The sound was not heard with my ears but felt up into the core of my body, as if I was a small body of water into which a stone had been tossed. The ripples of the paddle having hit my ass echoed within my inner core setting loose a deep-seated desire to have more. I begged him mentally wiggled my ass and another landed. Again the echo rose up inside my body giving me such incredible energy. Another thwack was laid into both butt cheeks raising me up on my toes pushing me forward and jerking me back onto my bound arms causing another form of pain to filter through my dazed mind. He worked my ass and thighs like I had seen an old lady beating a well-worn rug! Trying one paddle then another varying the sensations we both were sharing.

I was well beyond pain lost in my own nirvana when his cock entered me. It felt like his cock was a 440-kilowatt spark and I the receptor. Flash Fire; Fire in the hole, every pore of my body sparked blue flames as his cock connected us together. It was a tingling static fusion that made me totally crazy. His cock took on a life of its own as it transformed into a steam fed piston plowing my ass into churned butter. His cock began to swell as it moved preparing to blow his load deep into my bowels. He was pumping hard then he withdrew and was gone. GONE! I screamed long and low as I realized he had just about taken me over the edge and halted just on the edge of oblivion. He left me there until I calmed down. Ignoring my muffled pleas for him to shove his cock back into my hole and use it completely. He heard nothing. He was no longer present.

When he returned I was released from my position. Locked my hands behind my back and guided by his hand on my shoulder up a small flight of steps. I could not picture where I was and thought I knew the ship like the back of my hand. I was confused as he walked me around back down a step or two and returned by other steps. He lost me on my own ship. I had no clue where we were, nor did I care. We stopped his arms closed around me, and I felt as if we were the only ones left in the universe. Holding me pressed into his chest one of his other hands began weaving the fire back into my body, awakening me to more serious needs, his.

He backed away leaving me stranded. The boat under my feet rocked gently, but I held my place until hands closed over my head releasing the hood and unlocking my wrists. I damn near shit when my eyes cleared. Everyone or so it seemed was present and looking at me, handlers, slaves, the crew of the ship and a camera crew who were broadcasting this event to the other ships.

JD stood before me dressed in full leather, boots and a no nonsense grin, "9-745, turn and face your Owner."

I spun on my heels and found my owner, master and Lord standing behind me with his hands crossed across his chest. He looked good especially with jonathan kneeling at his left side and 9-777 head bowed to the floor on the right.

Sir looked down at me, "Number ONE!" He bellowed so all could hear, "do you accept the brand that will make you my personal slave for life and serve me even unto death."

I did not even think, I responded, "Sir! YES! SIR!"

He looked down at jonathan, "Number ONE of Buena Vista. Will you accept the brand that makes you as Buena Vista's and my slave until death and beyond?"

Jonathan looked up, smiled a big handsome smile, "Sir, I am yours use me, Sir!"

Then Hunter turned kicked out at 9-777, "you are my slave for constantly fucking up. you have no choice. you will receive my brand and will serve me one way or the other until I either sell you or bury you!"

Master stepped forward raked his eyes across the crowd, "YOU are my peers and witnesses of this event. I, Bruce Hunter, Founder of the Buena Vista manor and soon to be reining Deus of Castle Enterprises place my brand to these slaves. By doing so, I seal their fate to mine. They will serve me forever and beyond. So it is written, so shall it be!"

He stepped back and shouted clearly over the mumbling audience, "IRONSMITH! Let the irons be set!"

"Number ONE, 9-745, come to me!"

Every part of my body seemed to tingle with fire as I dropped and crawled the short distance to my lord, there I lowered my head kissed his boots lovingly and let him pull me to my feet. "Lock your hands behind your neck, spread your legs and look directly into my eyes, slave. I am your world, I am your only focus and I will drink your pain as we did earlier today."

"Number One, you are to carry the heaviest load in my life. You will be branded in two places so all know what you are. Look into my eyes, allow yourself to drown in them and do not move."

My peripheral vision saw two men approaching carrying cherry white-hot irons. One took position behind me the other stood between Hunter and I until master took the iron into his hand. I wanted to run away and I wanted to stay put. Still I starred into his eyes letting them be my only world. I heard the man at my back counting; "One, two, and I felt a deep numbing cold then saw my Lord place the second iron just above my right nipple. The air burned with a disgustingly sweet odor the smell of burning flesh. Then the iron that my Lord had used to mark my flesh was transferred to the man standing next to him. They withdrew breaking the spell.

The irons had been so hot that they felt cold. The places that they had touched me grew hotter tinglingly. Foolishly I closed my eyes shutting them and breaking the connection he had shared with me and I was drawn into a whirlwind of burning mind-searing pain. My mouth opened but no sound exited then my scream caught up with my voice and pierced the air, again I screamed for nothing more than to release the pain. My eyes jerked open and I realized Master had walked back from me leaving me standing alone in a sea of people watching the spectacle.

Master's arms opened, "Come to me, Number One. Only I can make it feel better."

It was as if my legs had turned into lead each step drug forward as each step took all my concentrated effort to move my torched body towards the only fire extinguisher. My arms opened and I fell forward being caught by his arms and pulled into his chest. Damn it if his touch did not quench the fire that my body seemed to have engulfed me. Tears were streaming unashamedly down my face as he held me to him. He leaned forward pulling my chin upwards and placed his lips to mine. There for all in the world to see we did the tongue dance and he sucked the pain right out of my body. My legs grew weak and he allowed me to drop to the deck there I stayed his left boot resting securely between my legs.

"Slave jonathan front and center," bellowed Sir.

Jonathan walked to the center stage, placed his arms like I had been ordered to do and waited until Master corrected his thinking.

"Wrong captain! Right arm behind your head locked. Left extended palm up! Slaves front and center, hold him in place."

Master walked to where they held jonathan, "I have called you Sir, Captain and Cappy now I call you your proper name, slave jonathan the last name you will be ever called. You will receive two brands for making me wait so damn long for this moment! Tell Me cocksucker how much you love me and hold your position!"

Jonathan started shouting, "Sir, I Love you more than my life, more than rain, more than sex. I love you more than boots, I love you more than leather, I love you more than....Arrrgh! He screamed loudly as the two brands were placed at one time to his skin. One brand went on this left forearm the other on his right butt cheek. The brand on his left arm was a stylized BV and the Hunter's brand went on his right butt cheek. Once the irons were lifted, he screamed and fell forward to the deck as if he had had a fist slammed into his gut and his head bowed forward. Slowly he looked up then over to his master. He crawled the short distance, placed his lips to his boots and was lifted. Hunter had the same affect on jonathan as he did on me. It was odd to watch a man filled with pain all of sudden when touching another man find it gone, whisked away like a leaf by a wind.

Jonathan dropped to his knees once he and Hunter exchanged long deep kisses and Hunter pushed my head in jonathan's direction indicating to me that I too should give him a kiss. The kiss we exchanged was more than just brother linked together by fire and brands it was a kiss of love that spoke volumes.

Now it was ex handler Dan's turn his new name and number 9-777 slave. Hunter raked the crowd of handlers, "Handler's" he shouted, "bring me the offending member of your class, bring me 9-777, now!"

Chains rattled as if 9-777 had tried to rise from its forced bound kneeling position then the handles descended upon it, caught it between them and lifted it. Together they dropped 9-777 before his new owner and master.

"Deck it men!"

One handler put his boot behind 9-777's head and pushed the others jumped upon its body and drew its fraying limbs out stretched using their boots against his body to hold it in place face up screaming in defiance of all that was happening to him.

"Ironsmiths front!" Bellowed our Lord.

Hunter took the glowing hot iron from the ironsmith, stepped away for us and moved towards the ex handler dan whose screams stopped when Hunter came into view.

"Your handler friends said you did not scream when they whipped you. I will get that scream from you now."

"HOLD him tight, men!"

Hunter placed the iron right above 9-777's breastbone near the bone. The smell of burning flesh hung into the air and dan's scream was wrung from its lips like an old dishrag of water until he was silent.

"Release it of its shackles, handler's. Slave crawl to me and I will ease your pain or stay there and suffer. It makes Me no never mind."

9-777 did nothing but collapse over on to the deck and draw itself into a fetal position, there it stayed starring off into space as master walked forward to center stage. Turned and with his eyes directed us to go to where 9-777 knelt there to wait until orders were given.

A slave removed master's rubber shirt and wiped his sweating body with a thick rag. Then Hunter started focusing lifting his arms over head and slowly focusing them down increasing and drawing on his Chi. He did this for a few minutes his eyes focused on all of us slaves kneeling a short distance away watching him draw energy from the air itself as if he was about to give battle to some unseen foe. He nodded his head. Two men walked forward placing an iron braiser containing hot coals and a set of heating irons.

The elder of the two men took an iron from the fire placed it onto a peeled potato checking the strike then turned towards Hunter who nodded his consent. The first iron was laid upon Hunter's flesh just above the left nipple a lazy spiral pattern was burned into his flesh. Once done the ironsmith turned and passed the cooling iron to a boy who dropped that into a bucket. Another iron was pulled from the fire, tested and placed to Hunter's flesh as he gripped his hands into a tight white-knuckled fist. Like the first it was passed and dropped into the bucket. A second was lifted from the fire, touched to Hunter's chest and passed to the boy. Then a third was taken from the flames and pressed to Hunter's sweat covered flesh, withdrawn and dropped into the bucket. The men drew away hurriedly and a slave stepped forward holding an over two inch thick plank of wood. Two slaves held it before Hunter. Slowly his focus found the plank, he put his fist forward as it to mark its place, pulled back then forward again. He shouted and stuck the plank splintering the plank into small flying shards of wood. Then he stepped back looked down and smiled. 9-777 had encircled his boots with his body.

A cheer broke out but people held back letting us his slaves crawl forward and help him ease down. His chest was covered with hot dripping sweat. Slowly his breathing altered changing back to a normal pattern. His arms opened as we rushed into them, all three of us, clutching our Lord as he gathered us together as one. Unlike the family into which I was born this family would not be separated. The brands that each of us would bear for the balance of our lives marked us as property belonging to our Lord and Master Hunter.

I noticed his eyes like ours were glazed and helped direct him with the aid of my brothers towards a huge pile of pillows. Carefully as if he would break we laid him back onto the pillows. He caught us, each one at time, pulling our heads down to his and raped our mouths with his tongue even 9-777 melted into him after the kiss. We were left alone as the handler's dispersed seeing that we needed time to share our communion one with the other. It was like a love fest each devouring the other the brands having enflamed our passions and heightened our sexual energy instead of taking it away.

Other slaves brought food and left it within a hands distance. We fed him while he dined on us and we on him. An orgy of paramount proportions commenced at our small section of the deck and seemed to sweep all the ships. Perhaps the camera continued to focus on us after the branding I do not know. What I remember is when I came up for air all the deck that I could see was an undulating surface of sex crazed people having their way with each other. I chose to ignore that herd and dove back into our waters they suited my tastes far better.

Hunter had grabbed 9-777's head placing it on his cock turned to me releasing my cock from its captivity, and I grabbed jonathan who was in route to grab 9-777's ass. Jonathan shoved his cock into 9-777s uplifted ass while I chewed on his nipples. Then Sir grabbed my face pulling me towards him dislodging 9-777s face from his cock. I was lifted and slipped down on his sword and he allowed me to control how he fucked my ass until he was over that. He lifted himself, flipped me off, grabbed at jonathan, pulled him off 9-777 and nailed that slaves butt. While 9-777 rose to the occasion, flipped me on my back, and impaled his cock to the hilt. Hunter grabbed 9-777s head pulling it in his direction and they sucked face. They turned and jonathan buried his face into 9-777s ass and Hunter turned and I did the same to him. Both Hunter and 9-777 rode butt for hours or so it seemed then as if on command that blew their loads. Hunter withdrew his cock forcing it into 9-777s gasping mouth to clean as jonathan sucked down 9-777's. Our orgy continued through the night as if all of us were insatiable whores having found themselves in a sea of men after years in a nunnery. We passed out somewhere nearing the dawn and lay there totally filled like kittens watching the dawn.

We helped our Lord up to his feet and did our damnedest to move amongst the bodies littering the ship deck making our way home to our suite. In route home 9-777 and jonathan grabbed a couple of trays of food for us to enjoy in our cabin. We undressed our exhausted lord, fed him, put him to bed and the three of us climbed in bed with him. I slept under his left arm, jonathan on his right and 9-777 at his feet.

This way all of us were present when he awakened. Together we slept the greatest part of the day until an overloud air horn signaled scmeone had found another of the treasures.

Like wounded soldiers with volcanic hangovers we crept up stairs to the brilliant laser bright sun that seared our eyes shut and made our minds ache. Like crabs we found our way under the nearest awning and a slave brought to us a huge pitcher of the poison that messed us up the n ght before. We drank it tenderly allowing the toxic chemicals from over indulgence wash away and clarity return to our senses.

One of the cooks stepped out of the gallery and approached our private love fest. Master was the only one seated in a deck chair. The balance of us either stood or knelt at his side. The cook was a small wiry looking man of an unknown heritage. He stood before Hunter holding out a wooden tub with a cork stuck down into it, "Mista Hunta, youse this," he said with an overly toothy grin "et healp with them burns. I saw what cha ded slast night. Damn Sur! Damn!" The berry brown man flashed a big smile turned and disappeared back into his domain.

Jonathan opened the container stuck his finger into it and pulled out a lemon scented pearly white paste and he rubbed it on his fresh brand. He looked up, smiled, "Sir, it stops the burning almost instantly. Shall this one apply it all around, Sir?"

Hunter didn't even say anything just grunted and waved his hand thereby granting jonathan permission to rub the ointment on all of us including master. The numbing agent worked swiftly and the tension that all of us were enduring seemed to lift as smiles broke out and you could have heard an audible sigh of relief coming from us all.

"One, go thank the man and give it back to him. Better yet find out from what it is made. With this and Doctor Phillips lotion we may have found two more products to add to our business line. They may pay for this trip." He laughed, "get moving and bring back some fruit wedges. We could all use something more than this spiked punch before dinner."

I found out from the cook that it was a family recipe that had been given to him by his great great grandmother. She had been a firewalker if I understood him correctly. I grabbed the plate of wedges was about to leave when he put the tub back into my hands, "you is gonna need hit for a cuple of days yet. Keps it I gots plenty more." He showed me a huge five-gallon bucket filled with the stuff and I departed. In route back I saw mike and he followed me back to Master.

Master took a huge slice of fresh pineapple and shoved the whole thing in his mouth. Juice dripped down his chin onto his chest and 9-777 licked it off without so much as an order. Seems the branding is what it needed to accept its true identity as slave to our Lord. By the looks of that slave he had beaten every day but Sunday he was bruised almost everywhere and wore every shade of the rainbow. Still as he knelt beside his Lord hands at his back head bowed he smiled telling all he was happiest here in his place.

Master and mike began an interesting exchange while we listened in silence. "So mike, have you found Mister Right yet?" Hunter asked the twin.

Jonathan was grinning like a Cheshire cat as he listened, "Well, Sir I have narrowed down the playing field considerably," mike laughed.

Mike looked down at jonathan then over to me, "Sir, may I switch to another ship?"

Hunter looked up from the plate as he took another piece of fruit, "what's wrong, JD cramping your style or you have run out of fresh meat on this vessel?" Master slapped his forehead with his open palm, "duh, mike. Yes you can switch. So my little snake charmer has found a bigger python on another boat. By all means but let your mother," Sir kicked his sandaled foot at jonathan, "let your mother know where you are or she will worry. Get over there while the launch is out. Have fun, boy!"

Mike leaned forward and kissed Sir on the lips then down and kissed jonathan, "thank you both." He climbed to his feet and was about to depart our area when Hunter called after him.

"If you see JD tell him to report in before nightfall. I got something I must speak to him about!"

Hunter was recovering nicely cause he started barking orders. He put his toe on jonathan, "get your lazy good for nothing ass up and go tidy up our state room slave," and then he turned to 9-777, "go with him, pull out my boots and give them all a nice spit shine. Oh and while you are down there go to the dungeon and retrieve my toy bag and toys."

That day passed at sea Sir went diving with jonathan and I was locked in a cage for the duration of his time out. He kindly placed me in fingerless mittens, hood, leg irons and took me down to the dungeon where the cages were stored. Once installed, the cage locked I was left alone to my own devices. Later another body was locked in with me without hands to see, eyes to feel I could not guess who it was nor did I care. The whole time I was within the cage I had only one thought in my head. I was craving my Sir.

Later that evening I was retrieved and brought to him by JD. Entering the stateroom I found him wearing a full rubber suit, the same one that he had worn when he came to me while I was still within his pit. Once inside and kneeling before him, JD was dismissed. He then ordered that I watch him, as if I had any choice. My eyes were already riveted on him.

The bastard that I loved so much leaned on his desk put out his booted foot in my direction showing off a massive basket packed into his satin sheened rubbered black body. He put spit on himself rubbed his spit into his growing mound and crooked a rubbered finger in my direction giving me one of those come here, slave. I got something for you looks. Like the pig that I am I crawled rapidly to him. God how I love a man that loves to tease those he loves. Not in a bad way mind you. His teasing was wrapped heavily in love. You knew how he loved by the way he teased you. He was the first to tell any associates that if he did not like you he would not tease you.

"Hey, pig, how you like me in my rubber?" Hunters eyes with all but twinkling as he knew what was going on in my mind usually better than I did.

"Oh, God, Sir! You look good enough to eat," I panted.

"Get at it," was all the invitation I needed to connect my mouth to his rubbered cock. While there I was thinking back about my first taste of rubber. It was that mechanic that had caught me stealing when I was a teenager. Hot daddy of a grease monkey who had turned my ass over a rack of rubber tires and fucked the shit right out of me nightly until dad found me and took me home screaming.

"Mind what you are doing pig. That's my cock you are biting!" His hand connected with a light slap making me focus more on him than my past.

That's how it all started. I was tonguing him and he was rubbing himself all over me. Using my tongue like a paintbrush to spit wet his rubbers. Some where during that encounter I lost my head and begged to be placed in rubber. He laughed,

"I wondered when you were going to ask for it."

He had seated himself, pulled me into the vee of his legs and kept me working my tongue over his growing leg sausage, "you think you can handle a total black out, shit head?"

"God, yes, Sir," I panted with his cock cupped by my lips and tongue.

He pulled my head away, making me look up at him, "If I take the time to put you into rubber are you willing to take the risk that I may just keep you there for the balance of this vacation? Well, are you pig?"

I groaned which he interrupted as my acceptance. Actually it was my cock straining against the padlock that made me groan but I was just to damn excited to care. My lips felt like they had been Teflon coated as they slipped around his hot rubbered body. He pushed my face away and ordered me into the center of the room stopping me before I got too far away. "Let me remove that padlock so My cock and balls can be encased as well."

He followed, walking beyond me placed his boot between my shoulder blades and pushed my face into the floor, "head down were it belongs, pig."

I heard the door to a closet open, then the door to the hallway and the patter of many feet as they entered the room. One of them was in chains. I heard the rattle and drop of a slave at my back, "jonathan, you know what to do, dig a trench deep enough that the monster can be seated!"

"7, you are with me. Come here slave, I need you to hold these as I pull them out." Hunter was talking to 9-777 and by the sound of it pulling the wardrobe apart.

Fucking A! HELL! Krist all mighty! My ass opened like a blossom spreading before the sun. Jonathan loved to eat ass better than any slave on or in the compound and you could tell by his dedication that he was good. The music from Star Trek began to play in my head as his mouth docked with my ass lips and his tongue penetrated my rectum. I could do nothing but rock back onto his face it felt so fucking good. I was jerking and shaking like a whore who had been released from jail.

"On your back jonathan, One climb up to a squat and hold that position. 7, get this rubber cock sheath on that pigs cock before he pops a nut." 9-777 dropped down on his knees grabbed my cock and rolled a heavy rubber condom over my cock then pushed my nuts into a tight rubber sack at the end of the tube. Jesus Krist it felt good, all tight and black and hot and if I could have found something to rub against I would have popped my nut in a heartbeat but I knew if I did Sir would have gotten even.

Master slapped the back of my head as I was craning my neck to see what he was doing, "eyes front, pig!"

The face that was buried ear deep up into my ass was withdrawn and I must have moaned my displeasure cause Sir laughed. Then spoke quietly to jonathan at my rear what I heard made me worry just a touch, "take your time but I want this plug in that hole. Get it seated!"

His tongue reconnected to my hole then was withdrawn and a cold blunt object began to slowly penetrate my open asshole. The sudden change sent shivers up my spine and made me clench my ass closed but not for long cause the tongue resumed its labors. My attention was drawn from my ass to Master's hands. He was working on a slipknot forming a noose from fishing filament. This explained his request from the Captain the other day about fishing line, God I love how he anticipates our needs.

The noose was slipped over my left nipple and tightened while holding the nipple away from my chest. Slowly more string was wrapped around my nipple until a nub projected from my chest looking more like a bound cock than a nipple. Sir only stopped winding the thread around my nipple when it was about a half an inch extended off the chest and had begun to change color. He lowered his head, studied his craftsmanship kissed my nipple, "now I can find it under the rubber."

9-777 approached with a handful of beige rubber. Hunter told me to keep my ass in place and the three of us worked the shirt over my head, down over my arms and pulled it gently over my throbbing tit. The rubber sent electric charges running like rivulets across my body and down into my prostrate.

Jonathan had changed from tongue to dildo as he worked my ass open in preparations to receive what Master had termed the monster. Slowly my ass seemed to yawn open and accept the huge log of a plug that he was working up and into my core being. His tongue had been hot, but this lip sucking ass master was making me feel as if my ass was being wedged open by a bowling ball. Once seated, jonathan pulled it all the way out and slipped it back into home plate. I fell forward dropping to my hands and knees ass elevated when my legs gave out. That damn monster was just making me all but purr and the sons of a bitches around me was laughing.

"Head up boy." Hunter said and when I looked up he slipped an open-faced rubber hood over my head and tugged it down my neck. Another hood followed that one, this one locked my head in all too familiar darkness my old friend. Tubes were inserted into each nostril and the first inhale pulled my mind back to that old garage with my ass bound over those tires and Papa bear fucking my ass royally. Handsome man was Papa Bear, heavily muscled, full beard, full pelt of graying chest fur all that poured into a grease cover jumpsuit and old greasy engineer boots. I don't know why I had to try to steal something from him; perhaps, to see if the rumor was true. They had whispered in the locker rooms at high school that if he caught young men stealing from him that he took their theft personally and made the thief work off his debt to him personally, under his heaving hips. I found out, boy did I find out!

My focus shifted to the invader that was being gradually forced between my ass cheeks deep into my bowels. It was fucking HUGE! The tongue that had danced all over my prostrate had kick started my engine and my ass ate that fucking rubber monster like it was a candy and wanted more! The continuous pushing forced my ass to open and snap together around the flange at the base of the monster plug. The bad boy was to the hilt and to prove it my tongue dropped out like a whacked out pup on Valium.

When they stood me erect I felt like I was sitting on top of the apex of the Washington monument. I have always thought that DC was anally retentive they have too many sculptures that have phallus shapes but try their damnedest to say no to cock.

As if we don't know the truth about our capital, it's the best little whore house around. Everyone puts out there, one way or the other.

They were guiding my bare feet into pants legs by the way it felt. One leg in and pulled up to the knee then the second leg and then they pulled the pants all the way up to my waist. With the rubber shirt over my torso and now these pants I felt hot like a cat in heat. Someone grabbed my cock and pushed its blackness through a hole in the crotch allowing it to extend out front in a vulgar display. I was lead around the room each step sent shivers up my spine, each step made me feel as if I was in bondage and each step cranked up my sex generator another notch. WoooHo! I was a turbo sex engine about to blow my legs off and they were not finished with dressing me. Gloves went over my fingers and were pulled up over my wrists. They stopped tugging at me forcing me to turn this way and that Hunter was making up his mind.

My arms were lifted and guided into what I can only guess was another shirt of rubber, hands within the sleeves pulled my rubbered hands forward while others pulled something over my arms and pulled a zipper down the front of my chest. Zowie! I thought, double layers, WOLF! Pig in a Poke was I!

My legs got lifted a second time and worked into another pair of pants, these they had to work over my other rubber pants and rubber booties were worked over my feet. Again my legs were lifted and slipped into what felt like extremely heavy pants until my feet were forced around a bend, meaning boots. Straps were tugged tight around my thigh another tug was pulled as another strap secured them just below my knees. Walking forward my legs felt like they were encased in lead cause they drug on the carpet, and I had to concentrate on moving each leg, not as before, when I was naked they moved easily.

Sir pulled on the back of my head releasing and pulling my hood off my head. "Walk around pig, see and feel the new you. Watch how you step cause your boot soles are lead, we are not taking you up on deck cause with your luck you would fall over board and I would lose my Number One." The room laughed at his joke and my expense but I just did not care. I was wearing rubber two layers and I felt hot as a raw butt fuck! Yummy I thought, fucking yummy! Then I saw myself in a full-length mirror I had to take a double look just to make certain that was this slave that looked back at me. WOOF! WOOF!

"Get over here, pig meat," Hunter called me to him, "I got something to show you."

I walked with a springy step to where my Lord was leaning up against the desk with his wonderful shit-eating grin plastered all over his face and body. He liked what he saw as much as I liked how I felt. He was holding up a hood that had an alien look to it. Yes, it looked like a gas mask but none that I had ever seen. Huge eyes, odd out of proportion nose with double tubes extending from the nostril area and an O tube for my mouth that looked like it had been sealed by rubber. "Once this is on, you are going to have to pay close attention to me cause you are not going to be able to hear worth shit," you understand pig meat?

I nodded my head and said, "Oh, Sir, yes, Sir!" I was just to excited to get into that hood and be complete.

He looked at me shaking his head, "a pig is born. Or is that a pig is hatched, whatever."

9-777 and jonathan helped me into the hood while Sir guided from the front. The back was laced down tight; straps were pulled over my head locking the gasmask tight to my head. Two tubes were inserted into my nostrils they were the ones that flared out and became the large accordion tubes that were pulled back and snapped at my shoulders. Then Sir inserted the mouth tube that I bet if I knew my Sir was just large enough to accommodate his cock. They backed away as if to say, there it's done. Sir signaled that I should walk around and the feeling was so damn good even with that monster plug installed in my ass. All of my whole body hissed like electricity in the high wires. What I wouldn't have done to been granted permission to jerk off at that moment. Sir caught my thought, laughed and shook his head, no.

He walked over to where I was standing, added two panels over the eye plates and locked me back into total darkness. Hands guided me backwards as if they were docking a stored piece of cargo. My ankles were bound spread; straps went around my calves, thighs, another around my waist. Then they pulled my arms down to my sides those too got strapped down and another strap was cinched tightly across my chest just below my bound tit. Then the hands disappeared and I was left to free-fall through paradise, memories.

Papa bear lived and worked at a place he called Hub Cap and Tire World. He had caught me trying to sneak out of the backroom with a moon hubcap for a friends ride. I really think I wanted to be caught so I could see if the rumor was true. Boy oh boy was the rumor true. Papa bear not only spanked the shit out of me while I laid over his legs but later after he had bound me over that rack of tires fuckied the living shit out of my ass. It was my first time and I cried like a baby into his lap and got an unexpected surprise when his cock got hard again. What could I do, he had striped me of all my clothes and hand me handcuffed in his back room. The bell rang out front saying a customer-wanted gas and he left me there all horned up and without any sense in the world. When he returned I begged him to let me go. He said he would after I had given him a blowjob. I learned that night how to give him a blowjob. It was a Thursday night that I had tried to steal the hubcap he kept me there for about a week. During the day I wore his old stinky greasy coveralls with leg irons and worked with him in the grease pit. No one saw me until dad came by on his Harley and found out whom I had been whoring around with. He and his brothers damn near killed him as they stomped him to death. Dad put me on his hog and drove my ass home. Chained me to the bed and there I stayed until all hell broke out.

What the fuck? Too my surprise, I hit the walls on both side of me, as well as, forward and back. Far fucking out, I thought! I could have freaked out if it had not been for my cock that was draining all common sense out of my brain as it filled with blood. My deepest darkest fantasy was happening. Master had locked me into rubber so that he could lock me into a coffin, bound and gagged. If I knew him as I do he is watching me somehow. He knew I was about to panic but I knew that if I could control my panic he would crank up the game plan another notch. I made myself relax forced my mind to control my desire to pant like a wild beast and relaxed. Relaxed and enjoyed my bondage, submitted to his game.

Somehow that bastard that I loved to call master had modified the breathing tubes cause I choked on the filtered air that was assaulting my nostrils and would have gagged if that had been possible. The bastard had to have inserted the end of that tube up his ass cause all I could smell was one of his raunchy wet ass busting farts. These farts of his could be bottled just for the methane alone and sold for automobile gas additive. They were so raunchy that wallpaper peeled off walls, paint flaked and chipped off and wood blistered. This my loving master was mainlining into my body via those damn nasal tubes and I was helpless to do anything but get high as a kite on his butt stink! Whew, I love it and if I had been unbound would have been between his legs; nose or mouth covering his farting butt cheeks. I was his fart eater and LOVED my JOB!

I sucked in a huge lung full of his fart-scented air and found out that I could not exhale. The bastard was playing me like a damn fiddle. He was on the other side of this coffin holding the tube in his hand with his thumb over the tube mouth and I was unable to exhale or inhale fresh air. I began to slam my body against the straps holding me in hopes he would realize just how much a panic he had put me within. He must have heard and removed his thumb. I exhaled a rush of hot putrid air and went to suck in fresh air and found nothing. Again that bastard was helping me realize how helpless I was. Screaming at him mentally calling him every term I knew did nothing. Stars began to spin before my eyes, sparks of light, fireworks went off before my eyes as I realized I was dying from oxygen deprivation. I was without hope then his thumb moved and I got a huge rush of air that sent my head reeling as if I had just taken a huge hit of poppers.

No sooner that I had gotten one good inhale of fresh air than my master closed the tube and I was plunged back into a new state of all out panic. He never tired of this game. I hated it and love it at the same time. Let's just say, my cock never softened when he had me in total oxygen deprivation. Actually if my cock was out it would be leaking mind you a fucking river of pre cum and my cock would be selling my body to him for more abuse. God how I hated my cock telling tales on me when I was helpless but master knew who to talk with when he was playing with me. No longer did he listen to what I said but watched my cock. It was a far better barometer than any as it could tell him when I was amused and when I was abused just by the way it waved at him. Sir controlled my cock better than I did, that is why he keeps it under lock and key. OH, God, please let him give me some air!

He allowed me to enjoy one of his cigars that day. They say second hand smoke is bad for you. It might be but hell if I care cause I love it the way he forces me to share his cigar. When he had finished his cigar, he pulled me from the box, put me on my knees and allow me to thank him properly but blowing him through the hood. Yes, he fucked with my air all the time I was blowing him.

Three nights and two days I spent in my rubber suit never going out of the stateroom. Being fed by a rubber tube inserted into my rubber tube as he did his cock whenever he wanted my attention. He allowed my ass out of the suit twice a day to take care of business. The second day JC, jonathan, 9-777, Lady Katherine and a new face entered the stateroom. I had been placed into the bondage chair strapped down tight and pulled up to the table next to where my owner and master sat with his people. They were getting settled while he made me watch him. 9-777 had brought over his humidor and placed it in the middle of the table. Lady Katherine who loved a good cigar took one, as did the new fellow and Sir made me watch as he pulled out a huge cigar that looked like a 60 ring. 9-777 offered a cedar match to all those that had gotten cigars. Master took his own sweet time lighting his making certain it was a well rounded light before he took a nice long draw and exhaled it right into my nasal tube. All seemed to watch as my eye sockets on the hood clouded with bluish white smoke and I did my damnedest to drink it all down and hold it as his thumb had closed off the tube. I started wiggling in my chair and he released the tube allowing me to exhale.

My cock was rigid like a fucking steel pole when his smoke hit my breathing tube. Fuck the surgeon general, all I wanted at that moment was to inhale his smoke deep into my lungs and hold it as long as I could. I did my damnedest to hold until I had to release then I couldn't but did eventually. Sir moved my tube so all their smoke would filter into my face and into my lungs. While they talked I got lost in the pleasure of servicing three cigars at once and knew if I were lucky all the ashes that would accumulate in the ashtray would be mine as well.

The first to grow an ash was the new person at the table he was about to flip the ash into the tray until Hunter ordered 9-777 to open its trap. Sir knew I was watching and chuckled as I groaned out loud when the ash fell into that fucking evil slaves mouth and was swallowed. Another ash went into jonathan. I must have started wiggling back and forth in my chair as JD had to add another strap, I was protesting the fact that those bastards where eating what I wanted, their ash. I was after all the only trained ashtray pig in the house, wasn't I? I wanted to shout that I was master's humanidor to tell them that I was his ash pig, his cigar boy, but all that came out was blubbering that drew all their eyes in my direction.

Hunter turned my head towards him. He made me watch damn him! Watch as he put the big cigar to his lips, as he took a long draw on the cigar, held it trapped within his mouth or sucked some of the smoke down into his lungs then he exhaled right into my tube. Yes! Yes, I mumbled! Awwh God it was good! I wanted his lips pressed against mine as he exhaled, I wanted him to run that hot tip over my body, over my butt, over my naked body as he had done so many times before. I wanted to feel his cigar tip roasting my nuts. Just the thoughts were making me batty, just watching him as he smoked and carried on business made me insane with desire. Just the thought of him doing all that to me made me into a blubbering idiot trapped in rubber watching him as he tortured me.

When the smoke cleared Hunter was walking the crowd to the door. The door closed and Sir lay down between jonathan and 9-777 both were on the floor. He laid back pinning jonathan's arm at his back with his body. Took a huge inhale from his cigar making the cherry tip turn bright orange, leaned over and exhaled his smoke into jonathan. Smoke and his tongue filled jonathan's mouth as they kissed. All I could do was rock back and forth in my bondage chair and scream through my mask in a mumbled way, I want that kiss!

Hunter turned blowing on the tip of the cigar, grabbed 9-777 and rolled his cigar down the slaves chest and damn it if that fucking betrayer did not arch his back to make the cigar burn a fiery path across his chest. I could not stop watching what was being played out for my benefit. Damn this rubber suit, damn him for putting me into it, damn them all for making me crave him and his cigar more than anything I had ever craved at that moment.

He played with both slaves that way. One would be fed smoke the other the fire back and forth between the two and I helpless as hell wanted it all. Even the ashes they were forced to eat. Still it was a hot scene especially how jonathan handled the hot butt as it descended down his chest. The closer the fire got to its crotch the harder his cock became.

Sir crawled closer to my bondage chair and the two slaves followed him as if drawn by chains on their necks. Sir's cigar rose to his lips. His teeth grabbed it and his lips rolled it around like a warm brown cock. He sucked in drawing warm liquid smoke into his mouth, down his throat and into his lungs. The tip glowed hidden behind a cooling gray ash a wicked red. As if to acknowledge my presence, he leaned forward grabbed my tube and exhaled. Again, warm billowing clouds of his rich tobacco smoke wreathed me. Through stinging eyes, I watched as he forced 9-777s legs wide. His cigar descended towards his target and touched the base of his slave's balls. The jolt when the cigar touched skin I felt in my rubbered womb. Hunter turned placed the cigar back to his lips inhaled then pulled the cigar from his lips, it too dropped now towards jonathan's open legs and touched the base of its balls. Another jolt I felt in my smoke filled tomb.

Hunter's cigar was about three inches long when he had jonathan stand and walk towards me. Sir followed in a less graceful approach on his hands and knees.

He turned jonathan so his hard cock faced me. Sir placed his cigar to his lips took a long draw, motioned with his hands that 9-777 should come to him and he feed that beast with my ashes. Another draw then exhaling and blowing on the tip until it glowed brilliant orange hot cherry red fire. The tip coasted up jonathan's leg making for his cock. The tip roasted that slave's cock as it pissed pre cum and Sir pulled it the length of jonathan's cock until the slipped it between the slave nuts and touched home. The reaction was not what I expected as jonathan shot one huge load followed by another. Both splattered over my chest up and onto my face plate and I shot with him. When jonathan stopped humping mid air he fell to the floor and crawled out of the way. Hunter placed his cigar in the ashtray and I enjoyed the balance of his cigar while he played roughly with 9-777.

A pair of hands took away my sight as duct tape locked my eyes closed. The cords that bound my body were released and the zipper that had held me contained for two days was released. I did not want it to end this way, Sir had other ideas.

Chapter 3

I hope you have not been leading a double life pretending to be wicked
and being really good all the time. That would be hypocrisy.
Oscar Wilde

I awoke when I heard a door thud shut. Looking up I saw jonathan wheeling in a huge covered tray on wheels. Whatever it was it smelled wonderful. He stopped just before the desk then walked over to our bed and shook Hunter before calling his name. His eyes fluttered open and he saw who was leaning over him. "Wwhat time is it?"

"Sir, its plenty past noon, Sir," replied jonathan.

Sleepily Hunter groaned, "let me sleep if its only twenty past twelve. I had to feed three hungry holes last night." He yawned and rolled over slipping his hand over my chest and down under an arm to grab my wrist forcing me to spoon with him.

Jonathan persisted with waking him, "Sorry Sir. It is plenty past noon. Actually it's near 2:00 by local time. Your orders and I quote, 'no matter how much I beg or whine do not let me sleep past 2:00. I have a conference call coming in at 2:30' unquote, Sir."

Hunter groaned, slammed his open palm down on 9-777's ass, "front, piss pig," and rolled out of the bed over me. 9-777 did not muster as ordered so I dropped before him mouth open ready to accept his piss.

Sir halted jonathan's dissertation long encugh to point at a whip on the floor. The whip was placed in Sir's outstretched hand. His arm rose swung backwards then down were it was laid on 9-777's upraised ass hard. The slave all but shot out of the bed as if it was an arrow shot from a bow and dropped before its Sir, wide eyed with its mouth open. Sir fed it his morning piss as it choked on the rush of fluids it had to drink.

"A slave rises first; unless, bound 9-777 lazy fuck, you were not immobilized," my Lord shouted.

Once Sir had finished his piss he pulled me into the bathroom and 9-777 was sent to the Captain's office to retrieve a briefcase that was in the safe. I bathed my Lord, shaved him and saw to it he was dried completely before he left the bathroom. I joined him a few minutes later having completed my chores within that room. 9-777 entered as I exited. I had placed papers down in the bathroom for its use before I departed.

Sir was seated at the desk as jonathar ladled out a handsome smelling fish stew. Once Sir was fed he signed that jonathan could fill our dog bowls. I don't remember now why I returned to the bathrcom but I found that 9-777 had not used the papers as all slaves would yet their was a ripe odor in the air which said that he had just taken a dump. I would speak to Sir about it when time was fitting.

I joined the others on the floor at one of the dog dishes. We ate on all fours, a position of humiliation for some, an honor for others. Sir dined above us as was his habit and flipped us tidbits of food naming the creature that was to catch it. Jonathan was the best at this game being able to catch food mid air. Having watched him time and time again I knew that he and Hunter must have had plenty of practice at this game.

Meal complete 9-777 returned the wheeled cart and bowls to the kitchen. It returned with a bowl of fresh fruit and a huge pitcher of Guava juice. One of Hunter's favorite fruit drinks. Lunch complete, Sir ordered 9-777 and I to pull out his boots and give them all a proper spit shine. I was to instruct 9-777 to the way our Sir preferred his boot polish applied.

I was half hearing the conversation that Sir was having with jonathan. They were discussing the balance of the two-week vacation after this trip was completed. Hunter was going to Europe to receive tutelage from Lady Beatrice in preparations for assuming the reins of Castle Enterprises. Hunter was attempting to detail to jonathan why he had to return to Buena Vista. "Nothing has changed, jonathan. You are still the best qualified to get Buena Vista back on her feet and back in running order."

"But, Sir. Then I was a freeman, now I am a slave with your collar and Buena Vista's brand?"

Hunter keyed open his brief case, pulled out a sheath of papers, "take these to Eric Wilson but read them before so you will understand what is going to be happening. Jonathan, you wear the brand of Buena Vista because you are as much the soil as the soil is you. That's why I had to make you the Buena Vista Number One slave. You know the earth better than anyone and have been her slave for years." Sir cocked his head and got a distant look, "actually jonathan when I am not there, you speak for me, you have a touch more clout than you did when you were my foreman. Besides, you can no longer run away from me this way. When you get home you will be placed in chains."

Hunter laughed as jonathan did a double take, "really, Sir? Oh, SIR!"

"Hell, jonathan, I need you more than ever now," Hunter said almost angrily! "I don't trust anyone but you and JD with our Buena Vista and with me taking over Castle, it's the beginning of our dream. As my Overseer you are the only one in contact with me and you have more power than when you were my foreman."

Jonathan responded, "but Sir, what if I screw up and loose my temper like last time?"

Sir laughed again, "you've always been a hot tempered little fuck, but this time I think I have out anticipated your actions. You are permitted to yell, scream, stomp and even kick but slave you will no longer run from me. Beside with the new man if you fuck up he has permission from me to clean your plow or plumbing as the case needs."

"Please Sir. Don't make me train another one like the last. True it was a gift from the German manor house but it was the dumbest creature on this earth. Hell a wood screw had more function than that man."

"Actually, jonathan, the man you will be training I have been watching for a few years. He is a black belt instructor, was on the Vietnam clean up crew and is use to commanding large companies and this you will like, demands absolute obedience."

Jonathan voice rose, "sounds like someone I might like to know, Sir."

"Hells bells, boy, you already do. I have recruited Eric Wilson or I should say you have recruited him. Seems you have a way with persuasion that I do not," Hunter smiled his big toothy grin.

It was jonathans turn to laugh, "Master Hunter, it would seem you are a sadistic yenta after all!"

"Go about your business, jonathan and take Number One, he could use some fresh air and sunshine on his back. When I am finished with 9-777 it will be sent up too. I need to make a phone call to Europe, dismissed Number One."

Two boots had been cleaned and polished when Sir sent me out for fresh air and sunshine. To my chagrin jonathan placed me on a chain gang swabbing the decks on our knees with heavy bristled brushes. I got my sunshine and plenty of fresh air but not in the way I had anticipated. When one job was completed another one began. The chain gang and I were put to hauling supplies out of storage way below deck and taking those supplies to the shore. Tonight was to be a rather huge celebration as the fourth prize had been found; that was a ten day vacation at any three of our manor houses world wide with all expense paid. Not at all a shabby deal.

One more prize the granddaddy of them all was still out there waiting to be found. The treasure hunt had been a huge success by the way the handler's had worked on those maps, star charts and runes. Each map got successfully harder and the last one was the bitch of all bitches. Not only was the map written in ancient Italian, but the land masses were encrypted with code, and the damn leaves that looked like a floral design was readable when held up to a mirror. The handlers were in a high state of anxiety while they poured over old dictionaries, worked their fingers to the bone on computers and muttered obscenely at whoever created those maps. Someone I know had a blast creating each and every one of those clues and for a bribe I just might tell them; but I think many of them knew. That's why he wasn't saying a thing. As he was just enjoying the trip and his people.

Interesting how at the first of this trip everyone was serious party hounds getting drunk, whoring around; being true hedonists until they found out the first prize was just what the maps proclaimed. Then the second prize was found and the third well everyone got serious. They still drank like fish, fucked like whore dogs but any spare time they worked on those charts and maps Some of them burned up more brain cells working out the logistics on this treasure hunt than they had done all year and for some others all their life time.

The last and greatest treasure was still to be found. The ship was almost as quiet as a damn library as everyone worked. Some worked in clusters combining their brainpower others as individuals. The deck was littered with people pouring over charts and laptops all focused like never before on one project winning the custom built Harley Davidson that would be designed to fit whoever found the key. If this treasure hunt went on any longer I dare say that people would be having anxiety attacks or worse yet begin to flip out. As it was right now they were very studious.

We slaves were taken to the island a few with each of the supplies loads. Some of us dug the fire pits; others lined one with rocks and set the fire blazing preparing it for the pig. While it burned we set up the knee high dining table, added pillows, flowers, grass mats and gathered more wood. Another team was out opening coconuts, setting up a St. Andrew's cross and even another team disappeared into the island with overseers to do what I could not guess Those that had completed their chores were returned to the ships.

Not finding jonathan on deck, I returned to my master's quarters and found a strange creature crawling around on the floor. It looked like 9-777 but its head was covered with a heavy inflatable hood that had no eyeholes or mouth holes only a leather grin and one large grommet hole near center. The creature was crawling around on its leather covered balled hands and rubber booties. Sir had bound it so it could not lower its knees to the floor but had to walk like a dog on two sets of paws. It turned towards me as I entered the suite and when I slammed the door it came towards me. Gently I brushed my hands down its backside and its back arched up to greet my hand. Its head turned towards me as if to sniff and define who I was. That's when I noticed that Sir was napping. I tried to return to my boot polishing duties but the creature would not leave me alone and Sir must have heard me.

"Come here slave, stop playing with it and come here. After last nights orgy you should be almost as tired as I am. Come on get in bed with me," Hunter yawned and patted the bed.

"Sir, I stink like a horse in summer, Sir. May I take a shower first so as not to offend you," I begged him.

"Get in bed with me slave," then he patted the bed next to him more forcefully than before. I climbed into bed next to his warm body. One of his arms went over my chest under my arm and found my wrists with a pull he had me spooning with him. There with his hand on my wrist he held me locked to him. Then it happened he moved his leg and blew out the most disgusting stench any body's body can produce. Too often I have wondered if that man had something rotten within him. Farts like those are unnatural, Exxon would have bottled his shit and sold it if they could cause my Sir was a grade AAA+ methane factory.

I had been in the pit for maybe 3 weeks when he had first started coming to me. Then anything, anyone other than myself was a great encouragement. While I was in that pit he trained me to eat his farts, hell, anything that smelled as rich as they did was a better than what I had. I would bury my nose as far up his ass as I could when he let loose one of those cell burning brain deadening farts. He got me addicted then and now, well, I was just as addicted to them. To me there was nothing finer than to have him blow the bed linens off his ass with a tremulous fart and if I were unbound I would dive for his ass or pray that he would trap me under the sheets for the Dutch oven. Damn I am a twisted pig but he made me this way.

An hour or more must have passed before any intrusion happened on his naptime. When it did come it was in the form of a phone call. I was about to answer the phone, but he beat me too it having put his hand on my chest and motioning me to stay put. He spoke to someone asking questions about her health. Then told them that it would take a day to lay the groundwork but he would be there. Send a plane to the last stop on the agenda. He hung up the phone coming back to where I lay poising one of my more seductive 'come fuck me' poises. Except he blew right past me into the shower, shaved and returned ordering me to do the same. By his abrupt distance, I knew the phone call heralded a major change in our lives. Hunter was leaving sooner than any of us had anticipated. Finished with my cleanup I returned to him and dropped to my knees, hands behind my back, head bowed.

"Number One, go get a pad and pencil. I need to take notes while I am thinking clearly." I ran off to find the items he wanted. When I returned he and JD were deep into a heated conversation. I stayed my distance waiting until he saw me and beckoned me to him.

JD was sitting on a chair near Hunter. They seemed to be arguing JD stood knocking the chair backwards and over. He turned as if to leave turned back. He pointed down at master who sprung to his feet and grabbed JD turning him around quickly to face him as he was stomping off. JD looked downwards while Hunter spoke then his head shot up and he said something. Hunter backed off as if he had been struck. I moved forward ready to jump JD and Sir saw my movement, put out his hand to stop me. They talked a few more minutes. JD turned, his face was beet red and he looked tense enough to have been a tightly pulled spring; then he stomped to the door, opened it, said something and departed slamming the door.

Master signaled that I should come to him. I knelt at his feet. He turned and studied the waves while looking out a porthole, turned back to me, "butt me slave." Then turned back around to watch a launch putter across the waves to the other ship. I was preparing his ordered cigar; cutting the end, spit slicking the cigar and lighting it when he turned around. His eyes showed to me the depth of his concern. His puppy must have realized something was afoot as he found Sir and pawed the chair until Sir's hand stroked its back softly.

He sat, took the offered cigar, took a long draw, and exhaled watching the smoke blow away on the afternoon breeze, "take notes, Number One."

"To Castle Enterprises, i.e. Lady Beatrice. Send the water plane. I will be at your side before you know it. Have a car waiting me."

I looked up in shock as if to say something, he held up his hand, "shut the fuck up, I do not want to hear anything from another slave right now." The way he said it told me volumes about his discussion with JD.

"Paragraph two, notify Eric Wilson of the changes and alert Black Watch in DC. Number three, inform England manor that their records are not up to date per Castle Enterprises this is their last chance to correct the situation. Item four," he sat back and sighed deeply letting the smoke just float out of his mouth. "Item four, notify the Scottish Watch to kick down the England manor's door find the records and find the problem. They have carte blanche on finding out the problem with the manor Lord. Item five," again he paused, "Find out how doc is doing?"

He looked down at me, "go find jonathan tell it to find my large suitcase and bring it to the state room as well hidden as he can. I cannot allow my departure to dampen the mood of this vacation for my people."

I ran onto the deck found jonathan and showed him my notes and he read them hastily, "OH Shit! I tried to warn then about this but it looks like the shit is about to hit! Those Corporate eggheads will not know what hit them after Sir is finished with their assholes! He is taking up the reins sooner than the Founder's think and he is about to clean some plows! He tried to warn them at Union that he would not put up with any of their shit and if given the power he would do what was right! They laughed at him then they won't be when he is finished."

No sooner than I had crossed the threshold into the stateroom did he hit me with orders, "lay out my finest leathers and my boots for tonight One. If I know this barge like I know my compound the word has leaked out and is spreading like wildfire that Lady Beatrice is real sick and needs me. Tonight we must present a fortified front."

The door swung open in walked the two slaves carrying what looked like a huge platform between them. Once the blanket was removed and the cardboard folded away it was nothing but his large suitcase. It was placed on the table and under his direction it was packed for his trip off the boat and back to civilization.

Hunter talking to the room, "I just came from the Captains office. He has a secure line. I just called Lady Beatrice's home, and I will be departing sooner than I thought. I want 9-777 to attend me cause you and jonathan must make certain all things go well here and back home at Buena Vista. The captain once everyone is on board tonight will make his way towards the last island in the treasure hunt. The water plane will find me there."

JD stepped into the busy room, "Sir, I have word from the Captain. He says that we are heading into a storm. Your plane may be delayed a day, Sir!"

Hunter stopped mid step, turned to JD, "What did you say?"

"Sir, your plane may be delayed for one day due to a huge storm front, Sir," replied JD!

"OK, OK, this can work for us. JD go find Lady Katherine ask her to join us for formal tea here in the stateroom. If she asks tell her it's a power meeting, she will understand. Jonathan do we have anyone with us that was connected to the Scottish Watch, think?"

"Yes, Sir. Billy Burns recently joined our troop after the last Manor run, Sir."

"Good, find him, have him report to me at the same time." Hunter looked at jonathan, "Go and find them, now! One can finish the packing!"

He turned to JD, "you I want here as well. I need your support and ideas, JD; you have a level head when in tight places. Go about your business and ask the Captain if he can out run the storm?"

They all left the room and he turned to me, "come here." His arms opened and I ran between them and encircled his torso with my arms."

"One," Hunter whispered in my ear, "everything is going to be alright. Believe me its going to be fine. Now do me a favor," he pointed to the beast, "take that one upstairs and give it to the head of the entertainment committee he will know what to do with it, then return."

Leash in hand and manimal in tow I all but drug its lazy ass up the steps by its neck and out on the deck. Luckily I bumped into the head of the committee and gave it to him, "Sir asked that I bring you this manimal for tonight's entertainment. Sir." He took the offered leash, stooped over and patted the beast talking in a soothing tone. Having given over my charge I ran back down the steps and into our stateroom to find my Sir.

He was sitting in his chair, naked smoking his stogie and starring off into space. Upon my entrance his head rose and he saw me, "inside that closet is a box with your number on it. Pull it out, take it to the bedroom and put them on. Go on, do it now."

I shit when I opened the box and the scent of leather rushed up filling my nostrils with that tangy acid bite that spoke volumes to our breed, leather. I all but tore the lid off in excitement. There inside the box was a gift like I thought I would never ever earn again. I had not owned leather since they cut it off me in the jail cell many long years ago and here before me in a box was the most handsome set of leathers I had ever seen. Tears started flowing down my face I was so overcome by that moment.

He must have been watching cause he yelled over to me, "something wrong, One?"

"God! Sir," I ran to where he was seated threw myself into his lap and covered his shocked face with kisses. He held me in his arms, "it is time." With a push he shoved me back towards his gift, encouraged me to dress as he showered.

I nearly flipped out when I realized the volume of clothing the box contained. Satiny-soft black glove leather chaps, black cock strap and dozens of chromed rings, a new pair of combat boots and the vest when I saw it I started crying again. He had the word's Number One written in blue leather down the right side. Damn how my cock hurt just looking at them and I remember bowing forward as if in reverence to kiss each piece before nervously putting them on.

It felt like the first time I had ever placed dead animal skins around my body. My heart was beating faster, my cock was hard and god the smell just made me sweat with anticipation. As fast as I could dress I ran to stand before him. His smile told me everything I needed to know about how I looked. He motioned me over to him where he was drying after the shower so he could adjust the laces more to his suiting.

"Let me adjust those straps. I want your cute bubble butt with my brand to show our team who owns it as if they don't know," he chuckled to himself as he laced my outer laces that ran the length of my leg. "Looks like you have put on a little more mass since you were last measured these chaps fit you like a glove and I love what they do to that ass. Nice!"

He grabbed my hard cock, "get this soft or those rings are going to hurt doubly bad. Never mind I will do it," he chucked opened a small ice chest grabbing a handful and placing it on my cock and balls as I danced around trying to hold my place. All the while he laughed at my antics. The ice did the trick. In no time my once hard cock was sheathed in his heavy chromed rings from the base to the final one that he locked through my piercing. "Now, if you attempt a hard on, all will know," he smiled his big toothy grin, "believe me, We will know!" His laughter would make my pain all worthwhile.

"Go to the humidor and prep me three cigars. Since your ass has been stretched you should be able to handle them easily." With a pat on my butt he sent me on my newest mission.

Lady Katherine, Burns, JD, jonathan and I were present for the next couple of hours where he detailed to all what was about to happen at Castle and Buena Vista. The next day and half would be critical to his plans, secrecy of his plans was almost as important as his intended departure. Hunter was to fly to New York headquarters. Lady Beatrice and himself have preplanned his ascension months before this accident. Once in New York all he had to do was kick the Lady's slaves into high gear and they would begin the transference of power.

Our team understood what was going to happen, what part in the transformation each played before Hunter broke up the conference suggesting all get ready for the party tonight. They said their good byes and departed.

Sir had been sitting there the greatest part of an hour typing notes on his laptop when the door burst open in rushed jonathan, "Sir your not even dressed and the last boat is about to leave, Sir."

"Then dress me you old fart, leather chaps, heavy chrome cock ring, boots and a Sam Browne will suffice for tonight. Number One bring me those cigars and bend over."

His slaves ran ahead to hold the launch and found it empty. We shoved off and flew across the water towards an sland beach that was awash with torches; the party was under way by the noise carried across the waves. Crossing through darkness into the light his people heard him approaching. En masse they stood, raised their glasses as we approached and cheered when we crossed from the darkness into the light of the party. Everyone had heard the rumors. Nothing could travel faster on our compound above or below ground than the slave vine.

They placed him on the dais where the winners would have normally been seated, yes, they knew all right and it showed. During the evenings announcements Hunter called for attention. He told them that an emergency situation had arisen with Lady Beatrice. She had been involved in a car accident and he was needed before his time. That he would be leaving in the next couple of days for New York. He reiterated that after the ships docked that each of us had another week of free time to take as they wished and another week of part time getting the base back to its standard level of operation. Many had wondered if that last week would be paid. Originally he had said no but tonight he gave them part time pay while they restored their homes to working order in the new caverns below. This way, he hoped they would help the Black Watch team get our house back in order sooner it was a calculated risk that he felt was worthy.

Being a slave I was not permitted to sit in the presence of my superiors. Like the other slaves that joined this event I too had to work serving all those seated at the big table so I was taken by surprise when I looked up and noticed. I was the only slave left standing and the others had disappeared. I had to supply all the handlers with drink that night and it kept me seriously busy being the only one on duty. Where had the others gone I wondered and poured another cup of ale?

I had filled everyone's cup and was returning to the kegs when someone slipped a bag over my head, closed their hand over my lips and began dragging me away. I began to fight them until they chose to play dirty. When I tried to break free my nuts suffered. I learned rapidly, stopped fighting, surrendered to the hands, and followed where they lead me.

When we stopped, I was backed into position. Ropes bound my arms outstretched. More rope was wound around my chest fusing it to a tree at my back; more rope bound my legs just as securely. When they finished I began to struggle within my bondage and found my tree wobbled as I wiggled. I must have been wiggling more than I remember cause the tree started falling forward gathering momentum in its descent but was drawn up taunt before swinging wildly in a slow arc. Slowly I felt a new sensation as my old rugged cross and I were being hoisted off the ground. As I rose into the air my hood was jerked off my head. No one was nearby that I could see and it looked like I was about 5 feet off the ground. Whoever had done this to me left me to suffer and anticipate what was going to happen next. I did not have long to wait as the brush parted out stepped a man dressed in an executioners hood, leather pants, boots who had two huge gold nipple rings.

He looked up at me, walked closer grabbed my nuts, "call your Master shit head slave or I will denut you were you hang!" I knew Sir had enough on his mind tonight that he did not want to hear me screaming out to him. I shook my head negatively. The man with the golden nipples rings laughed, grabbed my nuts and applied pressure. I screamed all right, I screamed loud enough to be heard over the partygoers and screamed again for good measure when he slammed his open hand into them.

Then I heard his voice calling out to me, "Number One, where in the fuck are you boy?" As he called out other voices behind him mocked him. It sounded like the whole party was coming my way. Yes they were as I could see a line of torches approaching down a well-chopped path in the brush.

The floundering party found me swinging in the breeze. Master stepped forward looking up at me, "how did you get up their boy?"

The man wearing the executioner's hood stepped out from behind some brush, "Good evening Master Hunter and guests," he said, "Tonight entertainment is called, Torture Garden. Torches illuminate the pathways that take you to some old and some new stations of the cross. Feel free to lay on your hands, use the toys that are displayed or apply your hands or mouths as you see fit. This garden is for you to enjoy. Libations and rest areas are scattered throughout the trail feel free to use any and all that we have provided for your pleasure and comfort." He stepped back into the jungle and disappeared.

There was no torch but the one illuminating my area until we heard a loud whistle. As one they all exploded and burst into full flame. Screams followed as if on cue luring our sadistic crew towards the sights and sounds of the garden. Hunter left me there while he and the others paraded past. I hung there until the man with the gold tit rings returned releasing me with an order "go find your master, slave and be quick about. If you are caught unescorted too long you will join those being tortured.

I found my Lord occupied. His hand and the greatest part of his forearm impaled into a sling boy's ass. Hunter had wanted to fist me, he would in time that was the reason that he had jonathan fill my ass with the monster or lovingly referred to as his hand cast in latex. He tried but my ass lips needed more practice. There he was standing tall arm almost elbow deep into a young slave that looked to be all of twenty. Damn if the boy wasn't begging for more too and Hunter obliged him by working his other hand into that pig boy's hole. It was a picturesque scene that I witnessed. A crowd had gathered around watching, some playing with their cocks others playing with others as Hunter fed that boy both his hands. The boy had entered pig heaven when his body arched and his cock shot one huge load onto the crowd. All cheered! It was a great way to start the night with an offering of boy cum so willing given up for the Lord of Darkness.

It was weird, no sooner than Hunter had withdrawn his hands from the boys ass then the boy started chanting fill me, fill me until someone filled him with yet another set of hands. Master saw me kneeling on the edge of the crowd as he was wiping down his arms and called me over to clean them, which I did without hesitation.

The background music of erotically charged sexual foreplay not unlike a whirling vortex sucked us up mingled our song and drew us down the pathway. Or next station of the cross called to us even as I bent over pulled from my ass a condoned cigar, tore the condom from the cigar with my teeth, cut the cigar, lighted it and knelt to present the cigar to my Lord's hand. He gave me in exchange a long smoke filled kiss followed by his tongue while we shared the flavor of his cigar. Walking the pathway as lovers, his arm resting lovingly almost protectively over my shoulder while one hand fingered a nipple we passed from the light of the fister's enclave into the darkness moving forward towards another well of light. In the bush as we passed we could see shadows of coupling people each engrossed it their own liberty's sharing their bodies with another.

A betting arena had been set up; one male slave his hands bound at his neck his ass lips spread over a rather large horse cock was being impaled. The cock was situated on the top of a steel pole, the cock had been inserted in the slave's ass lips and the slave had been placed on its toes. Only the tip of the rubber cock had been inserted into the ass when we were there. The rubber cock was held into the boys butt by a wooden seat and shaft combined. The cock could only go so deep but the slave did not know that. The game was not meant to damage the property only to stretch its hole. With the slaves ass impaled on the rubber cock it could not lift itself off without the use of its hands. It could walk around in a complete circle while on its toes. If it tripped the rubber plug would slide deeper into the hole. This was a waiting game handlers loved to play with us when they had time to fuck with our heads. The slaves legs would eventually give out and down the slave would slide, thus filling its hole completely. Bets were placed the length of time it took for the slave to be seated and colored sectors around the base of the platform allowed handler's to bet on the color the slave would be filled. This was a game many slaves had to endure in the slave camp in many forms as they learned their ass holes would stretch to fit any and all cocks that came there way.

The boy was active while we watched, twisting and walking his small circle around the shaft buried deep into the ground. He made a Herculean effort to push himself off the rubber cock but there was nothing that would give him enough leverage. His activity while on the pole was almost as busy as the bets being laid on how long he could hold himself off the plug. It was exciting to watch as the slave walked and turned like a pig on a spit and to hear his grunts of displeasure as his toes gave out sinking his hole down an inch onto the impaler. The boy tripped not soon after. The anguish on his face was so fucking hot as that mauler in his ass rose up another couple of notches triggering a betting frenzy by handlers laying odds on how much longer the boy would last.

Sir got bored so we walked on turning at a conjunction of the hewn pathway and entering a darkened area with less torches than had been on the main path. We wandered this way until we came upon a private scene. A handler that this slave had the unfortunate pleasure of acquainting while in the pit was suspended by his boots, arms bound over his head and locked to the ground. Another handler stood to the side of the bound handler with a heavy flogger in his hand. He turned and almost shit when he realized it was Hunter who was approaching their little scene.

Hunter broke the ice, "Handler did we stumble off the path?"

"Yes, Master Hunter. This is a private bet settlement. Sir? Would you mind helping me explain to this handler that it is not nice to welch on a bet."

"Oh? He wants to beg out of his bet does he? What's your name Handler?"

"Jeorge Reys, Sir."

"and what was the nature of the bet, Jeorge?"

"He bet me that I could not fuck twelve men and still cum down his throat in one night. If I could, he would serve me as my slave for the balance of this cruise. Serve in any and all aspects as my slave, Sir.

Hunter seemed perplexed, "how did you accomplish that Jeorge?"

Jeorge laughed, "I lined up twelve men, slipped my dick into each once then grabbed his ears forced my cock down his throat and blew my load, Sir."

"Sounds like you won the bet fair and square, Jeorge. Might I suggest that you place a heavy loggers chain and padlock around its neck as soon as you can and add shackles to it. It looks like an unruly beast that will need lots of cock and serious training." Hunter stepped forwards towards the bound slave, "next bet you need to clarify your bets better."

We retraced our steps once again turning onto the well-beaten path. As we joined the others making their way between Stations of the Cross; we found slaves bound, kneeling, being used as urinals at conjunctions of avenues, and small lean-tos being used to give away beverages, toys, and trinkets to remember this evening. We turned towards the sound of waves and ran into a huge spider web draped from tree to tree. Stepping aside the cobwebs we entered a den so to speak of well-spun spider webs. To the left was a huge woven rope web, which held a suspended, and rope encased slave. Upon close inspection we found the trapped handler was not only bound but was wired for sound.

Wires ran just about everywhere on that man's body. Wires seemed to squirt from his ass, copper wire bound around its ruts; another strand wound around its cock and still another electrode was attached to a metal sound protruding from his cock. More wire ran around his thighs on close inspection the wire was not totally stripped of its insulation there were nicks exposing copper wire that touched the skin. All I could think was evil, eeevil! From the rope webbing hung various Ten's units and electro toys that could be added to the bound form hanging in the web.

The slave had been quietly hanging in his spider web bondage until Sir went towards the Tens units hanging besides the slave. A few adjustments sent the slave bouncing in its web. By the boys reaction it looked as if it was getting fucked by some unseen cock. Sir seemed pleased by the slaves reaction an adjusted another unit. The boy was twisting and moaning to the oldies by the way it was reacting to the electricity working the plug in its ass and the sound in its cock. The slave's cock grew as if to tell those of us gathered to watch him hump the air with his cock and ass that he liked this treatment. All was going well until a man stepped out from behind a clump of trees and directed our attention to another scenario in the center of the clearing.

Where two slaves should have stood facing each other were two handlers dueling for superiority. Each handler held a hand crank generator the leads on the opposite generator running to the nuts of his opponent. Our escort lead my Lord to a small table with two chairs on the sidelines of the battling duo. Sir and the handler known as Edison, yes, Tommy seated themselves before the competition began. Switches were flipped giving life to panels with needles. Thomas explained that each handler would crank his generator giving the other handler a shock then the opponent would be given a chance to respond using his generator. This shocking event would go on until one of the handlers dropped to his knees or dropped the generator and the one standing would be the winner.

Handler's gathered and began placing bets on which handler would more than likely win the competition. On the right was a handler and trainer of the mule teams his name was Wolfie a big oafish fellow, dark hair, beard, hairy chest and back, with low hanging balls and a nice thick veined piece of meat. The other handler was his opposite in many ways. Al had a shaved head; goatee and mustache light complexion fair skin and had a swimmer's build. His cock was handsome well proportioned like a banana with a purpling cockhead and his nuts even bound down into their copper wound stretcher was tight and heavily veined. Both men were poised and ready to give each other enough juice to fry each other's nuts off by the way they were snarling and cursing each other.

While I was studying the handlers and listening to those betting Hunter had been listening to something that Edison was saying quietly behind his hand. I could not read his lips by the way he was covering his face. Edison gave Sir the thumbs up, rose from his chair and approached the two men.

"Gentlemen, we are here to settle a dispute. The winner will be the others superior for the balance of this cruise which means one of you will be the Master tonight and the other will be the slave. Agreed?"

Both men growled their answer. Edison looked to the crowd and to each man's seconds, "do you have chains and shackles ready for the winner, Seconds?"

They showed them to the crowd who roared their approval.

Edison pulled a gold coin from his pocket, "Call it mid air, gentlemen."

Al screamed, "Heads!"

Wolfie screamed, "Heads no Tails!"

The coin was flipped and the men shouted their call. The coin hit the sand and displayed heads.

"Al has his choice to give or receive, which is it Al?"

"GIVE!" Bellowed Al!

"OK, Gentlemen. Here's how it goes. First round you both get 30 seconds. Al will go first than you Wolfie. You will hear this and he pointed to Sir who depressed the trigger on an air horn. When you hear the air horn stop cranking. Fail to stop and your opponent will be given an extra 30 seconds. Each round goes up by increments of 30 seconds meaning for those of you who are dumb fucks. First round, 30 seconds; Second round, 1 minute; Third round 1.30 seconds and on and on until someone's nuts get blown off, or one of you drops their generator, or one of you drops to the ground. Do you understand?"

"AYE!" Said Wolfie, "let me at the fucker!"

"Fucking A!" Bellowed Al, "your nuts are Mine cocksucker!"

Edison walked behind the console turned to Hunter, "Would you give the call Sir!"

Hunter rose, "On my mark, Al, you have 30 seconds."

Hunter sat back down, looked to Edison and winked, "MARK!"

Al got off a few turns giving Wolfie one hellacious blast to his nuts. The air horn blasted and Wolfie cranked that generator like there was no tomorrow. Al's eyes rolled up into their sockets. This went on for what seemed like an hour, one cranking their generator harder then the other. When the time got up to 2 minutes I noticed that Sir or Edison would flip a switch making the needles on one or two of the lighted consoles flip back and forth behind their glass panel. Whenever they did that, the Handler giving his opponent hell via the hand crank generator would all but buckle at their knees and have to force themselves upright. Nearing the 4-minute round Wolfie got down into a squat and dropped his generator as he was trying to climb back upright. The air horn blared calling a halt to the contest and those who were Al's seconds moved into to shackle Wolfie before he could rise.

Hunter rose dragging me off my knees shook Edison's hand and thanked him for the show. As we were walking down the pathway Hunter told me the secret of the game that had just been played. Neither generators worked; they were only for show. All the electricity that was being sent into the handlers was coming from the console that he and Edison had controlled. When the handlers had flipped the coin that was how they decided who was going to lose the battle as Sir and Edison had called their own flip based on how the coin fell. Like always those in control held the power.

Walking down the pathway we found at the apex of an avenue a slave couple bound together writhing in their bondage. Interesting how it was a male and female pair bound crotch to crotch locked together on a roughly built bed. Neither seemed to mind the crowd as it passed by laying hands on the humping bodies. It was after all just part of the show. Sex was everywhere; the night was full of it, and if we could have bottled that night along with the setting and that big beautiful moon what a marketable item it would have been. When the couple tired of their dining pleasure long thin green switches were nearby to help them get back into the mood. Only Lady Donna knew for certain what these two slaves had done to displease her but she was corralling and handing out switches to everyone within arms length. Those two humping slaves would be kept at it well beyond their normal climax by the cold look on their owners face.

The other side of the pathway had gathered quiet a crowd. When Hunter pressed through to see what was the ruckus we found one of my friends where he loved to be. Loved to be bound like a monkey and servicing all takers. Slave patrick was a male nymphomaniac, needing sex to feel loved and willing to do anything with anybody to satisfy his cravings. Damn him, I remember being in the dungeon below with him in my cell. I had been cuffed with my arms extending behind me out through the cells wall and my feet had been cuffed as well leaving my cock within easy access of patrick. The slave struggled against his chains all night to find away to get to my cock. I was never so thankful as I was that next morning when the handler arrived to take me elsewhere and even then patrick whined his need. Tonight he was in his element men and women had gathered around him to use one or more of his parts for their pleasure. The slave just did not care who rode him or how he was ridden as long as he was giving himself and them pleasure. They had him in a suspension harness attached over head to a bamboo tower by bungee cords and it looked by the way he was being used that everyone was riding a hole to hell and back! The smile plastered on his face after his face was removed from a cumming cock said it all, patrick was in heaven. Like a pig in shit, he loved his time of service!

Hunter looked over to me as we turned from that action, "you would think I was the king of pig farmers instead of the Deus," his laughter told me more than most would have thought. He pulled me to him, forced me to drink one of his handsome kisses, placed his arm around my waist pulling us down the path only to halt in a couple of steps before the one handler that use to scare the holy-be-Jesus out of me when I was in the dungeon. Even now with my Lord's arm around my waist he had to have felt a shiver of anticipation. The handler was of Nordic descent blonde hair, blue eyes and built like a fucking concrete wall. There he stood like a child in a candy store trying to look over the crowd at patrick while fisting his cock.

"Sven, it looks like you need someone to help you with that thing," Master asked?

"Ya, Sir. that ma boy is othervise occupied."

Master did not even flinch but handled me over to the handler, "here use mine. Send him along when you are finished, Sven."

Hunter pushed me to my knees before the huge giant of a man without so much as a thought of what I might or might not want to do and walked off. The blonde giant looked down at me, coughed up a huge wad of spit, and spat. Like a fucking trained animal I caught it like so many other times when he did this game to me while I was under his care. Damn him, I hated the fact that I accepted his spit so fucking easily like a god damned trained dog catching a bone!

Sven slapped my cheeks until they dropped open, "Chew suck good or I fix chew!"

His broken English held enough of a threat coupled with his size and having been on the front of one of his gut punches before. I knew that I had better suck good or he would fix me.

His cock slipped easily down my throat. It was a nice long cock not overly wide. I closed my throat muscles around his cock and made that daddy moan with my new improved technique. Sven had only had my mouth once before and then I was still a rough neck recruit, now I was a well-oiled machine. What I could do with my throat, tongue and teeth made my Lord all but sit up and beg for more like a puppy. This was power, slave power, the ability to bring a grown over bearing mean son of a bitch to his knees using only my mouth and my specialized talents. I was proud when he popped his nut rapidly, prouder when I found myself surrounded by others fisting their cocks waiting their turn at my hole. Once Sven withdrew his cock another found my hole open and inviting. I must have blown about half a dozen cocks when I heard an all to familiar voice that almost made me choke.

"Where is Sven," my Lord asked the crowd? No one seemed to know where he was or a cone of silence had settled over us and their voices were sucked away like so many other by products.

"Number One, what are you doing down there?"

I tried to answer him but it's kinda hard to do that with a cock plowing your face.

"Slave," said Hunter.

Just the tone told me I as in trouble with him and the night was still young. I gagged about that time as the handler whose cock I was sucking chose to blow his load before Sir jerked me off him unsatisfied.

His large hand closed around my throat using it to lift me to my knees, "boys, this shop is closed! There are enough holes to go around boys. Go find your own," he laughed telling them he was not mad at any of them. Then he turned his eyes on me. Even in the low light I could see and feel his anger at me being unable to follow his order.

His hand never came off my throat as he pulled me into a small hastily built hut. We left a few minutes later with me in heavy leg irons, my hands bound behind my back and my mouth filled with a nasty gag. I loved the leg irons and bondage but the gag held a funnel at the end. He was planning to make certain all that cum that I had just sucked down my throat was well washed down into my gut. I could read this man like a book or so I thought.

We turned on a side path and found jonathan chest deep in a tub of piss. That slave was in his own heaven and even waved from his watery bucket as Sir passed him by taking me to a bamboo pole bound between two trees. There I was forced to my knees and bound by rope. Sir started the line as he grabbed the funnel attached to my gag, and let the piss fly. It was like choking down a rainstorm, which abruptly stopped. He patted my face walked over to jonathan's trough that slave rose up on his knees, opened his mouth and drank directly from Sir's spigot. My sight was blocked when another patron stepped up to this urinal and left me his deposit.

While I drank my fill of recycled ale, Sir was not far away enjoying something just as entertaining as his loud laughter was heard in the background to all the other sounds of the evening. Yes, it was a wild party by even our standards. Thank God we are on a deserted island in the middle of the South Seas. As the hours wore on the party became more wild, clothes were disappearing fast, nudity was rampant as was fucking, sucking and beating of flesh. It was a fun evening. It would have been more fun if my Lord had not locked me into service as a urinal. My stomach felt full just from all the fluids that I had been fed while he was away having fun.

When he sauntered into the glade I did not notice as my head was bowed and I was starring at the sand. Boots filled my vision and I felt my funnel being lifted. I sighed to myself, another load of piss coming my way, and did not look up until he forced me to look up. There he stood looking down at me, "are you ready to go yet?"

I nodded my head yes and amazingly I was released from the fence and my piss gag. He even escorted me to stand before jonathan and I was ordered to piss on my brother slave. Jonathan's back arched out as if the fluid was the kiss of life, like a child he played in his piss tub letting anyone that wanted to add their golden nectar to his body in or on he was overjoyed to accept.

Hunter leaned over, calling jonathan to him and kissed his property. While they were kissing, Hunter was releasing jonathan's lead chain from the tub, and when Sir rose he pulled jonathan from the tub, "time to let others have some fun. Heel, slaves."

We followed him passing a section where St Andrews, Tao crosses and other whipping posts were filled with occupants enjoying them. Mike was kneeling bound by its neck to a post with a freshly slathered back of welts and glazed eyes. He stirred when master approached and rallied when Sir released him to our care. Three slaves followed our Lord to what ends it did not matter.

Rounding a corner we literally ran into Lady Katherine who was leading her bitch by a lead chain. I must have winched when I saw her slave girls breasts cause Lady Katherine pulled her up close so she could rub on the bitches breasts. They had been bound like my nuts got often bound. Rope cinched them tightly pulling them away from the chest protruding grotesquely, each nipple held huge wooden nipple clamps that I knew had to hurt with every movement. But what really made me want to suck my cock into my body was that she had applied a half dozen of those brutal clothespins on her cunt lips! God, how that had to hurt with each step just those small appointments made me want to run but then I made the mistake of looking at the girls face.

Oh MY GOD! Lady Katherine had sewn the bitches lips closed! With big huge black nasty looking stitches that cris-crossed her lips like something you would see on a shrunken head. Lady Katherine's only explanation was that the bitch had sassed her once too often this trip. Then went on to explain that when the stitches would be removed she would look as if she had been given botox injections. Hunter laughed and looked at me, "maybe I should learn to sew." He kissed Lady Katherine and bid her a good night.

We stepped beyond an invisible barrier into the ladies den. It was like a fish fry that had gone horribly a rye. Too many women running around wearing strap on cocks fucking men with their less than little darlings. Other women were bound this way and that while being beaten or fried with electricity but what Hunter had drawn us into was to see the cuttings that Lady Jean was doing on the people beneath her blades. They were awesome! An intricate fairy with spread wings was being cut into a bound female while the slave under her seemed to be so far away. She had given over to the endorphins and the rush of being sliced, just watching it was an awesome experience and a small quiet crowd had collected to watch. We left there to watch another even more exciting scene as it was about to be taken up a notch.

Syringe needles had been placed, or so it looked, every few inches down a rather large bodied woman. The needles ran from her shoulder down the tops of her arms, down her chest, over her hips, thighs, and calves and up the other side. She had been laid on a large wooden platform. Scaffolding had been erected around the platform and women were in the process of attaching her to the overhead scaffolding using dental floss. Each needle had its own strand of floss to the scaffolding overhead. Once all were secured and checked the wooden platform on which the lady lay was removed and she hung suspended by nothing but the thin dental floss attached to the needles in her flesh. Her Mistress checked the slave's progress speaking quietly to her and added a strap to the above scaffolding that ran under her head acting like a pillow. It was an incredible sight to see this lady of 260 lbs held in suspension by nothing but needles in her skin and dental floss. Quietly we departed leaving them to their playtime and we rejoined the herd moving down to find the balance of our slave team.

We sighted a figure moving before us and Hunter whistled like a wolf at the man whose back was to us. The man was wearing knee high lineman boots and a rubber kilt. The man stopped, turned with a huge smile plastered across his face. To my shock it was JD.

"Hey little boy, I got some candy," said Sir.

JD cracked a big toothy grin and walked up to Hunter, "Oh, you do?" JD dropped into a deep squat before Hunter and was mouthing Sirs cock, "what type candy you got for this little boy, Sir?"

Hunter was laughing, his hand grabbed jonathan's nuts and pulled them towards JD, "peanut brittle, want some, little boy?"

JD rose up, "thanks but no thanks Sir. Peanut brittle gets between my teeth." They both laughed. JD leaned forward putting his hands around Hunter neck and gave him one of the biggest mushiest kisses I had ever seen him give anybody. Hunter returned the kiss pulling the boy closer releasing jonathan's nuts. When they parted both men were laughing.

"Take it you are having a hell of a good time, eh, JD?" said my Lord Hunter.

"Sir, I am having a blast." JD held his arms out spread; "this is like a smorgasbord only better you can't get full not if you try some of the elixirs they are serving down that path Sir. Guaranteed to wet your whistle and raise your sagging pecker that's for certain."

They exchanged banter for a few minutes until Hunter asked JD what he had on under his kilt. JD's response was interesting; he mooned Hunter and ran off into the darkness.

Hunter turned to jonathan, "looks like that boy has grown up, pappy! Go grab you some boy butt, slave, that's an order!"

Just like that Hunter was down to two slaves. We wandered down towards the watering hole and found an odd collection of men having a measuring contest, length and girth. We lost mikey as it seemed he had missed two of those rather large cocks on his mission to find the largest cock employed by Buena Vista. For all mikes sweetness he had a hungry hole that equaled none. Size queen, yes, that was mikey, but he compared other aspects as well. Not only did the cock have to work it had to have reloads as well, more than one man had died trying to satisfy that boys lust for cock but they died with a smile on their face.

Thus being parted from out merry band of slaves leaving just Hunter and his Number One to wander the lusty trails we found ourselves before an outpost. The outpost was serving elixirs that were guaranteed, according to the doctor who had been drafted to serve up the tonics to all that needed their masts hoisted yet again. Hunter had a nice long cold draft of one of his favorite fruit punches, while I was allowed to lap at one from a bowl at his feet. It was nice to share the ground with other distinctive creatures a playful feline was swatting at her Mistress's whip and a dog boy was showing his Sir some affection.

There is nothing greater than being on public display when one is with ones Master. Like tonight, I was so fucking proud to be wearing my Lords shackles walking beside or behind him amidst all these hot looking men and women. Their pride showed in how they handled themselves, masters of men, and we slaves had our pride. Damn few in the outside world could handle the level of dedication and pride we feel when we walk with our Owners. Damn few understand what it means to be a slave in our society. It's not about sex although there is good sex, it's not about serving and yet it is, it's about pride in being the best that you can be for another. It's about giving of yourself unselfishly without care for what comes and it's about acceptance. When people in the gay bars talk about pride they do not have one inkling of an idea what it really means as they are just mouthing the words like a parrot. Come up with an original thought just once before you think you know what it means to have pride in being a slave. Slaves are either born or made, it's that simple. Those that are born know it from the beginning that they were put on this earth to serve mankind you will be amazed how they go about finding jobs that allow them to serve. They are in every walk of life, literally everywhere serving their fellow man and getting their jollies doing it. Then there are those like this slave that were made to conform to a set of parameters established by its control. Which slave type is the best? That's a matter of opinion those that give freely and those that are a little rebellious. All depends upon the owner.

Sir wants a cigar. It's my job to squirt it out, cut it from its condom, prep it and light it for my lord. Once that use to embarrass me beyond reason, now its so matter of fact this slave almost embarrassed my Lord in polite public. (Polite public meaning where there were straights present.) We were on one of the island stops, tourist trap; Sir had placed some cigars in my shirt pocket since we went to the island as real tourists, dressed. We were sitting on a balcony watching the ocean with friends when he asked for a cigar. Without thinking I dropped to my knees and prepared to squirt one out when he tapped me on the head. "Polite public, boy. Don't you dare! One from your pocket will work best." He laughed it off the guests did not notice anything out of place. Still it happened as the training holds me tight within it's boundaries.

Another time, Sir was in a heated argument with a business associate. We were in a fancy seafood restaurant when Sir made a fist. My training being that I was trained to hand signals. I was in the corner of this huge round booth when the sign was given and I rose walked over the table top, dropped to the floor placing my head between my hands, ass in the air, kneeling legs spread. The maitre'd ran over to see what was the problem. Hunter did not even see me down on the floor holding position until he looked. This slave heard the Sir telling the maitre'd, "Oh, he does that when he is starving. His blood sugar is out of whack, bring him some soup and crackers so his head will stop spinning." After that incident Sir was more attentive to his hand signals.

Returning to the happy trail Sir lead the way as if he knew where he was going, and I clanked behind him doing my damnedest to catch up with him. We rounded a clump of palm trees and ran splat dab in the middle of an orgy. All they needed to look like a fish school were fins and silver backs instead of the multicolored bodies swimming in a sea of oil by the way their naked, near naked and rubbered bodies glowed in the torch light. Someone had laid down a huge tarp added oil and chained four slaves one to each corner the balance of the heaving mass of bodies looked to be handlers and some of the ships mates. A daisy chain had formed with 9-777 getting its ass plowed hard by a handsome Afro-American, while 9-777 gobbled down a big pecker who was blowing an Indian and so the circle went round and round. This ended the Torture Garden tour, somehow it was very fitting end as everyone was getting in the end all 30 or more bodies.

Hunter and I returned by the way of the well-beaten path to where jonathan had been sent after boy butt. Sir had me standing before him, his cock sliding up and down my ass crack while we watched the show. Jonathan had been placed in chest high waders that had to have been Sir's at one time. The waders had been cinched up under his armpits and filled with his liquid of choice, recycled water, piss! He looked like something from out of a really bad dream as his ankles up to his crotch were swollen almost to capacity. He looked like someone who was suffering from elephantitus but the boy had a huge shit eating grin plastered all across his face saying to all that he was in pig heaven. He was struggling to walk around and while we were there he stumbled teetered back and forth trying to maintain his feet, but he fell backwards bounced once before the piss found a weakened area. The fluid rushed and washed over him giving me the impression that a damn had broken and he could drown in his divine liquid. The pig loved it! Once the deluge was completed he bounced up asking for donations and laughing, "what a rush!"

Hunter slipped his hand under my chin, whispered into my ear, "open the ashtray pig," dropped in his ash, "hold it," inhaled a huge lung full of smoke, clamped his gloved hand over my lips, placed his open mouth over my nose and exhaled as I inhaled. This way we exchanged a lung full of smoke. His mouth came off my nose and his other hand pinched my nostrils closed as his hand pulled me into his chest. He wanted me to struggle, was holding me so that I could fight his hands and I did. My lungs were burning from too much smoke and not enough air. I tried clawing at his hands with both of mine, still they held. I tried to shake him off that was no use. I began seeing stars flashing before my eyes and knew my knees were giving away still he held on to my nostrils and face. My eyes begged him for release even as my mind shouted to him, please, Sir let me breathe. He must have heard cause his hand was released and I sucked in a huge oxygen rich load of clean air. God it was good!

He pulled me to my feet, stepped me over to the grass hut had my shackles released and bondage suspension cuffs bound over my hands and wrists. He had plans or so it seemed. He picked up a bag of toys that were hidden behind the bar, added heavy logging chains to my dee rings, and drug me behind the hut onto a private path. I was excited cause he was excited, taking my cue from him, always. We stepped into a well lighted glen. Directly in front of us was a St. Andrews cross with a hoist hanging down from a beam set between two trees. It was to that cross I was taken. He pushed me against the cross, put his body against mine and held me there pinned as he forced a kiss to my lips, down to bite my neck and dropped down another level to nibble and roll my nipples. God, I wanted him in me in a bad way!

While his tongue did a fancy dance to my right nipple both his hands were busy removing my vest. One hand held the vest the other drew my arms up, he stepped back long enough to connect my hands to the above chain then he stepped aside to the crank and lifted me to my toes. He folded my vest and used it on my back and front as the warm up tool making huge whacking sounds that echoed back from the forest around us. When I was cherry pink he devoured my flesh with his tongue and laid in a series of deep bites into my burning flesh. My squeal had to have been heard over the dim as people were drawn to our intimate circle of which he was not even aware. They stood like silent soldiers watching Sir play with his number one slave.

He tore switches from a nearby tree returning to me and layering those branches over my backside before tossing them aside in a fit of anger and grabbing, lifting me into his arms. My legs closed around him even as his head slipped down onto my stomach there his teeth found the necessary folds of flesh. He bit me hard and I could not stifle the scream as his teeth tore at my hot flesh. He tore himself loose, pulled a whip from his bag. A thin braided cat was used to raise hundreds of welts, and I danced for him like I had not for years. I sang our song with a muffled voice his fist having found purchase upon entering my mouth forcing it open. Another brutal bite ripped a chunk of flesh as he slowly devoured me. He was a cannibal devouring his slave, each bite felt like electricity running into my body forcing me to mewl and beg even as I screamed in delight of his pleasureful pains.

Sir walked towards me his eyes glowing in the fire of his sadistic desire but I was too smart for him. I raised myself up with my arms, spread my legs and caught him within the vee of my legs. His cock was hard, my ass wet and craving. The two met, joined and he was mine! The captive caught the captor in his trap. I held him as he struggled, working may ass muscles forcing him to fuck me and he did. Like a bull he fucked my hole raw and came with a roar of the king of the jungle. His lips found mine even as his hands found the chain and released my arms that dropped onto his shoulder. He carried me a short distance until he had me trapped between the St Andrews cross at my back and him at my front. His cock wanted more of my butt and took it. This lovemaking was as passionate as the first one was brutal! We both loved it and he came again up my ass and I swear my ass came when he did cause I felt his climax like nothing else before.

Chapter 4

If absolute power corrupts absolutely, does absolute powerlessness make you pure?
Harry Shearer

My Lord is walking before me. I love every pore of him and am intimate with every square inch of his body. He hides his true nature behind a gruff façade, but I have learned to read him like a well-worn book. He is nothing but a huge teddy bear loving to a fault, ok, I will admit it. A teddy bear with sharp claws and teeth but does it matter not to me? He taught me to fear him, I did, hated him and that I did too, so I was surprised when I woke up one morning and realized I loved him, like no other man who has been in my life. There is no way to rationalize my love for him. He kept me captive for years still this love for him goes beyond the Stockholm syndrome, this love is genuine and it affects us all. Even the handlers who are truly sadistic bastards love our Lord Hunter. They are devoted to him and he returns their devotion by giving this wild ass party on the South Seas. I wonder if they really knew who gave them this morale builder, team creator of a cruise how many would have paid their own way instead of him footing the whole bill. Oh, yes, Castle gave the prizes after he twisted their arms nearly off, but he paid for everything else out of the Buena Vista sales. The trip is his way of boosting morale; helping the handlers who are normally loners develop trust with each other and form teams that will be useful when they return home.

I was watching my Sir's heels move off before me and failed to notice in time that he had stopped. Rear-ending him didn't give him whiplash it did make him turn. Seeing it was me, his hand closed around my neck as he drug me forward and I saw what brought him up short. Seems that 9-777 had crawled out of the grease pit and was now holding private audience. If by the line that was forming you could call a private anything. It looked like three slaves were having a contest to see who could suck off the most men in one night. Hell of a contest! By the looks of it the contest was just about to start. Hunter would have normally allowed this contest to happen but for some reason tonight he wanted 9-777 for his own.

Sir stepped to the front of the line, physically picked up 9-777 by his throat and tossed him, mind you, I tossed him about 4 feet. 9-777 fell hard and laid where it landed, quiet possibly due to a big size 15 D boot held it in place. Sir was just a little testy at that moment when he proclaimed, "Who told it to think, slave?"

9-777 seemed to go pale and kept its mouth shut. Which was not to master's liking. I knew what was about to happen but could not stop or call out for fear I would catch his wraith. Sir's large boot rose and slammed down hard into the slave's solar plexus bowling the creature in upon itself.

"Number One, fetch me a bite gag and posture collar!" By his tone alone I knew 9-777 was about to really hurt and I flew to the grass shack, grabbed the items and returned. The bite gag was a brutal device that forced the mouth wide open, I think it had to originate in a sadistic dentist's office, ours forced the mouth open and buckled securely to the back of the head. Once in place 9-777 could not close its mouth around cocks nor could it swallow. Compounded with the posture collar it would collect flies as well, living flies and dirt and whatever else Sir wanted to feed it.

Hunter and 9-777 could have passed as brothers they looked so much alike, almost identical twins but I must have been the only one that saw this and the way they interacted told me volumes. Hunter was always on 9-777's ass, never giving it an inch cause if he did 9-777 would run a yard only to be stopped mid stride and stomped for the effort. There love for each other was intense, one loved to give pain the other receive. It was like looking at the Yin and Yang sign were Hunter and 9-777. 9-777 was only an inch shorter but built like Hunter. Strong chest, big shoulders, bigger arms, thick trunk like legs. Sir had a little gut forming whereas 9-777 being the younger did not. Hunter had hair whereas 9-777 was shaved as was its eyebrows, face clean of any hair. Its mouth yawned open fused by the dental device and its neck stretched up on a Victorian posture collar fused in place by thick leather panels under its chin and its arms were strapped at its back. Sir was standing literally on 9-777's crotch holding it to the ground while the other slaves started the contest.

Using only his fist inserted into 9-777 forced open jaw, Hunter lead us away from the cock sucking contest. We returned by way of the juice shack where Hunter had two of the power drinks and I was forced to drink one. Head buzzing from the powerful aphrodisiacs in the drink I stumbled towards our private alcove there I installed 9-777's hands into the suspension bondage gloves and helped Sir set his hands into the hoist. Sir hoisted its arms overhead, stepped away ordering me to strip it of rubber gear. Sir disappeared while I did as was ordered quietly removing 9-777 from his rubbers.

My Lord stumbled back into our private alcove a few minutes later with a bag of toys and a jug of fluid of some kind. Those he tossed down near me "chose a whip Number One!" My head shot up as if someone had fired a gun when he ordered me to choose a whip. He repeated the order, louder, "choose a whip SLAVE!"

I pulled the three he had in the bag out looking at them cautiously as if they may turn into snakes at any moment. I chose a light doeskin flogger and held it out to him. He had been sitting on a rock outcropping playing with a single tail when I returned to him with the light flogger. He took the offered flogger and tossed it over his shoulder, "not good enough for him. Get one of the others. If you are going to get respect from that piece of meat as his Superior he has to know you mean business else wise he will run over you in a rush to get to me."

"Take the one in your right hand and flog his back. Do It Number One! Hit him! Goddamn it!"

I was never so reluctant as I was that moment. I had more than enough reason to hit 9-777. I took a practice swing to see how the flogger would work mid air even laid a blow across my back to feel it. Moved into take position as I had seen Hunter do often enough but just could not get the flogger to move towards 9-777.

A gunshot cracked right next to my ear. I jumped!

"Flog him Number One so he can respect you as MY Number ONE slave! Look at his eyes, One, look and see a creature that wants you to fail at this order.

He would not have a problem whipping you nor did he in the past. I heard he loved whipping you among other things. You tapped that anger once let him feel it, NOW!"

Oh, I found my anger all right! After the first few light blows it all came bubbling up out of me into that whip as I laced 9-777's body with bloody red welts. I wanted him to suffer like I did at his hand when the roles were reversed. I needed him to feel my hurt, my betrayal. I slashed him with every last morsel of anger I could find within my body. Hunter had moved up behind me. I jumped again when his arms encircled me, the flogger dropped and I turned into his chest. He held me secure as I shivered but not from any cold unless it was the cold within my soul. "Sssh, you did what was necessary and you have shown him who is his boss. You did good, Number One, real good," he kissed me lovingly. Gave me the juice bottle, then ordered a cigar prepped and ordered me to sit over on the outcropping of stones to sip the juice and calm down.

He walked over to 9-777 slammed his fist into the slave's guts, lowered his arms and bound him to the St Andrews cross facing forward. Sir fiddled with his boot pulling out a butterfly knife and expertly flashed it into full extension blade exposed. One hand on the slaves head the other on his knife he showed it to the slave, "I could cut your skin off like Doc did in Vietnam for not obeying my orders 9-777 and no one would even lift a finger in your behalf."

Sir dropped the blade to 9-777's heaving chest allowed the blade to take a slow descent across the slave's panicked chest. The blade drew a red line from one nipple to the other then descended to the belly button and back up to the right nipple forming a bloody red triangle. He stepped away, commanding, "butt me, One!"

Hunter sat on the stone outcropping, I kneeling at his left boot, both of us sharing his cigar and the juice from the jug watching the blood crawl down over the slaves chest. He looked down at me, "go back to the shack, ask the bartender for my supplies and be careful not to spill any when you return."

I ran off on my new duty and returned carrying a small bag and a basket of what looked to be cigar ashes. He took the small bag and ordered me to rub the cigar ashes over the bloody lines carved into 9-777's chest. The ashes would halt the blood and would seal the wounds leaving a mark upon his skin to remind it of this day. Sir however was not finished with the slave.

Sir ordered me on hands and knees before 9-777 using my back as a table for the contents of the small bag. Hunter pulled rubber gloves over his hands snapping them loudly in a jungle gone strangely silent. I smelled an antiseptic and knew by the movement of the slave's legs that the location that it was being rubbed was not to his liking. It did not matter as the location pleased the Sir as his Dark Angel was now in control and feeding well from the meat hanging before him.

My Lord chuckled his deep bass sadistic laugh that told me all too well that 9-777 was going to hurt badly after this exercise in control. I saw the slave's leg muscles tighten and heard it squeal as Sir worked on the slave's body, modifying it to suit his dark tastes. First blood had been taken with the knife more would follow if I knew my Lord's darker nature. Plastic sheaths of two colors were dropped to the ground telling me more than I wanted to know. Sir was driving his miniature swords, needles, under and through his slaves flesh. Each needle represented a small sharp cock or sword tearing into the slave, forcing it to take Sir's pain. Oddly enough even with my limited range of sight I could see that the slave was maintaining a hard on even as it suffered Sir's pleasure.

Sir stepped back, grumbled something under his breath and moved back into position. Fifty or more plastic sheaths littered the ground most of these were colored a mint green. More antiseptic some dripping to the ground as Sir swabbed the slave's cock literally covering the whole surface with the brown acid smelling stuff. Sir pinched the foreskin together the slave flinched and groaned as Sir forced a needle with suture through the skin over the cock head and back out the other side of the foreskin. He drew the thread tight, knotted it and forced it back through the skin from another point drawing the sutures over the swollen cocks head. The slave's gargled scream had to be heard to the next island but Sir was not finished.

Sir dropped to one knee, tossed another sheath to the ground and drove the long needle through the base of the slave's cock. All the slave did was shutter as endorphins dropped into his system. Sir chuckled and added another needle up the shaft followed by another and another until the shaft of the slaves cock was layered with needles. As if that was not enough, Sir added dental floss binding each needle in a crazy eight cinching the flesh tight over the needle making the slave squirm and moan as he bound each needle in turn. Sir rose to his full height, the slave groaned as Sir went to work on binding his needles all across the slaves heaving chest. Then Sir removed the items on my back stepped away to admire his handiwork and ordered me to heel.

Master walked to the stone out cropping as I crawled on my hands and knees only stopping when he sat. There I stared up at him watching him as he watched his pain slave. I lowered my eyes for fear that his Dark Angel would want a donation from my flesh. Kneeling there I studied his boots, placed my hands at the small of my back, dropped my head and prayed silently that I would be spared. An order was given "go fetch me some cigars."

I ran to the hut and found none was sent to the other hut down near the piss station there I found three, grabbed them all and almost stumbled over jonathan in my haste to return. He followed, as did others once they realized Sir was in one of his darkest scenes, blood sports.

A blood-curdling scream pierced the air. It was one of those long drawn out screams that end's in a great sobbing moan that foretold incredible horrors. I ran faster than I thought possible whirling around people, trees and jumping over rocks with jonathan on my heels. We burst into a scene that would have made my hairs stand on end if I had any and stopped dead in our tracks. Two Dark Angels were feeding 9-777's eyes were glazed as badly as my Lords when I dropped to my knees beside him. Both were locked in a battle few would ever see outside of our society, the dance of Demons.

The jawbreaker had been removed from 9-777's mouth still nothing could have silenced that howling sound that was coming from his bruised lips. Hunter stood to the slaves side working with a Tens unit the leads attached to needles in the slave's cock and the slave was still hard and by the looks of its cock head leaking pre cum by the gallons. 9-777's right nipple had been pierced not once but by eight different times each needle seemed to weave under and over other needles imbedded in the skin under his nipple. The left nipple had been sliced and quartered by Sir's knife this way it would never hold a ring again. Master had inserted one large needle under the corona of the left nipple. Threads had been woven around the wheel of needles in its right nipple then run to the left nipple, down to its cock and the closest needle to the cock head and back up to the right nipple. As the cock strained against the threads it inflicted pain on all three areas. If that wasn't enough Sir had used his knife to make what looked like hundreds of nicks on to the slave's chest. Bloody cuts were all over the slaves heaving chest. Eight needles were embedded across the slaves abdomen. Each needle was woven with dental floss making it look as if it was held within a corset of its own flesh. The slave was panting like an animal and yet its eyes remained focused on its master never once faltering as he walked back and forth before it.

I knelt primed his cigar lighted it and offered it to his hand. Without so much as a glance in my direction it was taken and I was shooed away with a kick from his boot. Master smoked while he walked locking more like a steam engine as it blew smoke from its stack then my Lord pondering his next action. He dropped to one knee; pulled a package of needles from the bag at his belt they were long thick looking needles. Sir grabbed a hold of one of the slave's nuts, pulling it down into the sack, holding it there tight within its purse of skin. Sir held out the needle in his hand, grabbed the nut harder telling the slave just by feel what he intended to do with that needle. 9-777 became animated begging Sir not to ruin his nuts. Sir didn't even look up, "SLAVE do I own you?"

9-777 responded, "SIR YES SIR!"

Hunter bellowed, "then they are MY NUTS!"

He drove the needle into the slave's testicle and the slave screamed shaking violently. Sir did not stop pressing the sharp needle until the sharpened point exited the other side of the slave's nut. He pulled another needle from its sterile jacket and drove it in that same nut and added a third before he lifted the second ball and repeated the process. 9-777's screams feel on deafened ears. Then Master stood, took a long draw on the cigar in his mouth, grabbed the slave's chin and forced it to look Sir in the eyes, "a slave owns nothing is nothing save by the Will of its Owner!" Sir was quoting one of the maxims we had drilled into us slaves by the handlers. Hunter tossed the slave's head back as if to say I am finished with you. Did an abrupt about face before side- stepping to its left side. Sir had been studying the ground when his head shot up and caught it watching its Pain God working within his cathedral.

Sir took a long draw on his cigar, stepped close to the slave, "want some of this too whore dog? Well, do you, pain pig?"

Mindlessly 9-777 nodded his head yes. Sir closed the short distance, sucking up snot from below his belly button, cocked back his head and spat. The goober landed on the slave's forehead and crawled down the ridge of his nose, down to the cheek before its tongue could coax the master's snot into its mouth with his tongue. The slave smiled weakly and Sir laughed. Hunter sucked on his black cigar, exhaled blowing the ashes away forcing the cigar to grow into a cherry white brilliance before he stroked the slaves sweating chest with the glowing ember. The slaves response was a deep inhale of air and a whispered, "thank you, Sir."

Sir's gloved hand slipped over the slave's lips as he leaned his weight into the slave's body. Sir's elbow rested in the crook of the slave's neck. His other hand brought his cigar to his lips. Master spoke to the slave, "you love me don't cha 9-777?"

The slave would have lowered his head if Sir had permitted that movement, "Sir with every breathe in my lungs, Sir."

The cigar was pulled from his lips. Sir exhaled smoke into 9-777s lungs clamping his hand over the boy's mouth and pinching the nostrils closed while the other hand traced a red trail across the slave's chest. Sir released his hand and touched the fiery tip of his glowing cigar to the left nipple. There Sir roasted the slave's nipple black. Sir tossed the cigar to the ground as if in disgust. Looked at me for a second with a pained expression on his face that was swept away as he laughed. Master found a Tens unit within hands reach and bumped up the tone. Sir backed off, snapped his finger and pointed to the ground. I ran to my place and dropped to my knees.

Master turned to jonathan, "front, pig!"

Sir released a torrent of piss before jonathan could place himself before him still he caught all that he was offered. Hand signals flew rapid fire telling those that served his body what to do, jonathan knelt at his rear and I at his front, together we drove ourselves into his body. I tackling his monster sized cock and jonathan diving between our Lords butt cheeks, Sir stood over us, legs spread arms crossed as he studied the slave hanging from his St Andrews cross.

He must have known JD was there cause I do not remember him turning to see the crowd watching this dance of the Demons. JD was called forward and ordered to lower the slave's arms by attaching them to the hook and hoist. Its legs were released as well in preparation for the next lusty scene that would unfold. Sir stood there slightly bowed forward as jonathan wormed his tongue deep into Sir's cleft and I worked my tongue over and down his growing cock shaft. Silently, Sir gave over to the rising pleasure in his body, just as his hand worked the butterfly knife spinning it in upon itself then out again to its full extension. He stepped beyond us, ignoring us and our probing tongues to find a different pleasure in the slave writhing slowly to his beat as the Tens unit continued their burning cycle on its cock.

"You are my greatest folly," Sir said to 9-777 whose head dropped to his chest. His silence spoke more clearly than any words. He knew just exactly what our Lord was speaking. Without looking over his shoulder master shouted, "bring me a sharps container."

JD brought a wooden bench and placed the container within arms reach then withdrew calling jonathan and I to him. JD sat on the outcropping pulled jonathan and I close to watch what was about to happen. The scene had drawn a crowd who stood around in silence watching everything unfold. Their silence showed a respect that could not be found in the outside dungeons. Outside in the world beyond our gates few understood the union that had built to this moment in time.

9-777 was hurting I could read the pain in his eyes but master chose to ignore it. Driving a point home helping the slave understand beyond any and all reason that he was in complete control. I was summoned to Sir's side. There I removed his chaps, folded them, bent to kiss his boots and withdrew leaving him naked save for his Sam Browne belt and shoulder piece, boots and his chromed cock ring.

Mind made up, my Lord stepped forward, removed a Tens unit and relocated the leads to the slave's pinned testicles. Sir looked up, "you will sing for me tonight!" He depressed a button on the small console a jolt of electricity shot from the unit directly into the needled nuts. The slave opened its mouth and screamed a god-awful sound that had to have come from the depths of hell. Its song was the terrible sound of a man suffering his Owners pleasure. 9-777s voice cracked ending abruptly. Sir's head turned to me, "jug, here, now!"

I ran for what he ordered, the jug of juice. He snatched it from my hand with an angry gesture; stepped closer to 9-777, "open your fucking mouth, cock sucker!"

His slave obeyed and Sir poured the mouth full, "swallow, cock sucker, swallow it slowly. There is more."

Sir's beast of burden consumed almost half of the bottle before our Lord lowered the bottle, took a long swig and passed it to me to cap. Sir ran his hands over the slave's chest, tapping each of the needles with his finger before moving downwards to another. He was enjoying the little starts and jumps the slave made as he surveyed his slave's pain field. Sir leaned forward and kissed the slaves chest, looking up at the slave while he kissed and licked the slaves bloody chest, "I love how you suffer for me, 9-777."

My Lord, signaled to JD who on command elevated the slave's arms and locked the mechanism before walking across the playing field to lean onto one of the rocks calling jonathan to him.

Sir dropped to his knees before his slave, reached between the manimals legs and began flipping and moving the needles buried in the slaves testicles laughing and watching as his pain pig danced for him. Slowly one needle at a time was withdrawn until he had four pulled free. The other two were moved in and out of the same hole making the slave squirm as Sir fucked its nuts like I knew he would fuck his ass when he was ready. This entire prelude lead up to that final moment when Sir's cock would feed on slave butt.

Master stood flipped open the knife and embedded it in the wood of the St Andrews cross before talking to 9-777, "now, lift and enwrap me with your legs slave."

9-777 pulled himself up, opened his legs pulling Sir within the vee of his legs. Meanwhile Sir was busy aligning his cock between the vee of the slave's butt cheeks and as 9-777 came down Sir's cock entered the slave's ass and they were united. Sir moved forward until he could rest the slave's back against the St Andrews cross. Held in this position master began the thrust and parry we all loved as he drove his cock deep into 9-777's innards before pulling out and repeating the process. I could tell these two were made for each other just by the way they fucked. It was like choreographed dancing the way 9-777 would lift his pelvis as Sir heaved forward going for the greatest depth. They were awesome.

The pain was driving 9-777 faster towards the brink than master wanted. The knife was pulled and I saw fear sweep across 9-777s face as he watched Sir lower the knife between them. Quickly the corset of dental floss was cut allowing 9-777 greater flexibility. Still Sir wanted it to hurt and flipped each impacted zone with a finger making 9-777 cry out. Each needle was withdrawn slowly making the slave feel them intensely. Those needles were dropped into the sharps container before others were withdrawn. Hunter worked slowly across the slave's chest forcing it to take more and more pain as he inflicted one minor hurt after another while fucking the slave's ass. He took his knife slipping his fingers down the blade using the hilt like a hammer and drummed on to the right nipple with all its imbedded needles just to feel 9-777 arch his back lifting his pelvis as it screamed. The scream started in pain but ended in pleasure.

Hunter was in control, he stopped heaving his cock in and out of the slave's guts. Found a Tens unit adjusting the strength of electricity that pounded into the slave's raw nerves within its cock forcing the slave to fuck itself. Forcing the slave to lift itself with its arms in hopes of escaping the pain that was slamming into its cock before it fell back upon Sir's cock buried deep within its ass. Each pounding blow to 9-777s cock forced its ass muscles to tighten around Sir's cock making his ride all the more pleasurable. Still Sir wasn't lollygagging around doing nothing. He was removing those needles from the slave's cock that were not attached to electricity, prolonging the pain and dragging out their climax. Each needle feeling like someone dragging their nails across a chalkboard as each needle was drug across raw and tender nerves within the slave's sensitive cock. Every needle that was withdrawn made the slave work and writhe on master's cock making Sir concentrate on not blowing his load too soon.

Hunter pulled the slave's face to his forcing him to mount his lips, swallow his tongue even as he rose and dropped onto master's cock. One Tens unit fell to the ground followed by another. Those needles were flipped, tapped and flicked by master's fingers exploiting the slave for all his pain, forcing it to give master more pleasure. Sir leaned forward placed his lips over the burnt left nipple biting it hard and came up with blood smeared all over his face and lips. 9-777s face was pulled close and they joined with another long deep kiss.

Thank God our society believed in the screening all for infectious diseases. Time and time again our fanatical sense of purity allowed us opportunities that those on the outside could never afford without fear of transmitting a hundred known diseases and strains. This scene would have not been permitted elsewhere nor appreciated for what it was merely a waltz between a Master and his slave.

Master's knife flashed in the light, descended between the two heaving bodies and I assume cut the sutures that held 9-777's cock head sewn shut. The knife was dropped to the ground. Sir pulled the suture from its cockhead exacting a low crying moan from his slave as the sutures released one quarter of the his foreskin than the other.

Sir signed to those of us who could read, "release his hands." JD was the first to respond and releasing the safety latch allowing the slave to drop his still bound hands around his Sir's neck even as master leaned in taking the slaves weight and control.

Hesitantly, I turned my head from the scene and found many handlers's had their cocks in hand fisting them in rhythm with our master. Some, the lucky few had their slaves bent over rocks fucking them in concert with our Lord, all joining in sharing the unified energy of this gathering, treasuring it for what it was, a communion between God and man.

Claw like fingers closed around 9-777's throat pulling his body deeper into masters heaving thighs. No one noticed but me when the slave started fighting Sir's hand that had encircled its neck and was cutting off the air to the slave's lungs. Hunter kept thrusting his hips as loud howling like a wild banshee came from Sir's open mouth. Sir's hand dropped from the slave's throat and 9-777's beastlike voice joined my Lord in a duet proclaiming their rising need for a unified climax. Others picked up the wild animalistic cry joining them as my Lord and 9-777 climaxed. Sharing the moment, sharing the energy, and bonding with their unified energies. Sir's legs buckled forcing him to fall forward catching himself by wedging the slaves back to the cross and leaning his weight into the slave. His breathing slowed 9-777 wiggled still impaled by Sir's masterful cock. That's when I noticed water dripping between their legs. Sir was leaving more than a deposit of cum in the slave's ass he was leaving a load of piss as well.

JD stepped forward to assist Sir with the weight of 9-777 and signed for us to join him. I was detailed to care for our Lord while JD and jonathan released 9-777 from his bindings.

I lead a glassy eyed Sir to the stone outcroppings wiped his brow and offered him the jug of juice to drink as he regained some control over his Dark Angel. That beast had to be sated by what it done to 9-777.

Once down, 9-777 limped to where I was tending our Lord. There it dropped between his knees, leaned forward and cleaned his ass juices off our Lord's cock with his mouth. When it rose from its duties, Hunter opened its mouth and filled it with the juice. Ordered it forward and slowly began to remove the eight needles still woven under its right nipple. While he worked handler's stopped by to pat Hunter on the back and to thank him for as they worded it, "one hell of a scene."

Hunter rested, his creature 9-777 between his legs resting and Sir chatting with a few of his well liked handlers. jonathan and I policed the area making certain all-stray needles found their way into the sharps container. Finding his knife, relocating his whips into the bag, cleaning the St Andrews cross for future users before returning to kneel before our Lord.

"JD, thanks for your help with 9-777. Take jonathan if you want company, but I think its time for Number One and I to return to the ship with 9-777. We need time to clean it up from tonight's activities and just might torture it some more," said a very tired sounding Hunter. While the slave at his feet groaned at the suggestion of yet more torture when back on the ship.

"Sir, "said JD, "may I have your permission to mark jonathan?"

"Explain what you want to do, JD," replied our Lord.

"I remember a rather twisted scene from my youth involving needles and hot wax. I think its time jonathan visits the reverse side of the coin so to speak, Sir."

Hunter rubbed his face as if to wash it free of spider webs. This told me he was tired, very tired and if I did not get him home fast he would be asleep on his feet.

Sir chuckled, "as long as jonathan is with you. You may do that scene but promise me. If my memory serves me right he whipped the wax off your cock with one of his nasty crops. You may repeat the scene if you promise to fuck him like there is no tomorrow. Once you have beaten his cock like he did yours it will be out of commission for a while. Use him accordingly, JD and have fun. Dismissed."

Hunter rose to his feet pulling me with him, "Come One lets get back to the ship, I have something planned for 9-777 and my Number One."

As we left the party everyone was getting their third or fourth wind. We stopped to drop off the bag of toys and to pick up another two liter of joy juice and was handed a tub of lube called butt butter. Like joy juice it was an all-natural product with aphrodisiac properties. Joy juice was a combination of infusions taken from tropical fruits and herbs that when combined made even the dead rise and walk again. Where as butt butter was rumored to have a super jolt of THC incorporated into a rich butterfat and as a lube there was nothing like it on the market, yet. Used on a slave's butt, no matter how tight before the application of the butt butter afterwards that butt would eat whole watermelons and beg mind you for more. Its side effect is that you had killer munchies and if you had a horribly mean master you would munch the night away on his cock or parts.

Three blind mice made their way back to the ship. Once home Sir ordered a tray of goodies sent down from the kitchen along with cold buttermilk and two rolls of saran wrap. Before he did any clean up he gave 9-777 a tender massage with the cold buttermilk and wrapped it in saran wrap and added duct tape. Master and I left it laying on the floor while we showered and ran topside to indulge ourselves with a long soak in the hot tub. Together we mellowed out, allowing the foaming waters to release any tension.

When we returned to the stateroom, 9-777 was released and ordered into the shower as we nibbled on the goodies from the kitchen. We heard the water running then heard 9-777 enter the shower. No sooner than he had entered than we heard a god-awful shriek and he came running out as if his chest was on fire. Master was giggling like a bad child caught in some evil deed, "what's wrong 9-777?"

9-777 was moving around the room briskly all the while patting on his chest and dripping water as he moved. "God Sir, my chest is on fire! It feels like each cut has been rubbed with acid, Sir!"

He ordered me to fetch a wet towel and rub 9-777 until it was clean from tonight's accumulated activities. Even with only a little moisture on the towel it shrieked and ran around the room fanning his chest. Sir could not stop laughing as he watched 9-777s attempts to cool his chest.

Sir looked perplexed, shrugged his shoulders, "you always said I was evil, tonight I proved it. You are getting a taste of a torture called death by a thousand cuts. Except there will be no death from this just good clean suffering, each time you bathe you will reactivate the yeast culture in the cuts. Its that culture that is making your chest catch on fire!"

"One make certain its clean of all debris, put it in its bedtime shackles" Sir said to me.

I went about my assigned task cleaning off the dried blood until Sir was satisfied. We, 9-777 and I were allowed to strip if we had clothes on and joined him at his feet. He fed us from the platter making certain we both had our fill before ordering us to bed. Either the sun was setting or rising when I looked out the porthole before I dropped the drapes. Together we slept very well that night I at his front held in place by his arms and 9-777 at his back locked to the bed by steel shackles. We slept until late afternoon only to rise when he needed to piss or when he rolled over and took what was rightfully his. I was awakened by the sound of buzzing bee's huge ones by the way it sounded or a whole hive in attack mode. The buzzing seemed to come from everywhere, grew louder until I realized what it was a seaplane. Damn, I thought to myself, this isn't fair. I should be going with my Lord to New York not 9-777. The motor died and I snuggled back into his arms hoping it was all a dream.

I had just dozed off again when a knock came to our stateroom door. Hunter ignored it as he was still snoring lightly in my ear so I did too. The knock repeated itself then stopped. Loud too loud booming as a fist slammed into the door then stopped before being repeated the second time rattling the doorframe and us lying in bed. Hunter rolled over, wiped his eyes and yelled, "this better be FUCKING important," and pushed me out of bed as he waved his arm in the doors general direction!

Bleary eyed, naked and still half asleep I opened the door and a pilot wearing breeches and boots stepped into the room, "begging your pardon Master Hunter," he said overly loud to my ears. I had shut the door, offered the gentleman a seat and returned to where my master lay in bed besides 9-777.

Hunter rose up to one elbow, "what's the meaning of this ruckus?"

"Sir forgive me but Lady Beatrice sent me a head of the storm. She needs you as soon as possible. Can you come, Sir? Now, Sir?"

Sir had risen while the pilot spoke walked into the bathroom-splashed water on his face before coming into the room, "how bad is our Lady?" He didn't wait for him to answer as he walked over to the pilot, "come with me, we all need some breakfast." He took the pilot by his elbow and escorted him down to the galley returning with his cup of coffee. No sooner than he had crossed the threshold did he start barking orders, "One release 9-777, 9-777 go find jonathan and JD. Number One find my pre packed suitcase and check it for all my necessaries." His coffee downed, he stepped into the bathroom while I checked and added items he would need to his luggage we finished about the same time. I was sent to the galley to fetch breakfast for three and enough coffee for a small army.

Arriving first, jonathan was ordered to dress him while I took the luggage up to the deck and saw to the pilots needs. JD had arrived when I returned and was sitting taking notes while he sucked down coffee I assisted jonathan with the dressing of our Sir. Heavy leathers meant for New York weather, light silk tee shirt another shirt he would carry with him along with his motorcycle jacket and his ever present knee high boots with gold Founders spurs. I added gloves to his jacket, filled his miniature humidor, the travel kit, for his survival during flight. We dressed him as he walked around the room leaving final orders for all on the cruise, ignoring those that were attempting to dress him. He would stop long enough that we could get his legs into the pants and into his boots but we had to follow along besides him, pulling up zippers, buttoning flies, adjusting his cock and balls all the while ignoring us as he went about his last minute details that he needed to finalize before departure.

Once dressed, Hunter tackled the tray of sticky buns, grabbed another cup of coffee, and began pacing the room like a caged lion. "Eat and drink as you need boys."

"As you know Lady Beatrice has been involved in a major car accident. I must go to Castle Enterprises; she has sent me her pilot and plane, which means she has reason to fear my arrival on any other plane. Do not cancel the other plane that is to arrive here tomorrow. Let it come and delay it here for as long as you can. Hold a mock search for me on some island or something."

"Don't worry Number One, I am use to court intrigue and I am very good at confusing the elders; especially, those that would prefer that I did not come to power," he turned to 9-777, "go shower, clean out your ass and get ready you will attend me on this journey."

In his haste to obey 9-777 forgot what the water would do to his chest. Its shriek as the water hit his cuts and reactivated the yeast in his cuts made my Lord smile like a Cheshire cat then laugh, "God how I do love that sound!" His hand closed around his hardening cock as he laughed. "I really must be evil," he winked, "just like the Founder's think I am. They will eat crow before the Lady and I are finished with them!"

"I am taking 9-777 with me cause he will suit my needs and will add to the Founders confusion. One, pack one of my big bags with its gear, add another pair of my boots to its bag, the bondage shorts, pants, one of my plugs and other gear you think I may need. Our size and close body structure can confuse the hell out of the Founders."

Orders issued as he walked across the room to a cabinet Sir stopped, turned as 9-777 stepped out of the bathroom drying itself, "Stop what you are doing 9-777, turn around slowly." A smile crawled across his face and he began nodding his head slowly. He laughed and began issuing more orders to jonathan, "go get the slave clippers, razor, water basin and some of the bronzing cream, its time to pull the wool over their eyes." Jonathan never even blinked at the orders only laughed at what Sir was about to do and ran out of the room to fetch the needed items.

9-777 stepped towards Sir, "JD would you do the honors of getting that piece of meat dressed. Plug its ass with a chrome egg, lock its cock down and Number One dress it in my leathers and boots."

Jonathan entered followed by Lady Katherine she was up and had seen the plane. Sir stripped off his silk shirt, sat down and ordered jonathan to shave off his hair. The slave all but danced as he set about his task, giggling, "Sir, you are evil," then he laughed, "this one had wondered for years why you have groomed that one. Fuck, Sir, you are just too deviously evil!"

The electric clippers buzzed his hair down to a short crop and the old fashion razor trimmed off all the rest until his head was bald and shocking white. A bronzing agent was rubbed into his scalp until the lines were blended and his head looked as if it was all one color a rich warm bronze of healthy sun tanned skin. Standing Sir walked over to 9-777, "do you think we will pass as twins? Should I shave my eyebrows and goatee as well?"

JD and Lady Katherine agreed and his eyebrows and goatee joined the hair on the floor. A little more touch of bronzer and Sir could easily pass as 9-777. The ruse would keep them confused for hours if they could pull this off, what would the Founder's think? My only question that I kept to myself was why was this necessary? What was he going into that he needed a double?

While I redressed my Lord, 9-777s head was slipped into one of Sir's heavier hoods, its hands locked behind thick gloves and it along with its luggage was taken up to the deck to be loaded onto the waiting plane.

Sir gave us our final orders, "JD, Eric will be running Buena Vista while I am away, they will look to you and jonathan for guidance. Number One you will be taking care of the main house and all of you will be along with the handlers getting the place back up on its feet and in running order. We have twelve weeks before the October Manor run where all our Shield Mates join us in celebration. This year everyone will be there plan for about 20,000 less or more will show once they realize I am the Deus of Castle Enterprises. Be prepared, as Founders will be joining the party and make certain Castle sends in their medical records for all attendees. Dismissed, see you in two weeks."

They filed out while Hunter held me back. He pulled me into his arms and my arms closed around him. My head I placed on his heart and his neck curled over my head. We held each other then he pulled us apart, looked down took my chin and kissed me long, hard then tenderly nibbling my lips with his.

"When next I go to the Castle you will be at my side where you belong. You serve only the Deus no one else. I cannot take the very best to that hellhole in New York. I got to clean up a serious mess as our society is at stake," he kissed me again. "Come walk me up to the gang plank," his smile carried me to the deck.

To my surprise and his whole ship seemed somewhat awake. We stepped out on the deck and were greeted by a huge roar of cheers that stopped abruptly until they realized that it was a bald Master Hunter and their applause and shouts were huge. He held up his arms calling them to silence, "When I return to Buena Vista, I will be the Deus of Castle Enterprises!" Their applause drowned out the air horns of the ships. Again he held up his arms, "You are the BEST of the rest! Party hardy cause when I get your ass's home I plan to work your nuts off!" Sir laughed, turned and gave me another big kiss, stepped forwards out of my arms to jonathan and held up his arms.

He took jonathan in his arms, "This Number One is my right hand man while at Buena Vista, obey him as if he were me. Obey JD, Eric Wilson as well, they will not lead you astray, but forward to more profits." They drowned out the air horns on the ships as he bent down forced a long kiss on jonathan. He stepped forward to the gangplank, grabbed JD, gave him a kiss, saw mikey and pulled them both in his arms for a quick hug and kiss. Then he stepped over the side of the ship down the ladder to the seaplane, climbed aboard waving as the door closed. Everyone's shouts nearly drowned out the coughing sputtering engine. We stayed on deck until the plane was a tiny dot in the sky then dispersed.

A dull headache like gloom settled over our ships or so it seemed to me. Once the crowds had dispersed JD pulled us back down into Hunters cabin and we went over his notes and made some of our own. We decided after the last prize was found that we would out Master Hunter. Tell the troops who had paid for their luxury vacation and why. Perhaps with that knowledge under their hats they will like us return to Buena Vista and work their fingers to the bone to get her up and running before Sir returns home.

All left the stateroom save for jonathan and I. We set about cleaning it up, tidying the bathroom, making the bed, relocating items Sir had taken from the closet in his rush to get packed. Jonathan seemed to know where my mind was and worked along side me sharing the duties making things go faster. If it hadn't been for jonathan I would have slipped into a dark depression but that man saved me. Once the room was complete, he took me upstairs, got us drinks and food from the kitchen and we took it into a quiet corner were we would not be disturbed. JD came to check on me while we sat in the shadows of the largest mast and not much later mikey joined us as well. We were all hurting in our own way the sudden departure of our Lord.

Jonathan sipped his drink and nibbled at some fruit, "what none of you realize is that Hunter took the best possible slave with him this time. 9-777 was a Karate instructor before he came to us, he will watch our master's back better than any of us. Plus he is a dead ringer for Hunter's twin. Castle Enterprises is like being bloody chum tossed into a shark pit; the old Founder's will do their damnedest to bully their way if given any leeway. Hunter is about to enter the pit and show them a new sheriff is in town. He has more enemies than he does friends at present, but that is about to change. London, England's manor house is going to have its doors ripped open if he hasn't done that already. They have failed to send in any medical records for a quarter and the reports from there are even stranger. Once London Manor house falls the German Manor house will find itself in a quagmire of shit."

JD spoke up, "do you think it wise that we tell these people everything, Sir?"

"Not everything we slaves know, we keep our secrets close to home. But we tell them that,"

"Oh, there you are?" Lady Katherine was standing above us, "power pow-wow, should I leave you all alone?"

She went on to state her business, "I was wondering since Hunter has departed our company if I could move into his suite for the balance of the trip. My quarters are a little tight?"

JD didn't even blink and eye, "Lady Katherine, our Sir left orders that tells us to keep the suite his until he returns to it. Is there anything else we can do for you, Lady?"

Her lip dropped like a little child and she pouted. So uncharacteristic for the strong arming boss in the caverns who made her handlers salute her at every chance she could and would stomp a slave to death if it farted in her direction. Esssh! She would not look the same to me after this cruise. Here she wore flowing gowns and wispy things something totally opposite what she would wear in our caverns, her military issue black jumpsuit and combat boots.

Ever missed someone so badly that you felt like you were not whole or complete until they were with you again, that's how I felt with my Lord Hunter gone. Oh, I went about my business, running errands for people, helping the entertainment committee set up for the dinner while the handlers were off on their treasure hunt. This treasure hunt would require them to use all their limited brains to find the keys that were literally buried right beneath their noses. If any had asked all I could do was point at the coat of arms hanging from the central mast of our ship, the Buena Vista coat of arms. There on that shield held all the answers to his questions. No one had to run to the island to find the key as it was hanging right before there faces the whole trip. Luckily he knew his crew better than I as all had gone ashore to seek out the green valley carved by an Iron Fist and Lightening. All very viewable on the manor shield that held a green chevron above an iron gloved hand clutching lightening bolts. They had the whole day to search the island, dinner tonight and part of tomorrow cause we were to arrive in the evening back at home port and leave homeward bound on the next day.

No treasure was found today and the party on shore was kind of low key both due to Hunter's absence and the fact that everyone there was bone weary. During dinner JD called their attention to him. We had discussed how would be the best way to bring the trip to their attention without blowing their minds to badly. JD took the direct path. Their reaction was both shock and outrage. As JD spoke to them about the plans he and Hunter had laid out before his departure I withdrew into my mind reviewing a story jonathan had told me earlier today.

Hunter and jonathan were out west in New Mexico on a motorcycle run when an ancient Native American grandfather stopped Hunter on a street in Flagstaff. I, jonathan stated, still haven't figured out how the old man knew we would be there. As we had only changed our plans while in route, Hunter was driving and I was riding on the sissy seat. We were standing in a line waiting to register other leather men and women stood around us, we basically looked like clones all of us were dressed somewhat alike. The old Indian walked down the line of people leaning heavily on his walking stick and stopped before Hunter and I. He studied Hunter's eyes and even Hunter bowed his head in acknowledgement of the oldster's presence. Watching the grandfather carefully I saw him reach into a pocket pull something out and pass it to Hunter. Hunter opened his hand palm up there lying on his open palm was a black stone. I think it was an apache tear at least it was black and shaped like a huge teardrop.

Hunter stepped out of the line, indicating with his hand for the elder to move we followed him to a beat up rusty old truck and he told Hunter to bring his bike. We followed him down a dusty road until the truck stopped before an old adobe house. We entered the darkened interior of the house and found a young well-muscled man lying on the floor on a grass mat. Sir walked over to the man, dropped down to the floor and sat there talking quietly while I was sent to fetch a beautifully beaded bag within our saddlebags on the cycle.

I watched as Sir opened the beaded bag and pulled out a black leather cape that he pulled around his shoulders, on his head he placed a handsome beaded skullcap and then he pulled out a smaller bag. Using his spit he wet powder he sprinkled into his palm this he applied to the forehead of the man on the floor. When we entered the man on the floor was agitated fitfu and coughing up blood but once the paint was applied to his forehead he calmed and his leg spasms ceased. Another color was mixed and placed on the dying man's face. As Hunter did this he began a low keening that made my body hairs stand on edge. The man on the mat stopped struggling to breath as Hunter's song grew in strength as if he was drawing the pain out of the dying man's body. Hunter seemed to curl in over himself as he sucked the pain out of the dying man's body and into himself, he would cough hard and spit something into a gourd the old man had placed beside him. As Hunter sung people started arriving. It was really weird that they arrived wearing full headdresses and leather finery, each arriving guest would drop to one knee, touch the man on the mat and withdraw allowing another to approach. I thought it odd that they kept quiet and the old man spoke only to me even as his house filled with uninvited guests watching the man and Hunter in the center of the room.

The room seemed so full of people as the song changed in tempo and accelerated. A drum sounding much like a heart beat sounded in the room. Shrill reed pipes joined the drumming followed by low singing. The sun was well past its zenith while the old man and I sat watching Hunter as he worked on the young man on the mat. The room grew dark, but Hunter's face seemed to glow as if illuminated by a candle or fire light but there was no fire and the boy on the floor seemed to glow as well. The music seemed to grow in intensity giving life to the lifeless body on the mat. The drum beat grew louder making the body dance and vibrate on the floor until the man rose from the floor and stood like a puppet held by strings on his two legs the old man walked to where the man stood. They talked while the music played then the music changed. A huge toothy smile crossed the man's face as the drums called him back to his mat. Lying there Hunter stooping over him we could watch the pain that the man had been enduring rise from his body like stream then Hunter began to chant and sing with the drums. The song Hunter was singing was one I had heard often when we were camping in the woods. He always sung in at dawn and sunset as he offered a pipe to the four winds. Hunter referred to it as his Soul song, his prayer to the creator.

The song faltered, Hunter bent forward scooping the body of the young warrior into his bear like arms drawing him into his chest. There he held the boy, like a mother would cradle a baby and changed the song. The man's body was like watching a flickering candle filled with radiance of life slowly dying from lack of oxygen as Sir held him within his arms. Slowly the radiance faded, Hunter's eyes closed and his life bright color changed as he too faded. It was as if Hunter seemed to leave the room carrying the man in his arms as a lover would across the threshold. Abruptly the song stopped, the room grew cold and silent as a tomb.

There had been people, native Americans gathered all around the room while the music played once it stopped and I looked up they like the music were gone. I rubbed my eyes thinking I had been asleep, but there wasn't any one present except for Hunter holding that man and even he was not moving. No one but grandfather was present with me in the room. It was as if all had been drawn to the music and to share the moment of the young warriors parting. I would have freaked out if the old man had not taken my arm and ushered me towards a table. He placed a cracked bowl of something hot before me and ordered me to eat it was some kind of soup. He sat beside me drinking from an old gourd looked up and told me that I had witnessed something few white eyes would believe. Those that had come to see the boy were his dead ancestors. Hunter had summoned them with the song to assist with the transfer.

The room turned deathly cold; we could see our breaths in the air as we exhaled as if we were in the dead of winter. However I knew just outside the temperature was well over 90 degrees this room was as cold as any meat locker.

I had climbed to my feet and was about to check on Hunter when the old man stopped me. Hunter's body looked pale white even when the old man lighted a match and stuck it to a candle on the table. He whispered, "leave alone the Death Dancer, he walks where no man has ever set foot, leave him, he comes." Together the old man and I waited for hours as we watched the sun slowly setting just outside a window. Just before the last ray of sun had left the sky Hunter drew a huge breath of air and coughed hard.

Running to his side, the old man and I lifted the lifeless husk out of Hunter's arms before helping Master to his feet. Wobbly he walked to the table and I had to spoon feed him the soup as his hands were shaking so badly. The old man was busy elsewhere. By hand gestures Hunter indicated that I should remove the buffalo skin robe. Once that was off him his color began to return rapidly and his shaking subsided. When he had finished his soup, I helped him up and we stepped out into the warm night air and there he drew in the warmth casting the cold from him.

Once warm Hunter and I stepped back inside the adobe house. There the old man was dressing his son in ancient beaded leathers that the old one had hoped would contain his body never his son. The old man did not acknowledge our presence so we returned to the cycle. Hunter kicked it to life and let it idle a moment probably hoping the old man would set out and see him off. Hunter's head jolted up right as if to sniff the air, he turned to me, "the old man has willed his own death, tonight it comes." I had goose bumps flying all over my body and growing on top of others as Hunter turned to face the adobe house muttered something in some strange language, throttled the cycle, kicked it into gear and we drove off returning to Flagstaff.

I thought once we were back at the run all this weird shit would have been done and finished but I was wrong. We arrived late for registration only to find out that someone fitting our description had signed us in, gotten the run packets and rented us a motel room. All was paid in full for our stay. Friends showed us our motel rooms, passing the keys to us and when we entered we found the run packet and an apache tear on the bed.

I accepted jonathan's recounted tale easily. Too often I had seen that man do some weird things. Still that tale of jonathans fit along with other such stories about our Owner. He was weird but he was ours.

JD not to be out done by jonathan coughed and said, "maybe you, Sir, can shed some light on what I saw when I attended Sir on the Hawaii trip. I thought my eyes were playing tricks on me but when I saw the evidence I could not believe my eyes."

"Hunter had hired a local tour guide to take us on a car tour Sir's main interest was the volcano fields. The tour guide was walking ahead while Hunter was taking his time enjoying the view of the dark sinister looking crusty earth. Hunter had veered off the path the guide had taken. I was standing with the guide up closer to the edge of the volcano when I looked back and saw it happen. Sir was walking along jumping from one lump of stone to the next when all of a sudden where he stepped gave away. I must have screamed out cause the guide turned, saw what was happening and we vee lined towards where Hunter had fallen. We both knew he would have been cut to shreds if he had fallen into a ravine or worse.

We rushed to the place we saw Hunter drop and found him surrounded on a small black island that was slowly loosing ground as lava moved around him on both sides cutting him off from any quick access to less heated ground. I was panicking, the tour guide was no longer at my side and I simply did not know what to do for him.

Hunter waved at me motioning me for silence; it was as if he was not upset. You would have thought he was standing in the middle of a cold river instead of hot flesh eating hot lava! The tour guide joined me and we yelled our fool heads off trying to get his attention, but he was holding his hands out from his sides, thumb to forefinger like I had seen on one of his Buddha statues.

Then the oddest thing happened, hot air escaped on the shore opposite where my Master stood, Hunter looked to it and began talking. The steam rose to form a pillar of hot fetid air oddly shaping itself like that of a female standing on the opposite shore. Sir extended his hand as if reaching for something, stepped off the island right into the hot lava flow and I screamed.

He walked across the lava flow, as it was nothing more than sand on a beach. One step, two, his boots burst into flame and he did not seem to notice. I however had gone beyond panic and was trying to figure out if we should call a doctor or a pastor for his last rights. I knew his feet were being burned beyond his ankles and I knew he would never walk again.

The tour guide all but carried me down the hillside to get to the other side of the lava flow. I ran to Hunter's side while the tour guide called for help. When I found Hunter he was walking down the side of the mountain, oddly he walked right past me as if he did not see me. I followed him at a respectful distance just in case he fell. This way I followed him down to the parking lot to where the tour guide was standing next to a paramedic team.

Hunter was in some kind of a trance. The paramedics said he was in shock. They cut off his boots and found to their shock that he had his feet intact and no burns. None! Not even any cuts from walking on the sharp lava glass! They applied water to the soles of his feet this and this alone made Hunter snap out of his trance. He looked around and asked where was the Lady?

Driving back to our guest quarters Sir spoke about the Lady. All he could say is that she was very beautiful with long flowing hair and that she called herself, Palau.

Chapter 5

Hero-worship is strongest where there is least regard for human freedom.
Herbert Spencer

The flight home was intensely boring as I was assigned to a seat in the back of the plane along with the other slaves. It took two long days to arrive home in our familiar turf. All of us as one groaned when we arrived at Buena Vista found bunks set up for us and dropped like the dead. Most of us slept two days without so much as stirring; at least, I know I did.

All but a few returned to Buena Vista to help get it back upon its feet and in full tilt running order. Eric Wilson was in charge at first getting everyone reacquainted with the changes, new corridors, reassigned new living quarters and handed out maps so we could find all our old haunts. God had they done a masterful transformation to our underground.

JD sent out buses to return to us our manimals, mules mostly that had been taken to other farms while ours was undergoing renovations. The hive began to swarm with renewed life, as everyone got busy getting their housing quarters rejuvenated and filled with their personal belongings. Mountains of cargo had arrived from Castle to help with the renovations, these the mules would be moving into the tunnels once they returned.

I worked on getting the pigpen of a house back into master's concept of pristine. Those that had lived within the house while we were gone had made one exceptional mess after another even the slaves who cooked for them could not keep up with their needs or so I found out from the chef that had replaced mike. Lets just say the house looked like a wild weekend at a frat house, turned upside down and scattered to the far corners of the wind. It was a pigsty!

Sir called us when he had chance usually late each night. The distance seemed to shrink when we spoke after everyone had had his say during a conference call. I so wanted to tell him that everyone had returned but was sworn to secrecy. I just about bust a gut holding back on the secret project that everyone including the guilds was working on after all the assigned tasks for the day were completed. It was to be our gift to Our Lord something that would give back a touch of what he had done for us.

All that joined him on the cruise in the South Seas had left here as loners but returned as a cohesive team. The cruise had done more for us as a group than any other planned event he had held for us. It changed everyone's out look on their world and made them more focused. They worked harder than I had ever seen them in getting things laid out according to the plan and on their gift to him. Time literally flew past and before we knew it he was home. He was supposed to have been away only two weeks but our Lord was apart from us for more than a month. Thankfully it gave us enough time to complete the project to our level of perfection.

JD, jonathan and I met him at the Washington D.C. airport. We had been given clearance to drive a huge black and silver Humvee limo out on the tarmac to meet his plane. Actually JD met him while two slaves wearing brand new livery waited by the Hummer. It was a brisk fall day, first of October and we felt as hot as we had to have looked. Two slaves dressed in the uniforms we had designed that night many months ago. Black leather bondage pants, waist jackets, Dehner boots, black gloves and two chauffer hats cocked rakishly low on our heads with a dress blue uniform shirt under the jacket. We both stood hands locked behind our backs, eyes locked forward watching the plane as it taxied up to our limo.

JD waited until the door opened to extend his hand out to Hunter welcoming him home. Damn he looked good standing there, so good my cock tried to harden making me wince as he had left me in chastity when he departed that day. I wanted to throw myself into his arms instead I stood my ground making him come to me. 9-777 stepped off behind Sir, uncovered, unfettered and yet it walked with a new certainty that spoke volumes. 9-777 seemed to be tense, alert, watching in all places as he followed his owner and JD to the limo.

I held the door open while jonathan ran for the luggage, "Welcome home my Lord."

He grinned his toothy grin, removed his mirrored sunglasses, put his hand to my chin and kissed me lightly, "damn you two look good enough to eat." He climbed into the limo and I shut the door before running to assist jonathan with the luggage. I was about to climb into the drivers seat when the window flew down, "slave get your ass back here were you belong. 7 up front co pilots seat, jonathan can you handle this barge?"

"Sir, I can drive anything with wheels, Sir," jonathan replied with a huge toothy grin. I heard, as did everyone else in the vehicle as jonathan slipped into the seat a loud moan escape his lips.

"Something wrong with you jonathan, should I have 7 drive?"

Jonathan laughed, "Sir Eric got a little to heavy handed last night, Sir. I am fine, Sir."

I climbed in the back seat with my Lord and Master. At first I was confused with where I should go but he directed my path, pulling me between his handsome thighs settling his boots around me and tenderly pulling my face towards his, "damn I have missed your ass Number One among other things." He raped my mouth and I his. When he released me the Hummer had started and drove into traffic that surrounded the D.C. airport.

He flipped me around allowing me to rest my head where I so loved into his crotch before I spoke, "Sir?"

"Yes, One what is it?"

"JD would you care to explain." JD looked at me with a puzzled look on his face.

"Ah, right. Sir, mikey has gone AWOL. We just found out where he is would you mind if we go fetch him home,"asked JD of our Lord.

"What do you mean he went AWOL? Explain yourself!" Hunter leaned forward trying to read JD's face.

JD, looked at the floor, "Sir, its not as bad as it seems. While you were gone Eric and the doctors started the implants, all of us here including mikey has a microchip implant. We were the first. We know just exactly where he is, Sir. May we go get him?"

"You fucking better go get your brother!" Hunter exclaimed. "How in the fuck did he get off the mountain and why? Would someone tell me?"

JD had pulled a black box from a duffle bag handed it up front ordered the plug inserted into the cigarette lighter and it turned on. We heard in the back a slight pinging noise that could be only mikey's chip radiating along the green board. I had the pleasure of watching the tracking device work when we were testing the tracking board.

I looked up to my Lord, "Sir its all my fault, mikey and I were hanging back in one of the shops at the airport after we arrived from Hawaii when he saw this man walking down the concourse. The man either had a summer sausage stuffed down the left inside of his leg or he was a porno star. Well you can imagine mike's reaction seeing that piece of meat. The man turned into the men's restroom and mike followed he came out a few minutes later with a piece of paper and a smile. Mike confessed it was real and that the man would marry anyone that could take it all. You know, Sir, mike's tastes better than any of us. He had to find out if he could take it all."

"Who is this man, what does he do, and how did mike get off base, will someone answer me?" Hunter was demanding answers.

JD spoke up, "Sir, all I could find out is that he owns a restaurant called the Crazy Pig down in old town. We had a shipment outbound all I can guess is that mike hitched a ride."

JD turned to watch the screen in the front seat, "turn right, ah that must be the place, 'Le Restaurant de Cochon Bizarre'."

Jonathan stopped the limo before the vacant looking resturant, "JD you and 7 go find mikey and drag him out here to explain himself." Sir ordered while the turned his attention elsewhere.

"Damn boys you two look really good in those uniforms. How do they feel?"

Jonathan was the first to speak, "Sir they feel awesome even with the extra additions we added to them."

"Ohhh?"

I laughed, "Sir we have missed you badly. When we suited up we installed into each of us one of your special butt plugs. We are ready to rock and roll at your command."

Sir only laughed then pulled me up for another kiss, "both of you are sluts! God, I am now a pig farmer! Esssh!"

We had been making out in the back of the limo when Sir looked down at his watch and exclaimed, "Shit, what in the fuck are those men doing in there? What the fuck is taking them so damn long? jonathan, go find them and get their asses out here I am tired and want to get home. I have been away from home to damn long!" Hunter showing a touch more exhaustion than we had anticipated.

I thought I would draw his attention more to me, turned my head and began nibbling around his cock.

"Boy, what the fuck are you doing down there?" Hunter's hand pulled me from his rising mound.

"Sir, I am hungry, starving Sir. Haven't had a decent meal since you left, Sir!" He laughed and opened my jacket and shirt to get at a nipple.

"Hungry huh? You little shit, you are up to something." His fingers tightened around my nipple making me squirm then his fingers tighten even more, "confess, slave, what are you all up to?"

The pressure he was applying to my nipple was about to make me break and tell him all that was planned, but I was saved by JD who jerked the door open fast. "Sir, we need your help, 7 is down and mikey is in trouble!"

Sir shot out of the car like an avenging angel making a beeline for the front door and I following him. He ran up the steps two at a time, I at his side. JD was running before him, together they burst through the front door into a central foyer. JD directed his path by running before him, up a flight of steps turning through a small door. He burst into the darkened room, the lights flipped on and we of his immediate family screamed, "Surprise!"

It took him a minute to realize that mike was not in trouble. He looked around the room as if to find someone to target for his anger as his breathing calmed, "What did you say, boys?"

Five voices shouted, "SurrrrPRIZE!"

Hunter turned to the door where the fifth voice screamed. A stately Mae West looking Madame stood blocking the door in full drag. She was awesome looking in an emerald green floor length sparkling evening gown with henna red hair layered up on her head like a beehive or volcano about to blow. She entered the room in a voluminous cloud of perfume and make up talking in a southern draw, "Mmmm, Leather men. My my my am I a lucky girl tonight!" She walked up to Master Hunter put her arm around his waist, tippy toed up and gave him a big kiss on his right cheek then purred, "they call me Dixie Tricks but tonight big boy you can call me Dixie. I am your hostess for the evening."

She escorted Hunter to a big wingback chair gently pushed him into the seat before she turned an swept the room with her eyes and hands, "are all these men yours Master Hunter?"

He coughed stifling his laughter at the comical face she was making, "Yes Madame they are, but I seem to have misplaced one. A blonde haired boy with blue eyes would you know where he is Madame?"

Dixie put one hand on her hip and the other one she waved around with a limp wrist, "I can be butch when I want too." Her left limp wrist straightened and she walked around like a cowboy grabbing her crotch, "but it hurts my wrist to do that. Still I can toss a mean flogger when I want, boys, so mind your pee and cues cause Dixie knows all the tricks!"

She politely blew him off as she walked around the room opening curtains that gave us a view down on the dining room floor, "you are in the only private dining room so make yourselves at home, gentlemen." She moved to a antique burled desk opened it to show us the bar, "help your selves to a drinky-poo or two." Then she swirled her way towards the door took a hold of the doorjamb and thrust her hips into it, "our guest chef has prepared you boys a masterful dinner. I will be back in a few with ice and mixings for your drinks." Quietly she shut the door and we roared.

Hunter looked at us," what is the meaning of this? One explain, now!"

"Sir, we have waited a month to celebrate with our Master and Our Deus. This is only a private celebration with our Lord. We knew as soon as you got home you would be under attack from everyone wanting something and we just wanted our time, that's all, Sir?"

The door opened quietly in stepped Dixie with a humidor and a bucket of ice,

"I was told to bring you cigars and you need ice for your drinks. Anything else I can get for you gentlemen?"

Hunter looked to 7, "go with her to the wine cellar pick out a bottle of bubbly for us and check on dinner I am starving, better yet get us some appetizers."

JD was preparing drinks for jonathan and Sir. Master indicated that we should get comfortable, he could see that we were sweating like two stuffed pigs. He took his drink and ordered us to strip to our boots. Gladly we obeyed.

Master was seated in the wing back chair, a small hearth warmed the room at his side, I was on his left side kneeling, jonathan was comfortably seated at his right and JD was seated in a chair near the linen covered dining table. Sir had been telling us about the excitement he and 7 had created once it was revealed.

Hunter was saying, "I arrived with all my luggage, slave and all were taken to Buena Vista quarters a huge suite you all will see eventually one day on the 11 floor. Our people meet us, took the luggage and my slave to the suite. Our people did a customary bug sweep while I went to check on Lady Beatrice. She's over the worse of the accident. When she sent for me she had been put on methadone for pain control and she was unable to run the business. Her slaves could only do so much and the man-eater's (other Founder's) were already waiting for her to die. Some would have killed her if they could have gained access to her quarters. We did find that someone was slowly poisoning her that could have been why the accident occurred in the first place. Thank the Gods she had chosen to drive her Bentley instead of a smaller car. What we could piece together is either she wasn't paying attention to the road or it happened so fast that she was out of control as two semi trucks wedged her vehicle driving it into a bridge support column.

They had to cut her out of the vehicle and when they got her out she had broken her right leg, fractured T 11 and 12, broken ribs 8 and 9, which made the breastbone, shatter. Poor girl was in agony until they put her on methadone."

Jonathan spoke up, "Sir, they know me well there. Should I return to assist Lady Beatrice?"

"No need, jonathan." Sir smiled, "your job and loyalties are where they belong on Buena Vista. I know how you hated being at Castle. Besides, Lady Beatrice will be arriving later tonight via plane, picked up by one of our ambulances and taken to our hospital. Here she can recuperate, and I can have her slaves help me handle the paperwork of Castle Enterprises until I have a team trained. This way, she is safe, well cared for and we have a feather in our cap."

A quiet knock came to our door, I rose to open the door. With a flourish of many years on a runway Dixie entered carrying a covered tray with 7 following her carrying ice bucket of chilled champagne and tulip glasses. Dixie set her tray down and began putting out plates of appetizers then turned to our master.

"Master Hunter, the maitre'd has informed me that you are an old patron. He promises that he will see to it that you are not disturbed if you can guarantee that you and your naked, oh my, men do not get too noisy in here. Or as he put it, 'no screaming, fuck me, fuck me Jesus!' and I can guarantee a peaceful evening. Did you really scream fuck me, fuck me Jesus, Sir?"

Sir blushed bright red, choked on a cheese laced something, "Dixie its why I haven't been back here in about five years. I did not scream the fuck me routine it was one of your so-called straight waiters who became really confused when he waited on a friend and I up here. He wanted to be part of our discussion and became our dessert."

"Well, you do not have to worry about any more squealing straights. All of us here are queers and very happy to help a man. Besides with all the Congressmen and Senators that come here you would not believe what goes on in the basement bathroom. Believe you me if it is lobbying than I am a fairy god mother!" She closed the door quietly and departed.

We were feeding and being fed appetizers when I heard a pop turned and saw 7 standing quietly in the corner serving the champagne. JD was talking to our Lord with jonathan interrupting to give up dates on progress while I watched 7 quietly going about his duties. Interesting how he had changed while away. He hadn't said more than two words since arrival kept his eyes and body on alert even here within our private room. He saw me watching him as he poured the glasses of champagne one for each of us, took the first sip, swished it around in his mouth and swallowed then waited eyes closed. That very glass he took to Hunter the second to JD, I got the next, jonathan and then he looked to Hunter who nodded affirmative and he the last.

JD stood and we slaves joined him, "To our Lord and Master our Owner and now the reigning Deus of Castle Enterprises Unlimited, welcome home Sir."

We raised our glasses and drank the contents before JD turned and tossed the glass into the fireplace shattering the glass, "no other man compares to Our Lord!"

We followed suit and the door all but burst in when Dixie entered, "Boys! Boys! That's gonna cost you extra," she laughed before sweeping up the glass and disappearing out the door.

Hunter looked to 7, "strip."

Once 7 was out of his clothes he took a position between Sir and the door, hands behind his back, eyes focused, attentive to all action in the room and to any sounds in the hallway. I felt him tense up and watched as he flung himself at the door as it had quietly begun to open. He held the door as Dixie entered bringing another bottle of champagne and more glasses, "Compliments of the House, shall I open it, now?" She turned to see a naked 7 who took the ice bucketed bottle from her and walked to the far side of the room her eyes followed him.

"You leather men are so damn silly. Why place jewelry where no one will ever see it. I just will not understand. Who ever heard of putting jewelry in a boy's cock or nipples before a drunk drag queen missed her ear." We all laughed she turned towards the open door, "dinner will be ready according to our guest chef in about thirty minutes." Again the door closed and we fanned the room to push her vapors out into the dining room and down to unsuspecting dinners.

Hunter was watching 7 as he studied the bottle. We all turned to watch before 7 turned to Sir, "its been tapered with Sir, the casket had been opened and resealed, Sir."

"Take it outside the room, just place it in the hallway bucket and all." Hunter sighed. "Our world has become a dangerous place too soon."

"Thank you 7, join us."

"Our ruse worked better than I would have thought," Hunter was explaining to when my ears finally cued back in on the conversation. "I had to be at two sites at the same time, one place I had to do nothing but be a body there 7 filled in and I was elsewhere handling business matters that the others could not find out about. Interestingly 7 or someone like 7 in his heavy hood was about me at both locations."

Sir was laughing hard, "now they really think I am a voodoo witch doctor being able to be in two places at the same time!"

"You men are the first to know that I am Deus of Castle Enterprises at the stroke of midnight tonight the word will go out to all Manors, Shields and mates. Those poor bastards that have felt the whip of Lady Beatrice's last days in office most are seriously apprehensive about what I will do once I take office. Little do they know I have been in office for a month and it was I not Lady Beatrice who was axing a lot of Manor houses. You were right in trying to warm them jonathan shame none of them listened. Fools!"

Sir was getting mad would have launched into one of his favorite lecturers if the door had not opened; again 7 all but sprang to the door. In swept Dixie with mike on her heels both of them pushing wheeled carts laden with food. Platters of food, family style, were placed on the round table. Mike announced each dish as he uncovered it, Acorn Stuffed Pheasant, Leg of Venison, Mock Oysters, Peas in a Potato basket, Mexican corn, were only some of the treats that many of us had not had the luxury of eating before. Hunter made us all take a seat around the table another unaccustomed pleasure.

We were seated, all of us, to my dismay and served by mike's own hands. 7 was about to take taste tests of all Master's food but mike halted him and an argument would have broken out if mike hadn't have put a hand on 7's chest halting him, "He is after all my master too 9-777 and I have been preparing his food longer than you have been with us. All this food has been prepared by me and brought up here by me and Dixie."

Hunter caught Dixie's arm, "Dixie, we thank the house for the last bottle of champagne, but I believe we have had enough liquor to drink." Hunter was whispering to Dixie. "We are unaccustomed to a lot of that stuff. Would you return it to whoever had sent it to us with our thanks." He handed her a twenty-dollar bill, "don't tell them we did not drink it. Just let them think it's our way of saying thanks."

She placed the money in her bra and winked, "thank you I will be happy to take it to the couple they are sitting below in the dining room next to the red column. If you look out later you will be able to see them enjoying their bottle of bubbly."

Once Hunter's plate was stuffed to over flowing and he had taken his first bite we were permitted to fill our plates according to our rank within the household. Meaning JD and mike came next, then I, then jonathan and finally 7 got his plate full. Believe you me we had more than enough to go around. Mike had made us a huge meal that was fit for the king or in our case the Deus.

We ate in relative silence until our hunger had been abated then Hunter continued the conversation with JD. "We got to see the medical records of German house, they have a new breeding program that is creating awesome looking mules. They could pass as a combination between mules and bulls, huge shoulders, legs and small waists. I could not get a suitable answer from them about their lifting strength but it looks like their weakness is in their lower back."

Thus they chatted throughout the meal about the breeding programs with jonathan speaking in turn about what Eric was doing. The meal would have been more pleasant if a ruckus down on the main floor had not erupted. Having wolfed my food down before anyone had really gotten started, I was up serving drinks to everyone and was asked to see what was happening. I peered beyond the sheer drapes then parted them wide to look down. A man was laying face down on the table while his wife was screaming. It was a heterosexual couple by the looks of it sitting before the red column. I had begun to describe the unfolding scene below to those at the table behind me. I turned when I felt a body press into mine; it was Hunter looking down on the screaming woman who at that moment looked up at our private dining room.

Sir did not even turn away from the scene but spoke over his shoulder, "7 call Castle local tell them we need a clean up crew. Those people are from the London Manor. Interesting isn't it? Come on back to the table boy. If I know my mike we have a killer dessert coming our way," I must have visually paled, "let me rephrase that," he laughed light heartedly, "one of his famous party desserts."

"Mike?" Hunter was walking towards the table, "who is this man with the sausage down his leg I heard about?"

Mike choked on his food, "Sir only an excuse to get down here and make arrangements for me preparing your dinner, Sir."

Hunter laughed, "you never could lie well, mike. I had better meet this man of your dreams if he is reality."

"Sir, alas he is already taken. Dixie and he own this restaurant together. Well that's not true either, Dixie and the man of my dreams are one. Dixie is the sausage King!"

A light tapping echoed on the door, it opened revealing Dixie, "I thought I heard my name called," she smiled and winked at mike, "begging your pardon gentlemen. This envelope has been passed throughout the restaurant and no one will accept it. Does anyone within this room answer to the name, Deus?"

Hunter, JD and 7 all but choked in unison. Looking sheepishly at Hunter, jonathan spoke to Dixie and stood up, "I will take that, Dixie." Jonathan felt around his hips then realized he had no pockets then looked to Hunter who only waved indicating he would take care of her.

Jonathan felt he needed to explain to her, "it's a nickname from my old lover. Thanks for bringing this up to us."

In stunned silence we sat there thinking who could have known we were going here. Eric, yes, cause he would not allow us to drive the Hummer unless he knew where we were going complete with a detailed itinerary map and any proposed stops. Man, I thought when I handed it all over to him how paranoid could one man get about a damn vehicle but I would have done the same if it had been my pretty red corvette instead of that damn bulky overpriced gas guzzling Hummer!

Jonathan handed the envelop to 7 who studied it under a light in the corner before returning to the table. He slipped a butter knife under the edge of the gummed flap slitting the paper along the creased edge. Slowly he pulled the paper out away from his body as if something might fall out into his lap. He opened the doubled paper and read the letter, looked up at master and laughed.

"Sir, it reads, 'the jig is up!' Sir"

Hunter studied 7's face then joined him in sharing a long low laugh we all joined in not understanding why we laughed just that he did so we felt like we should too. Hunter held up his hands for us for silence, "its from Lady Beatrice. She just informed me that the grapevine has burst into flames. The world will know before we finish dessert that one of the most powerful corporations in the world has a new leader, me."

We resumed our private party without any more interruptions. We tried our damnedest to update him on all that had transpired while he was in New York working just as hard as we were down here on the estate. Mike had slipped out to finish what he called our dessert and Hunter tried to fill us in on the petty intrigues within Castle.

The door opened in walked mike carrying a flaming dessert behind him wasn't Dixie but our own Eric Wilson. Eric turned to us slaves, "dress, now!" Then turned back to Hunter, "Sorry Sir for the intrusion on your little party, but we have a problem."

"Oh?"

Mike went ahead and cut Hunter and Eric a piece of his dessert then ladled out bowls of the stuff for us once we finished dressing.

Eric took a bite, looked up to mike, "damn mike this is good, what in the hell is it?"

"Baked Alaska, Sir," replied mike

"What problem, Eric?" replied Master was a mouthful of ice cream, "You are right this is extra fine mike, boys, get dressed and try this, its good!"

No one was rushing around getting anything done except we were dressing as fast as we could in hopes that we would get some of that dessert before we had to depart. Dessert mind you is one of those things slaves rarely if ever get the pleasure of enjoying.

"About an hour ago the phone lines at Buena Vista started getting hit by hundreds of calls concerning the Deus. One in particular spoke about an attempt on your life tonight. That got me really concerned the others are being screened by Squirrel and a few others. One threat and your limo had not returned by its appointed time," Eric starred in my direction, "someone had failed to note a change in plans, I see. Anyway to make a long story short we came looking for you with the other slave sonar we knew only those on Buena Vista had been chipped and that we could find you. Damn that sonar works like a charm!"

"Take your time Sir, finish your dessert and we will be waiting in the hall when you are ready to leave." Eric said all but licking the plate clean of the dessert.

"Have you and your men eaten, Eric?" Hunter asked then turned to JD, "see that rope and tassel over their pull it."

"No Sir but we can get something back at the estate," Eric turned as Dixie entered the room.

Hunter spoke up, "Dixie does the club still have those baskets for the congress persons who want a quality meal in their office? Yes, good have your chef prepare…Eric! How many men are with you tonight? Two baskets, no alcohol, enough to feed six starving men, give them juices, coffee or cola. How long will that take Dixie?" Dixie was turning to leave when Hunter called her back, "Any reporters snooping around outside Dixie?"

She stepped out into the hallway, "back in a shake and I will check on the reporters."

"How did you get here Eric?"

"Two vehicles both Hummers, Sir?" Eric looked stunned when Dixie swished into the room.

"Bad news is good news. We have reporters at the front door demanding entrance and at the side door the only exit it the kitchen door and it's a pigsty out there in that alley and too small to get even my fat ass through. Baskets will be done in a few more minutes. Do you need a diversion, I can ask some of the girls on the other floor?" She departed to check her resources and to retrieve the baskets.

Dixie returned with two heavily laden baskets that Eric took from her, opened and whistled, "damn, this is even a better feed than mike would prepare. Sorry mike." He pulled a cell phone from his pocket and called Jorge. The man appeared a moment later.

We had dressed by the time Jorge arrived and were gulping down our bowls of baked Alaska when he knocked, "Castle clean up crew is here, Sir. The couple will be taken out now and hopefully lure some of the reporters away from the front door."

"Let's not even worry about the reporters we could wait them out. We could have all your men come in and dine here or we could play with the reporters by giving them something they cannot actually print or could they?"

Dixie entered our private room, "Master Hunter we have six drag queens at your beck and call. Our side of the show is more than happy to get into the news; besides, it will help business.

"Mike, cut Dixie a slice of your dessert and get her a glass of champagne. Dixie Tricks we got to talk, Eric, JD and 7 join us." Hunter and his friends drew closer and began whispering among themselves while I policed the room to see if we had everything we came with and spoke to mike about getting the bill for this evenings dinner and private dining room.

I got informed that mike had paid for the event and all the food by working in the kitchens and preparing enough for all the guests in the main dining room. By the exchange the patrons were surprised by a wonderful change to their standard bill of fare and had the pleasure of meeting a budding new master chef. Mike was all but beaming that tonight was such a success. That is if you negate the possible poisoning due to bad champagne or was that tampered champagne the end result was still there; mikes big debut was a success.

Hunter looked up, "Number One, strip down to your boots," then turned back to the whispering crew. "Jonathan go bring the limo around to the front curb and take One's clothes."

Jonathan was just about out of the door, "Jonathan wait! Ask Jorge to bring their Hummers around as well, one to the front and one to the back. If we are going to do a motorcade we might as well do it right. Check the trunk and see if we have or if the girls can make up some mini flags for our bumpers. Dismissed!"

Jonathan laughed as he departed, most of us did at the thought of having flags on our bumpers like you might see on a head of state from some foreign country. However that wasn't a bad idea, we were in a way a country within a country. Hunter was about to make that splash he was always talking about. He use to always say that its time that people knew what we are all about. But was it time for Castle Enterprises to come out of the closet. The world commerce already knew about our success in sperm production and our Obstetrician hospitals were the best in this nation. But is the world ready to learn about genetically altered slaves who produced the sperm? Are they ready to believe like we that everyone should have a slave within their homes thereby allowing the parents more time with their siblings or giving them the possibly to enhance their mental abilities or for sexual pleasure? Was the world ready to find out that we are not like themselves we are a untainted by the diseases that plague the world; the same diseases made in their own labs for controlling our masses which have backfired running amuck among all sexes not just ours. Are they ready to find out we are free from disease and that some of our larger manor houses are perfecting cloning of humans for profit?

JD and 7 left the room to find out if the limo was ready to accept passengers, 7 returned. Mike in his chef whites and 7 in his black leather had to make an interesting contrast when they departed by the front door. Mike was first into the limo and 7 guarded the limo door.

Master was informed by Dixie cf mikes contributions to the success of tonight's dinner party and was somewhat stunned by the restaurants generosity and demand to have mike return anytime as their guest chef. Two fair ladies if you could call them fair were poised at the door ready to fling it open for Master Hunter, Dixie and I to exit.

Dixie stood on his right, Sir in the middle and I on his left when the doors opened and we stepped out to the sea of flashing bulbs and microphones. We stepped lightly through the shoving crowd to the bottom of the steps, Sir turned putting Dixie before the cameras as 7 opened the door of the limo they exchanged a kiss and he climbed in. Naked came I into the world and into that throng of flashing lights. As Sir climbed in my ass was literally glowing in the light of flashing lights. I held my ass up for all to see as I rocked back and forth on the curb half in the car and half out. All they got was some great pictures of my branded moon or a man and a drag queen kissing out in front of a very popular restaurant socialized by the political leaders and the avant-garde of society. 7's hand to my butt helped me into the back seat with my Sir. He shut the door with finality and joined us in the front seat.

Hunter rubbed warmth back into my shivering limbs as three vehicles in a motorcade sped off joining the traffic of the city. He had me where he wanted me on my knees between his legs. There he put me to work on my favorite task. Sir dimmed the lights within the limo allowing the lights of the city to give us our only filtered light in the back. I rolled his cock around in my mouth, tasting him and teasing him until he ordered me into his lap. Spit slick, I climbed into his lap, lowered myself while guiding his cock between my cheeks and into my craving ass. We sat that way for the longest time just kissing, him rolling my nipples, and I nibbling on his neck or licking on him. We let the bumps and curves of the winding country road work his cock into my ass and churn my butter.

As one, we flipped onto my back. He lay between my legs, cock buried deep within my ass. He took my head between his hands. A light from a passing car caught the silvered thread of his spit dropping from his lips to mine. I opened my mouth and caught it sucking it into my mouth. He pulled his cock out and drove it hard against my prostrate. My back arched, my ass pushed into his crotch trying to force him to go beyond. Together we worked each other into ecstasy, one nudging the other faster, deeper, harder, longer. We shot as one in unison with the other and I had never laid my hand to my cock. He slept the balance of the trip to Buena Vista with his head resting on my thigh, home at last.

We put the house on our concept of cool running that is everyone wore padded boots. Not actually, but we kept any sound down to a low rumble and allowed him to sleep. A smile crossed our collective faces when we heard his morning trumpet, a bellow. God it was so good to have him home. We really did miss him while he was away.

Running to him with his coffee mug in my hand he asked what time was it?

"Sir its only 1:45 PM, Sir."

"WHAT time did you say, One?" demanded Hunter after his first sip of coffee.

"Sir, its 1: 45 PM, Sir."

"Who thought I needed more sleep than normal?"

"Sir we all did. We tried to waken you when we arrived and you were out cold. When we carried you upstairs last night you did not even stir. We all concluded that you were entitled to a good nights sleep in clean mountain air. You got it and if I may say so you look far better than you did yesterday, Sir."

"Any reports from last nights photo shoot before the Crazy Pig?" asked Hunter.

"Nothing much only a picture of Dixie and you kissing and a small blurb about who they thought it might be. They were more interested in the people taken out in the rescue vehicle especially since one of Dixie's girls leaked information about it being the Deus. No doubt that couple is being photographed in their hospital beds even as we speak, Sir."

"Sir, begging your pardon, I was ordered to get you dressed, shaved and ready for a gathering set for 3:00."

Hunter's eyebrows crinkled across his forehead, "I don't remember calling at meeting did I, One?"

"Sir the staff of Buena Vista have called the meeting as they wish to discuss something with you."

"Oh, ok, get me ready then, One."

I dressed him in formal Buena Vista attire, normally a kilt would be worn, but he balked when I pulled that from the closet and ordered that I, if I must dress him in formal wear, at least give him leather. So I dressed him in pants, a chamois cream shirt, boots, the woolen sash and the pin that declared him as the Lord of Buena Vista. His eyes rolled heavenward when I pulled out the sash and he would have questioned me but he saw the set of my jaw.

Sir was fed a meat pie while he worked off some of this tension in his office. There I collected him near the appointed hour. I lead him down the houses main flight of steps into the underground and halted before a new steel door without to his disapproval a guard. Using a plastic card that now hangs from my right wrist, I swiped the card slot and the door slid aside allowing us entrance into the slave caverns. A guard at the guardhouse met us and directed us onwards down the left corridor. We passed another guardhouse checked in and turned another left we were now entering the new section that which had been opened while we were away.

I grabbed up an old wooden torch lighted it on another hanging from the wall and lead him deeper into the bowels of the earth. A new cavern had been opened beneath the mountain while we were away. The walls on either side of us were machine cut lacking the uneven edges that were present when slaves cut a tunnel. He commented that it looked too new but kept following me down the machine cut steps. Our steps rolled to the right around an extremely large handsomely polished stalagmite running into jonathan, and JD who were waiting before a huge wall that held one very intricately carved door with dragon fashioned hinges.

Hunter whistled at the size of the wall then turned to the waiting men, "what is the meaning of this, men?"

JD stepped forward, "What you are about to see was done by those that returned with us from the South Seas once we outed you and what you had done for them. This is their way of showing you their gratitude to you, Sir."

Jonathan stepped forward, "Knock on the door and proclaim yourself Sir."

The mouth of the cavern had been covered by large hand cut planks held together by hand wrought hinges and bolts, the wall was fucking huge! Into that wall were two large carved doors held on the wall by dragon hinges and one held a fist shaped iron doorknocker. Hunter stepped up to the wall, lifted the fist shaped knocker and let it drop. A loud resounding boom echoed out and back behind the door. Telling us that the room was as huge as the wooden wall was wide.

A small door opened within the bigger door and a face protruded, "who goes there" asked the voice?

Hunter laughed, looked around to all of us and announced, "it is I, Bruce Hunter, Founder of Buena Vista."

The voice behind the door laughed, "impostor, he is still asleep the lazy bum!" The little door slammed in Hunters face.

Hunter looked around at us as if asking what he was to do. Jonathan stepped forward, "Sir allow me."

Jonathan knocked on the door, again the little door opened, "who goes there?"

Jonathan spoke, "the One of Buena Vista and his Lord and Master."

The voice spoke, "I see the One of Buena Vista but the Lord is still in New York."

Again the door slammed and jonathan backed away it was my cue, "Pardon me Sir." I stepped around Master Hunter and faced the door, "Sir, allow me." I beat the door hard with my fist. The little door creaked open and the voice called out, "who goes there?"

I yelled back, "a humble servant and the Deus of Castle Enterprise bides you make ready and open."

The voice called back, "ask the Deus to show me the sign of power that I may know that he rules according to tradition."

Sir began to strip off his sash and began pulling off his shirt. "One pull my shirt up slowly."

I had slipped his shirt over his head before he turned his back towards the portal. I had seen the laser cut across his left and right shoulders but only thought it was another embellishment to his already handsome features. Hunter turned his face to me and spoke over his shoulder, "behold the mantle of power, I am the fist that holds the reins!"

He flipped around and held up his forearms. They held pinkish scars from his wrist to his elbow an intricate Celtic knot design. They were new as were the burns that ran across his shoulders and across his shoulder blades. Intricate burns that had to have taken many strikes as the brand ran across his arms and shoulders.

Hastily I tried to put him back into his shirt as we heard the echo of huge bolts being pulled releasing what we hoped would be the double doors before us. They cracked open swinging in silently. Eric stood on the inside of the door, "Stand and Receive the Deus of Castle, Master Hunter has returned!"

The room went wild with screams as an outburst of cheers for our Lord issued forth. The sound was so loud it had to echo down through the caverns into New Market and deep into the bowels of the slave pens.

Sir stepped over the threshold, and I could have sworn that my Lord's chest swelled as he drunk in the ovation of his people. This meant more to him than any laurels that would be heaped upon him in the future. He stood there, leather and booted legs spread, hands to his hips, chest bare displaying to all that could see the brands of power that embellished his skin and was burned into his soul.

As the cheers quieted, he looked around, snapped his fingers and we slaves joined him. The cheers resumed increasing in volume as we strode into the great hall, down the two huge wooden tables that looked to cover the length of a football field towards a single chair on a raised dais.

Proud like a peacock he walked; hell, we all walked to that dais. He climbed the three steps as I followed him and walked beyond to my position on his left. He stood there poised like a movie character having come to life in a pagan setting and threw himself into the throne. Cheers lessened but never actually quieted as he studied the room from his throne. He stood, held his hands aloft for silence walked down the dais to the corridor studying the room and its contents. The room was medieval splendor right down to the shields hanging from the ceiling. Huge fire pits heated the room; torches lined the walls giving the room both high and low light. The tables could have easily seat over a hundred and the room had enough space that another row of tables could be placed behind the third row.

He stopped his sight seeing tour, "You are supposed to have been on vacation!"

A spokesman stepped forward, "Sir, this was our vacation. We heard from little elves that you had paid for our vacation in the South Seas. This and what follows is our way of repaying your kindness. This is OUR gift to the Lord of Buena Vista and the new Deus!"

Hunter extended his arms spread wide, "this is incredible! I thank you as does the Deus of Castle. You have shown with this act what the Castle will strive to generate through out its holdings while under my rule. Union, a unification of brothers and sisters, united for one purpose. Together We are strong, divided we are easy prey!"

Cheers followed his announcement.

Sir looked towards me, "this calls for a toast. Wine for everyone!"

I ran behind the throne returning with a large silver flagon of a fist holding a bulls horn he took it firmly then looked down at me, "due to this special occasion Master's and Mistress's wine for your slaves as well. They too have worked doubly hard for this occasion."

We sang our praises of our wise master with a loud outburst of cheers.

Wine was poured into his cup by 7 and Sir began walking down the long length of the tables once there he stopped, turned and raised his flagon, "A toast," he shouted, "To Buena Vista," he began walking back towards the dais as he spoke, "may she be a good teacher to Castle Enterprises and may she be a good pupil and thank you dear friends for being the best of both!"

All lifted their cups and drained the contents before clanging their cups down hard on the wooden tables. Their roar of approval of his toast and him as he walked back to the dais and stopped before it.

He studied the three steps and his throne. Abruptly he turned, "But ladies and gentlemen can we loose the dais? I am still Hunter the same man you have always known. Besides," he laughed heartily, "I get nose bleeds at certain heights."

Their laughter and negative response negated his idea. They wanted him elevated. He climbed the steps and settled into the throne.

He snapped his finger and I moved to his side. He signed and I dropped where he indicated with his boot, jonathan took the opposite position. JD sat nearest the Sir at one of the flanking tables and 7 was poised behind Sir ever watchful on duty. Mike was strangely absent, but then he was working inside the kitchens preparing yet another feast for our Lord.

"We have an opportunity coming to Buena Vista soil like our world has never seen. Our October Run will be happening here on our soil in less than four weeks. Its one of our annual events for our shield mates in the outlying countryside; however, this time the world will want to be part of our little known event. Let's not let the assholes throw a wrench into our party. We have years of experience and the know how to pull off this event no matter what size it may become. We have resources and manpower on loan to us from the Black Watch. It will take some work but it will be worth it for ALL of us! Extra measures have been taken to safeguard all our safety. Eric would you please report."

Eric walked up one step of the dais so all could see him. "When you folks ran off on your vacation Lady Beatrice sent in all the troops. She sent all the people at her disposal to work on ripping open this mountain. We have transformed it into a modern hub of commerce from which our Deus can run Castle Enterprises stateside. We will be close but we hope to be putting the final touches on the new computer security and subsystems by this time next week."

A murmur of approval ran through the handlers and guests.

"My Lord Hunter, my commanding officer has been recalled to base, and I am at liberty to offer to Buena Vista our full garrison of trained security personal for the October run which will free up the handler's for other more important jobs."

Eric stepped down from the dais, "another thing, Master's and Mistress's we need you to bring your slaves in to the security post in medical for a chip implant. This will safeguard your property and allow them free access to your quarters as well as limit their access in forbidden zones. Handlers, we need you to come by the upper level security outpost for your encoded badges that you must wear daily or you will be halted at each door as they scan you and will open at your approach. With these chips in place we limit access to all but those that are suppose to be in the underground."

Everyone seemed to groan including Master Hunter.

Eric went on, "the badge is a burden only if you allow it to rule your life; however, it will give you access to your living quarters should the mountain need to be shut down should a breech occur. Without a badge no one can enter our world this will stop unwanted outsiders from finding our deepest secrets. Plus no slave or guest can use a stolen badge to gain entrance to any part of the mountain. Believe me when I say we will be tighter than a virgin's ass."

Master cleared his throat, "Eric, you and all your garrison are welcome to our camp as long as we have enough room for everyone. The badges, as much as I hate the idea is a great idea that we will learn to use, like a whip these badges are only another tool to our arsenal."

A lone figure dressed from his head down to his toes in stark white walked around the dining room tables and stood at the end of the tables, waiting to be noticed, it was mike. He was following high court protocol. I plucked at Sirs pants getting his attention and showing him mike. Sir looked up and motioned mike to join us.

Mike walked down the double tables head held high, secure in his talents and craft. Not a slave but a man in full knowledge of his skills as a master chef for Buena Vista. Casually he bowed his head to his Master and Deus then he turned to the people at his back and cleared his throat, "Master Hunter, Deus, We of Buena Vista are jealous! Buena Vista is jealous herself! Tonight Sir is OURS! Tonight we celebrate the return of Our Lord and Master who just happens to be the Deus of Castle. No more business, Sir."

Everyone jumped up shouting and pounding their fists on the tables agreeing with everything mike was saying.

Turning in his place mike raked the crowd with his eyes, they quieted but stayed afoot.

"Sir, by your lips you proclaimed me as Master Chef of Buena Vista. Sir if you will forgive me. This," mikes arms opened wide as he turned around in place, "Is my dining room. For one night, Sir, you are not its ruler, I am!"

I watched Hunter's face transform from a smug look to that of open laughter then acceptance. Mike was carrying this off better than we had planned. He was the only one within our ranks that could have pulled off this stunt or so we hoped as we coached him on his lines.

Hunter bowed his head to the Master Chef, "Tonight, Master Chef Michael these hungry people and even I am at your command. This dining room is yours."

Michael turned and began issuing orders, "Captain of the Guard, recall all the unnecessary personal, have them report here double time!"

A heavy baritone voice replied to mike, "Sir they are all present, Master Chef!"

"Gate Keeper, Keeper of the Door. Shut and lock the door, Let no lady or gentleman take leave!"

We heard the door slam and bolts being slipped into the walls thoroughly locking the gate from the inside. Then mike turned to the right looking over the people seated there, "Let there be music!"

It may have been real music or a CD who cared as a soft stringed quartet began to play in the background.

Then mike turned to our Lords slaves, "Make the Lord comfortable bring him a table and wine that he may dine with his fellows. Slaves bring pillows that you too may be comfortable when permitted." He stepped up on the dais to the left and clapped his hands loudly, "let the festivities begin!"

Everyone cheered when a pair of naked oiled slaves marched down the corridor between the tables carrying a huge baked fish on a bed of kelp. It was first presented to Hunter who indicated that I should place a small portion upon his charger before the fish was taken down served back and forth between tables to the other guests. Flaming shisk-abobs were carried by four slaves, "game birds cooked in honey and brandy," was announced to the hungry crowd by mike. Either jonathan, 7 or I served Hunters plate as each dish was first presented to him before being served to everyone else. We lost the count of dishes brought in by mike and his naked kitchen slaves; however, like all good things they come to an end. While we dined jugglers entered followed by a team of wrestling mules. Once the wrestling bout was finished mike reappeared to serve us dessert. Medieval dining at its best something even King Arthur and his court would have problems saying they had it any better.

After dinner the party grew in intensity as each of the team leaders were to stand, propose a toast and drink in our Lords honor. The drinking bout went on most of the night until many of our family began dropping like flies, passed out on the tops of the tables. It was a celebration that would be remembered for many years to come.

A celebration that commemorated the return of our Lord and Master to his beloved Buena Vista and the new reigning Deus of our entire world with our Lord in control of the slave market our profits would soar. All the hard work that many of us had done prior to this time was about to pay off. Had the hard labor, long hours, shitty details been worth it? Each free man and woman that stood beside our Lord knew deeply that their rising star was about to shine out over the whole world.

Chapter 6

The wise are instructed by reason; ordinary minds, by experience;
the stupid by necessity and brutes by instinct. – Cicero

Not unlike the squealing of tires of a car tearing out from a stop sign Buena Vista leapt forward with master Hunter at home and at the helm again. A meeting late in the afternoon after the huge success of the new throne room was called for all team leaders. For a time, it seemed that everyone had a job title but we slaves, yet we knew our places and our jobs.

Unlike the outside society, Hunter was not into being the Deus for the glory and fame that it would bring him it was so he could increase our, Buena Vista's, profit margin. As long as Castle and Buena Vista turned a tidy profit he would rule. Shame it wasn't always so in the outside gay societies. If more of them united and kicked out the glory hounds they could have a community that would make most governments sit up and take notice.

We all worked but it seemed at first that Hunter worked hardest of us all. Late hours in the evenings with team leaders and early mornings were his standard routine. The Buena Vista dig as we called it installed Hunter into a private office below ground. What had once been his substantial dungeon was now his office and a small alcove hidden by a sliding bookcase gave him access to a private dungeon.

Seeing him for the first time sitting within his circular desk, computer monitors rising out of the desk surface I had the strangest feeling I was watching a spider spinning out his web. Actually the symbolism was more correct than I would have desired to imagine at that time. Five slaves in an entry office before him acted as his personal secretaries were on loan by the retired Lady Beatrice who now is recovering from her accident within our hospital. They would remain here until Sir's staff slaves completed their training. Seven and I were there to attend to his personal needs, all in all the new system worked far better than the old one to everyone's shock.

Sir's hours were long and seemingly endless the first week home prior to the run. One major problem continued to surface giving Eric, JD, and jonathan where were they going to put all those that where wanting to attend the run. Jonathan wanted to house all that came to the gate. By our rules of life we could refuse no one entrance; however, Sir settled the problem by giving jonathan and his team one stipulation. They were in a meeting while I served coffee it being rather late at night and most of them were yawning as the meeting went on and on forever. Master had raised him self out of his chair and was leaning forward on both hands as he talked to JD, "let's do something totally unheard of within Castle. Let's fry the Founder's nuts! Unlike Lady Beatrice who spoiled those Founder's until they were rotten I do not want to see those crazy fuckers! In the New York office they have their own suites, some had their own floors, and they did not have to mingle with the commoner's. We just do not have the space to give them private suites do we Eric?"

"No Sir, we turned the old ones into quarters for handlers and some of our full time security personnel as they needed them more than the Founders who rarely visit Buena Vista cause it's a working farm," said Eric as he slapped the map they were holding between them on the desk.

Hunter had seated himself while Eric spoke. His hands were clasped before him two fingers holding his chin as he thought then his face lighted up, "jonathan can we relocate a few handler's to tents topside. Let's relocate the Founder's into the old handler's dormitory. They will be trapped in one location forced to use communal showers and mingle with common folk. Can we do that jonathan?"

Jonathan rolled his eyes heavenward, "Sir they are going to bitch like dogs turpentined, but I think we can do that. We take these handler's located under the topsider blacksmith shop and put Founder's there. They will be blocked from accessing the underground without the special badges Eric has given us and they will at least have access to an elevator."

"They are going to bitch cause we do not put candy mints on their pillows at night or have slaves to tidy their rooms during the run," JD intervened.

"Do it that way jonathan. Let's make them hate coming here again," Hunter bristled his response.

One more problem to solve then we can all go to our own beds if we are so inclined, "who do we want in the main house besides Eric and the command team? Anybody think of any one that needs special care? No? Ok then dismissed," Hunter rose with his men and all of us left his office in search of something to eat.

The solution to the problem was so easy once it was figured out. The Founder's would not like their new quarters; but what the hell. They were here only to brown nose Hunter who would have none of that from them. Besides he has two brown noser's that love doing it on command and that's quiet enough. We had the dream team within the main house and working towards one goal, profit! Big profit! When the coffers of Castle increased the Founder's with their hurt egos would soon deflate. Besides with that simple act of putting the Founder's down within the slave caverns he set his tone of command. The Founder's would have to shit or get off the pot!

As time drew closer I was less and less in the office with my master. I worked for jonathan helping with a team of slaves to measure and erect a tent city, pounded in hundreds of torch pipes into the ground so all the main arteries of the camp would be well illuminated. Helped direct slaves at setting up fire pits, shock piling wood for each fire and helped mike raise his outdoor kitchen tents. Nearing midweek huge 26,000-gallon tankers from a local brewery arrived. We no longer had keg parties we had tanker parties when it came time for October run. One tanker would usually last the whole weekend but due to the unknown quantity of persons that may attend we had a second one delivered just in case. My team shuffled papers for hours every evening as we prepared the run packets complete with run pins and patches for those that would be joining us on the run.

There were a few glitches, but aren't there always when a big event kicks off. The run pins got misplaced but were found in time to stuff into the envelopes. The commemorative beer buckets were slow in arriving; hell we were unloading them as the first guests arrived. Security was having problems controlling the mundane's who wanted to crash the party and even Pappy was mobilized to assist with his local police.

We did have to give one concession to the Founder's. When they arrived at the D.C. airport all they had to do was hop on one of the piper cubs that was flying back and forth from our local landing strip thus cutting their travel time down just a little bit. The trip alone would tell them that they have left the civilized world and gone back into primitive culture, hell they were with rednecks, now! The airstrip at New Market was nothing but a flat section of sod, a windsock, two old barns and one old two-seater outhouse. The outhouse alone should scare them back into the plane if they got to use it as it hung over a creek, too much movement within the wooden structure could easily upset the apple cart so to speak. Hell as one of the old boys said, "hit has running water what more du ya want?"

All of us know that when Hunter ascended to power as the Deus that everything would change, but none of us were prepared for how abruptly the change would come. We slaves were use to regular injections of his cock, daily, sometimes more than that. Just within the first week, I had been fucked once and that was in the back of the limo. It just wasn't fair to us, our asses were itching badly and just watching him cross the room made my mouth salivate. Chastity sucks; especially, when it is due to everyone being to damn exhausted to do a damn thing! With him working all hours of the day and night oftentimes he came home and dropped like a lead weight into his bed. More times than not we were right beside him as he had set the pace that everyone on the mountain was attempting to maintain.

Christ Almighty! I was horny and temperamental as a cat while nearing the final stages of the run countdown. I had been working closely with Hunter when the tension of the event, the lack of sleep caught up with us. For some odd reason, Hunter asked what I considered at the time to be a real stupid dumb ass question; my retort was just as smart-ass as they come. His reaction was merited as he turned and backhanded me across my chops for starters followed by a chokehold. He must have liked the way it felt or he realized that we were all suffering from lack of association. He dropped me to the ground as I was struggling to breath cause the damn phone rang.

He picked it up and sat down hard in this leather chair. God, I wanted to grab that fucking thing out of his hands, slam it down on the receiver and drag his ass out for some much needed RandR, Rapeing and Raping, but I didn't. With a sigh, that he had to have heard, I dropped to my knees and began kissing his boots in hopes of distracting him. He watched me for a few minutes then stood abruptly shouting into the phone before slamming it back to the receiver. He stood their hands on his desk fuming, punched a button on a console and bellowed to his secretaries, "Hold All Calls!"

He walked out from under my adoring lips and snapped his fingers, "heel slave!"

Damn if I didn't get goose bumps just by the sound of his tone! I could have skipped to the dungeon, but I knew it would not have made him any happier. We made our way to the old dungeon door; opening it we found an office and a secretary looked up with one of those looks. Stepping back into his office he looked totally disgusted then looked down at me, "where did they relocate My playroom, God damn it!"

Like a lost child I returned him to his office, "no shit head, the dungeon, where is it?"

"Sir, forgive me, I thought you knew or I would have shown it to you earlier.

Place your hand on your computer monitor, just to the right, feel the indention, press your finger there, Sir."

He followed instructions to the letter and we heard an audible click on the wall with all the books, a secret door opened and we passed through. Once our bodies entered the room the lights came on dimly and elevated until full brilliance. There in the center of the room was a huge red bow and card from Lady Beatrice. It read, "the modifications were for your convenience. 'They say behind every good leader is a woman or man supporting this or her weight and convictions.' I prefer for every good Deus there are slaves suffering for him. Use this room daily if you want to keep your sanity. Monitors and cameras can be trained to cover one area or the whole room, and you can watch while you work at your desk. Cheap thrills, No, motivation for you to get your work done faster and join him. My room kept me sane and if you remember I was always watching one of my monitors whenever we had a boring Founder's meeting. Now you know the secret of my smile. Enjoy! B."

Cabinets lined one wall, he opened them removing one of his favorite items, an arm binder which he worked up my arms and laced tightly across my back. A small drawer gave him a leash that he attached to my guiche and another door gave him a bishop's hood that he buckled around my head. Opening the door we stepped back into his office, "it is high time you help me find my way around this dig. Ok, guide dog, take me to Commander Schmidt's office."

More than half the day was spent traveling from one site to the other and every place we turned up phone calls or messages awaited him. The presence of security was everywhere we went. Buena Vista had been lucky that we had not had a slave revolt like other manors, but then we had more handlers and our iron guild provided us with more cages than most. Still the newly installed security system did away with many of the little idiosyncrasies of the old slave training sites. The new caverns allowed us to house more slaves expanding our profits by a thousand fold. Our underground hive-like society was empowered before the modernization now it was a virtual fortress harnessing the underground rivers for electricity, powering underground plant nurseries as well as generating enough energy for what ever we needed. They kept the slave turbo room active allowing the energy it created to be sold to the local electric company as before so as not to frighten the outsiders. The less they know about our world the better neighbors they make. We had grown from a small underground village to a huge fucking metropolis with one exception our city ran more efficiently than one of those outside. In the outside world their cities were too often filled with lost souls, our people knew their places, could rise above their stations and prosper.

We were making our way towards security when Sir's cell phone began to chime. He chose to ignore it as we were tucked between a wall and a staircase, necking to hide, if only for a minute when we heard the unmistakable patter of boots on stone approaching. The boots stopped just before where we were hiding, "Master Hunter are you lost again?" came the voice.

Sir stepped out chuckling like an errant child pulling me along with him, "not really, just tasting the merchandise." His smile could be heard in his voice, "what's going on?"

"Sir, Rob Roy and his horde are at the gate house they will be arriving in a moment. Shall I take you up the nearest lift," said Paul whose badge I read, a heavyset full bearded bear of a man?

Security took us up a lift that deposited us inside what was once Hunter's private art studio that had been transformed into topside security. The room was a buzz with people watching monitors as the bikers roared up the mountain and we made a beeline for the main house.

JD stood on the front steps looking great in his leathers with 7 standing beside him holding the silver tray, pitcher and Welcoming Cup. Eric and jonathan joined us both wearing sheepish grins as if they had been caught doing the nasty deed. At least they were getting some, I thought to myself, but I would tonight.

The sound of engines filled the air with a roaring sound that equals none and speaks volumes about the wonderful world of bikers, leather, greasy pits and boots. The very sound of the engines as they echoed off the trees got our hearts pumping harder and our blood coursing through our veins. They were coming home, all of them; the boys were coming home to Buena Vista.

The roar of many engines drew closer and the first biker popped over the edge of the mountain as if thrown at us scattering dust marking their passage. The huge man riding an even larger bike arrowed directly at our team and Hunter stood there waiting his hands on his hips one holding my leash and I kneeling beside him in bondage. Others clustered around us waiting for them to pull up and shut down their bikes before we spoke the words of tradition.

The big bearish man swung his leg over his cycle and stepped closer to Hunter when our warrior Eric moved forward putting out a hand between Hunter and Rob Roy, "halt who goes there," demanded Eric in his most authoritative voice!

Rob Roy seemed to stop mid stride, we could hear murmuring among his people on their bikes. Then he smiled, nodded his head, "tis I Lord. Keeper of the Iron Collar and Mace, Shield mate to Buena Vista Manor." Rob Roy turned to his people, "present our Lord with our shield of honor." Two men stepped forward carrying a covered placard of about 2 feet by 3 feet and halted beside their Lord. Rob Roy turned grasped the cloth ripping it off to reveal a shield that had a red border all around its edge in the center was a broomstick and chain with a spiked ball and an iron collar.

Two slaves ran forward at jonathan's hand signal, they took the shield carrying it to a tall telephone pole. Normally they would have climbed the pole but due to an accident four years ago they used a cherry picker to get the shield up to the upper most top. There it would hang in honor as the first to arrive.

While it was being hung, JD stepped forward and passed to Hunter the Welcoming Cup. Sir poured a little of the honey mead to the ground, all said in unison, "for those departed." Hunter lifted the cup high for all to see, lowered it to his lips and spoke over the rim of the cup, "How do you some to Buena Vista, Lord of the Iron Collar and Mace?"

Rob Roy's face exploded in a huge grin, "we come in peace Lord."

Hunter took a small sip then extended the cup to Rob Roy, "be thou welcome!" The cup passed hands and Rob Roy tossed the cup back drinking the contents before passing the cup over to JD. Both men opened their arms and I nearly got trampled in their rush to be in each other's arms. Cheers went up from everyone around to witness the first arrivals.

Hunter dropped my leash, while he and Rob Roy stepped aside to thump each other on their backs and grab each others asses, "damn its good to have you folks home again!"

Master looked over his shoulder at us all waiting for his next command, "Rob

Roy you knew this one as Cappy, that was his free name, he has been reduced to where he has always been and is now called jonathan. Eric Wilson is now chief of security he has some badges that you need to keep on you. We have had to change some thing's since you were last here. Eric and jonathan will get you settled. Go with them and when you are settled come find me Rob Roy if you can," Sir laughed and they broke apart.

Rob Roy walked to his bike, kicked it to life and with a salute to Hunter from he, and his leather clad people; they roared off towards tent city. There they would have the pick of the campground as was fitting for first arrivals.

We had just stepped back into the main house as I was freezing my tail feathers off being naked except for the arm binders and bishops hood when JD approached, "Sir may I have Number One for the afternoon. Founder's are arriving at New Market in the hour and we need to take the limo to pick them up?"

"Wait JD, since I have fulfilled my duties with the cup its your job as the manager of Buena Vista's soil, besides its your turn to get shit faced on that damn cup. Who is coming in that you need the limo and One?" smiled my Sir.

JD stepped into his office returning with a clipboard. "Sir, it's the Columbian Manor, Julian Reyes and three slaves."

Hunter laughed hard when he heard the name, "if I know Julian he has brought more than any limo can carry, send two vans, two handlers and two slaves. Sorry JD, you are stuck sucking that cup today, nice try." Sir hugged JD to him, "Besides I am taking Number One upstairs and I plan to pound his butt into butter. Sooo," Sir winked and JD laughed, "cover for me will you?"

He had said the magic words and my dog like nature took a hold of the leash with gusto as he talked with JD. I was jumping and pulling at the leash doing my damnest to pull him up the steps and into our private suite where we could do whatever we wanted without any intrusion for the outside world. His laughter made my jumping eagerness all worthwhile as he let me pull him up the steps. He keyed the security lock on our domain and we entered. Before we entered I was already on him burying my face into his pits sniffing around him as if he was rauchy smelling meat. Right then, I had only one thought in my head, I wanted meat and soon. He had other ideas as he pulled me to him closing the door with our entangling bodies he kissed and bit my neck making me growl like a wounded animal. In a way I was his manimal wanting him to breed me like the wild pup I was for him.

His hands found my nipples rolling them as he buried his neck into mine and sucked my skin into his mouth so he could get a big bite. Teeth set, I howled like a wounded animal grinding my ass and bound hands into his crotch. We both knew what we needed. His hand released my arms from the binders even as his face sucked on my lips. Once the binder was off my hands he went to work removing his shirt burying my head under it to get at his ripe armpits there to suck up his sweat then across to his meaty nipples. Those I ground into sirloin before passing down his stomach with my tongue over his cute little stomach into his belly button and down. Opening pants with my hands as I knelt on the floor begging with my eyes to open his fly with my teeth. His nod gave me the much need approval, and I went to work growling at each hard metal button until I released my pet cock that was trapped in his pants. It sprung up waving a friendly hello to an old friend my lips. They spread wide and sucked him in to his old familiar haunt. Together we got reacquainted until he was spit slick and ready for more action. I bowed before my Lord grabbing my toes knowing that my juicy butt was self-priming no lube needed. He sunk his cock into its hilt held me there as I shivered in anticipation of what as about to come my way. Together we walked to the footboard of his bed as I laid over it was ordered to hold on. He slammed his thighs into me so hard with his need others outside the house had to have heard our slapping sounds. He came fast as was normal for his first climax removing the edge off our need thus allowing his next climax to build in passion as we joined taking pleasure from each other. Someone started knocking at the private entrances door, Sir stepped over and looked through a peephole, "damn them to hell they have found us. Well fuck them, come on boy we are going to a place they would not think of looking, my office and its dungeon." Like children hiding from parents we hopped into his private elevator riding it down to his office. We stepped through h s office keyed the dungeon and entered. I knew but he did not that a light just went on in the secretary's office telling them he was in his dungeon. Still they were very aware of his presence should an emergency arise.

Master looked comical walking from his suite upstairs with his pants down around his boot tops his cock jutting out from having its first taste of boy butt for almost a week but I dared not laugh although I did my damedest to stifle a giggle or two. Sir and I entered the dungeon and I dropped back on my knees. Our eyes were equally lust filled when he looked down saying in a commanding tone, "Get him ass slick, boy, I want more of that butt."

Master's words seen to have come from a great distance, but they could not have come at a better time. A pearly drool tear was attempting to tear itself from his cock in route to the ground. I caught it in my mouth following the silvery drop up to its source. Gently since his cockhead was still sensitive I lapped and circled my tongue around his swelling cockhead, strolling over his corona before gliding down the pulsating cock sucking him into the depths of my moist cavern. Master's moans told me that my next course of events and I set my head in motion. Sucking his cock even as I impaled my face on it driving him nuts with the strength of my throat muscles pulling him deeper into my throat begging him mentally to make me gag by burying his cock deeper than ever before until I reached his pubic hairs. Eternity faded into nonexistence while I held myself so, letting my throat tease his cock unmercifully, milking it slowly with only my throat muscles as he has taught me to do, but master had other plans his hand closed around my throat choking me and forcing me to give him back his cock. Using his chokehold he lifted me to my feet, held me tight to his chest and whispered, "not so easily will I give you my next load, little pig."

He dropped me, turned and went back to the cabinets searching and tossing items out on a floating bondage board before he called me to him, "you and I both know they will not allow me to have too much pleasure with you today with all those that are arriving. Too many expect me to greet them but I can have you where I want you when I return," then he laughed sadistically, "right where you belong, ready, willing and able."

He helped me slip into something more comfortable a wonderfully worn canvas straight jacket that he laced up the back before he added two bicep bands and pulled my arms around to my back. Additional straps were added over my arms in front as well as a large strap that ran the circumference of my arms locking them tight making me unwilling to attempt escape as I had in the past. Once within his jacket he nibbled my neck and began sucking on my earlobes. He added straps around each thigh others around my booted ankles before helping me to kneel on a raised platform.

His hand began to grab my ass then began slapping it working for what he called his cherry ass; a paddle was added to heighten his pleasure. Acquiring the color that he sought the paddle was laid aside and his fingers began to work into my happy hole. Two fingers started the ball rolling; three helped me appreciate his love followed by rubber balls on a string. Inserted I felt like the Easter bunny still nothing felt so good as his control over pulling them slowly out. Each ball seemed to make my mind melt as it was withdrawn we were both having a great time playing together when an annoying buzzing began within our chamber then as quickly as it came it dropped into silence. We returned to our play as he pushed a large dildo between my ass lips and began slowly feeding it into my hole. I was grunting like a whore in heat it just felt so damn good.

He had begun to swat my ass when the annoying buzz returned filling the chamber the most irritating nerve grating sound known to mankind. His voice sounded as disgusted as any body I had ever heard when he asked me, "what the fuck is that noise, Number One?"

"Sir," I panted, "over on the wall near where we entered is a one way monitor, press the on switch. You can see who is calling but they can not see you."

I heard him speaking to someone, telling him that he had left orders and I heard someone apologizing to him. Then I heard his exclaim, "How in the fuck did that bitch get here! Right! I will be along in a moment. Detain them at the gatehouse, ad lib check their records, but do not let them on the base. I will call when I am at the main house."

He turned back to me, "God damn German manor house! Boy I got to go but before I do, let me leave you with something to think about."

He set about plugging my ass with a plug that looked like a huge fucking trailer hitch, locking it in place with straps that ran around my butt and waist before he helped me to my feet. I was ordered to walk around while he dressed. Having completed his dressing he grabbed me in his arms, "I will train the monitor on you…be a good boy until I return." He pulled me to him and raped my mouth with his tongue, turned picked up a ball yoke pulled my nuts out from my body and attached it to them. He placed me between wooden uprights, tossed a thick foam pillow on the floor and helped me to kneel. Once kneeling the ball yoke was pulled back into the bow of my ankles there secured by ropes. Thankfully my balls had become low hangers over the years of hard work and play, the forced position would be pleasantly uncomfortable. Rope was woven from my thighs to the wooden uprights as he sewed me into place kneeling bound between two large wooden beams planted in the ground. Another longing kiss was followed by the installation of a bishops hood and he used the straps with more rope to freeze my head in space. I watched him from my immobile position as he adjusted the cameras, changed the lighting to halo my body and without even a look back he departed.

I settled back to enjoy the ride that he had set in motion. I tried struggling within the straight jacket but the additional straps refused to allow me to pass beyond and gain freedom like I had done once before. I tried tampering with the ropes by leaning one way then the other but he had seen to it that they all had equal tightness and my body would not shift in any direction. A dull ache began to creep into my awareness due to the forced position of my nuts, they were not uncomfortable at present but the ache would increase as time worked against me. My butt was pleasantly stuffed and I found for entertainment that by squeezing my butt muscles it would tease my cock into wiggling, some movement was better than no movement.

Slowly as if in a dream I shifted my focus inwards adjusting to the dull aches and moving beyond like a dancer moving to a private song. Mirrors flashed up all around me giving me back reflections of myself then beyond as I turned back the hand of time. He had let me wallow in my own self-hatred digesting my meal resigning myself to whatever fates looked down upon the creature in the plexiglass box beneath his butt lips. The pit had broken me now it was his turn to remake me according to his image.

Hands drug me out of the box, clipped my long nails, and forced my hands into thick neoprene gloves. The fingers got folded in upon themselves before a half of a hard rubber ball was placed into the palm of my hands and another glove was formed over the ball and hand giving me a pair of paws where I had once had hands. I no longer struggled with the transformations but waited patiently enjoying the touch no matter how rough anything was better than that damned pit. Calmly I watched as a blacksmith set a heavy gauge cocking at the base of my cock and balls while mules held my legs wide. Nor was I upset when he added a heavy ball shackle, added shackles around my ankles and added one length of chain between the two. I was bemused when they added a metal belt running around my waist, set wrist shackles and secured my arms at my side. I thought all this I could live with if it kept me out of the pit.

Like a monkey jumping from foot to foot I was lead by two mules holding my leash into an adjoining room. There sat my Master in all his rubbered glory waiting, watching another slave kneeling at his feet, mouth open waiting anxiously for his cigar ash. I was lead before my master who looked down at me and passed sentence, "once an animal bites its owner it no longer trusted as before. I plan to take the bite right out of you forever."

The mules scooped me up, placed me on a slab of metal at master's back who rose to help strap me down. A doctor the one we slaves knew as the jawbreaker stepped into view and master spoke as he looked down, "rip out the animals teeth, no more will it bite the hand that feeds it!" Master turned and walked away. I opened my mouth to scream as they had anticipated. Scream I did but not before they got my mouth wedged open and they had begun the procedure. It took me a month or more to recover from having all my teeth removed during which time my head was locked into a sightless hood. They fed me at first through a tube later when my mouth healed I was put on the bucket.

Everyday while I was in the underbelly of the cavern, locked within the chambers off from my pit master came to me. There within the caverns he taught me to fear him and I learned to understand him completely. Being sightless and hobbled I found his touch no matter how rough or harsh to be pleasing. One of his strong rib breaking kicks may have sent me sprawling nevertheless I crawled back to him and begged silently for more. He took his pleasures with my body as he desired. His fist filled my void as did chain even as it slipped down the back of my throat and I gagged for his pleasure, no matter how horrified I may have been at the time I knew it was I who was giving him pleasure, not others.

When he was not present others helped me maintain focus as they forced me to work on machines that forced my body to return to its once powerful exterior image. No matter, we both knew the exterior façade was a lie for the interior was broken. No matter how strong my body may have been it was a weak mindless thing mewling within. This creature owned nothing now not even the air it breathed and its Sir taught it well that he could take what he wanted and make it suffer or die. This creature ate what pleased its owner, drank what came from His body, breathed as it pleased Him or suffered as it was forced to suck air through tiny tubes while it heard its owner laugh. No longer dare I raise my hand to him the thought was driven from my mind, body and soul. Through my Master all things came to me. Freedom came only when Master ordained it not before. Life prior to the pit was a lie whereas life after the pit was reality.

My body now His body was never so alive as when he used it. Its cock and balls were never so fully used as when his boot occupied them, nor was its mouth so fully filled until his cock, fist, piss, boot or ass filled its void. Its ass was constantly full, had it ever been empty? This creature soared when his whips cut its hide his pain teaching it that true pleasure was serving, serving the One.

Shots were given to it three times a day for what purpose this creature did not know or care as it was alive and living to serve its God however He wished. This one had forgotten the tone of his voice no longer did he order me about but used his whip, a jerk on a chain, or a kick from his boot to direct. The hood took away more than just sight, smell it took away hearing and his paws took away all but direct touch and my taste buds died along with other parts of this creature. His will was strong, this creatures will was dead, it along with its fight died in that pit. Even as this creature was being remolded to serve he was implanting his seeds so his will would take hold and grow within.

When this one displeased him it was locked within a crate, forced to bend in upon itself until it was secured by straps then wooden panels would be sealed around the beast until only its head jutted from the top. Absence from his touch no matter how brutal this one craved, needed to know it was alive. The crate taught me about brutality. To serve him was good whereas being without him was bad, it meant emptiness, worse yet, it meant living in a void of no sensations. Without him this creature did not exist with him it lived. Day after day this lesson was repeated until this creature was boxed and he withdrew his touch. From that day forward this creature knew it must remain within close proximity of its owner or else it would surely die.

The following day its hands were released from the belt and it was taught how to walk like a dog, not crawling on its hands and knees like a human but walking like a dog on both sets of front and back paws. It walked on all fours for hours, pacing besides Masters boots, feeling him brush against it and when it faltered a strip of leather encouraged it to move. When pleased with the awakening dog at his feet Master would ideally scratch his pet. Like a foolish slave this one spoke of its pleasure; but Master helped it realize with a brutal kick that speaking was forbidden to his pet. It learned thereafter to speak only in simple barks, whines and yelps. His dog grew with each passing day found pleasure eating from a bowl at his boots, loved the simple joy of wagging its tail to feel the tail striking its own backside. It took pleasure in walking beside its owner and feeling his owner's hand lovingly almost ideally stroking its loins gently with his fingers. Some aspect of how it gave its owner pleasure must have pleased its master as Sir give it full rebirth, meaning he lifted off its hood.

This dog squatted before is owner on its haunches, tail within its ass wagging back and forth in excitement of being with master. Master had placed its front paws so that they stood on his boots while he released the padlock, zipper and laces that kept it locked within darkness. The unexpected suction on its ears made it yelp and whine as he pulled the hood off from around its head but when his hand brushed its hair it was given over to pleasure so supreme that it could barely stand still with the excitement. His rich deep voice cautioned his dog to keep its eyes closed and to calm down. Just the sound of his voice no longer muffled by the folds of leather was rich with colorful overtones. This animal wanted to look up at his owner to see if it remembered his face and tired but found it impossible from its position. The room had been darkened nevertheless once my eyes stopped tearing it could see his boots; and yes, it jumped in excitement, those were my master's boots. My tail started beating both sides of my ass cheeks my butt was wiggling so hard from the excitement of the moment and his hand touching my sensitive scalp sent shivers down to my cock. He held me in place just rubbing my head, feeling my face, and scratching lightly behind my ears while his dog licked whatever part came into its path. This one found its voice and barked elaborately of its own pleasure of being free from that nasty hood and having his hand on my head again. It was delirious pleasure that he was giving his dog, and it could not speak more than barks, chirps and whines to celebrate the moment.

He took that happy time to change my headgear. My mouth was pried open and he installed a small ball that was bounc at the back of my head, "human speech is forbidden to my dog blu, this ball will help it to remember." Two round tubes of leather were fitted over my nose and eye sockets, those were tied at the back of my head, "these will be removed once your eyes adjust to the light, blu." A chinstrap was pulled into place and buckled at the back of my head; more cups and straps were pulled over my face. All these were woven around my head and buckled at the back before being locked in place by a thick collar around my neck. His deep bass laughter came down to where his dog blu stood, "tomorrow or the next it will see what my dog blu looks like. It's a handsome beast that's my blu."

He stroked the length of my body, rose to his feet, his dog felt a gentle tug on its collar and heard him say, "heel blu." His dog blu shook his head once testing to see if the straps encircling his head were tight and trotted off following his master as they explored the lower caverns together. Master started off at a slow run and found his dog blu keeping up with him, his laughter excited his pup that replied with loud barking. Together they ran until blu was winded and his tongue was hanging out of its mouth. Master reined blu in and together they walked down a corridor cut in stone. Blu was whining by the time Master squatted and drank from huge underground lake. Blu walked belly deep into the water before he drank all the while master was laughing, "look down at the water blu," said master. When blu did master struck a match and blu jumped back barking his fool head off as he looked into the water and saw another dog looking back at him. Master started laughing at blu's antics that excited blu who splashed in the water before running to jump into master's lap as blu did his damnedest to lick master's face. Neither blu nor the slave that was quiet within had ever seen its master so happy as he did that day. Master was so pleased that he removed blu's tail plug slipped his cock into his dog and fucked it as it bayed in pleasure. My devotion to my Master awoke with his rising need and his pet give to him all that it had to offer.

I was lost in my mind; worrying about needless things when I first noticed the scent that told me he was near. Yes, I could smell it a cigar. If I could have looked around the room I would have found him standing their quietly watching me as he fisted or rubbed his bulging cock.

"Miss me?"

My reply took him by surprise as I yelped and whined to him. He crossed the space between us his laughter floating down to my sensitive ears, "Ahhh, back in puppy space I see, good boy!" He stood a thumbs distance away form me. I could have tongued him if he had so ordered.

While he was topside he had turned cold and he needed someone to suffer for him. He needed my pain and my acceptance of his power over my life as much as I needed him in me. We read each others minds as he stooped forward opened the front panel on my bishop's hood and forced his cock into my mouth. He allowed me to suck his meat while he worked on loseing my strained and sore parts as I transferred to him by way of his cock my pain to him. With a wet plop, his cock was pulled from my lips. Like the dog his pet was I actually whined my displeasure as his bone was taken from my hole. I tried to capture it again as I forced myself to wiggle forward stretching my tongue obscenely out like a snake trying to catch a bug. He leaned back; looking down at me, "cock hungry, huh?"

Stepping back he leaned onto the wall, his hand grabbed his cock and began fisting it all the while he was starring at me, mentally commanding me to beg for his cock. I started barking, yelping and whining when he did not give his cock. Pre cum was dripping from his cockhead and being transformed by the action of his fist into a white froth within his palm. I just could not stop myself as my whining rose a notch as I as transformed into his bitch in heat. His crème filled hand slammed into my mouth greedily I licked his hand clean. Slowly too slowly for my hunger master straddled my torso his cock humping midair as he leaned behind me to release me from the straight jacket. My mouth caught his cock before he could reach the straps and I drew him into me. He was caught off guard his laughter told me so even as his backhand forced me to spit it out.

Laces that held me tightly centered between the two uprights were cut and I was lifted, tossed over a nearby bench. His cock found my mouth and drove deep to his nuts while he busied himself over my back working on removing the plug in my ass before I could drain yet another load down my throat. I had control, his cock was after all in my mouth and my ass muscles were not going to permit him to remove the plug any time soon. Helplessly he knew he was being bested by his pet blu and gave himself over to pile driving his cock deeper into my yawning throat.

He let me work his cock down my throat. There he would grab the back of my head and hold me impaled gagging, spewing phlegm, choking as I tried to breath around his cock. He held me there until I was starved and frantic for air then he would release me. Time and time again this was repeated until he could no longer hold back the rising surge he heaved his hips forwards, locked his hands around my collar and power drove his cock down my throat. One hump, two before his jism shot deep, and I was forced to swallow or choke on his cum as he pulled his cock from my slack jawed mouth. He pulled me upright, weakly I smiled, and he laughed and pulled me to him.

"Bastard slave, you knew I wanted another piece of that ass, but you had to have it your way," his kiss told me he would have what he wanted whenever he wanted.

As we were walking up to the elevator and taking it up to our private suite my mind started thinking as it always would after good sex. We could count our lucky stars, I could especially that Castle and their Shield mates maintained such strict health codes. A file was kept on all mates within a Manor house. Each house was required by Castle law to submit monthly if not biannual updates to their files along with their profits for the time period and send their findings to Castle data for proofing. All those that were chosen for medical training were loyal followers taken from within our ranks, many of them had been slaves that showed dedication and a natural tendency towards medical care. Our doctors had a level of loyalty that bordered on fanaticism. One of the major reasons for their unyielding pledge was that they had risen from the same slave pits to their esteemed position. Each doctor had attended schools for many years. Schooling completed they were assigned to one of the medical facilities within one of the Manor Houses. Further bonding to Castle arrived monthly. The doctors were some of the few individuals that could buy their freedom from their own earnings.

The doctors were responsible for testing all slaves, mates, handler's anybody that was part of our society including the Founder's for any sexually transmitted disease, as well as, taking controlled samples of sperm from all willing and not so willing donors. Even the Founder's had either sperm or eggs on ice, no exception to the rules were permitted. The doctors thought highly of themselves, some used their power to help while others used it to intimidate. The sperm bank had become over the years a great profit. When the plan was instigated, everyone laughed; nowadays, the laughter is heard as we bank our credits from its exchange on the open market. Just imagine how much profit drops down a slave's throat or shoots up his ass in a day worldwide and your head will swim with the wasted profit.

Hunter utilized these pre-tested males often in some of his larger scenes and to teach lessons to uppity boys like me. When I was raped in the jail by which I thought to be redneck hicks and the sheriff's men. It was his pre-tested males were actually raping me. He wanted to teach me a lesson in obedience boy oh boy did I learn that lesson well. Each cock that rammed over my tongue drove that fantasy and lesson home. My fantasized rape was never as brutal as the real thing. Nothing prepared me for the horrified realization of repeated oral rape. Now more than ever I am more sympathetic to women who have been raped. The rape was orchestrated by the one man who owns me for his pleasure mind you and the bastard had the gall to videotape the scene and market it. If he had not used those men I would not come full circle to where I stand now at his side as his Number One.

Before any open forum such as the Halloween run or any of the great gatherings data had to be withdrawn from Castle's computers. Only those houses that have the five star rating could openly participate. I had overheard Hunter speaking with jonathan about the Audit ruling and a few other rules that required a board's approval to invoke. If a House failed to submit proper data within fifteen days prior to deadline internal auditors would kick open the doors of any manor house and search out the records. Should the auditors find more than the average mistakes the house can be disbanded, its lands confiscated, its slaves assimilated if healthy and the balance of the staff used elsewhere as slaves. This ruling included even the Founder's however the situation had never come up to justify that Castle ruling until now. The rule merits enough fear to make certain that all records are submitted in a timely fashion. That rule and a few others is one of the main leverages the Deus has to control other Houses.

Of all the records that had been flooding our data collection centers, only one was earmarked as potentially hazardous, the London Shield. The final act of Lady Beatrice or was it the first act as Deus for Master Hunter was to have the doors crashed on the London Manor. The Founder in question was not home when the raid was pulled.

When Hunter and I returned to the surface we were both in a much better mood. I ran to prepare him a bath, laid out his shaving gear while he spoke on the phone to one of our team. I bathed him and he me. In turn I shaved him and he left me to shave myself. Returning to the bedroom, I found him laying on the bed his hand indicated that I should join him by his side; together we took a short power nap.

We were woken by the phone. He grabbed the phone while I prepared to dress him in formal livery of Buena Vista. He was shouting into the phone, "Hold that son of a bitch at the front gates, and better yet, quarantine the whole party! Do not let them loose within the compound. Put the Founder in a private cell away from his slaves, separate them. I have my reasons. Follow Orders, Damn it!"

"God damn him!" Hunter turned slamming the phone down on the receiver, "Sir Frederick Black with slaves no less has approached the main gate for entry. We raided his manor house in London less than two weeks ago for failure to comply with rules and regulations. Sir stomped in my direction stopping abruptly, "Dress Me slave, I am fucking waiting!" I knew his anger wasn't aimed at me still he caught me out of the corner of his eye me start from his outburst. He caught me and pulled me into him arms, "sorry shit head, my anger is not with you," he squeezed me tightly to his chest.

"Get me dressed, I got to meet the assholes that are giving JD hell and go down into the underground to find out what the fuck Freddy is doing here. He should have known better than to show up here." Sir tried to hold his place so that I could dress him but when he is agitated he tends to pace that makes it hell to get him dressed. All in all, I got him dressed in under 30 minutes and out the door then I could kick back and dress as he had ordered for me, my Number One outfit. Show time was upon us.

I ran downstairs only to find him trapped in a corner by an outraged Founder who looked like a raven in black leather. She was poking her finger into Hunter's chest as she screamed her outrage at having to be located below ground with others and she demanded to be shown to the Founder's suites. He told her as politely as he could the room that she was sharing with other Founders was the private suite and that he had more things to consider besides Castle's Founders. Gently he pushed her aside took my leash and lead me outside to the gathering throng of partiers. Rob Roy's club had already bellied up to the first tanker and where threatening to drink it dry before other revelers arrived.

The screeching raven that was more upset by the fact that he had dismissed her than she was upset about the communal dorm room followed Hunter and me. Hunter stopped mid stride, turned and caught her off guard, "Frau Hummel, I highly recommend that you secure your bunk space, three other Founder's have just arrived and are taking the whole dorm as their space, go duke it out with them." He was about to dismiss her again and was preparing to turn when he laughed to himself, "Or Frau Hummel, you could go back to New Market and take a room in the bed and breakfast. I hear it's very nice, of course it's at your expense; but, I will gladly see to it that you are taken off base."

He had been making his way down to the Rob Roy's camp but turned when he heard the roar of more bikes arriving. JD was offering them the welcoming cup when we arrived and stood behind him watching him as he preformed his duties as manager of Buena Vista. The Wildcats M.C.C. had arrived from Norfolk. Their president once completing the welcoming tradition saw Hunter and ran into his open arms. She was a smallish woman, a petite Dolly Patron, decked out in full bright red leather. (Literally full with that set of knockers), her brawn, a handsome mule slave held her cycle as she thumped Sir on his back.

"Sir, you didn't have to become the Deus to make me love you any more, you old fart," she yelled at Hunter. Then she gulped air and realized who she was addressing and tried her damnedest to correct herself. Master went formal on her, making her stumble over her words of apology, along with forcing her to repeat her commitment to Buena Vista. Then Sir, looked down to her, "You know you could be whipped for calling the Deus an old fart! There are zealots everywhere some even think the Deus does not shit. I am here to prove to them that not only does the Deus shit but he can be just a mean old fart when he wants, don't you agree, Maggie?"

Hunter had wrapped his arm around her waist as he walked her back to her bike and brawn, "how's your brawn working out? Ready to trade it in on a new model?"

Hunter looked up to the brawn, "She treating you like you deserve or better?"

The brawn coughed them smiled, 'Mistress treats me too well, Sir."

Maggie had climbed back on her bike when Hunter put out his hand to catch hers, "Can you stay a spell after the run, Maggie? I need your advice on something. Want you to think about something while you are partying, think about coming home. We need a few really good people here. We will talk later. Go party before Rob Roy's crew drinks the tankers dry."

Turning from Maggie, we just about ran over Frau Hummel, "what else can we do for you? Hunter said with disgust in his voice.

"Ve have three slaves. Do you have cages for them," asked the Frau.

"Lady are they trained?"

"Very well trained," replied the Frau with her hands now on her hips.

"Then, Madame, they are your responsibility unless you are submitting them to be used for tonight's entertainment. Even in New York, you are aware that every Founder is responsible for your slaves. Ahhhh, now I remember. You are the one that created the scandal and was barred from Castle headquarters. Lady Beatrice told me you tied to switch out slaves, your badly battered slaves for fresh stock." Hunter turned to her, "if you try any of that shit here, Lady or no, you will find yourself caged. Don't fuck with Me or you will live to regret it!"

The lady put up her hands, "It was a misunderstanding my Deus. Our boys wandered off and got lost in the complex, that's all," the lady was now backstroking in attempts to get away from Hunter.

Sir looked down at me, "go get JD. We will clear up this matter once and for all, Madame."

JD was on the porch talking to an elderly lady in a wheelchair with a cast on her right leg. I dropped to my knees and waited for his attention while I racked my mind trying to remember where I had seen her last. The elderly lady pointed in my direction, "I believe, the Deus's slave has more need of you. My boys will care for my needs."

Returning with JD, I found Hunter about to blow a gasket as his face was beet red and the Fruline was just as bad. The two Founders' could hold their own but the poor slave on Frau's leash was looking as if he was being choked to death by the leash held by his irate bitch of a Mistress. Each time she raged she pulled on his leash and the collar was a choke collar.

JD and I stood to the side overhearing their conversation, Hunter was speaking, "I will not tolerate any shit or shanigans from your house while here on Buena Vista or I will see to it that the imposed suspension on your house is not lifted, that your house is closed, and your stock sold to pay past debts to Castle."

Sir saw us, "JD, ask Eric to ear mark all this woman's slaves. Put her on the watch list, she is a known troublemaker and I will not tolerate her bullshit this weekend. See to it for me, JD."

The Fruline was screaming something in German when Hunter turned his icy cold eyes back upon her. "You have better go with him, sister! I want you to know that you will not walk out of here with something that does not belong to you unless you have a signed bill of sale with my name on the sale. Start anything here, sister, and I will rip that whorehouse of yours down to the ground and burn it! Good day!"

Hunter manned the welcoming cup while JD was off with the German house. This gave Hunter time to unwind while talking with Lady Beatrice and a chance to get enough mead into him that he began to unwind, a little too much so. Being the good slave that I am I took it upon myself to relocate JD and asked him to please take the cup away from Sir. JD returned and joined me as I fed them both sandwiches before more guests arrived and I took Sir back upstairs to get him ready for this evening.

I had placed him in the hot tub to soak while he relaxed I ran about preparing everything that would be needed to dress him after he napped. Laying out clothes, shaving gear, the usual stuff, prepping his boots until I heard him calling me to him. He was sitting in the shallows wanting me to scrub his back, no problem. The back turned into his chest, into his crotch that got his cock hard. He pulled me down on to his cock and had me wash him while plugged on his antsy mast. Whoo hoo! He was making up for lost time!

After I had completed his shaving, I was ordered to shave while he watched, that for some reason always makes me nervous. Him sitting there in the barbers chair watching as I denude my body of all imagined hairs that had grown since my last shave. I think he just loved watching me twist and turn as I worked to keep my body parts smooth to his touch. He gave me orders to shower and douche as he rose from the chair and walked into the dressing room.

When I joined him squeaky clean, I found the Master of some of my more jaded dreams standing before me waiting for me to assist him with his boots and spurs. He was dressed in a full leather motorcycle cops uniform. Every detail correct and the leather molded to him like it had been painted onto his body. My cock sprang to attention as a salute to him and his powerful presence.

He laughed, "I take it this old thing meets with your approval, slave?"

I was dropping to my knees before him when I looked up, "yes, My God, yes! May I help you with your boots, Sir?"

The custom was to hold the toes of the boot under my balls and to balance the boot between my thighs. He used my head as support while he inserted his foot and stomped his foot into place. Finalizing, I leaned forward and kissed his boots lovingly.

"You are not finished yet, tonight I need the golden spurs." He was unaware that I had them in my hand when I had dropped to my knees. One must always be prepared.

I had gone to fetch him a requested cigar from the humidor. A suit box was lying in the middle of our bed. He must have seen me paying attention to the box as I passed to hand him his lighted cigar, "the contents of the box is for you. Something special for tonight."

My hands shook as I opened the box. Inside was a pair of black pants, a brown shirt with black piping and my old motorcycle jacket. I was ordered to dress.

As I dressed I found myself shaking from lust or excitement. The pants fit me like the glove leather they were made from. A chain male mesh codpiece would be fastened over my cock and balls after he had decorated them according to his preference for the night. The leather shirt laced snuggly over my chest. He called me to him.

He adjusted my pants, so that, his brand on my ass could be viewed through an encircled hole in the rear of my pants then he re laced the shirt making it skin tight like he loved on me. My nipples could be seen jutting out from my chest detailing to all who came close that the right one was pierced and both hard.

"Put on your Hiatt's, they will set you aside from others who love the Dehner look."

He rose, walked to cabinet and called me to him, his wolf whistle made me want to strut to him to best show off to him what he had given me. He slipped my balls into a heavy chromed cock and ball ring, added another chromed extension ring that went around just my balls and drew then down tightly into their sack. Over these he snapped the chromed mesh. He walked to the middle of the room, turned and ordered me to come to him, "Now, you are what I envisioned the first time I laid eyes on you. A slave fit to be envied. Come the party awaits."

His words started me thinking as we opened the door and stepped into the hallway. Look how much I had changed over years to suit the one man that I once hated and now love. His will and strength made me change. His love and my need for him made me change as I drew to understand how much I needed his love. Never had I known a love like this, nothing compared to my devotion and his.

We started down the steps. His hand resting casually on my butt, fingering the brand that marked me as his property, true, he had branded me but I him. Each in our own way together we serve each other's needs. His is the hand whereas I am the glove.

We stopped on the landing, he turned to me, pulling me to him and holding me within his arms. We both must have been reminiscing, "I love you so much, slave, it hurts!"

My hand went to his face, cupping it gently, "I never knew love could be like this until you showed it to me. Sir, you made me love you." We kissed and only when our lips parted were we aware of the cheering crowd gathered around below our landing. They cheered for the Deus or for his confession of love or both it really did not matter as we stepped down the few steps into a circle of awaiting friends.

There was enough leather in the room to scent the warm air with a rich heavy musk that spelled only one thing, leather people! The room was awash with black and colored leathers a virtual sea of men and women enjoying the gathering. Two huge fireplaces illuminated the great room where all were mingling. Kerosene lamps were placed along the walls to increase the light and yet keep the room filled with sensuous overtones of light and dark interplay. We like intimate sections within the great room, so that, people could pair off and talk without being bothered by too much light. The combined flames within the fireplace and lamps made the room warm and pleasant compared to the chill that awaited us outside.

Stupidly I had thought 9-777 needed assistance at the bar and was about to lend a hand when Hunter wrapped his arm around my waist and basically told me that my place was at his side, that is, until he wanted a cigar. Going to get him a cigar from his humidor in JD's office was interesting if you don't mind being groped, pawed on by strangers and otherwise man handled in passing. I found him upon my return speaking to a man he called Jorge. He turned opening his arms to me and acknowledged me by turning his face, "ahh, good to see you made it past the man handlers. Where's my cigar, slave?"

He took the cigar eyeing it, noticing that I had not lighted it as was normal and eyed me casually looking down the end of the cigar as he put it to his lips. I had to stifle a giggle at his antics keeping my stony face and offered a cedar flame to his cigar. He sucked on his cigar drawing some of the smoke into his lungs and exhaled it in my direction his way of saying thanks.

Jorge spoke, "your boy eh likes a good cigar? Does he like it in all ways?"

Hunter's arms wrapped around my shoulder pulling me close were he could share the cigar with me, yummy! "This little pig loves cigars and normally serves as my humanidor but tonight I have plans for that hole other than cigars." Sirs laughter stopped when he pulled my face towards mine, his hand clamped over my lips and his mouth closed over my nose this way he exhaled directly into my lungs.

I drank his smoke into me. His hand moved but still I held my breath waiting like a good slave for his permission that was given with a nod of his head. He was talking more to Jorge, the head of the Columbian Shield and I was about to be introduced.

"Lord Jorge this is my number one slave, One."

No hand was offered nor should there have been. I was merely a slave. Instead, I dropped to my knees and kissed the man's alligator knee high boots. Looking up for my position was my way of welcoming him to Buena Vista soil.

Lord Jorge looked down, "Your Lord has you well trained, One. Few know or care to show proper etiquette, but what's this I hear that you Lord Hunter have two number One's? Something new for only you, eh, my friend?"

"Actually, not at all, Jorge. This slave is my personal property, the other Number One you have known for many years as Cappy, now jonathan. He is where he belongs you might say in charge of the soil he loves, Buena Vista."

Lord Jorge put up his hand, "Too long you thought you two have fooled us! My shield and we who know the art of love like Lao's knew all along you two were only fooling yourselves with those little games you two tried to play on us. This is good, very good for you and this soil."

"Ah and where is that big buck you brought to Castle that is all the scuttlebutt. Is it true he beat the Castle's reining champion in the arena wrestling for your honor?"

"Yes, Seven is around here somewhere. It is not very far from his ward, ever since the was implanted at Castle its always around guarding me." Hunter was turning his head this way and that as he stood a head taller than most of the crowd looking for 9-777, turning his body around to Jorge he noticed 7."

"There he is Jorge, standing on the fireplace hearth. Dare you to try something Jorge and watch his reaction? No?"

"Hunter, always the kidder. I am a slight man, that brute would snap me like a twig! Perhaps later in the run we can see him in action. No doubt some of our angry Founders will try something after you placed them in common surroundings. Jorge laughed then exclaimed, "pigs! They don't know what's good for them!"

"Pardon me, Jorge. I see someone who is wearing an inappropriate uniform to this gathering. Slave's with me."

All I could do was follow in his wake with 7 following in mine as we pushed our way across the room aiming towards what looked like a Royal Canadian Mounted Policeman in full regalia. Hunter stopped at this man's back watching people around the policeman before grabbing the cop's ass, "who let this Jezebel into our house?"

My heart stopped and 7 moved closer when the RCMP turned abruptly scowling at Hunter. Hunter scowled back puffing on his cigar and blowing the smoke like he was a damn locomotive. Seven moved up to Hunter's side, a slave in a red jock moved before the RCMP. The confrontation was about to happen, people started moving away from the men.

Hunter cleared his throat, "fucking crazy Canuck! Don't you know I am the only one permitted to wear anything but basic black to high moo functions?"

The RCMP took off his gauntlet gloves slowly as if he was digesting what Hunter had proclaimed then spoke one simple word, "Harlot!"

Master absorbed the verbal retort like a fist placed into his gut then the corner of his lip curled upwards, "BITCH!"

The RCMP spoke in broken English," Qui, mon captain et vous?"

Our little circle got closer when the two guard slaves pushed between the two masters. Seven was attempting to stop a fight but became the center of attention. John Claude whistled then spoke something in French the smaller slave darted behind his owner. Whereas Hunter did not code 7 to call him off preferring to allow 7 to remain the center of attention as 7 stood between the men quietly tense anticipating movement and being ready to respond.

The RCMP removed his hat handing it to his slave along with his gloves and stepped back. 7 held his place just to the right of master, left hand at his side and the right one poised mid air as if waiting to strike. The cop moved his hands to his waist, 7's response was to move his left hand towards Hunter. The room around us had gone strangely silent and when I looked back towards the crowd I noticed it was as if we were encircled by backs. People were watching the exchange quietly while continuining their conversations in polite hushed tones.

I looked up to Hunter, studying his face. Then I knew this was a game being played out for all present. He had a straight face but his eyes were twinkling and the corner of one side of his lip was up-turned as he was trying to stifle a smile. Hunter coughed, "It would seem your training holds better than you thought, Jean-Claude?"

Jean-Claude spoke in perfect English, "when was it implanted?"

Hunter, "Four weeks ago and got a booster before we departed."

Jean-Claude, "damn! Look at it! Its ready to rip off my head if I so much as move my hand towards you! Damn! Call it off will you Hunter?"

Hunter spoke something in his native language and I watched as 7 deflated like a balloon and stepped to Sirs side. Hunter said something else in his Native American language and 7 became attentive, focused and a smile covered his face.

Jean-Claude and Hunter stepped towards each other with arms held wide, "Damn that new programming machine works great," said Hunter, "its been too damn long since you have been here Jean-Claude with your little slave Pepe. Bear hug over they parted and Pepe was sent for drinks while I was introduced to Jean-Claude and his lovely boots. Drinks returned while these two old friends were talking about the Maple shield and the problems brewing within the Canadian government.

Jonathan found us and together with the aid of 7 we drew our social butterfly towards the opposite end of the great room closer to the fireplaces. He went on his own time greeting friends, making everyone welcome, as was his duty until we got him to where he needed to be. He saw friends at every turn as we walked the long room. I actually thought I was moving him when in fact I was being lead by him by an invisible leash.

"Sir, everyone is present, all have arrived, Sir," said jonathan.

Stepping upon the huge stone fireplace hearth he called the room to attention, "Ladies and Gentlemen!"

They quieted respectfully. Jonathan with the help of slaves from the room was busy dispensing steins and boots of beer. 7 brought Hunter his stein, stood before him and tasted it before passing it to his master and gave me an engineer boot full of beer.

Hunter announced, "By your leave, Dominates, a boot of beer for your first mates/slaves."

I looked at 9-777 questioningly when it placed into my hands one of Sir's engineer boots filled to the rim with beer, then I looked up at my Sir who only winked, the other slaves had small glass boots that held about a pint I was stuck with a fucking gallon as my loving master with the aid of my brother 7 had handed me one of his knee high boots. God, how I loved those two! Bastards! I thought quietly to myself. It would seem by this presentation that more than the other boot would hit the floor before this night was over.

Hunter was watching the crowd, seeing to it that all got their necessary drinks before the toasting began, then he called out to the room, "Ladies and Gentlemen, some of you have come from great distances to join with Buena Vista's Shield Mates in celebrating our highest time of remembrance our All Souls Eve and tomorrows All Hallows Day Motorcycle Run. Tonight the dead walk with the living; tonight they join us in sharing our libations. Take a moment, speak the names of those that have left the land of the living; so that, they may realize that they are welcome to this celebration and will join us for this night."

Hunter began looking around the room, watching and nodding his head to Shield Captains as they began to intone the names of brothers and sisters who have died within their clan. Hunter began his litany of the dead and I was shocked to hear him mention the name of Doc. He saw me look up at him when he said it but said nothing more than that twisted little fuckers name and went on adding names of others. Others within the room were reading their list of loved ones and it seemed the ranks of the room swelled as the dead were summoned to our party. I know for a fact the room became filled with a light fog whether or not it was ghosts or not I could not say but if I had had hairs on the back of my neck they would have stood up that's for certain.

Hunter continued with his list of fallen; boy jim, dannyboy, Bill, Colt, Grunt, Dr. Dave, Helena, Jerry, Harold, Annie, Ben, Morris, Willie, Lady D, Mistress C, Scooter before falling into silence and waiting patiently until others finished their naming of names. Silently Hunter hoisted his stein towards the ceiling the company joined him they lowered their drinks spilled some of the contents on the floor then took a long drink on their drinks. The clamor of people celebrating life filled the room like a brilliant flash in a dark cave.

Hunter bellowed down to them, "let's kick this fucking party into High Gear!"

"Tonight we celebrate UNITY! May this run prove to be all that you have come to know and to expect from your Lord and more since I have been awarded the title of Deus!"

Cheers like a huge wave from the ocean washed over the crowd and spilled out into the night where more people were gathering around fires waiting quietly for their leaders to exit the house to officially begin the party. Cheers from the guest's showed their appreciation as he joined them in downing his beer stein and 7 was there at his side to hand him another. I cut 7 a look that should have killed him in his place, as I knew what it was to manhandle a big tall drunken master when he was in a party mood.

7 extended his hand towards my stein and I passed it to him, he chugged a goodly portion and passed it back to me as if to say, join the party or else.

Hunter belched loudly and continued, "First of all let me introduce to you the team that has made this party and all its fixings come together without whom I could not function properly. 'Jonathan, front and center!'"

The crowd parted for jonathan as he made his way to were his Lord stood, "you use to know him as Cappy. He is still in charge of Buena Vista as its Number One slave known to us as jonathan. If you are upset about your housing accommodations 'tuff shit!' But jonathan can get you first aid and help you if you are lost. His commander and soon to be Master is Eric Wilson."

Eric made his way through the crowd to stand next to Hunter on the fireplace.

"Eric was commander of the Black Watch but I stole him away with the lure of fresh meat, jonathan, and the promise of better times. Eric is in command of our Buena Vista Security team if you and your brothers behave well you may never see him in action. Hold your applause until I have introduced them all."

"You saw me smooching on this one," Hunter's hand encircled my neck and pulled me up to stand at his side, "this is my personal property, my Number One."

Hunter snapped his fingers, 9-777 stepped around from behind Hunter to stand below him. "This one was once a handler is no more, this is my personal bodyguard and Number Two, this slave is 9-777."

"This team along with a small herd of other slaves has put this event together; now you may applaude."

They went wild and I honestly did not know what to do but I was not alone we all seemed to draw closer to Hunter as the wave of energy from the cheers and clapping washed over us. The noise would have continued if not for a loud bang that sounded like a gun shot came from the front of the house. Everyone seemed to turn towards the loud noise and we heard a quiet voice speaking.

"Make way for the Grand Deus, said a boy standing beside a lady in a wheelchair."

Ahhh, that's the same lady I had seen with JD earlier that day. The puzzle pieces just keep falling in place. She had been on the ship when I was uncrated many years ago.

The crowd parted to allow the slave-propelled wheelchair as it was driven through the crowd as she made her way towards Hunter. The wheelchair halted at the fireplace, its metal leg supports moved as one boy stooped downwards the elderly lady looked up to Hunter, "care to give a feeble old lady a hand up big boy?"

Hunter all but picked her up from the chair and placed her next to him. Two slaves moved to take positions on either side of the Lady acting as support while she tried to balance herself on one leg while not putting weight on the one on the cast. She was radiant with energy and style. Late 60's, perfectly arranged white hair, black leather corset and a long black dress with a split up one side and one riding boot with gold spur. The normally white cast had been painted during the afternoon a nice glossy black and had even been fitted with a mock golden spur.

The crowd had quieted while she got squared away. She looked up to Hunter and smiled her cherub like smile. The same smile that had foretold others that the axe was about to fall and another body would be added to her count.

"Share a part of the spotlight with an old lady, Hunter?"

"Lady Beatrice, my friends please welcome the recently retired Deus."

The crowd gave a quiet applause to show their appreciation for her presence.

She raised a wine glass over her head, "I am suppose to be the first one to officially congratulate you on your promotion to the head of Castle Enterprises Unlimited, but I have been told by my spies that you dear Hunter have already been honored by two parties and," she looked in my direction, "a few unofficial celebrations, too!"

I didn't know I could still blush; but hearing it coming from her the guests seemed to love my discomfort.

"Slave, Open the doors and Windows so all may hear what I have to say."

Those outside once the doors were opened began to come inside of the house until the room was packed even more than it had been and the music outside died. A slave gave her a microphone so those outside would be able to hear clearly what she had to say, "Friends, Shield Mates of Buena Vista, Founders of Castle, lend me your ears. As the recently retired Deus, I, Lady Beatrice do hereby command that you raise your glasses and boots to a toast. To Lord and Master Hunter, Lord of Buena Vista the new DEUS of CASTLE Enterprises, may he rule with an Iron Fist, may he make us richer than our wildest dreams, and may his slaves keep him healthy and happy so we all reap the profits of his talents!"

"Here, here's" were heard throughout the room and cheers were heard from around the room as they all finished off their drinks and started mingling around wanting to get outside when Hunter called their attention on more time.

"Before you go. First drink outside is for Lady Beatrice to welcome her home to Buena Vista she will remain with us until and after she heals. One last thing, the Master Chef has prepared well for the likes of you. Meat eaters there is food everywhere, vegetarians look to the green tent there you will find plenty for you to eat as well. When you get time read your run packs it tells you when the run begins tomorrow. Now, Go, Let's party!"

They bellowed their thank you and it looked like someone had called a fire drill, as the room was once full suddenly empty only Hunter, Lady Beatrice and his team were present. We got Lady Beatrice back into her wheelchair and made our way towards the front door. In passing we checked with registration to see if any last minute calls had to be handled. Eric and jonathan excused themselves on the pretense of needing to get out and secure the fields leaving Hunter in the care of 9-777 and I.

We weren't paying much attention to any one thing as 9-777 opened the door and we stepped out on to the front porch as we were totally absorbed into each other and we got the shock of our life.

Every one, every damn one of those who had come to the party was gathered below us, gathered before and around the main house. Hunter was looking at me when we exited the house, and I was guiding him when I came to an abrupt halt just before the steps going down to the ground. He looked at me kinda confused then turned his head and stepped back one step that's when they began chanting, "Deus, Deus, Deus!"

Hunter stepped forward bowed to them rose and extended his hands toward them, opening his arms in a way of suggesting to them they were in his arms and began clapping for them. The mob began cheering their approval and even rose a pitch and the clapping took on a rhythmical pattern. He stepped back pulling me into his arms then pulling 9-777 who dropped to his knees before his master. Sir leaned over, kissed me hard, and the crowd went fucking nuts. He turned, leaned down pulling up 9-777's chin and gave it a kiss as well and they went fucking nuts with catcalls!

9-777 had taken his rightful position on Sir's right and to show to all my devotion to my Lord and Master, I dropped to my knees at his left leg, put out my right arm and encircled his leg and my head dropped over to rest lovingly on his leg. His hand settled down around my shoulders and the other hand on 9-777's neck. There we stood for all to see the Master, his slave over and his slave. Both 9-777 and myself looked up from our position radiating our love and total devotion to the man we called Master.

Sir held up his hands, "my friends, brothers and sisters of Buena Vista, thank you all for coming to our little party." Everyone laughed at his little joke, this in no way was a little celebration actually this was by far the largest get together this estate had ever seen.

"Tonight, Ladies and Gentlemen join US in celebrating Our UNION by the common brand!"

Hunter leaned forward, snapped a leash to my collar, and snapped his fingers at 9-777 who moved before us parting the crowd for his brother slave and Master. You would have thought it was planned but it wasn't. Together we descended the steps and merged with the chanting horde. 9-777 plowed a path through our people and in mass we moved towards the main feasting tent. He had his people eating out of the palm of his hands, they loved him now, but how would they handle the changes that he would bring about with the Castle Enterprises with him at its helm and the master plan implemented. We knew for certain a lot of the Founder's would absolutely die if not be terminated since many of their houses were no longer making profit for the greater company. Times were a changing but how much would change?

Chapter 7

Restraint with the eye is good,
good is restraint of the ear.
Restraint with the ear is good,
good is restraint with the tongue.
Restraint with the body is good,
good is restraint with speech.
Restraint with the heart is good,
good is restraint everywhere.
A monk everywhere is restrained is released
from all suffering and stress.
Dhammapada, 25,
translated by Thanissaro Bhikkhu

Master and I rose fairly early the morning after the opening welcoming party of the Buena Vista Halloween Run. We joined the heads of security in the dining room for a debriefing breakfast from last night's events to hear their verbal report of the incidents. The Halloween run was a huge success. As usual there were a few major and minor problems, but this is normal with any successful run. A few local kids crashed the party and found themselves in a world of trouble. A local sheriff had told them that we were a nudist camp, partly true. The boys had assumed we were holding a huge orgy, again true. So they thought it would be cool if they joined us, wrong, all wrong! Twelve young men from 16 to 19 tried to crash the party. They sneaked in by walking over three miles up rugged terrain to get to the party they knew would be a blast. God only knows what visions those young men had dancing in their heads by the time they saw the campfires, chromed cycles and heard the riotous laughter.

Security caught three of the twelve when they crossed a trip wire on the edge of the forest. Number Six security team wearing night vision goggles caught the boys unsuspectingly and made them scatter like a covey of quail still they caught three at that site. I know I would have shit too if four big men in pure black carrying machine guns stepped out of nowhere and aimed their guns at me. Six more were found later at the beer wagon and were taken in cuffs to the underground security center for a strip search and detention. I know those guards had fun with the boys at their own expense. It is within securities behavior to take advantage of certain situations and these boys were ripe for the picking. One more was caught when he tried to save a female slave from a bullwhipping demo. The little shit decked the master with a rotten limb he had found. That poor boy was tackled by onlookers, nearly stomped to death by our guests before politely being handed over to security when they arrived, that boy was taken to the infirmary before being taken to a cell. The two others were still missing and a slow search would be conducted just in case they got taken to someone's bed during the night. One other thing that made that weekend stand out in our scrapbook was that our security team caught a major drug dealer, a Founder. The Founder that was caught attempting to enter our estate with illegal drugs was none other than Sir Frederick Black of the Avalon Shield hailing from London, England. He was one of those that had been investigated by Castle's security accounting team prior to Hunter becoming the Deus. The stupid fucker appeared at the main gate with his crew of slaves as if nothing was wrong. When security intervened halting them until records could be produced Sir Frederick became openly belligerent. He calmed down when a security Humvee arrived to take them to processing, but he struck the driver of the vehicle when he realized that instead of being taken up to the main house they were being taken towards the underground entrance of the slave pens. Force was used to stop Sir Frederick when he tried to jump from the moving vehicle and a slave tried to flee the scene carrying a suitcase both were halted by an electric tazer. The other members of the party were docile.

Sir Frederick was housed separately and per request from the docile slaves, one male the other female the one who attempted to run got locked in chains in his own private cell. Both the male and female slaves in separate interrogations named the third slave as the one who has gained control of Avalon Shield by addicting Sir Black to a new deadly drug combination part meth and part ecstasy, SNAP. Sir Black recovered easily from the stun gun's affect but seemed agitated and paced the cell constantly moving like a caged animal. He did however have a seizure around 1AM. A medic was called to attend Sir Black during which Sir Black's luggage was searched in hopes of finding his medication. During the search they found 897 vials of the drug SNAP and conclusion was reached that he was undergoing withdrawal. Sir Frederick was transferred immediately to our hospital at least there they could control his fits and hopefully help him withdraw from his addiction.

We found Sir Frederick bound solidly to his bed. White blood flecked froth was running down his cheeks, his eyes were not focusing on anything and he was sweating profusely. Hunter spoke at length to the attending medic. They had tried normal procedures to lessen his withdrawal, methadone did nothing for him, the medical team wanted to see if Hunter would permit them to use one vial of the drug. Maybe giving him small doses would lessen the anxiety and hopefully weaken the destruction his body seems to be undergoing as it underwent cold turkey withdrawal. Sir Frederick was close to death all depended on what Hunter and the security guards could get out of his drug pimp. An interrogation was in order hopefully they could retrieve enough information to save the Founder's life.

SNAP was a new sex drug that gave its user euphoria compounded by brilliant colors and extraordinary sexual energy. An addict could not perform sexually without the drug as it made the user have more pronounced erections, impervious to pain and food did not lessen the high. A jolt of SNAP made a body burn for three brilliant days of constant stimulation coming down from the high was often deadly. On a man SNAP would not allow your cock to go soft. You could literally fuck the skin off your cock and not care. On a woman, it was worse; she would literally fuck anything to satisfy the itch, many women bled to death. Use SNAP once and it was fun, use it again and you were helplessly hooked. The downside of SNAP addiction was the brain began to malfunction and the body went into overdrive burning rapidly leaving a living breathing shell where there had once been a human being. Most burnouts became wards of the state if they did not die during withdrawal. Too often in the serious addicts their hearts would implode due to overworking the muscle. SNAP addiction was a one-way ticket to death; but those that used the shit did not seem to care, as every day was an orgy of sensual intercourse. SNAP pimps were called on the street the Angels of Death or in slang, Angels. The worse thing about SNAP it came from out of the United States medical labs like so many of the street drugs and like so many of the diseases.

Master Hunter was an avenging angel when he made his way to the slave pens that was housing Sir Frederick Black's slaves and the slave that had attempted to escape with the case full of SNAP. In route to the slave pens, Hunter stopped to check to see if the boys that were caught last night were fed breakfast and saw to it that they would be collected by Pappy. Cold shivers ran up my spine at the mention of that evil fucks name. By the looks of those young boys, more than one would have their tail feathers plucked by Pappy and his gang of rogue cops. Hell they would have a fucking field day, and if I knew Pappy he would have them all branded as official police equipment and convince each of their parents that they had to do thousands of hours of detention just for his intervention in their behalf. Sick thing is, the boy's parents would all but give the boys over to the sheriff in hopes he will lay the law into their hides. Little did they know what I knew, his law would get deep into their butts before he was finished with them.

I thought Hunter was in deep thought as we traversed the underground passages in route to the slave pens when he abruptly stopped and turned to me.

"Number One, do you trust me?"

I had no clue where he was going with this and answered him honestly, "Yes, my Lord I trust you completely."

One hand encircled my waist and he pulled me to him, "They want to test you. They want to test my Number One. I laughed in their faces but they did not laugh back."

"Sir, what type of test?" I asked him confused about where this was going.

His sigh spoke volumes, "I honestly do not know. All I can say it that it will be harder than you imagine and nothing you cannot handle. You know I would never put your life at risk. The ones calling for the test knew you when you lived in outside society they need proof positive that you are no longer that being."

He pulled me to him as a way of comforting me and helping me to overcome the hesitation, "Sir, will it hurt?"

"On one level yes but nothing you cannot handle," he smiled then, "they want to see if your love and devotion is true. That's all it can be but they have a right to make certain that the Deus has the best of the best at his side. Lady Beatrice was put through hell for her slave pup's mine can be no different."

We walked on in silence for a few minutes, "what if I fail the test, Sir?"

He stopped, turned to me, "nothing will change between you and I. I need you more each day. Its how they will behave around you that's at stake. Pass the test and you are in their eyes the true Number One of the Deus. It makes you in their stupid minds my associate, lover, slave, tiffle," then he laughed again. "Besides no matter what happens you are MINE and I am yours!"

Our journey down the corridor left me in considerable confusion. When he arrived he stopped by the security desk told them to bring the two slaves to him in interrogation room one and to take the stupid fuck of a slave that tried to run to the medical exam room, secure him to the table and have someone wait with him. Just his tone of voice made me thankful I wasn't on the receiving end of any of these interrogations nor was the officer on duty who all but jumped to Hunter's orders.

We had not been in the room more than a few minutes when the door opened and two scared slaves were ushered into the room both greeted Hunter in a way only our stock would know. At the door they dropped to their knees placed their heads to the floor and kissed the floor as a sign of respect for Buena Vista their home training grounds. Sir named them, the female was known as Clara and the male Gene both had been trained on Buena Vista soil and given to Sir Frederick as a gift from Hunter when he took over running the Avalon Shield. The two slaves blurted out in unison what had happened to their master.

Their master had become addicted to the drug SNAP about 6 months ago and his only means of paying for the drug had been to introduce the pimp, Rodney, to his friends and associates. Rodney was not a real slave, he wore a collar as a fashion statement and knew that the collar denoted a well-trained service animal, something Rodney was not. For all his looks, Rodney was a self centered egotistical manipulative weasel who had wormed his way into being one of the largest drug dealers in England with the help of Sir Frederick Black who himself had become a slave to the drug SNAP.

The guard was summoned Clara and Gene were transferred to medical where they would be given a full examination. If they passed they would be put to work above ground within the kitchens for the completion of the run afterwards depended upon if Sir Black survived his withdrawal. The two seemed genuinely happy to be home and went easily with the guards that came for them.

Exiting the interrogation room, Hunter looked over his shoulder and caught me yawning widely. He stopped mid stride turned and caught me in his arms, "You are exhausted Number One. Get your ass back upstairs and into my bed."

I tried to protest saying something stupid like, I needed to be with him but his hand over my lips stopped that nonsense. He ordered me to bed and told me that I did not need to witness what he was about to do to another human being. I was overjoyed in away that I was being sent to bed cause I really did not need to see him do to a human being what doc had told he had done to them many times. This was not an aspect of my master that I needed to witness. It was bad enough that I knew he had a dark side a very still cold and dark Angel that was about to be released on a pimp for SNAP. No, this I did not need to witness.

He pulled me into his arms, held me tightly as if he would have much preferred to be going back to bed with me than to where he needed to go, raped my mouth, hugged me close then opened his arms. "Get going, One. You will need your rest to pass the test" and with a pat on my naked butt I was away.

I ran down the corridors enjoying the pleasure of running, turned a corner that would take me upstairs and nearly ran over Eric Wilson who stopped me abruptly.

"Ho! Is the house on fire?" Eric had a well-bound jonathan at his side on a leash.

"Sir, I am sorry Sir. Master sent me to bed while he does one of his special interrogations on the English slave, Sir." I replied while panting.

"I need a moment of your time One, my worthless slave here won't tell me or doesn't know where Master Hunter stores his Harley. Hunter has asked me to let Rob Roy look at it prior to the run."

I must have looked at him oddly, jonathan should have known, true he was gagged but he should have been able to lead him to the garage.

I heard the elevator chime, the very one I was planning to use to get topside, and Rob Roy carrying a duffle bag of tools stepped out, "Eric, where in the hell did you two go! Oh, there you are. Anyone find the hog in this fucked up maze? Christ what they have done to a simple compound dun gone and made it into a fucking crazy maze. No self respecting slave could ever get out of this damn place that's for certain" Rob Roy was talking a blue streak as he made his way towards Eric. It all seemed so normal to me I should have suspected something but I didn't.

They would not have found the place where Hunter stored his Harley without guidance so I took them through the underground passages, up a lift, to a metal garage located behind the larger one. When I got there my exhaustion from the previous nights activities must have caught up with me. Looking back know I should have seen it coming, the lock on the door was removed, that was a first. Only Hunter had the key to that and I knew he was down below working on a helpless animal.

The garage had a huge door that moved on a track and a smaller human sized door, it was to the smaller door that I went. Eric asked me to go ahead and turn on the lights and like a fucking fool I did. I should have seen it, but I didn't. I flipped the switches, no lights turned on. Eric had poked his head through the door and caught my attempt at turning on a light.

"One?" said Eric, "do you know where there is another light or should I send jonathan to get a flashlight?"

"Wait one moment, Sir. There is a light over his work bench."

Bastards knew I would never make it to the workbench! No sooner than I got to the middle of the room I was jumped! A bag was tossed over my head, hands grabbed my hands and feet and I went down in a flurry of swinging hands and kicking legs. They were not going to take me easily. I know my feet slammed into some flesh nevertheless there were too many. They got me down, rolled me around and tied me up. I was as mad as a wet cat bound in burlap and god helped any of them if I got loose.

Damn if they did not let me roll around and try my damnedest to get free. I rolled over and over until I bumped into something than rolled back the other way until I bumped into something hard again. No one seemed to be present while I worked myself into a panic. I honestly don't know how long I lay there worming around on the floor but it all halted when I heard a Harley kicked to life.

The room was suddenly filled with the roaring voice of a finely tuned engine and I was stunned when I heard Hunter's voice, "lift him carefully boys and tie him securely, can't have him rolling off when I drag his carcass to the test."

I felt the heat of his bike as he rolled near me and had the pleasure of feeling his boot on my stomach when I attempted to roll closer but was shocked when arms scooted under and lifted me. I tried wiggling in their arms and a gruff voice ordered me to stop or be dropped. They carried me a short distance and lowered me to a bumpy surface and tied me to what I thought were old tires. There were a stack of old used truck tires in one corner of his work shed, could they have made some type of sled.

They did not give me much time to think about it as the motorcycle engine was gunned and I moved forward carried on a sled made from tires. Inside the garage the light was dim, the burlap bag gave me limited light so I was basically blind. My sled jerked forward then shot like an arrow out of the shed. As we picked up speed I could hear a screaming mob as if it was all around me.

I knew the route we were taking I was trying to scramble for a handhold when we hit the curve and my sled skidded around the curve spewing rocks and gravel at the cheering crowd. As abruptly as my ride began my sled of used tires skidded to a halt and Sir's motorcycle engine died but the cheering from the crowd rose in a pitch. I could hear the crunch of boots approaching, not just one pair walking my way and then I heard him, yes, my Master's voice, what he said chilled me to the bone. Hands went to work releasing me from the sled. They tore off the burlap bag but kept my hands and legs bound. I watched as Hunter dismounted from his Harley and walked towards me.

He held up his hands for silence, "not unlike a lamb brought to the altar for sacrifice, I do now bring my most trusted and valuable slave, Number One. Do with us what thou wish!"

He grabbed my chin and the men holding me allowed him. A rapid kiss to my lips and a whispered order, "follow your heart, boy!"

I watched in horror as men closed around him, placed a burlap bag over his head, cuffed his hands and took him away. We went in opposite directions as I was being carried towards the barn and he was being taken towards the security center. I had opened my mouth to scream something when a ball was inserted by Rob Roy with a cautious warning, "we will have none of that. He has his ordeal and you have yours," then he winked, "you two will be back together if you both pass the test soon enough."

Rob Roy and his brothers carried me into the manimal pens I once loved this time I was frightened half out of my wits from the uncertainty of what would come next. They took me into one of the empty stalls, released my hands and feet as Rob Roy moved forward. He held up to white patches of cotton, "I have to cover your eyes so that you can see nothing until its time. Part of your test is obedience to orders. Once you are without sight you are to stay here unfettered until they come for you. Do not try to escape this stall or it will really go hard on both of you." Then he whispered in my ear as he was taping the eye patches over my eyes, "your Master said, ' be the pig that he knows you can be and you will survive the ordeal.'"

"Lay down and rest while you can slave, we have things to prepare. Leave this stall and you will curse the day you were born!" Rob Roy's final words left me wondering what were they preparing to do to me. I sat down when I heard the stall door close and the door latch slipped into its shackle. Men were talking just beyond where I was lying in the straw strewn floor sadly too low for me to understand, still there chatter made me realize I was to stay put until they came for me. So I shut my eyes and fell asleep, might not be master's bed, but it was good enough for me. Besides when I was a mule in training I called a stall much like this one home.

The fresh straw awoke memories buried deep in my subconscious mind. Living life as a mule had its perks. Sweet apples were the best fed to me by my handler after a hand days work on the fields and those long rub downs and cooling baths given to me by my handler after a hot day plowing fields. Suddenly I realized how much I missed those days of certainty each day was like the day before it, some would have thought it a boring life but here working with my trainer I thrived and loved the hard labor. Memories flooded back once I had allowed myself to relax, great memories, learning to run in horse hoofs, the first steps how they felt being elevated above others, the simple pleasure of feeling the wind in your face as you run pulling a carriage and the simple pride of being one of the master's trained carriage nags. Simple pleasure, simpler times...

Oh, God they are here for me! The door to the stall was opened, "Get up on your feet, slave," barked a deep bass voice that was new to me. He did not give me time to rise but grabbed a hold of my collar and lifted, others grabbed my arms pulling them backwards and cuffing them. With his hand on my collar I was lead out of the stall, turned a few times to get me confused in which direction I was taking and then we were off. The stall had been warm and out of the weather they escorted me out into the chill of the October day naked save for collar and cuffs. They walked me this way and that, other party goers were still enjoying their run by the way they greeted my escort. We must have walked a good mile, turning this way, then another way until I was completely lost and shivering down to my boots. A door opened, we moved forward inside a tight room by the echo the hands on my arms withdrew and the bass voice spoke again, "stand right there until we come to get you. Move and your ass is mine!" Booted feet withdrew, someone lighted a cigarette by the smell and I slipped into parade rest stance, waiting and shaking, as the cold of the room seemed to bore into my bones.

My body had begun to chill uncontrollably as I stood in that cold ass room. Voices of men and women were outside the shed. I could hear them talking about their breakfast, the run, how the weekend was shaping up and over heard a Master berating his slave. I was forced by the cold within my body to extend my mind farther than this room, hoping to hear anything that would take my mind off this numbing cold. My teeth had begun to chatter when a warm hand touched my shoulder. It was as if someone had placed a cattle prod between my legs and had depressed the button. My jump and scream had to have been heard outside and was by the returning laughter of those outside the shed.

The hand on my shoulder pushed me forward. Hesitantly, I shuffled my feet fumbling for each step, a door opened and the warmth of the room waved out to greet me and I hurried into the room. Tobacco and reefer smoke hung in the air as the steady hand pushed me forward into what had to be the lion's den. My hands were released once the hand on my shoulder called a halt to my progress. Each hand held by someone while the hand itself was fed into warm leather gloves. Each finger was slipped into its own leather condom before the soft glove was pulled over my open palms and down over my wrists. Straps were cinched around my wrists before being fed between my legs and I was turned into a human pretzel. In such a position I was locked, head down, legs spread, ass open and ready for whatever was next on their agenda.

By the sound a wooden chair was drug across the floor in my direction, someone took the seat and begin fingering my butt hole, teasing it by inserting their finger slowly until my ass and I began to relax. Whoever was working my hole knew what he was doing to me, my rosette unfurled to his whistled surprise. He spoke to someone near, "Give me that tube of butt butter, and let's see how far that thing will stretch." His finger withdrew only to be replaced by a cold metal tip. A metallic click followed by another as their butt butter was pushed past my rectum into my bowels. Butt butter is cannabis based herbal butter that I knew would heighten my enjoyment of the task before me. Using this stuff they meant for me to relax two clicks suggested they wanted me really relaxed if not comatose. The cold metal tip was withdrawn only to be replaced by a large bulbous instrument that was pushed steadily past my rectum until my butt sucked it in deep and started chewing on it like a pacifier. Once my butt was stuffed to their specifications my hands were released allowing me to stand upright giving me time to adjust to the heavy plug in my butt and to a new sensation of euphoria as it washed over me. They must have used someone's private stock to make that butt butter cause by the time I had stood erect I was feeling the buzz nicely.

Again my hands were chained out stretched in a cruciform position. I could move my arms only in tight little circles but not allow them to drop. My feet were kicked outstretched; straps were added to lock them into their appointed place. No one spoke as they worked to get me into their chosen position. Those within the room began to shuffle around, doing what I had no clue as they went about their jobs.

A hand cupped my chin and lifted it. The scent of leather filled my nostrils. Over my head was pulled a heavy drape of leather. This was tugged over my head, worked into position down my arms and over my torso. A quiet female voice spoke; "arms up," and my arms began to shift upwards. Two people, I think, began working under my arms in my armpits, one on one side the other opposite. Together they began drawing the leather over my torso and tightening it as they laced it down my sides securely. The front of the leather shirt seemed to hang long on my torso, draping almost to my thighs. It was through a hole in this leather that my balls and cock were pushed. Straps on either side of my nuts were pulled between my legs crossing over if not around the protruding stub of the butt plug. My arms were lowered. The leather on them was laced extremely tight or so it felt as they went about their job of sewing me into a shirt of leather.

My arms were released one at a time. Heavy straps were wrapped over my forearms up to and crossing my gloved hands. My thumb was inserted into something located within my palm then my fingers were molded over that round of leather before a leather strap bound them locked into place. Once done the hand was reconnected to the chains so they were out of the way for their next application of leather to my body.

Someone who must have been kneeling below me started cursing a blue streak, "his fucking boots are locked on!" Hands started pulling on my boots as if to rip them off instead they nearly unbalanced me. "God damned it! Look into the shed they might have bolt cutters." Boots ran out of the room and returned a few minutes later, "thank God, Hunter's anal. He had them on the peg board above his work bench."

A HA, I thought; now I knew where I was located. They had just walked me around until I got confused and brought me back to his work shed. I am in the office off from his forge. I relaxed and listened intently as they cut the bolts holding my boots firmly locked on to my feet. Someone whistled when they were removed, I knew they had to stink like rotten fish if not worse as Hunter had locked them on just before we went downstairs the first night of the run. Hastily my feet were washed and placed into warm woolen socks before rebound into position.

The sound of papers ruffling followed by a heavy thunk then another thunk, "nice looking boots," said a male voice in the room. Then another voice spoke, one I knew from the caverns below but where, "ok, this has to go between his legs, one of you hold it back there, raise it up, hold. Let me buckle it around his waist then you can release." Heavy leather was buckled around my waist by the feel of it, chaps, pants, I knew not which. A zipper was pulled from between my legs up between my butt cheeks then another was pulled up the front covering my erect cock and balls in folds of leather. I mistakenly broke silence with a, "woof!" A backhand taught me to remain silent.

Leather panels were pulled into place on my legs, each were laced snuggly downwards towards my feet. My hands were released once they had then secure and I was ordered to squat, adjustments were made to the knees so that swatting was possible still the pants were amazingly comfortable as they molded becoming a second skin. I know in my minds eye I had to be hot looking, covered in black leather laced securely to my body as if the leather had become my second skin, fucking awesome.

My feet were lifted one at a time slipped into a boot and laced upwards towards my knees. I overheard a males voice below me exclaim, "Look how the straps have locking luggage buckles, this slave cannot get out of these without a key!"

My cock threatened to go into overdrive but they must have sensed that cause the front fly was jerked open. Someone's calloused hand grabbed my cock and balls pulling them front and center. He forced my balls into a tight little bag that was cinched tightly around them. However, my cock was laced into a heavy piece of leather that encircled my cock up to the head. Once my cock was secured in its leather sheath my cock and balls were pushed back into the confines of the pants and strapped upright so my balls were an easier target if you knew where to hit once the zipper was closed.

Hands ran over my new skin, testing for firmness, adjusting the suits tightness until they were satisfied. Once they were happy with their inspection I was basically left alone. A match was struck, the smell of another joint was lighted and the smoke exhaled in my face. A gentle touch to my face made me jerk away. That gentle touch turned brutal when it pinched my nose closed and another set of hands locked my lips and jaw closed. Panic overtook me when oxygen deprived lungs began to suck in nothing. I tried to buck them off; they did not loosen their grips. Oxygen starved lungs generated stars that flashed before my closed eyes. I felt my body weakening sinking towards the floor when they released my mouth and I sucked in a ball. A hand forced the ball past the obstruction of my teeth, held it while I choked and sputtered until it was buckled in place at the back of my head.

I heard scraping as if something heavy was being dragged into its place around me. Silence except for my own breathing could be heard from those that had helped me into this suit of leather. Scissors began to gnaw at the gauze that bound my eyes and I heard a voice from behind me say, "keep your eyes shut slave until I say then open them slowly. The light's are kinda bright in here."

The tape and gauze was peeled away from my eyes. I held my eyes tightly shut allowing the light of the room to help them adjust even as something heavy was pulled into place at my rear. "Open them slowly, slave.'

I let my eyes slowly test the view for fear that they would be blinded by the brilliance of the light. What I saw before and around me took me totally by surprise! They had positioned mirrors around my body so that I could see every angle of what they had created over me. They had literally sewn me into a suit of rich satiny black leather that ran from my neck down to my feet. The suit was a masterful creation fitting me in all the right places; zippers ran between my butt cheeks and up the other side over my bound cock and balls. The suit made me look as if I had been painted in black glove leather it molded to every muscle and fold of my skin. I was hot enough to have fucked myself I looked fucking good, even the drool running down my chin looked awesome!

Those that were in the room had departed when they set up the mirrors. I was growing tired of my forced position when a bracket of mirrors were removed by a muscular slave to allow his petite mistress to enter. She eyed me up and down turned to her slave, "release his arms, remove the mirrors and let's get this show on the road."

She stood back to let him work and he followed her orders to the tee. My arms were dropped, mirrors stacked before he returned to her side. She pointed at my boots, "release his feet, let him walk around and get some circulation going. Help him if you must, but first bring him here. None of us like a fucking ball gag, let's loose that besides have something else in mind for you that will work better.

The heavy muscled mule lead me to his mistress, he pushed me to my knees before her. She grabbed my head and pulled it into her crotch, "heard tell, that pussy isn't your favorite dish? Hunter said that if you fuck up this test, I can have you." She laughed evilly, "after awhile slave, you will learn to eat my stinky fish like a professional muff diver, right mule?"

The mule behind me only grunted a response. She indicated with hand signals to hold my head so she could remove the ball gag. She was gentle and even wiped clean my chin from its heavy coating of drool.

She produced a half face hood. My chin was placed into the molded cup and my nose was slipped into the nose cuff the balance of the leather was pulled snuggly over my cheeks and eye sockets then all was buckled at the rear of my head. Once completely secure no light entered the facemask. I was totally helpless. The mule helped me to my feet and lead me by my arm around the room so I could get a feel of my new leather clad body and boots before I was made to do something harder.

He lead me or so I thought around the room however he was leading me out of the room, down a corridor towards the testing grounds. As I walked with him I was lost in my own headspace thinking if I did not have enough motivation to win through this test the threat of having to eat pussy was plenty of motivation. Hell I could probably walk on water if I was ordered to right now!

Up steps, steps I thought, where in the hell are we now? We stopped and the facemask was released and they backed away leaving me in a darkened room. My senses told me others were present within that room. No movement, just that six sense told me I was not alone. Their silence was disquieting.

A voice shattered the stillness and startled me, "around you stands the honor guard of the Castle, sworn protectors of our Deus. Master's, Mistress's, and their slaves that have survived this test and now stand before you on the eve of your greatest test. Master Bruce Hunter is the Deus in name, but it is up to you if he is to become the embodiment of the Deus and have power over all. Both you slave and Master Hunter are being tested today."

"Each slave enters this ordeal wearing something as a reminder of his Master's love and devotion to that slave. Your master made the suit that now encases your body, so that, as he stated, 'you will feel his love protecting you.'"

"Extend your arms, slave and stand ready. The test is upon you."

Heavily muscled slaves picked me up as if I was nothing but a bag of flour and carried me across the room to a suddenly illuminated St. Andrews cross. A panel on the back of my suit was opened exposing my flesh to whatever was to come. The voice spoke again, "you will be canned, slave!"

The room exploded with the sound of canes sucking the air, swooshing sounds seemed to radiate from all around the room. The first blow was laid not on my back but across my ass cheeks making me suck that plug almost up to my tonsils. Other blows struck my back and tripped down my back. Some strikes were merely light taps others were swift and brutal, forcing my lungs to dump air in a throaty scream. The rain of canes started abruptly and died just as fast. Before I knew it I was dumped from the cross on to the floor there I waited sucking air as my body tired to adjust to the suddenness of the attack.

A boot from out of the darkness caught me in my ribs flipping me upwards. Leathered and booted legs were dangerously encircling me preparing to take me apart if I failed their test. I could not see shit so I was amazed when a well-aimed boot found my nuts bowling me over onto that leg as I retched. My retching gave them time to flip me onto my back; a hand grabbed my head and forced it to look one way. A brilliant light illuminated one spot it was to that spot my head was focused.

People entered the illuminated door dressed in black robes wearing black leather conical hats with red crosses etched in the forehead. Master was drug into view. He was naked, filthy, cuffed and I tried to go to him but the boots held me in place when they turned his back to me. He had red angry looking welts across his back and buttocks!

I was forced to watch as they humiliated him before his peers. They lubricated his ass and forced a plug into his ass, by the grunts he made he was not pleased. I could read the pain on his face when they bound his handsome cock and balls. Hands guided his feet into black leather Jodhpur pants. In the past I had always thought that those pants looked silly on men, but seeing them placed on my master this moment they suited him well. They helped him into his knee-high boots that we loved so well. Released him from the cuffs long enough to place him into a black leather shirt that like me was sewn over his torso and down his arms. Heavy gauntlet gloves were pulled over his hands before they were cuffed again and then he was forced down onto his knees before a smallish figure, a female, I think. She pulled a hood over his head, laced it tightly, and adjusted the lacing until it was secure. She cupped his chin turned his face so we could see that the hood had a devilish grinning red face painted over the leather. Yet when he looked in my direction I realized there was no painting on his hood, merely black leather, either my mind or the butt butter was working overtime. His eyes were crimson red haloed by the black leather they shown with evil fury. She went on to add a heavy metal spiked collar around masters neck then a leash and she lead him around the room bound, plugged and humbled as he was for the others to gloat and humiliate him.

The woman spoke, "he will stay My slave; until, you take his place. A gauntlet of your peers is forming around you. Get to him and I will stop."

Master was forced onto his knees using the leash his face was drug down to her boots and his ass was upraised. I watched in horror as her arm rose a silver metal cane was held within her hand it fell suddenly landing on masters ass, his scream was torn from his lips, again her hand lifted.

Without so much as a second thought I started my journey to him by pushing off the boots that held me to the ground. Booted legs stood open before me as I crawled between them and they let me pass without a blow. The second pair was not so kind they rained blows down on my upraised ass and back as I wormed my way between their booted legs moving as quickly as I could to get to my master. A third pissed on me, hell I didn't even stop to think about it only hearing yet another muffled scream from my master echoing and spurring me forward. Six sets of legs had I passed, a little wetter that I might have wanted still it allowed me to slip and slide past other booted feet before they knew I was near. Whips slashed at me, canes slammed into my butt always driving me closer to my master, faster to him the quicker she stops beating on him. All I wanted to do was to jerk that cane out of her hand and break it.

I was panting hard, struggling to scoot past those that stood in my way. I was a rat running from one hole to the other as I scurried across the room drawing closer by each passing second to my master and the bitch that dare hurt him. I was nearing exhaustion when his scream no longer muffled punctuated the air. His outcry made me madder than I had ever been before in my life. The last few legs, boots flew past me in a blur. I no longer felt the rain of canes and whips as they rained down upon me when I reached him and grabbed her cane from her hand mid air. No one was more surprised than I when I bent it over my knee and tossed it out towards the bastards that had held me away from my master. I jerked the leash from her hands, released the collar from his neck and pulled him up right, and kissed him longingly trying to tell him in my kiss that everything would be all right now that his slave was there. He returned my kiss and we seemed frozen in the spot until bodies jumped on both of us and we were pulled part.

They seemed to be holding him not me. It was as if they were all waiting to see what I would do next, then I realized what was necessary. I dropped my head, placed my lips to her boots and submitted for his sake.

The boots beneath my lips shifted then she spoke "go to your Master, Number One."

I crawled the short distance; his arms opened drawing me into his chest. His shaking hand raised my head, his hood had been removed, his worn smile filled me with expressed gratitude and he put his lips onto mine. We clung like that until they came for us again. Our world became that kiss as hands drug us apart. We both were struggling until the Lady stepped between us.

"Lords and Ladies, this slave has taken his Master's place, do all accept the replacement?"

"Aye's filled the room,"acknowledging the fact.

"Master Hunter you are free to leave this room or stay as long as you do not interfere in any way with our tribunal. Do you accept our terms?"

Hunter looked over to me, winked and then up to the Mistress, "yes, Mistress. I agree to the terms."

She pointed her hand in my direction, "That slave has passed two of the three tests chosen by his peers within this court. We have followed the old rules and move into the new rules. By rights of tradition both Master and slave would be branded but that has already been done. So we are now forced to move forward applying the new rules. Slave look up at me when I pronounce sentence."

Hands held me tight within their arms; one such hand grabbed my chin forcing my face upwards to look at the mistress when she declared my sentence.

"I was told during our interrogation of your master that you dislike extreme bondage. The third test is long term bondage in a fashion that only We can appreciate."

"HE," as she pointed to my master, "proclaims you are ready for anything We can dish out."

My heart was racing a hundred miles a minute when she said extreme bondage and that they had gotten it out of him during an interrogation. I could have hugged him to death this was my forte, long-term bondage, yummmmmmmmmm!

Hands lifted me, others grabbed my legs no matter how much I tried to struggle another hand grabbed hold of my body and refused to let me drop. While I was held off the floor by a cluster of arms my ankles were bound with rope, more was wound around my thighs. I could not fight them off there was just too many holding on to me. I did get in some nasty punches and grabbed someone's boob in an attempt to flee. My thinking was why give into them, let them think I would hate this long-term bondage. Master did give me the clue to use, so I fought them and they won and were satisfied by there winning over a slave.

Once bound to their satisfaction they lowered my feet to the ground and held me between them. Master approached wearing a big shit eating grin holding out a bite guard, "open up for Master, Number One."

The guard was seated between my teeth when I realized it was one we used when we shipped out slaves. It had been carefully designed with tubes for breathing. UGH! Oh! Everything was beginning to take focus. He watched my eyes until he saw that I understood what was unsaid between us.

I was helpless to stop them as they fitted a leather neck brace and chinstrap beneath my neck. Another section went over the back of my head and the two were fused together by straps. My face was open for now. The neck brace and head helmet was a modification from the teaching-programming shield we used below in the caverns. With the neck brace in place my jaw was locked firmly, the tubes protruding beyond my lips.

I was lifted onto a refrigerator dolly, straps secured me so I would not fall from grace and they rolled me to my next station. They wheeled me up to a long rectangular box that could have easily passed for a coffin except it had an old ratty bouquet of flowers deposited on its lid. No, I thought, they were not going to put me into that thing. I nearly shit when they removed the flowers tossing them haphazardly to the ground before lifting the lid. When I looked down into that satiny box I knew they were no longer playing with a full deck. The bastards knew of my rising concern and discomfort at the thought of being placed within that rank old smelly coffin. The bastards holding me on my dolly were giggling at my discomfort. Fucking assholes, sons of bitches is all I could think about their heritage. Then I saw Hunter walking up with his shit eating grin plastered all across his fucking sadistic face and I knew, I knew I was about to be had!

Damn it if my master didn't stick his hand into that coffin and grab hold of that satiny material and give it a mighty tug. Fabric ripped out of the bottom of the coffin to reveal what was hidden under the satiny surface, sleek black leather, chrome buckles sprouting like weeds from the bottom of the coffin. Boy oh boy, master knew how to make me sit up and beg any day. His toothy grin told me more than I needed to know, he had planned this from the very start and they took his bait, as he knew they would. Damn I love my man!

Only the memories began to flood back into my mind as they lifted and carried me to that coffin. Memories of two other times where I was packed in such a coffin and carried away to my masters. The first trip was a disaster; the second such trip was to be with he who I adore and worship daily, my God, my Lord and Master Hunter. I had the weirdest feelings as I was being lowered into my sarcophagus. My cock was hard as a steel pole threatening to rip away any binding to get to any hand or mouth that would have it. Yet, my mind was horrified, filled with abject terror at the prospect of one of my darkest fantasies coming true. Would he, could he, of course, he is after all my master.

Touching the bottom surface of the coffin I was surprised as the surface gave way under my weight and continued to shift as did I. It felt like a waterbed and yet more like gel except it warmed to my touch. Odd this casket of his; like my master to create something unusual for me to be buried within. The rope around my legs was cut; hands guided them into their new location and straps held them. Almost gently they helped me to settle into my coffin. My arms were placed at my sides straps held them secured. It was odd to lay down inside a coffin and watch as heads and hands work on your body, adjusting straps, checking for tension, circulation then all of a sudden they departed. My head was locked into a well that cupped my neck and helmet. No manner of wiggling my neck or head would get it to move from its locked position.

A voice the female was speaking again, "let the journey to hell begin with a final viewing. Pray that he is willing to endure the hardships that will soon befall him in his last trial by fire."

Now let's talk about a strange ass feeling. Ever watched people from the bottom of a coffin as they cruised by the coffin to view the body. It is fucking weird! Each person walked by looked down at me and moved on. Some stopped, said of all things a prayer, crossed themselves and left. Others stopped, removed their hoods, placed an offering of sorts into the coffin and went on past. A few from my own household stopped before me, removed their leather conical hats with the red crosses smiled, leaned in and gave me a hearty kiss before moving on. Some faces I recognized others were just faces in a crowd. Hunter was the next to last; his kiss and whispered reassurances helped me more than all the rest. Then came the last person, she removed her headdress revealing who I had anticipated it to be, Lady Beatrice. She took Hunter by his shoulders, "come away Hunter, there is nothing you can do for him now. Nor can you miss what is waiting for you either. Come my friend, come."

HE stepped back his hand rested on the side of the coffin edge and the lid began to slowly close. It shut with a finality that sent shutters of fear coursing through my body. A key on my right locked the damn box with me inside as if I was planning a major escape. Hell I couldn't have farted by the way they bound me. Straps bound me securely to the bottom of that box, even struggling was limited, I knew I was doomed to take this coffin to whatever ends they had planned.

I felt my panic rising. Me breathing was short, panic induced breathlessness. I had a battle on my hands that I had to win if I was to survive this journey. Always before his voice or another calmed my fears, talking quietly, not this time! This time I was alone in my box. The silence, the darkness, the bondage was part of the test, so I could conquer my fears. So, tell me why was my cock still hard? Why was my body humming like a high-tension electrical wire? This box was the most jaded dream in my arsenal of jack off material, how did Master know? This bondage, delicious as it is extremely tight and very comfortable. My God, My Master knows me too well!

The box moved and I screamed with the shock of its movement. The scream came out of my tubes so it went unnoticed by those outside of my coffin. I had the distinct feeling of being lifted and carried. Darkness had become my old friend; the pit had taught me to enjoy my solitude. My darkness wrapped around me like a warm blanket, warm, too warm. The panic tried to raise its nasty head again. Was the air in the coffin going stale? The warmth of the air doesn't that indicate that the fresh air is going with each inhale? No, get a hold of yourself, breath deep, suck in deeply that's a boy. Plenty of oxygen in this old box, plenty of fresh air for me, yes, relax. That's it be a good boy and relax. My heart is running in hyper drive, soon I would enter warp speed and into the unknown. Could I be the source of heat or are those bastards roasting me alive over hot coals. No my Master would not permit them to burn me alive even if I was a royal screw up, which I am not. I did pass two parts of the test and by damn I will pass this one!

Son of a bitch! The box did move! There's light just above my head. Yes, light coming through a filigree grill just above my head. Light and yes, there's the big blue-sky high overhead. With a bump and a deep bone jarring thump my box came to a rest. Something hard was drawn over the lid, resounding deep within my coffin. Whatever they were dragging over my box's lid was being fed through the handles on the sides. Ah, its chain being secured over my box, they are locking me to something but why?

When they finished with the chain I could finally hear the voice, many voices, all excitedly chatting about everything but me in this box. It was like listening to a garbled radio talk show, everyone was talking at once.

It had to be the bike run. They were preparing to take to the road on their tour de force. The latecomers were standing around drinking a beer breakfast, the hair of the dog that bit them; others were just shooting the shit while everyone was waiting for the leaders of the pack.

This was unfair. Hunter had promised I would ride with him, cuffed to him like the first time. Damn I was a fucking fool when I walked out of that bar that night, so filled with dreams of servitude, never in my wildest jack off fantasies did I believe what I know now! Never in my wildest dreams would I have thought....

The coughing roar of hundreds of engines being kicked to life nearly deafened me. It had to be Gay Day at Sturgis by the sound of all the engines warming in idle. Damn I wish I were out of this damn box. I would love to see all those men and women getting ready for their annual bike run. An air horn shrilled piercing even down into my quiet resting place sounded as if it was right overhead. The caravan began to move out, I could hear them as they passed. The roar of the engines as they drew nearer to where I lay bound within their coffin. Deep rich thumping motors loud with power drew close making my body jar within its bonds then they sped past kicking up rocks as they gunned their engines. The sky overhead began to shift and move forward as my box and I joined in taking our place within the caravan we too were on the move.

Gravel and bumps made my shoulder's hurt as we descended the mountain making our way towards that big beautiful black snake that wound its way down the mountain and throughout the ridge. Hot fucking damn! I was now part of the run. Hopefully, Hunter is carrying me at his back as he promised but on a trolley. Oh, God! I am in a coffin. Damn him, the bastard knew what was coming up! We are in a fucking funeral procession and I am the guy in the box!

All the padding in the world did not stop some of the bone jarring bumps to get past and into my trapped little world. I felt every turn, bump within my aching shoulders. Nor did they allow for any movement so I could shift and relocate so the bumps would constantly be hitting the same spot. Looking through my minds eye, like Master had taught me to see beyond the hood, I could see us traveling down the highway. Men and women on bikes two to three hundred strong and in the middle of the pack is one lone biker pulling a trolley carrying a black coffin. The very air was alive with the sound of our passing hogs. My mind became dull lulled by the constant roar of the engines and my mind went to another death, my moms;

It had been three weeks of hell! No one wants to sit by a bedside in a strange hospital and watch as your mother fades into nonexistence. No one wants to do that horrible job; at least, not willingly. When the call came that mother was dying and asking for me. He sent me. Why—need I go back to the palace of dysfunction? He said, so say my last farewells, but I knew he wanted me to have closure. He needed to be the only pain in my life. Only because of his order did I go.

He presented me with a knapsack filled with clothes that I had never worn, flight arrangements, a ticket and even took me to the airport on his Harley. The chain that bound his Harley to a steel pole once held me to another, I was afraid I would never see him again. The padlock that locked it in place often held my nuts, there was no peace of mind in leaving him. He escorted me to the security gate. There standing at its side he removed my final remaining connection to him, my chain collar. He held me in his arms while I cried at my displeasure. Here I was strong, outside of his arms uncertain and fearful of what was to come of me. The click of the padlock, I felt within my heart, as the chain that had encircled my neck for five years was free. Standing back from him I switched into remote control and with his kiss still lingering on my lips and a teasing slap to my bruised and sore butt, I boarded the plane.

When I landed and had visited the hospital, I dutifully submitted my report. He called me nightly when I returned from the hospital; his words were my lifeline to sanity. It was hard living away from him, first time in five years. Everything made me feel uncomfortable, out of control and uneasy. I slept on the floor the beds were too soft. I had to buy a dog bowl; I was too uncomfortable sitting at the table to eat my meals. His training stuck with me. I missed my collar, his boots occupying my body, his cock tucked within my ass; most of all, I missed him.

At the hospital, I found her wallowing in her born again morality. I liked her better as a street whore; then, I knew what motivated her. Over the next weeks she asked repeatedly if I had been saved. Tears began to streak down my face, God, how I missed him. I gave her the only answer that would quite her fears. Confessing to her that I was saved five years ago by my Master seemed to ease her mind. I am dedicated to his disciplines and allow him to rule my world. The words had double meanings but they gave us peace. She died two weeks later on her birthday.

The old friends that came to the funeral did not know me. Had I changed so? True my head was bald (but so was my crotch and the rest of my body, it was a ritual I loved to hate). He liked me that way. What did I do for a living? I am a personal valet, manservant, (actually a boot licking pig slave); but, we liked it! Where was I living nowadays? In Virginia on the Blue Ridge Mountains in a remote cabin. (slave to a mean son of a bitch, I didn't lie as I snickered to myself). Yes, I had filled out and gained a lot of muscle. (you would too under his guidance.) The climate suited me. (As did the heavy shackles, the collar and his cock up my ass while lying in his bondage, it suited me, well!) They were envious; I could hear it in their voices. (I who was property of another man, owned nothing, am being envied!) Was I married? No! (Owned). Secrets, everyone had them, I, mine. When I cried at the funeral they thought I was being a dutiful son. (God, how I missed him!)

"WE ARE ABOUT TO LAND, TABLES AND CHAIRS BACK INTO THEIR

UPRIGHT POSITION," proclaimed a canned flight attendant over the loud speakers. My cock is hard just thinking about him.

Exiting the plane, I saw him, my heart raced as I ran to him. Dropping to my knees without thinking, I kissed his boots. The reaction garnered from the crowd was as if I had shaken my cock in their faces. With adoring eyes, I looked up as he looked down, our smiles met their fusion carried us to his bike and home.

"It's the first harvest moon. We will do it proper, tonight."

He bound me between two hugs oaks, arms outstretched. His knife made quick work of the Salvation Army issue, as they became rags at my feet. My cock sprung free to stand erect saluting him. His hands and lips made the rest of my body and mind follow suit. My body hummed like a high-tension electrical wire.

His switches began to rain down upon my body. The moon and I ascended into the ecstasy of the night together. He purged my soul of my heavy burden and renewed my life's devotion. Stretched taunt between two oaks I was a silhouette of black fire as He coaxed me to burn brighter than the orange red moon in the sky. Like a spark caught by an upward draft I rose on the wings of darkness into His light.

His cock entered my soul. Like a pump working within a well; he coaxed black crude from my embittered heart filling the gaping maw with his love and his needs. My soul drank his essence like a heady wine enjoying the sweetness of his kiss upon my lips. His liquid fire turned all sadness into ash as two more voices joined the conquests of the night. I was home returned to the peace of our valley.

Joyfully, I sank to my knees before the only man, my artist, who loved me. His hand encouraged a deeper devotion to his boots, to his sweat-drenched chest, and to lovingly clean his cock. The only sounds with our world were the whisper of the wind in the pines and the river singing in the moonlight and his moans of pleasure as my tongue danced across his body. Lost in our world, frozen by the light from overhead, we were transfixed like a pair of deer caught in a headlight waiting expectantly for something to shatter our peace. An icy chill encircled my neck, goose bumps traveled down my spine and with a click, I knew.

Here beyond any doubt, I was home.

Awww, God! We have ground to a stop, abruptly! Where in the fuck were we? Shit that hurt! Felt like every drop of blood in my body shifted to my brainpan! Finally, we are moving again, turning to the left, where? What time is it? My shoulders are starting to hurt, my neck and God what a headache I seem to be building. Does he care? Need I even ask that?

Where did I get this desire, this fantasy to having all my control taken from me? Why did I have a morbid fascination not so much about death but being in a box that they lived within? Everyone that I trusted enough to tell my deepest darkest fantasy shit when I told them about being in a box. Most of them thought I was crazy. Maybe I am, but Hunter heard me out and helped me understand my desires. Hunter helped me work up to long-term confinement, damn that man, he made me love him; I didn't want to do it....

God how that fantasy gave me many wonderful hard on's and just thinking about it triggered all sorts of wild haired scenarios. The scene of confinement has been my mental toy for years. First, it was a cardboard box with bondage; next, came steel cages fun but not confining enough for me. We progressed to trunks, steel boxes and then settled on a beautifully crafted wooden box. Hell, during our exploration he even took me to the Compound to enjoy a day in their sweatbox, what a pleasure! Still nothing pushed all my buttons and pressed my limits. Then Dan shipped me out to my first owner, Gawd, now that was a trip that pushed all my buttons! Hunter took me through various scenarios each time extending my incarceration forcing me to hold out for longer and longer periods of time. Bastard! You knew all along this was coming up! You are one sick fuck dear Master! You knew and trained me accordingly so that I would not fail you or embarrass you in front of your friends.

Heh! Driver watch those curves! Who's driving now some wild-eyed New York City cab driver? Let me see your license, can you even speak English, and where did you learn to drive a cab, Russia? Oh, fucking Shit! Bumps! Potholes, where in the fuck are you bastards taking me. The box may have wiggled around on its trolley but not I who was trapped within, every bone jarring slam was felt down to my gonads.

Heh, Sir. Thanks for this cute little box. You sick motherfucker! Wait until I get out of here to show you my appreciation, just you wait, cause I can barely wait to really show you how much I love this trip. Goddamn! My teeth rattled on that one, where in the fuck are you taking me? If you continue to drive like a manic I am going to be sprouting an antenna, as the butt plug will have been forced out my belly button. Holy Shit! Are we riding down a fucking railroad track? Finally or so it seemed we leveled out and my little caravan coasted to a halt. Yes, we have stopped. Engines are silent; people are talking about the beautiful ride. I thought to myself this run does not count; I did not see any fucking beautiful scenery. Then I chuckled to myself, who cares if I did or not, I am merely Hunter's Number One slave or worse yet, only the body in the box.

Oh thank God, they are getting ready to let me out of the box. Chains are rattling, as they are drug over the top of my coffin. Instead of having the lid lifted as I expected they decided to lift the whole coffin, oh now I am fucked I thought! They must be carrying me by the way the coffin shifts left then right. Carrying me where? Where do they plan to uncrate the boy in the box? Hey, guys, I thought to myself. You can set me down anywhere. That's ok; I can walk, thanks really.

Nothing doing, the box was set down once; perhaps, to change the pallbearers. Just where in the fuck were they taking this coffin? Panic returned, my heartbeat began to run steadily faster until I was panting through my tubes. I had a fight on my hands just to control my mind and heart from running away with me. While struggling to control my fears I lost the balance of the journey that is until the box stopped moving.

New sounds filled my coffin as something silky was pulled under and around my coffin, it wasn't chains this time what could it be? Rope, oh God, now what? The coffin was scooted forward then dropped and halted abruptly swaying back and forth as if it was hanging mid air. Was it or wasn't it?

Gently rocking back and forth told me it was rocking back and forth. Then I realized, oh God no! I had failed the tests after all and they were placing me into a grave, burying me alive and there was not one fucking thing I could do to stop what was about to happen. Rationalization tried to surface, hell; Hunter won't do this to me, not his Number One boy, but what if he wasn't in charge any more? Maybe they had already chosen another boy to take my place, was it 9-777?

Rationalization flew out the window, full-scale panic set in making me crazy within my bonds as I tried to claw my way out of them. My arms shifted within the straps maybe there was a possibility I could exhume myself from this grave. Yeah fuck them all over to have me come back from their grave. I fought on even as I felt my box swinging wildly and spinning as I descended into their chosen grave. An eternity flew past my eyes as I struggled with my arm bondage, one thumb broke free then a finger was wormed out.

The coffin thumped something hard jarring me within my coffin and gravel fell from above. What the fuck! Are they intending to bury me in this coffin? The coffin fell fast something had happened up above, someone had let loose too quickly. My coffin fell and hit the bottom of the grave bone jarring hard. I heard the tell-tell sounds of wood cracking then saw the lid crack open. Loose gravel at the bottom of the grave made my box slip down a small embankment until it halted with a deep cracking groan of splintering wood. Silence after too much sound was deafening. Then a wet thud hit the top of the coffin lid, could it be the rope? Deep oppressive silence pressed me into the soil that now surrounded my coffin. I started blubbering like a baby while thinking why couldn't they just have sold me instead of burying me alive?

Hunter! I wanted to cry out to him, but I knew he could not hear me. Instead I raged within myself. Oh, you fucking bastard Hunter, you knew all along what plans they had for me. God, how I hate you! My mind raged even as my hands struggled to release at least one arm, maybe with luck, I could claw myself out of this coffin and teach those bastards a thing or two about abandonment. Anger abated with each cursing thought, breathing calmed as the soil that was striking the coffin pushed me into cold sobriety. God, Hunter I love you.

I will improve Sir. Give me a second chance or a third or a fourth. True, Sir, this was my fantasy the coffin, the ride behind bikers, the burial and even now the cold earth covering me. It's all wrong! I want life and to serve you until I die. Please, dear God let him hear me and stop my burial, please!

I renewed my struggle with my bonds for the hundredth time since the journey began, one thumb was free but it was doing damn little to free the rest of me. Still my cock raged with my pants threatening to rip its way out of the coffin. If I could just reach it, I would blow the hinges off this coffin with my jism. Damn it, the air is growing stale again, I knew it would once they cut off the air from above with the soil that was being used to cover my coffin. Its getting harder to breath with each passing moment, the air smells funny, sickly sweet like rotting funeral flowers on a grave. Stars begin to flash in front of my open eyes and my head feels giddy and my lungs hurt from too much labored breathing. Oxygen deprivation, I have been told is not a pleasant way to die. The person begins to hallucinate like I am now.

HOLY FUCK! What was that sound? Krist! It sounds like nails being scraped across a chalkboard but it is running the length of my coffin from my feet up to my head. It's a cold bitter sound that is forcing what little hairs I have on my body to stand erect. My coffin was lifted, placed so that my feet would be touching the ground. Lack of oxygen was playing tricks with my eyes. I could no longer stand up my coffin in a standard grave then I could walk on water in the summer. Lungs burning, the air in the casket almost depleted. Was my mind playing tricks with me? Was I standing or lying in the bottom of a well dug earthen pit?

Click! Was that a key in the lock? A wave of coughing hit me hard as my lungs drew in their last gulp of air. Just then, the door was ripped off its hinges, hot fetid air rushed inside forcing my lungs to fill until almost bursting. Again my head was reeling not from lack of air but too much and this air burned, tasting of sulphur, brimstone and the furnaces of hell. There beyond my coffin was a vision from out of a twilight zone. A ghoulish throne cast from human skulls was elevated from a bone-scattered floor. A man if you could call it a man, larger than life he seemed was seated on the throne. One leather covered leg thrown across the arm like I had seen Master do all too often. The other stretched out before him both booted and did my eyes betray me but where those Founder's spurs on his boots? He was looking at me with interest as if I might give him some diversions from his boredom. His chest was a heavily muscled, huge blackened rings protruded from his nipples, and his skin was awash by flickering flames making it glow with a rich reddish color. His arms looked more like slabs of corded muscles than any muscles on a human and they were heavily tattooed with male bodies writhing in sexual frenzy. His hands were huge and he was using one of his long black nails to casually pluck out an eye from a fleshed bloody human head that he plopped into his mouth smacking his lips with relish.

The face was Hunter's and yet it was not. A much longer broader face than my master's, drawn down narrowing at the chin making the face look more sadistic than Hunter's. His eyes were definitely not Hunter's as they looked up catching me watching him the creature had eyes like a big cat, yellow, disgustingly yellow. His eyes were cold, distant speaking volumes about cruelty as well as sad. Watching him as he played with the human head I was both disgusted and drawn to him. There was a power, a feeling of loneliness yet such a feeling of all consuming power that I was drawn to him and I knew he wanted me. I could not take my eyes off of him as he slowly plucked out the other eyeball held it out to me as if to say do you want a bite laughed sadistically and sucked the tidbit into his mouth with gusto. I rolled my eyes downwards when he put the eyeball into his lips and bit down squishing liquid out between his lips, as it was only a juicy grape that's when I noticed the movement around his feet.

It could have been the flicking firelights playing tricks but it seemed as if his bullwhip or black snake was crawling down his leg and moving its long tail around between his boots. Perhaps there was a breeze whipping over the throne, but I could have sworn the snake's smaller tail was flickering like a cat's tail just prior to it pouncing on its prey and I was his prey. How could they be pulling this off? Who in the family knew enough about theatrics that could put this scenario together for my benefit and why? This was not play-acting for my part, that man on the throne was real; his tail is real, where in the hell am I?

He looked up as if he had heard my thoughts and spoke softly, "Yes, exactly," then turned his attention back to the bloody skull as he worked his finger deep into the socket dragging small bloody bits of meat to his lips and smacking them loudly with relish. A blood-curling scream rent the air it was a long drawn out scream that started loud and slowly drew quiet before it ended in a wet sounding gurgle followed by a wickedly evil laugh. In the distance I could hear a whip striking flesh followed by soft screams that seemed to echoing in a chamber behind his throne. None of it seemed to take his attention away from playing with that damn human head. The outcries were too common for him; it was like, living next to a railroad first time there you hear it loudly but after awhile you no longer take notice of the passing trains. So were the screams and falling whips in the next chamber.

He looked up as if seeing me for the very first time, held up the human head with its gapping eye sockets, "Ever skull fucked someone?" He asked, "I have, its not as much fun as it sounds." He laughed at his own joke, tossed the head to the ground before him and turned to stare at me, "Look here children. Someone has gone and thrown away a perfectly good looking slave." The voice was deep bass with just a touch of metallic twine to make it seem other worldly, "Children, make it feel welcome."

Children, I thought, what the fuck were children doing down in this hellish place? When I landed my head, my feet had halted in a higher position than my head. Hands if you could call them that, grabbed a hold the edge of my casket and pulled until my head and feet were on an even keel. Then I saw them worse yet I smelled them, his children, disgusting putrid looking and smelly things that no real man could call children. They smelled of putrid rotting meat. I would have been happier if they stayed on the outside of my bondage coffin, but the smaller ones jumped in to release me. Foul smelling crud encrusted blackened moldy looking testicles hung above my face as the balance of the body rubbed its nasty unwashed self down my body to get at the straps holding me within the coffin. Never was I more thankful for Hunter's helmet that I was at that time cause it reflected the creatures swollen pus oozing member from rubbing around my face and I helpless to brush it aside.

Hands began to run across my bound body and a head swam into view; if that was a head, I was on some really awesome drugs. Just what was in that butt butter they shoved into my ass? Now I knew that butt butter was laced with something other than just pot cause the face that was standing before me looked nauseatingly out of proportion. I tried to laugh thinking it was Hunter and his gang dressed in Halloween costumes and rubber masks but the eyes were just too vivid and glowing yellow orange. The three or five children that were playing with my helplessly bound body all smelled like rotten flesh, or putrid garbage, and my gagging as they rubbed their malicious paws over my body only made them giggle. Their giggle was too intense to have been anything but real unless someone had found away to keep inhaling laughing gas and helium without being too wacked out by the combo. Their gibberish was totally insane sounding combination of words half spoken and gutteral grunts.

The children, as he called them were neither fully man nor beast but more of a combination, manimals, shaped like our mules bulked muscle devoid of hair, faces covered by pieces of leather, their bodies covered in ripped rags and they smelled like one of those slag slaves that had been locked within a pit too long. Nasty, foul smelling beasties were pawing all over me flipping drool as they ground my nuts within my pants. It was as if they could not unbuckle the straps instead they pulled on them until with a wrenching of metal they pulled the whole backboard out of the coffin. I remained bound to the backboard, as if glued in place. The manimals ran their disgusting paws over me; no matter how I struggled to fight their affections it was to no use as straps held me tight.

The man-creature sitting on the throne eyed me causally while sipping from a gold encrusted human skull goblet. One finger arched away from the morbid cup, the manimals that were holding me giggled. My front zipper was jerked down while a dirty paw ran within to grab my cock that was attempting to crawl back inside my belly. They would have none of that; fingers busily released my cock bindings and a hot mouth dropped over my cock head. No matter how much fear I might be feeling at that moment, my cock betrayed my fears as it resumed its flag waving poise. Once erect to the servicing manimals preference my cock was bound tightly trapping the blood in my engorged cock. Backing off, the foul manimals showed their captive to the Master sitting on the throne.

His eyes bore into mine even as he smiled a toothy grin. No word that I could hear set the excited manimals working on the straps that held me to the board.

I dropped into the arms of one huge mule like manimal. He held me easily over his shoulder while another pulled the second zipper, the one that ran down between my butt cheeks and spread the panel to show the Master on the throne my cute bubble butt. Roughly my cheeks were spread revealing the bottom of the butt plug. Fingers roughly pulled on the plug; luckily the butt butter had spread down the shaft of the plug making the flange too slippery for the manimals to grasp.

The beast on the throne spoke, "Hold it children, Jackal comes to remove the slaves plug. The children lifted me by my hands and feet carried me a short distance before draping me over the shoulder of one huge massively morphed brute muscle mule. Ghoulish giggling dwarfs held my hands while one hand held my legs from kicking as I struggled to get away from these beasties. Jackal stepped out from behind a stalactite and I added my horror filed voice to their excited voices at what I was seeing. Another muscle mule with a grotesquely mishapened head one eye looked at the ceiling the other into some other space, huge pouty lips that seemed to be covered in a yellowish drool was being lead in by a delicate looking woman. The odd couple walked around me as she lead him by one hand and it was her voice that I kept hearing shriek into my ear ordering him to dig in and get her the shiny toy. I could have sworn Jackals tongue burned a path beyond the toy seated in my ass either that or it corkscrewed its way around and down into the center of my being. I loved and hated the feelings this creature was giving me. One moment my whole body would be in the most incredible feeling to ecstasy the next agony and all of this was focused within my ass as Jackal did his magic. One moment it felt as if his head was buried ear deep the next it was filled with a cold empty void. They flipped me mid air and dropped me to my knees before the throne. I found myself within kissing distance of the big mans boots.

Stupidly my hands grabbed a hold of my cock and balls seeking security in a world gone fucking nuts and I began slam fisting them. His boot rose looming huge as it halted close enough that I could smell the leather of the sole then it shot out slamming me in the face. Out of balance I flipped backwards falling down a pile of bones scattered before his throne. I righted myself and looked up to the throne to see what was coming next.

He peered down at me transfixing me with his yellow eyes, Naughty, naughty slave you know better than to play with something that does not belong to you. You have no secrets I do not know david. I know everything, E-v-e-r-y-t-h-i-n-g there is to know about you. Nor can you hide ever again from your Lord and Master.

It was as if I was spellbound. I heard my voice repeat what he said, "I cannot hide anything from My Lord."

His wicked laugh echoed down to where I lay. He looked down crooked one finger summoning me to him, "belly down and crawl to Me, kiss My boots and beg forgiveness, dog slave!"

Just the way he said slave made goose bumps run down my spine. Here was a man that knew how to direct his voice to get the best results. I felt Him shift in His chair as He leaned forward. He pointed his claw like fingers in my direction and made as to brush the air with his hand. With a loud shriek this hellish children swooped down over me and began ripping away my leathers leaving me crumpled naked on the floor save for my boots winded from the struggle of fighting them off. I found myself looking up at him sitting on his throne looking down watching as a smile crept across his face. He pointed his claw like hand in my direction and the beasts on the floor attacked me, ripping away the skins that had been so carefully sewn on my body until I lay winded and naked before the beast on the throne.

Without so much as a glimmer of thought I dropped onto my belly and crawled over the human bones to get to his boots. His boot tilted up on its heel and He presented me with His boot sole. I had no choice but to clean off God only knows what disgusting filth from the soles of His boots. Chunks of filth fell into my mouth as I worked my mouth over the soles whatever it was I gave it no thought as I chewed, swallowed and continued my duties on His boots. As I worked on His boots I came to realize that my ass felt as it was burning deep inside but not unpleasantly. It felt like I was developing a very hungry hole any time soon it would need to be filled or it would start dripping. The more I worked on His boots the more my butt burned until I became a hungry-hungry hole.

God, how my ass was on fire for something hard and He knew. Tilting laughter flowed down from above me as I was tonguing my way across his legs. Yes, by God, He knew what was happening to me as I wormed my tongue up his boot shafts while begging with my eyes to climb higher. The higher He allowed me to tongue the more I got to study his face. He looked like my Master; could he be hidden under theatrical make up, could it really be him? The nose and chin were longer and yet his head seemed larger and kind of distorted. His hands were huge; one could easily palm my face.

His finger indicated that I should rise to my feet. My hands went to the small of my back their customary location for inspection as my eyes and head tilted down to his boots. I felt him chuckle as He fingered my iron slave collar, felt His heated breath on my shoulders when He turned me and He saw the scars on my back, signs of an unruly slave. A finger touched the brand on my butt. When He rotated me to face Him again, without command I dropped to my knees before Him.

The sharpened point of one of His fingernails elevated my chin; His eyes commanded that I watch. He poured a dark heavy looking fluid into His human skull goblet. He put the goblet to His lips taking a sip smacking His lips in relish. He coughed hocking up a giant goober of phlegm this He spit into the cup. The cup was lowered, as did my eyes following the cup to His cock. With one hand He milked His cock gathering the precum into the goblet. His precum shimmered reddish gold as it oozed out of the piss slit and dropped hissingly into the goblet. Again He refilled His cup then stirred it with one black nail. The finger rose. His tongue snaked out and caught a drop from His fingertip.

The heat in the room was oppressive as my body was covered by sheen of sweat, I was so thirsty. I had been sweating like a pig working the bathrooms of a leather convention. I was in heat and hot as hell too boot! My tongue at that moment felt like it was glued to the roof of my mouth from lack of moisture, I had cottonmouth badly! The cup that He was dipping His finger into became my focus as I thought of nothing more than how it might quench my thirst. Everything He did to that cup only made my thirst grow more intense in me. True the slime ball that He spit into the cup made my stomach queasy; but, there was liquid in that cup, I saw Him pour it. His precum wasn't a problem only a sweetener. At that moment all I wanted was something wet, liquid and I would have drunk bitch piss if it were readily available.

He played with me teasing me with his cup of liquid. Putting it to His red lips and sipping slowly sucking the liquid into His mouth making me watch His every move. Making me crave whatever was inside of that goblet. Making me want it like I never wanted anything before. I even reached for the goblet, a daring move on my part, and was shocked when He passed it down into my hands.

The goblet was huge, like a goddamn soup bowl only deeper and hot when He placed it in my outstretched hands. He had been sipping on the liquid, but when I looked into the cup I found it nearly full filled with that soupy looking black liquid. I wanted to drink, but I didn't want to drink, He made me. A finger under the cup lifted my hands with the cup to my lips. It was as if I had switched gears and was all of a sudden a robot, as my hands would not obey me. They rose placing the cup at my lips. Horror filled me when He pushed the cup forcing my face to tilt back and my mouth to open and I drank rapidly swallowing the contents of the huge cup. From the onset of the first sip to the bottom of the cup my throat burned as if I had just drunk a caustic acid. The black fluid rolled over my tongue like thick heavy cream tasting like mulled wine before it oozed down my throat like snail slime. It made me choke on its heaviness and the fumes that rose to my nose smelled like hand-warmed brandy.

At first the liquid soothed my parched lips and throat; until, I neared the bottom of the upturned cup. The dregs held a wicked fire that awoke in my throat making me gag and sputter the few remaining drops of fluid. It felt like shamba, a whiskey made from fermented hot peppers, burning into a raw throat after being orally gang raped for hours. My sinus's caught fire, sweat poured out of my body in rivulets, my heartbeat shot up rapidly, I felt dizzy, would have fallen if He had not planted His huge booted legs on either side and ordered me not to move with His commanding eyes. The bastard rocked back into His throne and laughed a deep bass laugh that seemed to echo throughout the chambers. He was amused by what I had just drunk and its reaction within my body.

He looked down on me, "Want the fire to stop? Well do you slave?"

I was nodding my head furiously, "Sir, Yes, Sir. Please, Sir!"

"Get down where you belong you cock sucking pig slave. Open your mouth to its widest and place your lips under My cockhead. Drink My precum slave, it's the only thing that will cool that fire, now."

My second big mistake was to put my lips to His cockhead. His big fist slammed into my head picking up my body and tossing it like a leaf to the floor below of the bones. I lay were I fell hoping beyond all reason that I would not have to do what He had proposed. Initially it felt like just heartburn but it this was being transformed rapidly from a minor thing into a major pain. Imagine a oil lantern with one wick burning compared to someone spraying lighter fluid into the flame every second I did not do as He commanded the hotter my insides burned! Even as I struggled to rationalize my body flipped over onto its hands, knees and I began crawling back up that mound of human skulls to get back to Him. His boot on my shoulder slowed my attempt to get to where He had ordered as He berated me, "Waste any more of My time hu-man and I will give you to my children they deserve a new toy. On your back foolish man, hands under your back, now crawl, open your hole wide, WIDER shit for brains. Now, drink and find peace!"

Like a fool, I crawled between His legs planning to kneel before Him to drink His cum; He would have none of that. I was flipped onto my back, feet tucked as closely as I could to my butt and held open wide for one of His boots to rest. There trapped as I was below Him did He aim His cock and began milking it of its pre cum. Imagine how I felt, my stomach, lungs and body were on fire internally and this man-creature said His pre cum would put me out of my misery. Lying below Him watching as

His big hand with blackened nails fisted His huge cock slowly stroking down the huge heavily veined shaft milking it until a large pearl of pre cum formed on His cock head I was transfixed. My mouth opened without a thought as the pearl slipped out of His piss slit, gained momentum and size before it pushed itself over His cockhead. Like a spider it spun out its own golden web connecting it to the source, and I caught it on my tongue. My tongue rolled back inside my mouth with its prize then the taste exploded within my mouth it was incredible the sweetest nectar of my God! One pearl was not enough to quench my thirst as the fires kept burning within my heated ravaged body. One pearl followed another until His cock transformed into a river of pre cum. All I could do was to keep up with the flow as His pre cum filled my mouth and I drank it steadily. Was I in heaven or hell, did it matter, no? Each mouth full made me want more; never had I witnessed so much pre cum fall from a man before. Once He started the flow His hand withdrew and His cock took over as the pre cum ran like a rivulet filling my gaping mawl again and again. My groans of pleasure were not to His liking. I heard Him issuing orders to His manimals. His boot lifted from my crotch, hands grabbed my legs and drug me out from beneath His throne and I screamed clawing the ground in hopes of staying below him, serving.

Unwillingly I was drug from beneath His powerful legs and carried on my back by many shoulders away from Him. My head rolled back unsupported. I could not take my eyes off of Him as He pushed Himself out of His throne rising to His full height and followed. God what a man, I thought as they carried me out of the chamber. When I lost sight of Him I fought the many hands to get back to Him. My struggles were useless too many hands held me tighter than the bonds within my coffin.

Chapter 8

All that I ask of thee Lord
Is to be a drinker and a fornicator
An unbeliever and a sodomite
And then die.
Claude de Chauvigny

Out one chamber around a crystalline stalagmite His manimals carried me as they laughed and teased my body with their disgusting hands. I screamed out to my Lord and was relieved when He joined us in the corridor. Watching following seemed to calm my fears of being taken to some unknown hell by His minions. We traveled down a small corridor illuminated by torches set in wall brackets they carried me as if I was nailed to a cross, arms outspread, legs held tight, with my head dangling loosely on a rubbered neck. The throne room had been hot still nothing prepared me for the blast furnace to which I was taken. The heat literally sucked the cool air out of my lungs and made me have a nonstop coughing fit until my Lord took my head forced His lips to mine and raped my mouth. His tongue seemed to go down my throat once in my mouth He breathed deeply filling my lungs with the air in His lungs. When He removed His lips I could breath without coughing. His deep bass laugh followed a command for the manimals to set me down and prep me for a tour.

Sweat covered my body as fast as the air around me sucked it off. Here I was dropped to my feet, roughly my arms were bound at my back, a tether was drug between my legs wrapped around my cock and balls. Using the tether, three manimals helped me to see the sights, whipping me if I slowed on their tour. Even as I walked around the huge domed torture chamber I could not stop turning my head back to watch the Master of this hellish pit. He walked across burning waters to stand casually on an outcropping in the center of a fiery lake. There He stood as other creatures crawled out of the murky waters towards Him bowed down and worshiped.

The walls shimmered from the heat of fires ringing the room. Flash fires seemed to spring from any crevice or any pool of water making even the pool of water in the center of the room shimmer with flames walking across the surface. A blood-curdling scream caught my attention and a manimals hand on my neck helped me locate the reason. A large heavyset man was strung up by tiny threads that were attached to needles in his body there must have been hundreds of needles running from his feet to his shoulders sewing him to a ladder overhead. His screams were intermittent as one devil headed manimal shoved his cock into the bound mans mouth and others played the strings like a harp. Another man was stung up and swinging with meat hooks through his back muscles, his eyes were glazed and blank even as demons pulled on his feet. A jerk on my tether and I was moved on down the line to the next victim. A female whose neck was trapped in a thick posture collar, her mouth fused open by what looked like a spider inside her mouth was seated open legged on a reverse V that forced her legs wide. Her clit was spread wide with clamps; her breasts were brutally bound and bluing by the forced position. The manimals drug me around the back of this female to show all of her to me. Her back was laced together by thread that ran through her skin, she was wearing a living corset made of her own skin. Walking back around the bitch, I saw my Lord standing in the center of the room flexing His muscles. He looked as if He had grown bored of the worshippers while I was being drug around to see His aspect of Dante's vision. Many were bleeding at His feet still their hands sought to rise in praise and their cries could be heard over all the others as they sought His pleasure over their pains.

With a jerk I was moved to the next scene of a innocent looking boy who had been bound on his back over an outcropping of stone. The boy was literally bound down in upon himself like a sandwich of torso, arms and feet there held tightly to the stone by rope. A line of naked men with distorted faces and tongues hanging out of their mouths stood around him jerking and pounding on their grotesque looking cocks. The boy's balls were bluish purple bound to a leash that was being pulled while a grotesquely fat man sat straddling the boys face feeding the boy his ass. Others were pissing on the boy and the boy looked to be in heaven as his cock stood tall and proud. The next scene had two men bound together spread eagle facing each other, lovers by the way they kissed while two devilish looking men gleefully cut their skin into bloody ribbons with steel whips. If this was torture why were the devil's victims so sexually excited? Torment, pain was everywhere I looked nevertheless my cock did not go soft as I watched and heard the pitiful cries of those being tormented.

We stepped around a column of silvery rock to which both male and female slaves were locked in heavy chains. Their heads were filled with hollow blank stares their heads and bodies bowed by the weight of their chains as they stood silently awaiting their turn. My captors jerked my tether drawing me ever forward towards one scene after another. Crates of human cargo with heads and hands protruding from opening seemed to grasp the air silently screaming their displeasure. While cages of iron swung from chains hosting various hues of bodies, waiting, resigned to their fate at the hands of the devilish imps who seemed pleased by their wards suffering. Small tightly packed boxes that looked to squeeze the life out of a trapped individual or teach the occupant about the value of freedom. Square and rectangle steel cages hung from the walls, some crammed full of bodies, others singled out for solitary torture.

My tormentors made me watch as an iron mask was fitted over one screaming souls face before being locked around its pitiful moaning head. The demons took a stick to the bell shaped device laughing as they hit the mask and heard a hollow scream return for each blow. My tormentors dropped my reins as they took their pleasure by torturing the man in the iron mask. Forgotten for a moment I attempted to flee this hellish place. I ran for all it was worth ducked into a cave mouth and found myself in a placed filled with even more horrors.

A solidly built man with chiseled features was bowed down to half his height seemingly locked into a frozen position. Walking around I was shocked to see the man locked into place by a single steel rod that ran through his left cheek, through his tongue, out the right cheek, down under his chin and around his neck like a collar before it dropped down between his hands encircling both thumbs then down into the solid rock. The forced position gave his captors total access to his ass and no say in how it would be used as if any here had any say in anything. The scent of a good cigar lead me forward where I found a man smoking a cigar or so it seemed from my position at his rear. Walking around him I noticed his legs were strapped to a wooden board so that he could not bend his knees and fall forward. His hands were locked on either side of the board and straps held his elbows tightly across his back. Looking up I was shocked to see his head wrapped in heavy plastic the only opening in his face was an O and that was filled by a huge cigar. His eyes were alive with fear as a small monkey crawled around on him. Held in place by rapt fascination I watched as the man inhaled through the cigar and exhaled then the monkey ignited the cigar. Again he inhaled filling his lungs full of cigar smoke and my cock hardened. He exhaled smoke and inhaled more, exhaled slower this time before coughingly inhaled until his head slumped forward caught on a collar encircling his neck. The monkey crawled forward removed the cigar placing it in his mouth and waited as smoke curled out of the man's open mouth. With a start the man came around and horror filled his eyes as the monkey replaced the cigar. As I turned to leave I was caught by a pack of demons and set up on by their whips. Once subdued they drug me forward past a man in a sling with his ass spread wide who was shitting human hands. The demons howled at the shock my face must have registered.

My tour guides marched me back towards the heat returning to the circle. Upon seeing Him my cock sprang erect, such power He had over this unholy mess. My Lord was bored all His worshippers were gone. No more three pieced business suits crawling before Him begging for His favor, gone were the lawyers, politicians and doctors they were where they belonged on the crosses around the room giving Him His due. He watched them as they brought me closer having made the full circuit of His playroom. A moat of fire ringed a central stone that looked like a stone altar it was to that stone I was carried by my three tormentors. I felt the heat of the flames as they walked across the flaming waters to where their master stood. They released my bound balls and hands flipped me around, lifted and dropped me like a dead fish on a chopping block. My hands were drawn forward and bound parallel to each other against the stone. My legs were spread wide, then forced wider before being bound open and exposed.

His hot hands ran slowly over my body, reached under me and found my nipples. Those He rolled expertly before setting alligator clamps into them and chuckled deeply as I writhed for His pleasure adjusting to the pain radiating across my chest. He leaned onto my butt adding His weight to mine sandwiching his cock between my ass cheeks and slowly fucking them with His huge cock. Using only His sharpen talons slowly He clawed an awakening tremor from my hands down to my bound feet and He laughed as my ass twitched. He draped his weight across my body pinning me to the rock face, leaned down and whispered into my ear "Finally, I get my pound of flesh!"

I screamed, "NO!"

His deep rumbling laughter told me otherwise even as his rancid breath swirled around me and his face turned to me, "I know you want it pig, you can deny me nothing. I have owned you for more years than even Hunter. I was there when you first jerked off with your finger in your ass, helped you get up the nerve to give your first blow job to that sailor at fourteen and pumped your ego up for that walk down the runaway." His laughter echoed off the chamber and crept down into my soul. He paused, pushed himself off my back and casually walked around my body until he stood before me. He walked out before me, "Time to start this red masque! Let the blood flow!" He bellowed to the room and the screams rose in a rising crescendo, "now watch little piggy I have something special for you, my piggy-piggy!"

I could not take my eyes off of him as he struck one pose flaring out all his chest muscles, turned bending his biceps popping out other muscles as his corded muscles grew out from his chest then he turned showing me his back. His hands glided over his waist and down until they cupped his firm meaty cheeks with the huge black tail trailing out and around his legs. His hand took hold of that tail and He began to pull. The muscles on His arm began to bulk, as He pulled hard on His tail then His hand dropped the tail and withdrew. I watched in rapt fascination as the tail began to crawl out from between his butt cheeks. By God, it grew thicker as it crawled out of His ass hole. It grew like a boa constrictor until the head popped out and would have fallen to the ground except He grabbed it. When He grabbed it the snake changed into an evil looking bullwhip thick as an arm with multiple braided ends. He arched the whip over His head the resounding pop of the cracker sounded like a shotgun going off in the domed room and this He planned to use on my backside.

I began screaming and He had not even struck me with that evil looking whip, "no, nO, NO!" I knew it had no affect on Him as He would have whatever He wanted whenever He wanted. I was helpless as a lamb on a sacrificial stone.

He stepped forward draping the snake around His neck, "I got something just for you, my piggy."

Hands lifted my head as one of his minions pulled a hood over my head. It had no eye or nose holes only a wide tube that was forced into my mouth before the hood was laced doubly tight. I could breath and scream and be orally used but not see who or what He allowed to ride my face. Nor could I clamp my mouth closed with the rigid tube holding my mouth open. I tried pounding my head against the stone in hopes that I would be knocked unconscious but even that was halted when the hood that I was wearing was inflated taking all sounds with it. Now I was left to feel and feel intensely I would. He walked around me dragging His snake over my body and I could have sworn it moved with snake like grace as it crawled over my backside and down between my ass cheeks.

Waiting for the whip to land was like waiting on the edge of a cliff two wheels over the edge rocking back and forth at any moment the whip would land and I would slip over the edge into the abyss. The bastard let me wait and anticipate the blow. I had been grinding my teeth against the tube in expectation when a greasy finger inserted an even nastier rag that had to have been taken from its stench from some things private region. I felt the whip singe the air just above my helpless bound body and knew the next blow would eat human flesh mine! Like Hunter He was finding His placement so the whip would find its mark and rip my back to shreds for His pleasure.

In my minds eye I could see Him standing about 3 feet from my head. He stood proud like an avenging angel His whip curled around His feet. Slowly He moved His arm and the whip ripped into the air rising high before arching back in upon itself then down. I could feel the rush of air as it passed over my back then heard and felt simultaneously the crack of the whip as it collided with my left butt cheek marking it with His sign to balance Hunter's brand on my right cheek. The rag did not stop the rush of air as my scream tore past my teeth neither did it stop nor did His whip stop with that one connection. I felt it rip out a mouthful of flesh gobbling it down as it rose into the air before it sailed over my back spraying blood before returning to land in the same spot. I thought Hunter was good with a whip but this Lord of Darkness made me want more from His bloody whip then Hunter ever did. Even with the gag crammed into my face

I begged around it for more blood, my blood to be spilt upon this unholy soil. He gave it to me, slowly, methodically cutting my back and butt cheek to shreds. The whipping hurt, bad, real bad but not so much as when He stopped. Somehow I had dislodged my gag during the whipping session. I heard a pitiful whiney voice crying out to the Lord of Darkness and giggled thinking it how familiar it sounded and yet so out of character for anyone to beg for a whipping. I was stunned to find out it was me begging Him for more.

I felt Him approach, "Look what you have done to me hu-man." He held up his blood-engorged cock, thick like a man's forearm, heavily veined, and the head was massive. "you got me excited hu-man. Now you will know real pain."

Heat radiated from His body as He stood before me. He was talking to His underlings, "hu-man's are such pigs, watch and learn."

The tube that kept my mouth forcibly open must have been too small cause his arm wrapped around my head taking a hold of my chin. With a mighty twist of the tube it was ripped out of the leather hood and my mouth. I was in the process of closing my mouth when His fingers wedged my mouth open. With one hand holding my bucking head the other reached into my mouth dislodging my teeth and ripping out both the upper and lower plates. Mocking laughter shook His huge frame, "only a few like to feel teeth on their cock. Normally, I don't fuck ng care but today I want to sheath my cock within your body, pig."

Hastily I swallowed remembering back to the time they were pulled and the reasoning. Once again the lesson was fitting and the absence of my teeth whenever Hunter helped me to remember my place was constant. Now more than ever without teeth I served Him best as His pleasure slave.

The Lord of Darkness would have His way and as usual I had no control over how I was to be used. With one of His thumbs on either side of my mouth forcing my jaw to remain open He forced His huge cock over my fighting tongue, past the ring of muscle as the back of my mouth. He laughed even more sadistically than Hunter when His cock triggered heavy gagging but continued inching its way deeper into my expanding throat. It would have been an awesome experience if my lungs were not starving for oxygen. I had to have been flopping around on that slab like a beached fish but He paid me no attention. All He wanted was to bury is cock to His balls. To go deeper than any others cock and He did not care one iota if I survived or not. As usual it was all about His pleasure not mine.

Lights began flashing before my open eyes; tears had cleared the path for their departure even as I died of suffocation impaled as I was to His balls. My world was spinning out of control as He bruised my lips with the rampaging thrusts of His loins. My life began to pass before my eyes; Hunter holding me in his arms, Hunter whipping my torn back, Hunters boots in my crotch and I laughing at one of his twisted jokes. Images flowed before my eyes like my life flowed out of existence here within this hellish caverns held captive impaled on a cock. Any moment I knew would be my last and yet I continued to endure His thrusting hips slamming into my face then I felt it. Hands were prying my ass cheeks apart and another cock entered me. What had been terror at first at the thought of having His mammoth cock wedged down my throat turned into wonder who was driving?

Finally, I thought as I sensation of pressure pressed into my rectum. I giggled and choked like a schoolgirl on an old joke, rectum damn near killed them, as His cock head pushed through the gateway of my hole. I had seen His cock while below drinking precum but not until He was pressing His affections upon me did it dawn on me how huge He was. With only His cockhead buried within my fully stretched ass lips I started trying to crawl away only to wriggle up the shaft that was buried into my lips. I was insane to think I could take the whole of His colossal cock and I tried to crawl away. He had His plans, and I had mine. His would succeed and mine as usual would fail. His cock that was assaulting my mouth and ropes locked me securely in place no manner of wiggling would pull me off what He had begun to feed into my hole.

I had handled Master's hog cock well enough and even his rather large fist still nothing had prepared me for what He was pushing into me. Thankfully He would press His weight into me then halt allowing me to adjust as if any one could adjust to having a safety cone shoved slowly into one's hole. The more He pushed in the more my ass spread to handle what He was forcing into me.

Every begging moan that escaped my lips was followed by His laughter and a push for greater depth. Then something happened to change all the pain within my asshole. It happened as I fought to draw breath one moment my ass and mouth was filled with ripping pain and then everything, someone flipped the switch within my head and everything, He was doing felt pleasurable. My outcries of pain transformed into gurgling outcries for more as His cocks began moving out. Slowly like a giant serpents exiting their lair one cock slithered over my prostrate making every nerve in my body twinkle with brilliant pleasure while the other nibbled on my heart. God, I was ad-dick-ed to His talented cocks and the feelings they awoke within my whole body. It was as if I was a sparkler burning like a flash fire brilliant white-hot matching His blackness. What a feeling to be so alive that every fiber of my being cried out acknowledging His power over my being. He was the Superior male I nothing but His hole.

I was trapped in feeling. Feeling sensations that I had never known existed. Colors washed over me, and I became them as His weight pressed His cocks back into my holes. Light fled before darkness when He sawed His way out drawing every fiber of my being with His departing cocks. His cocks did not use me they possessed me, owned me down to my molecules. Once a hu-man now transformed by His need nothing but a pleasure hole to be used then cast aside. My ass rose to meet His descending weight no longer was I bound to the rock face beneath me as I had passed beyond limitations.

The pain in my ass, backside and tits was acting like an aphrodisiac stroking my boiler to reach higher pressure. Always pushing me forward, driving me before Him, making me beg for more and making me love His gifts of love, pain beautiful pain. I heard Him mimic my long dead mother's voice, "don't make me hit you!" His hand followed mom's voice as it slammed into my jaw jerking my head nearly around. Then I heard dad's voice, "hey boy, got something for you. Made it myself." The flashback hit me. Dad had me bound to a chair all day when he returned home with my first pair of home made shackles after that I was kept in the cellar locked to a wall when he was away at work. He mimicked Hunter's voice; "open wide Daddy's got a big surprise for you."

Insane laughter filled the air around me then the hood was ripped from my head allowing me to see the ghastly visions of others around me being worked by their tormentors. I looked out of the corners of my eyes into the flaming waters and saw His Herculean body's hunched over taking His pleasure as He fucked my ass and plowed my mouth. His huge hands holding my hips as He jackknifed His hips in and out. Driving me forward with each thrust, forcing my lips to spread wider as He pushed me further down His other cock lodged within my mouth. Then His hands would pull me back with each withdraw, holding me, keeping me locked in place between two heaving body's. His focus was supreme and when I dared a look His face was awash with intense concentration as He too had given over to pleasure.

The cock in my ass was an unholy piston driving a steam locomotive up a hill while the other cock was reaming me from my teeth to my toenails together they were designed to destroy me totally. I was lost, confused and in a state of total euphoria. Time stood still as both cocks ripped into my deepest subconscious minds reworking my wiring making me want to give more of myself to them. This slave existed only for their needs no more was it necessary to think only to be the hole that it had become.

Both cocks halted their pace. I rose up and out of my body watching two equally matched Lords of Darkness as they stood on opposite ends of a slave that was spread out before them. One Lord had His cock buried to His balls the other had His buried to the slaves lips. They waited for a sign from the slave. A sign came as oxygen deprivation made the creature locked firmly between them tired to crawl, scramble away and found no place to go. Its body quivered as I watched in rapt horror then the Lords moved withdrawing their cocks as one. My body sucked air into its lungs swelling as it did and they returned their swords to the stone grinding their balls into the vee made of the slave. Again they halted their progress, waited and watched the dying slave as it quivered beseechingly them with its eyes for air. The Lords laughter resounded around the room still they waited watching the slave then they moved again as one withdrawing their cocks. Their game was on. They took their time toying with the slave between them as I without a body toured the room. A silvery gold rope attached me to my body beneath the Lords heaving hips; the umbilical cord would allow me only so much distance before it would halt my progress. Death was not a part of the Lords game slow oxygen starvation was their cruelest of games.

I floated like a balloon tethered to my body between those heaving Lords. I would have normally been invisible except here in the underbelly of hell the manimals and devilish looking tormentors were very aware of my presence. Almost all would look up and point to me and laugh as I freely floated towards any scene other than my scene of debauchery.

Eight fresh slaves were being brought in from another chamber. All of them had their hands bound at their backs the extra rope ran between their legs around their balls before being connected to the arms of the one before him this way one demon lead them easily. One at a time they were dropped off at various torture stations they seemed resigned to their fate as none of them struggled, until they were put on or into a device of torture then they acted as if they just awoke. Fresh screams rent the air, spurring the Lords to grind my body like hurdy-gurdy between their loins. I wanted none of it as they were cleaving life force from my body at any moment they would kill me by their cocks, but what a way to die! Like well-oiled pistons they were regrinding my cylinder according to their needs. Periodically they would slow down change the cadence and alternate their speed while I lay between them transfixed by the power of their thrusting hips, their need was important mine no longer mattered as they drove their cocks into my helpless body.

With a jerk on my tether I snapped back into my body and I felt every nerve crying out in unison, cum fuckers, cum so I can die peacefully! Instead I overheard a conversation that left me wondering to whom the Lord of Darkness was speaking.

"You got a sizeable piece of meat that could easily match mine," said the Lord of Darkness at my rear as He laughed and sped up His tail splinting rage, "looks like you know how to use it too! You like choking him about as much as I do." More sadistic laughter echoed around the chamber and was picked up by the demon tormentors working on their charges. Screams ripped through the air followed by His deep bass chuckle.

"Is it yours?" The Lord of Darkness questioned the room.

It was a struggle to breath, a struggle to keep focused, as I was nothing but a fuck hole to them. Something to be used abused and tossed aside when they were finished. So, why was I so fucking excited by how they were using me? How they were raping my holes and how I had no way of stopping their affection even if I wanted to do so? Oxygen deprivation was getting to me. The world was spinning out of control and I must have blacked out. For when I came to the cock was out of my mouth but only for a short time while I hastily filled my lungs then the bastard pried open my mouth reinserted His cock and raced at a gallop to catch up to the Lord of Darkness..

"Is it yours?" Asked the bass voice at my rear.

"Yesssss," hissed the voice as His cock slipped past my Adams apple. "Broke it to suit all my jaded needsssss!"

Were my ears playing tricks with me or did that voice sound like my Hunter's voice. How could this be? I saw the Lord of Darkness as He pushed His cock between my teeth, not Hunter, the Lord of Darkness. Still even with the drawn out sss's the voice sounded like Hunter's. God, please let it be Him.

The Lord of Darkness spoke again over my rear as His cock plowed deep into my stomach. Damn if it didn't sound like Master Hunter's voice; but then, who was riding my face? The Lord of Darkness even had Hunter's looks, distorted, and elongated but still my master's face. Who was who? Was I caught in some hellish nightmare, was the drink He gave me drugged? No, no, I began shaking my head negatively giving the cock in my mouth a run for His money until a fist slammed into the side of my head. This is all too real to be a fucking dream....

Fire white hot and brilliant exploded across my chest when someone grabbed a hold of my alligator clamped tits. The pain was real and it alone snapped me back into focus. I would have screamed if the cock in my throat had permitted. Instead, I gulped air around that massive invader filling my lungs even as the cock drove past my tonsils stretching my windpipe to new levels of extension. I couldn't help to feel my windpipe stretch as His cock like a steel rod was rubbing it raw forcing the walls of my throat to expand to His needs before pulling out. Each time He leaned more of His weight into my face forcing His cock to meet the other one plowing my ass.

"Will it remember any of these rites of passage," panted the voice at my rear. It was Hunter speaking I knew it beyond any doubt. But how did he get from my front to my rear without removing his cock from my mouth?

Their hip thrusts were getting harder and faster. My jaw snapped loudly making me think that my jaw had become dislocated. Their laughter at the sound made me furious but their cocks did not lessen in speed as they were drawing close to their unified climax. I was caught up in a whirlwind much like that stupid cow in a twister. I felt totally helpless, just two holes with arms and legs attached. I think that is when I started praying that Hunter would give me deliverance from Him. It was blasphemous to the very core what I prayed within my mind still it gave me a measure of reassurance cause I knew any moment they would cum and I would drown on the loads of two elephant sized cocks.

"Does it matter that it will die on our cocks this day? After all it's only a slave. You like having it around cause its like a well-worn pair of boots. It no longer puts up a struggle. Haven't you always enjoyed the conquest, the hunt, my Hunter? What makes this lump of meat any different?" The Lord of Darkness panted as He reamed out my ass hole yet another time.

Then I heard clearly master Hunter's voice, "I love him. He may be my slave but he is also my life partner, friend and confidant. Something you would not understand."

The prayer was a stupid litany from a helpless slave trapped in a fantasy of an overly fertile mind. Everything that had happened to me today was part of my fantasies. Being sewn into a suit of leather, the coffin, buried alive, the Lord of Darkness using me and even this fucking scene. All of it was plucked from my feverish mind and put into action for whose pleasure surely not mine?

Then I heard Hunter's voice coming down to my ears from the hips assaulting my lips, "You are so right! This slave has been fun to break. I am glad that We had a great time doing it, you and I!"

My prayer however so humble said everything that needed to be said. If they could see my fantasies then Hunter would hear my prayer...

Master Hunter you are my universe, let no one come between us,

Let me give you pleasure, here on earth and beyond.

Let the song of your whip and voice correct my errors,

Give me pain that I may know your pleasure

For You are the Keeper of my soul, my breath and my love for evermore.

The cocks kept plowing their furrows. Two locomotives chugging down the railroad track, a mindless fuck lying between them as they worked up their steam enough that they could blow their loads. I could have been a field-ripened watermelon cored and being fucked by two young boys for all the attention I was being given. My ass felt like raw hamburger fresh through the grinding machine on its way to someone's plate while my lips had been stretched so wide that they had long gone numb as had most of my face. Except for an occasional slap to my backside, I was as mindless as a rubber dildo being used to hit some ladies G-spot. Only a tool, a fucking tool, a slave to Master's cock!

The body plowing my face spoke is a sarcastic way, "Do you really care? It is after all only a slave. By topsider antiquated standards; a slave is to be used as the Owner deems correct to suit his needs, abused and tossed away like an old beer can. So what if its whole life has been devoted to serving its Owner, it's a thing that can just as easily dumped into the garbage like some other kind of refuse. Right?"

The Lord of Darkness who now sounded like master Hunter interjected from his position at my rear, "Yes, I care! This one is special to me. I plan to change the value people place on slaves, especially a well-trained slave like this one. They are an asset to any body powerful enough to own them."

"Your profit margins will crash down hard if you do that. Those that own slaves will hold on to them instead of trading them in for younger or stronger models. Trading will come to a stand still, the slave market will crash if you do that!" Said the voice above my head.

"No, margins will go up! More slaves will be sold this time on the Open Market. The training and conquest will continue as the old slaves learn to lift burdens from their owners shoulders allowing their owner's the chance to made additions to their stable.

Slaves trained in specialized fields will become a rage. Slaves dedicated and trained in martial arts and given intense focus training will serve to protect their master's with life or limb. The market will escalate, watch and see," relied my master's voice as his cock made points in my ass come back to life.

The cock in my mouth began to swell; the end of this ride was finally drawing to a close. With a mighty thrust his cock shot past my tonsils and began spewing his cum down my gullet. Hot cum rose into my nostrils threatening to close off any oxygen reaching my lungs. Slowly his cock softened and pulled out giving me time to swallow and clear my nostrils.

My head fell back to the hot stone beneath me. My mouth hung open, slack jawed as cum too much to safely swallow oozed out of my mouth. Still the cock in my ass kept plugging away, thrust, withdraw, thrust, withdraw, thrust, constant as rain falling on a tin roof.

The Lord of Darkness or was it Hunter that was talking again, "This is after all your rites of passage as much as it is his."

Again I was confused and gave up trying to figure out who was speaking as someone continued, "all great leaders have their connections with slavery and magic. The Light and the dark, I am your dark side. This has been your test as much as it has been your slaves. Tonight we merge as one. No longer separated by the boundaries we will become a great ruler. People already fear and love you after this our union they will be shown new reason to fear, love or be devoted to you. Like Lady Beatrice and others that have ruled the Castle, each has met their darker natures here on our soil. Some let their darker natures rule others did not. You, Master Hunter, are strong in the ways of the Light. Our union will transform Castle and you."

A fit of coughing took me as I was having a hell of a time swallowing the gooey cum that was frozen in my throat. The voice at my rear said, "Attend to your slave, its choking on your cum."

His cock rested on my tongue the flow began as a trickle that turned into a torrent of piss. The pressure of the flow washed deep into my throat drilling by pressure alone a hole through which I could chokingly gulp air and swallow both his piss and his cum. His piss was coming faster than I could swallow. I seemed to no longer care as my airways became blocked and I slipped into darkness.

The last thing I heard the Lord of Darkness say to my master was while I was fighting to stay conscious but was losing the battle, "Hunter, you were born from magic, ancient magic. They will expect more from you than any leader. Unlike Hitler, Castro you do not seek power activity through the use of your magic; but it comes to you like a moth to a flame. Your reign will be successful beyond your wildest imaginings. Over the broken bones of the old ways you will march them into a new era. You march to a different drummer, some will hear that drum beat and join you others will not. Let the music carry you and now the one beneath your heaving hips shall hear it too!"

Hands slipped under my ribcage lifted and I was rotated while his cock was still within me. I lay there eyes held tight for fear if I looked up I would see the Lord of Darkness still plowing my ass and I really craved seeing my owner Hunter. His cock was thrashing around my prostrate slamming into it milking it for all the pent up cum it could muster. My back arched and I rose placing my arms around his neck as he slammed his cock deep within me. His arms closed around me and he lifted me from the stone his cock swelled larger and spew forth his fiery hot jism deep into my bowels. I was lowered back to the stone as his cock slowed its power thrusts where my hands touched they were fused as if bound. His sweat slick body collapsed over mine pinning me as he ground out the final drops as his cock slowed its dying rhythm. We were spent. Locked together in an oblivion that comes only after a mind-altering fuck like this one was. Winded as he was he lay draped over me pinning me to the surface of the altar. Slowly his cock softened within me and with a disgustingly wet plop heralded its exit from my ass. That noise seemed to echo around the chamber and set off the manimals in fits of giggling. Still I dare not open my eyes even as he pushed himself off my body and stepped away. I knew if I opened my eyes and I found myself still bound within his hellish cavern that I had somehow stepped outside of time and reality I would be lost to my master.

Something disgusting was held under my nose. I coughed and my eyes fluttered open. Where was I? The scent of his cum was all around me. It made me cough again. Dimly as if it was far away I heard a voice calling to me.

"Here," I called, "I am here."

"He's beginning to come around, thank God!" Master's voice registered concern for my welfare. "Inhale this One, its only ammonia salts, come on, snap out of it boy."

While my eyes remained closed, I took a quick inventory of my body. My back was sore from His whipping, my arms were numb from the forced position and bondage, and my body was cramping from the position.

I screamed in terror with my awakening consciousness! The scream allowed me to vent my fear, rage and terror at the abuse. Nothing I couldn't handle, they said. Correction, my fucking Master said!

"What the fuck?! You are safe boy, relax, Master has you. Relax. That's it breath normally, relax. I am here."

"Open your eyes boy!" Hunter commanded.

They fluttered open and the room spun out of control. I was still within the cavern. I had been tricked! Hunter wasn't calling to me but that other, that demon thing, the Lord of Darkness.

I heard boots hit the ground and someone approaching but I refused to look. A hand took me and lifted, "sit up nice and slow, boy." A hand held out a canteen when I did not take it he put it to my lips and force the liquid into my mouth. I did not swallow fearing it was another trick instead I held the liquid in my mouth, still some trickled down my throat and I realized it was only water. I swallowed and found the water was good, clean and cold. It alone helped cut the fog from my mind.

Pushing myself up with my arms. I found that I was no longer bound to the rock but had been bound over master's Harley. He stood beside me. Sweat had cut streaks down his black ashen chest making the streaks brilliant in the low light. The cleaner places on his chest were places showing fresh welts and a new brand. He looked almost as bad as I felt. Almost as dirty if he had been drug behind a cycle himself. He stood there holding the canteen taking a drink teetering back and forth he looked barely able to stand. I put out my hand to him and he flinched where I touched him but he said nothing. We shared the contents of the canteen in silence, neither speaking only touching. Speech at that moment would have been too much for either of us; touch conveyed all that was unsaid.

I sat astride his Harley while he stood beside me for what seemed like an eternity, each of us lost in our own thoughts. Both of us looked sex dazed to the point of being stupid. Looking beyond my Hunter I saw myself in the center of a huge domed cavern. Fires raged in pits around the room casting weird shadows on the walls. Tools of torture, Stations of the Cross were placed strategically around the room, but all were empty now. Hunter and I were the sole occupants in the cavern.

Master slipped his arm under me and lifted, "Let me help you off that cycle you have been bound too long. We need to get your circulation moving. Come on, boy, help me get you up." Master seemed to speak too loudly for this room, his voice echoed off the walls and around the room. He held me, lifting one leg then the other as he twisted my body and forced it to work. He lifted me off the bike, I stood for a moment before my legs dropped me, and I fell to the rock strewn ground. The pain in my knees helped me revive by shocking my system into awareness. The pain was real as was Hunter.

With his help I clawed myself up him and stood shakily beside him. With his arm around my waist, he half dragged me while I forced my legs to work regaining circulation with each step. I felt like I had been on a month long drinking spree. My head was foggy, my tongue could have easily been the bottom of any ashtray and my legs were weak. Together we traversed the greatest part of the outer fire circle walking slowly past all the various torture stations without saying a word. Whipping posts laced with dried blood and cats dangling in the warm breeze gave dark contrast to the fires glowing embers. Tools of torture, iron spikes laid in a row, brands glowing beside the fires cooling who other than Hunter carried a new brand? I felt as if I had been branded and yet without closer inspection with better light I could not say. We completed our circuit of the Cathedral of Pain finding ourselves standing beside his Harley. He pulled me to him tenderly took my face into his hands and pulled my face towards his. I did not hesitate as I joined him in sharing a kiss. His kiss breathed life back into my charred body from such a simple gesture. I drew light and life back into my bitter cold soul. It was for him that I lived and he for me, together we knew we were one.

"Come," Hunter, whispered, "you are shivering. Let's find your leathers and get out of here."

Together we walked around a stalagmite that shimmered light with reddish brown crystals. On the opposite side I thought I saw a throne and struggled free from Hunter's supporting arm to investigate. I found a knoll covered with bleached white roots from a tree overhead, no throne just a rocky outcropping and the back board to which I was bound rested as if tossed hurriedly away by manimals as they ripped the straps off my body to the side. My clothes Hunter found to his astonishment near where I knew the throne had been. He brought them down to me and helped me dress as if I was unable to dress myself. Dressed in his leathers my shivering finally began to subside.

Again he kissed me, but I did not respond being lost in my thoughts. More forcefully he grabbed my right arm, pinning it at my back and forcing me to turn to him. Clutched to him, his arm pinning me, the other hand drew my face towards his lips and he raped them as easily as he or the Lord of Darkness had raped my body. I surrendered to his will returning his kiss with the same velocity and strength that he had mine. Like lovers long separated we made love with our lips, touching lightly caressing deeply saying volumes about the cruelty of imposed separation. Thus we made our way back around the stalagmite and to his Harley.

Climbing on, he seated his cock beneath my ass. Trapped between the vee of my leathered ass crack and the seat. His arms encircled me as I tilted my head back for yet another kiss. The engine roared to life echoing the anger and vengeance of my

Lords temper. Slowly we moved forward and it dawned on me. Hadn't we traveled this way before when I first came to him? Yes but he sat at the front and I to the rear my cock was restrained by his ass. Had we come full circle? Had I become that which he had always sought, the glove to his hand, the ultimate slave.

"Ladies and Gentlemen. Thank you for allowing me to tell the story of how I became my master's Number One. My part of the tour is concluded I hope the story did not bore you too much. Are their any questions?"

"What happened to Sir Black of the Avalon Shield?" Asked a single lady in a prime cotton blouse.

"Sadly Sir Black died and is buried here on these grounds. He was unable to withdraw from the drug SNAP. If you would like to visit his gravesite please ask any of those slaves in a yellow jumpsuits they will be more than willing to guide you to the site."

"Anymore questions?"

"Your luggage has been brought up by other means and it will be found in your guest rooms. Dinner will be served tonight at 8PM sharp. Formal attire is suggested. If you failed to bring formal attire, ask one of the yellow jump suited slaves and they can help you find suitable attire from a few of our guildsmen."

My cell phone rang, "Forgive me, Ladies and Gentlemen, there is only one that knows my number. I must take this call."

"Sir, yes Sir. Right away Sir!"

"Now are there any final questions before I report to my master?"

"Yes, how can I assist you Master Pitchford?"

A man dressed in head to toe black leather rose to his feet, "One question if you do not mind Number One. What happened to the two boys that crashed the October run that did not turn up when your men did a sweep of the tents?"

I laughed, "well Sir. They did turn up at the end of the October Run. They were found in the entertainment tent and by the way they looked had been there since the beginning of the event. Needless to say they were well used, extremely well used by the time we found them. They are on this docket as mule 92-432 and 92-587. For those of you who do not know the numbering system, 9 denotes mule, 2 the year of induction and the next three numbers explains their talents. One is a master chef while the other is a trained body guard."

"If you will be so kind as to follow the slaves standing outside in the yellow jump suits that will take you to your guest quarters. Please take time to read the profiles of the slaves on the docket. Breakfast begins at 7 A.M. and the auction begins at 9 promptly. I would suggest that you arrive early to get good seats. Now if you will forgive me, Ladies and Gentlemen, my master is not known for his patience when dealing with a tardy slave. By your leave."

I ran to the nearest outbuilding, there I striped off my jump suit as slaves are forbidden to be underground clothed. I ran down the flight of steps passing through doors without having to open them. Each ranking slave had been implanted with special security chip that allowed the new security system to keep track us on, in or off the grounds. No more could we slaves flee and get away with it. Nor could a slave remove the chip without doing extreme bodily injury. Security knew I was in a hurry as I was in route to his office so they conveniently triggered the sliding doors as I ran. I ran through all the doors save one, His, there I stopped took a deep breath, knocked and entered.

For all his rush and drive to get me down to him when I entered he did not even look up but demanded where in the fuck had I been. I knew that tone of voice, he was teasing me cause he already knew where I was. All he had to do was look on his monitor to see where I or a hundred other slaves were at any given moment within this compound instead he slammed his fist on the desk and growled at me, "Where have you been Number One, I needed you?"

"Sir, a newcomer's bus, Sir. As if that would explain where I had been when he needed me."

"Ohhhh! My roster says that it was 9-777's turn at meeting them. Didn't it show up?" He looked up from his desk his eyes twinkling with mischief, "so you told them your story did you?"

He motioned with his hand, "Get over here, stand right beside me, One."

He moved his leather chair out from his desk as I walked to where he pointed, "what do you have to say for yourself, One?"

"Sir, I told them 'Our' story, Sir!"

He chuckled, patted his lap, "sit here, One."

I sat in his lap. One arm encircled my waist while the other busied itself. A pencil was placed in my fist; duct tape locked it in place. He was giggling as he did this and I began to struggle trying to remove the duct tape before he got the other one penciled and taped. He could have ordered me to halt at any moment, but we were playing together. I struggling to stop the tapeing of my hands he struggling to get them effectively taped. Eventually he won and pushed me to my knees between his legs. "How many times must I ask you to write Our story? Must I tape pencils into your hands, chain you to my desk, plug your ass and beat it until you write the story you so love to tell to newcomers. It is time that it be made public, now I am serious, slave!"

I held up my hands showing him my penciled hands, "Sir I can see how serious you are about making me write the story. It has all ready been started, Sir, and Sir, I hesitate to think you would expect me to write like this?"

"It is time that Our story enters outsider society. How will they learn the true value and devotion of a good slave if you don't teach them? How will they understand the strength and power we can yield when we endorse a political leader that is gay active? There is power in our vote; especially, when our one vote equals a million plus voices worldwide. Unity is the answer. Unity under the rainbow flag, the pink triangle, the black, blue, white and red and the perfected union of the hand and glove. As long as we are united we can be the driving force that rights the wrongs in our world today. It will take time for them to accept us as equals. More than likely we will be seen as a hostile threat. They have tried to kill us before, we survived and even grew stronger in our convictions. We have been here for centuries, they are not going to destroy us easily and if they try to destroy us they destroy themselves; their lab created diseases have taught them that folly. Yes, One it is time that you wrote the story. Some will believe and come seeking us and others will see us as just another euphoric society, another pipe dream. Those that seek us shall find their reality within our civilization."

I had allowed my head to sink into a submissive pose while he rambled, "Sorry about that meat. Got caught up in a train of thought, a speech for tomorrows opening ceremonies."

The phone rang on his desk, he announced to the room, "this had better be fucking important!"

One hand pulled my head into his leathered crotch while the other picked up the phone, "Yes, Hunter here!"

I felt him twist in his chair while I was busy elsewhere, then I heard him shout, "Hold ALL my calls, Louis. I am out!"

I heard and felt the snap as he attached my leash to my collar. He rose pushing me to the floor before him and with a jerk on my leash I followed. He walked towards the bookcase, pulled out a book and the panel slipped quietly aside. 9-777 his back turned towards me hung limply on a cross his face was laced into silence but his eyes showed me all I needed to know, 9-777 was content. His front was deeply bruised and red from a very recent whipping. That explains why 9-777 wasn't present to meet and greet the newcomer's bus. Hunter had known all along where I was. A Number One's job is never done.

Hunter is hungry and not for food that he will have much later after he has dined on the pleasure only his slaves can provide him. Dan's back looked pretty raw too but what is a whipping boy for if it's not for whipping. Besides, 9-777 likes it rough; he is better than any old Timex watch. What was their advertisement, ah yes takes a beating and keeps on ticking. That explained all of us, all his slaves that is, we took a beating and kept right on ticking.

Hunter caught me eyeing 9-777's back again as I looked up to see him watching me. He laughed, "I started without you shithead! Come on, let's dance."

He slipped his hand into a comfortable well-worn leather glove and flexed his fingers. Feeling the cool leather mold over his flesh, covering him with warmth. He made a fist and the glove moved with him. His fist struck and the glove offered his hand power and protection from harm. Together the hand and the glove were strong. Apart, complete in their incompleteness, a mere shadow of their combined power when united as one.

The Beginning

About the Author

Born where "good ole boy," applied to both men and women. Where "honey and darling," was applied to all women and they did not think it to be a sexist statement. Where being politically correct was something city folks did cause they failed to respect, honor and take pride in all those with whom one associated. Where a man's word and handshake was more binding than any piece of paper. Where honor, pride and respect were a state of mind the 'hum' in humanity. Experience they say is the key to being a great artist. If that's the case well, I am a frigging Picasso or one hell of a writer cause I done my share of hell raisin' and placating while here on this good Ole Earth of ours. One thing I have learned that is an outstanding truth that we tend to forget and that is, "Everything is connected to everything." Poison our Earth mother and we ourselves are poisoned, heal her and we are healed.

Graduated high school in '69, went to Morehead University for a start on my degrees. Been a retail merchant, badge carrier, training and educations officer within a branch of the Old F.E.M.A., am a healer and medicine man within the Hiawatha Shawnee Hidden Society out of Kentucky. Came to Florida to cross reference Woodland tribal magic with that of Tropical tribal magic and found an expanded universe that's absolutely awesome. Moved to Miami, Florida in the early 1990's to undertake the fire vision and survived. People either love or fear me it's just that simple. Moved from Miami to Ft Lauderdale also known as Ft. Leatherdale due to the amount of leather men and women who have moved into our beautiful city. Once in Ft. Lauderdale, I immersed myself within the leather community became a public figure. Became a leather tailor later ran a leather business with Amy O'. In '99 was the president of Leather University which was an educational faculty teaching safe, sane and consensual SandM, BandD arts and sciences.

In 2000 was involved in a major car accident that broke more parts than I thought was possible. The accident awoke a sleeping child hood disease, polio, bringing it back as post polio syndrome. I was told I would live the balance of my life in a wheelchair, but a Sensi taught me water karate and I regained my limbs. In 2003 I found the love letters that my slave had returned to me while he was on road tour. The love letters is the premise for the story Hand and Glove.